# DAUGHTER OF THE
# CYBER DRAGON

### C. T. PHIPPS

### &

### MICHAEL SUTTKUS

MYSTIQUE PRESS

I dreamed of the past, which was always a pain in my ass. It was one of the reasons I took lethe, which was the street version of anti-nightmare medications that had replaced opioids as the preferred narcotic of the masses post-Eruption. Unfortunately, when you carried around my kind of baggage, lethe didn't cut it unless you wanted to take the hardcore pure stuff that left your brain a little pile of mush. I was a recreational user but not ready to take the step into full-blown junkie like so many of my other fellow citizens.

I'll spare you what I dreamed about because I don't know myself. The benefit of lethe was, even if it didn't repress your nightmares one hundred percent effectively, you didn't remember them when you woke up. Opening my eyes and feeling an enormous hangover, I stood up and tried to take stock of my surroundings. I was lying on my mattress in the middle of what could charitably be called my apartment. It was more properly the top floor of a junk shop that just so happened to have someone living there.

The interior of my apartment was four metal walls, a leaky roof, and a floor with one-bathroom downstairs that I shared Joe Kepler's crew of scavs. The walls had beams of light streaming through a few of the bullet holes I hadn't managed to weld metal to yet. I probably wouldn't feel motivated to finish that until winter. I should probably at least put posters or other paraphernalia over them. I had a variety I'd collected.

# CONTENTS

# Foreword

## By C.T. Phipps

Cyberpunk is one of my favorite genres. It's the place where the dreams of tomorrow meet with the problems of today, only for things to get worse rather than better. The Agent G series gave me a chance to write how our world became a Gibsonian dystopia from the perspective of a corporate samurai. However, there was something missing which I felt needed to be addressed.

The answer to this came to me while chatting with my frequent collaborator, Michael Suttkus, specifically that I was doing a great job writing up the cyber element but not quite the punk. I was missing a perspective from the streets and those people who do the awful things which allow the corrupt high-tech society of the future to function.

Basically, in cyberpunk worlds, there are the Haves and Have Nots but there're also the Will Takes. The best cyberpunk stories are full of antiheroes and criminals who will do just about anything to escape the poverty and despair which afflict the planet. Much like noir fiction, these protagonists straddle the line between the ultra-rich and the impoverished masses. Agent G was very comfortable with the former but rarely got a chance to walk around with the latter.

Part of the appeal of cyberpunk is that there are a million new ways for the super-rich to keep the poor down. As we see in the modern day with data mining, debt, and omni-surveillance—technology can be a useful tool for those who want to dominate those below them. It also has inspired whole new kinds of criminals with black hat hackers having gone from being products of science fiction to a lucrative criminal trade.

This inspired Michael and I to brainstorm the Cyber Dragons series, which is a spin-off of the Agent G books (*Agent G: Infiltrator,* *Agent G: Saboteur,* and *Agent G: Assassin*). They take place in the same world, even incorporate the main character, but star a different protagonist. Kei Springs is the view from the ground up of the new century, a woman who has experienced the worst of the corporate dystopia and come out swinging.

*Daughter of the Cyber Dragons* introduces the concept of Riders, which are an element that has appeared in many prior cyberpunk novels. They are the mercenaries like *Neuromancer's* Case and Molly, people who do the bad things that keep the high-tech black markets of the future going. Each of them is disposable but they are also valuable for as long as they survive. None of them like their richer-than-God clients but they also are willing to do the clients' bidding because no one survives without patrons.

This is a pure adventure story with a lot of comedy, and I think folks will like it from start to finish. I'm hoping to have at least three novels starring our heroine, potentially more. The world of Agent G is one which I've become extremely fond of and examining it from another perspective will only help broaden its appeal.

No matter how many bodies get left behind.

# Foreword

## By Michael Suttkus

Keiko "Kei" Springs began her life as a character in a sci-fi table-top RPG. If you've been reading C.T. Phipps' books, you may have met characters based on her in his *Red Room*, *Agent G*, and our *Lucifer's Star* books. Charles and I have been friends for over twenty years now and often played tabletop RPGs together. That's role-playing games versus rocket propelled grenades, though plenty of those appeared to.

The character is one I carried in my mind for an exceptionally long time since she appeared fully formed in my head and has stuck with me for literal decades. Beautiful, sexy, dangerous, and more than a little crazed, Kei Springs is her cyberpunk equivalent and a woman who managed to survive the worst the streets had to offer her.

I've always enjoyed cyberpunk as a genre, though my famil-iarity with it is more things like *Cyberpunk 2020*, *Shadowrun*, and anime than Charles' extensive literary background of it. For me, it's an aesthetic to reflect the kind of action-packed sci-fi adventures you see on the big screen like in *The Matrix* or *Equilibrium*. Indeed, I take credit for introducing Charles to cyberpunk as a genre when I first lent him my old *Bubblegum Crisis* OVA and *Serial Experiments Lain* video tapes back before DVDs were a thing. I never thought I would be actually writing in the genre, though.

When Charles asked me to first collaborate with him, I was initially skeptical as I was more used to creating worlds than I was writing. However, he pointed out George R.R. Martin's *Wildcards* and James S.A. Corey's *Expanse* novels had both began their exis-tences as roleplaying game sessions. His Supervillainy Saga novels drew a lot from our *Halt Evil Doer!* game and I had often thought we could achieve something great with our shared visions of worlds.

These books take place in the same timeline as the Agent G series, but you don't need to read those to understand the plot, though they might give a better appreciate of Case and Lucita. You can consider the Agent G series to be prequels to these novels and we all know how prequels are hit and miss (just kidding, Charles—you know I love them). They do, however, incorporate the same themes of action movies, spy thrillers, crime, class warfare, and cyberpunk satire on the possible future.

*Daughter of the Cyber Dragons* is basically a freeform novel created as a kind of literary tabletop adventure. Kei, Paradise, and Case all come from the kind of characters I would like to see the adventures of play out. There's a lot of benefits to this style of writing as it is both unpredictable and constantly moving forward even when it's perhaps better to slow down. It's an action-packed work that shows the underbelly of a fictional world I'd certainly like to visit. Just not stay in.

So please enjoy.

# Cast of Characters

## Lead

**Keiko "Kei" Springs:** Our (anti)heroine. Rider. Ex-Trikuza assassin. Lethe addict. All round nice girl. Supposedly.

## Supporting Cast

**Miles Ashe: Rider.** Ex-cop. Ex-boyfriend of Kei. Jerkass. Some redeeming qualities.

**Terry Ashe:** Miles' estranged sister. Mother of Becky Ashe.

**Rebecca "Becky" Ashe:** Miles' thirteen-year-old niece. Not exactly a criminal mastermind.

**Winston Billions:** An exceptionally famous weatherman and comedian who (apparently) dabbles in organized crime.

**Lucita Biondi:** A beautiful Italian assassin turned executive. She is a Shell and can throw small cars. Trans. Has a teeny, tiny good side that she denies exists.

**Chastity Chambers:** Rider. Former member of Kei's crew. Now sports a new identity.

**Fate Firenze:** Rider. Ex-Trikuza assassin. Another of Kei's exes. Really awful person.

C. T. PHIPPS & MICHAEL SUTTKUS

**Case Gordon:** Formerly known as G and an international man of mystery. Bioroid. Affably evil or evilly affable. Maybe just a cheerful amoral neutral.

**Jimmy "Slick" Hernandez:** Rider. Rival of Kei's who is being suspiciously helpful lately.

**Solomon Jones:** Techjack. Sleeper. Genius hacker who dabbles in terrorism and the occult. Thinks he should be a billionaire when he's not spouting anti-capitalist anarchist slogans.

**Snake Juarez:** Trikuza boss. Master assassin. Surrogate dad of Kei and Fate. Seems to be under the impression he's a ninja master and enlightened spiritual killer. Also, not Japanese in the slightest.

**Joe Kepler:** Junkyard owner and friend to Kei. Formerly a master cyberneticist and doctor. A bit of a pervert.

**Zero Kepler:** Joe's son and friend to Kei. Also a bit of a pervert.

**James Madison:** Billionaire tech guru who is horrible at business and dependent on his backers to keep him afloat. But very good at programming.

**Evie Principle:** Owner of the This is Paradise brothel and safehouse. Former political activist and revolutionary. Mostly fabulous.

**Paradise Principle:** Evie Principle's daughter. Rider. Way too naive for her job. Supposedly. Raised by the media.

**Sun:** Lead singer of QuantumCrab. She is internationally famous and releases all her music on infospace. Heavily involved in charities and Third Age spirituality.

**Helen Troy:** Ex-model, ex-actress, and businesswoman turned trophy wife. All of this is a lie.

**David Yagami:** Kei's friend on the force. Operates drones. Nicer than anyone should be in a cyberpunk dystopia. Except, you know, if you're a target.

# Chapter One

## Why Yes, I Do Live Inside a Junkyard

I dreamed of the past, which was always a pain in my ass. It was one of the reasons I took lethe, which was the street version of anti-nightmare medications that had replaced opioids as the preferred narcotic of the masses post-Eruption. Unfortunately, when you carried around my kind of baggage, lethe didn't cut it unless you wanted to take the hardcore pure stuff that left your brain a little pile of mush. I was a recreational user but not ready to take the step into full-blown junkie like so many of my other fellow citizens.

I'll spare you what I dreamed about because I don't know myself. The benefit of lethe was, even if it didn't repress your nightmares one hundred percent effectively, you didn't remember them when you woke up. Opening my eyes and feeling an enormous hangover, I stood up and tried to take stock of my surroundings. I was lying on my mattress in the middle of what could charitably be called my apartment. It was more properly the top floor of a junk shop that just so happened to have someone living there.

The interior of my apartment was four metal walls, a leaky roof, and a floor with one-bathroom downstairs that I shared Joe Kepler's crew of scavs. The walls had beams of light streaming through a few of the bullet holes I hadn't managed to weld metal to yet. I probably wouldn't feel motivated to finish that until winter. I should probably at least put posters or other paraphernalia over them. I had a variety I'd collected.

They included my favorite bands like Sun and QuantumCrab, naked individuals of both sexes that in previous centuries would have been called art, plus a few road signs I'd stolen just for the hell of it. There was a used couch, ripped up chairs, and a top shelf infotainment center that couldn't have looked more stolen if it said, "Property of the US government." It was not the sort of place you would call classy, but I never would have used that identifier for myself anyway.

I was lying naked on my mattress with my blanket having been stolen by my partner, a naked Caucasian girl with red hair. Lisa, I think her name was? No, wait, Ariel. Wow, I hadn't even been close the first time. She was just a one-night stand since my last boyfriend and I had broken up over the fact I'd shot him. He'd been shooting me at the time, though.

Sliding out of bed, I checked to make sure my supply of lethe was still untouched in the false-bottom drawer by the bed just in case my partner of the evening decided to make a break for it along with any spare cash I had lying around, not that anyone still used cash except criminals like me. Slipping on a cheap synth-silk kimono from the local Japan-And-Stuff, I headed outside the back door where I'd set up a crude shower surrounded by metal walls. It was next to my pseudo-apartment with a metal staircase leading to the shop beneath me.

The sun briefly blinded me before I covered my face. I'd been hoping the smog would have kept the hateful orb away, but no such luck. Surrounding Joe's Recycling Lot (AKA Joe's Junkyard) was a big metal wall and beyond that was a vision of New Los Angeles. No one really called it that, it was still just LA, but the sight was still damn impressive.

Mega-skyscrapers a mile tall or higher were everywhere, with flying cars moving to and from. Automated flight paths meant the rich never had to deal with the massive traffic we mere mortals had to deal with every day. It also played hell with my business that required me to know how to use a motorbike for the ground and little gyrocopter when delivering packages to the people who lived above the clouds.

"Keiko! Gonna give us a show?" A voice called from the base of the stairs.

Standing at the bottom was Joe Kepler, a still-beefy sixty-year-old African American man who thought Steven Seagal's hairstyle was the height of cool even in his mid-sixties. Standing beside him was his son, Zero—no, I didn't know his real name—who looked like a thirty-year-old version of his father. Both were perverts but neither of them went beyond language, which was practically sainthood among landlords I'd dealt with.

I felt a gust of wind and pushed down my kimono bottom with one hand while using the second to flip them the bird. "Frick off, you two. Also, I go by Kei, not Keiko."

Zero looked hurt. "Hey, what did I do?"

"You're related to your father," I said, dryly.

Zero nodded. "That's fair."

Since Joe was already here, I decided to ask him about something relevant. "How's my Nina?"

My Nina-172 bike was as close to a lifetime partner as I was ever going to get, especially after what had happened with my previous attempts at more human partnerships. The cerulean vehicle was the key to my business alongside my copter Jill. Unfortunately, it was a credit pit and where the majority of what few profits went when I finished paying off my debts and medical bills, plus ammunition costs.

Thankfully, Joe Kepler was a genius with mechanics and charged me less than the cost of replacement parts. He also maintained my cybernetics for free, which was probably illegal, but the man knew his stuff. I was still waiting for the other shoe to drop on that one since he hadn't asked me to sleep with him in the two years I'd been living here. I'd long since lost my belief in the kindness of strangers, friends, lovers, and everything in-between.

"Your Nina is all better," Joe said, cheerfully. "Despite how you abuse her so!"

"Hey!" I snapped. "Don't blame me, blame the Russian! She sideswiped me during our last race. I had to bang it against the wall to get back my momentum!"

Street racing was a way I supplemented my income. It was equally as illegal as my primary profession but arguably less dangerous. The big problem was that virtually every other Rider I knew was just as good at it. I was fast but I wasn't the greatest racer ever. I also had to keep up on my shooting, fighting, and hacking skills. Jack of all trades, mistress of none. Snake had taught me to be perfectly well-rounded, but I'd never been the best at anything even with his training from hell.

"How does that work?" Joe asked, correctly guessing what I just said was bullcrap.

"Very well thank you," I replied, lying my ass off. I'd ended up coming in dead last.

"Did you win?" Joe asked.

"No," I admitted, grimacing.

"Then it wasn't worth it, was it?" Joe said, shaking his head with a *tsk-tsk-tsk*. "You're going to come to a bad end if you don't watch yourself."

"Comes with the job," I muttered. "Being a Rider is a guaranteed live-fast, die-hard lifetime contract."

You wouldn't think in this day of drones and automated driving that there would be a need of militant couriers. However, you would be wrong. All the amazing technology that made things easier also made them easier to hack. Want to send an e-mail of super-sensitive material? That could be intercepted or redirected by corporate saboteurs. Want to get a package sent to your house of super-embarrassing pornography or sex toys? Well, guess what, that will go on the delivery drones' private files before being sold to whatever Big Data company wants to share it with everyone else.

Then there was the primary source of Rider income: illegal items that no one wanted any trace of on a corporate or government server somewhere. Things like black software, illegal body mods, weapons, drugs, total experience dreams, and the occasional prostitute. Delivering these goods was as much about making sure clients paid up as making sure they arrived. It seemed there were no end of people who thought that once they had the object in question, they could just pass on paying. Either way, there was something like six thousand Riders in New Los Angeles and plenty of us took our jobs deadly serious. That was a pun by the way.

"You should find better work then," Joe said. "I knew a Rider decades ago. Beautiful, smart, and funny. Dead now. Maybe she'd still be alive if she found something less dangerous—like the army."

I snorted. "It's better than porn."

"Pfft, like people would pay to see you naked," Joe said, chuckling. "You're barely modded!"

Zero looked embarrassed. "Have a good afternoon, Kei."

I rolled my eyes. "Will do."

I turned around and headed into the shower, shutting the metal grate door behind me before locking it with a tiny chain attached to a steel spike. The interior included a shower nozzle attached to a pipe, a tiny sink, cracked mirror, drain, and a piece of soap that had seen better days. A bottle of soap flakes was in the corner. Slipping off my kimono and putting it on the side of the wall, I hoped no one made off with it and turned the water on. I wished it would have hot water available today but, unfortunately, no such luck. Still, freezing cold water was better than nothing and I washed my hair with the soap flakes before taking a moment to look in the mirror.

I was twenty-eight, Japanese American, white-haired due to weekly hair dye sessions, and possessed of an athletic yet feminine build with several scars from where I'd had cybernetic implants inserted into my body against my will. The first body mods I'd undergone were strictly ornament, necessary for the first line of work I'd been in, but most of the current ones were designed to make me function like a machine. Faster, stronger, and harder to kill.

A pair of steel-colored dragon tattoos flowed up and down my arms before entwining on my back. The mark of the Cyber Dragons clan. I often considered having it removed but they were built far into the skin and getting a new epidermic was costlier than I could afford right now. Instead, I just kept it covered up and it was only an issue between me and my lovers—which was sadly a lot more people than I probably wanted to know about them. But hey, sex was still the cheapest, most entertaining pastime available to everyone.

"Kei Springs, you have seen better days," I muttered, sticking my tongue out. It had a piercing I hadn't remembered getting jewelry for. Wow, I really had forgotten the night before. "Work hard, play hard, because tomorrow you'll probably get killed by a disgruntled customer."

Finishing up, I put on my kimono and headed back into my apartment. I was planning to spring for coffee when I realized that Ariel—if that was her name—was out of bed. What I saw irritated me. She'd put on a pair of booty shorts and a ratty t-shirt from the night before. She also had a tiny purse hanging over one shoulder. That wasn't the part that was irritating me, though. She was trying to boost my infotainment center. She was unplugging the monitor behind it while trying to lift it up off its CPU desk.

"Ahem," I said, pausing. "One-night stand lady, that is just rude."

Ariel reached into her purpose and pulled out a tiny R7 micro-pistol. It was made by Atlas Security and the preferred weapon of suburban housewives afraid of minorities everywhere. "Back off."

I rolled my eyes. "Do you think this is the first time this has happened? I removed the bullets from your gun last night."

Ariel blinked and looked at her gun. That was enough of a distraction for me to rush to her side, grab her in a headlock, and rip the pistol from her hand.

"Dammit! You tricked me!" Ariel hissed. She proceeded to call me a litany of names that don't bear repeating and were anatomically impossible anyway.

"No, I really did remove the bullets," I said, dryly. I escorted her to the door and threw her down the stairs, causing her to bounce on her rather shapely ass. She growled and gave me the finger. Which was deserved, I admit. "I don't think we should see each other again, Ariel!"

"Lisa!" She shouted back, making me feel slightly ashamed despite her attempt to rob me. "At least give me my gun back!"

"No!" I said, slamming the door behind me. It caused my walls to shake. Man, I really needed to get a better apartment. The problem was that if I roomed with another Rider, they'd almost certainly rob and kill me. If it wasn't another Rider, I'd probably get them killed. Maybe if I got a boyfriend or girlfriend I wasn't terribly fond of...Hmm.

I was going to say more when I heard my infocomm ring. Despite their impressive sounding title, they were just cellphone watches with a better voice control. I kept mine in the drawer beside my desk where I put my lethe, which was probably not the smartest idea I'd ever had given my infocomm was the third most expensive thing I owned.

"Maybe I should upgrade," I muttered, checking the drawer and finding it not there. I had a brain implant, an old Maelstrom 90, but it was spotty as it had exceeded its data storage for as long as I could remember—which admittedly wasn't long some days.

The watch's ringing continued until I found it behind the bed where it must have been knocked off by my rather energetic love-making session—minus the love—with Lisa. One annoying thing about the modern day was that you could now pick whether a phone continued ringing versus going to voicemail. My customers rarely respected my promise that I'd get back to them.

Finally, I managed to get the infocomm and slapped it on my wrist where it immediately clasped itself. The object then presented a holographic image of Jimmy "Slick" Hernandez's face. He had a thick black mustache that attached itself to his sideburns. Both his eyes were artificial, having a neon yellow sheen to them that I felt had aged poorly in the two or three months that it was popular among cyborgs.

Jimmy was a fellow Rider that I considered about twenty percent more trustworthy than most of our kind—which was to say twenty percent total—due to the fact he'd managed to score a regular gig delivering prostitutes to and from a hotel downtown. As such, he had as close to a steady income as any of us and didn't need every job the others competed for. Oh, and I'd saved his kid brother's life once. Between the two, his likelihood of screwing me over was small. Well, unless a rich client paid him to. Then all bets were off.

"Hey Jimmy," I said, staring at him. "Let me guess, you have decided you're madly in love with me and need to rescue me from this horrible lifestyle I've found myself in."

Jimmy snorted. "Maybe if you grow a penis, *chère*. You're way too feminine for me."

"So noted," I said.

Jimmy stared. "You alone?"

"That's usually an intro for sex or killing," I replied. "Not a great way to start a conversation after saying sex is off the table."

Jimmy shrugged. "I was curious if you had time for a high-paying gig. The Big Boss Man said to contact you directly."

The Big Boss Man was the nickname for the organizer of the Rider bulletin system for a good quarter of New Los Angeles. I didn't know his name and I was surprised he knew mine. "Really? What's the job?"

"Fast delivery," Jimmy said. "Parcel pickup and delivery within one hour. New Post Office Building Seventeen-B to a mansion in Neon Hills."

I shook my head. "Can't be done. You'd have to be Superman, Sonic, or the Flash to carry it out. I am none of the above."

"Are they Riders?" Jimmy asked, pretending like pop culture hadn't existed before the Eruption.

"Funny," I said. "Anyway, I'll pass. Sorry to—"

"It pays forty thousand credits," Jimmy said. "It's for the New

Post Office and can set you up with some long-term work."

The New Postal Service was a front for the Russian syndicates and ran about half of the courier jobs around the city. Drugs, guns, illicit electronics, and even the occasional pizza were things they guaranteed to be delivered within an absurdly swift timeline when the United States Postal Service was no longer a factor post-Eruption. If you got in with them, you didn't have to worry about where your next meal came from. You just had to worry about a bullet to the head if you failed them. I had a bad feeling that Jimmy had set me up for this without bothering to get my permission.

Goddammit.

I blinked. "When does the hour start?"

"Now," Jimmy said.

I barely had time to put on my racing leathers before I was out the door.

# Chapter Two

## My Early Morning Death Race

I should have read the fine print before I barreled down the high-ways of the world's most wired city on my Nina. It was a monster of a machine to ride and had streaks of light circling with every turn of its wheels. I drifted with each turn, trying to make it to an impossible deadline where a difference of seconds might literally mean the difference between life and death.

Jimmy had done me dirty by putting me in the service of the New Post Office, supposed favor or not. I wasn't afraid they'd cap me if I failed to deliver on time, I was afraid they'd do much worse. The contract I'd viewed in my cyberfeed stated that I was liable for the price of the package if I missed the deadline, and it was valued at two hundred thousand credits. That was more money than I made in two years, and I was doing well for myself as a Rider.

"Frick, I'd rather go back to serving Cyber Dragons," I muttered as my long hair trailed behind my helmet as I passed under the super-structures that made up the city skyline.

An enhanced nervous system and reflexes, illicit back-alley jobs or not, let me maneuver through the automated cars that were the preferred transport of the masses. My helmet let me know the NLAPD's drones had tagged my Nina, but I didn't mind as the bike was registered under a false ID number anyway. What I *was* worried about, though, was the fact I was ten minutes from my target with the clock ticking down from twelve.

"Ooop, curve!" I shouted, driving my bike between a crowd of people to get around an automated dump truck.

I had managed to get the package, a six-inch tall and foot-long black package in a "lock box" with a timer ticking down on it. It was a subtle reminder of just how much the New Postal Service liked to keep their people under foot. Two hundred thousand credits would ruin me but defaulting on the payment would get me killed—or worse, in debt to people like the Trikuza.

New Los Angeles was a gleaming forest of hundreds of buildings constructed within the last two decades, replacing the old City of Angles with a virtually unrecognizable skyline that looked more like someone combined Tokyo with New York. Much of the old city had been rendered in the calamitous series of earthquakes that had torn through the world following Big Smokey's eruption in Yellowstone and it was hard to believe this was still the same city. Then again, my grade school history teacher had once said that change was like the tide: sometimes it came in little waves and other times it was like a typhoon.

Personally, I loved the city. The constant beats of crowds smashing into one another, horns, buzzes, and engines running. Most of the city was jobless now, unemployment numbers having skyrocketed to something like thirty percent with bots handling virtually everything. But those were just official numbers. People found ways to occupy themselves whether it was street artistry, black marketeering, scavenging, or fighting over turf that they could claim was theirs.

I didn't mean to say that much of the city was criminal but that the definition of crime no longer really applied. The law had failed to keep up with the changing standards of life. I knew entire families that risked carcinogens to pick over the massive garbage pits outside the city, all to recycle metal for the hungry machine of commerce, and if that wasn't a job then I didn't know what was.

That was when my bike's alarm went off. A chipper male voice said, "You have been scanned by three auto-targeting computers. This is your DangerSense App responding. Thank you for using DangerSense App."

"Tell me something I don't know!" I shouted.

"I do not understand your query," the dummy AI responded. God, why did I even install it?

My helmet's vid-link was a box in the upper right-hand corner of the faceplate, and it showed that three heavily modified Trikuza bikes were coming at me, one of their riders holding a carbon-fiber laser katana with one hand and the other two riding on autopilot as they were pulling out gold-plated Uzis. They were three men in colorful track suits with black helmets like mine. They looked a lot higher class than the usual thugs I had to dodge around even if the katana made the one look like he was trying *way* too hard.

"What the hell?" I asked, blinking. "Did I ride into the set of an action movie?"

That was when one of the Trikuza with an automatic submachine gun fired wildly and the bullets shot out the back of a vehicle passing beside me. The head of the driver exploded onto the windshield while the car merrily continued forward with its pre-programmed course. Crap. This was for real. What had Jimmy gotten me into?

"Map display!" I commanded. "Now."

The interior of my helmet gave me a full sense of what was going beyond what my eyes could see and I prayed it was displaying things correctly. Plenty of Riders relied on automapping and got themselves killed by slamming into debris or new buildings.

Why the hell were they trying to kill me? The box? What the hell was in it? Normally, Riders didn't need to fear anyone but the occasional pirate over the contents of their deliveries. We were all serving the same masters after all. The suits were the government for all that it mattered. Atlas Corp, Karma Corp, Green Foods, and a half-dozen names that meant more than countries these days. I hated all of them and wished they'd all fall into a volcano somewhere.

The package was clearly something somebody wanted and somebody else wanted for them not to have. Simply taking didn't seem to be the end goal, because that would make shooting at me at these speeds really stupid, unless whatever was inside was made of titanium. None of which mattered right now. The New Post Office wouldn't bother sabotaging their own job to get me into debt because, honestly, I wasn't worth that. I was good but I'd kept most of my skills hidden to avoid just this sort of attention.

What mattered was getting to my destination on time—something that was hypothetically possible according to my mapping routine—without dying in the process. That might mean I'd have to kill the three guys trying to kill me and while that normally seemed like a no brainer, people like the Trikuza tended to treat that personally.

I couldn't make my bike go faster and the jackasses pursuing me were talented enough to keep up even with two on autopilot.

They had to be using much more sophisticated hardware than the cheap corporate-produced crap that normally went into bikes. I preferred to ride my Nina the old-fashioned way but that was keeping me from shooting back.

It might shave off precious seconds if I could go down an alley or two or five and hope my superior skill got me through while the Trikuza crashed into some dumpsters. Feeling the whizzing of bullets beside my head, I decided that this plan had more merit than just hoping that they weren't bloodthirsty enough to indiscriminately fire into traffic—as they apparently were. Criminals with no sense of public safety! What is the world coming to?

The first of the Trikuza managed to catch up to me, the result of me having to slow down for maneuvering. He took a swing at my head with his katana. It was a stupid weapon and a stupid action, but no one gave the New Los Angeles Trikuza credit for originality. Even their name was a play on words that made no sense in Japanese or English.

"Die *gaijin!*" the very Caucasian man shouted, using his comm system to pump it into my ear.

"You first," I said, reaching over to his bike controls and turning off his auto control before sliding into one of the alleys I knew well. Sword Boy ended up getting smashed into the back of a delivery truck. At the speed he was going, it was extremely unlikely he'd get to a hospital before his brain flatlined and was unrevivable by even the best cyberdocs. It was technically murder under the laws of the arcology—the United States Emergency Government was not big on self-defense—but it wasn't like I hadn't done worse to survive.

The infinitely more dangerous jackasses with actual guns followed me, firing all the way and probably getting other people killed in the process. I gained some distance on them by maneuvering past dumpsters and street trash. It didn't matter in the long run because I knew they could track me—I was set up to interfere with the cops' systems not the locals. Which gave me an idea. Unfortunately, it would mean burning one of my few remaining favors and those were almost bigger, more valuable currency than actual currency.

By the time I got out of a crisscross of dumpsters, the homeless, and back alleys, I'd already made an ultra-quick call to a friend and brought myself to a complete stop in a parking lot I could never afford the hourly rent for. I was going to be wasting even more time here, but it wasn't like being dead was a better option. As these two punks were about to find out. Both aimed their guns at me but stopped their vehicles first to get a better aim at my prone form.

"*Sayonara*, suckers," I said, feeling oddly racist despite being half-Japanese.

A drone marked with the NLAPD's colors descended from the sky and shredded them both with machine gun fire. It was a cold-blooded execution but the kind that was legal these days. The police kept its drones flying at all times over most of the city to make sure they could be redirected as "support." The public didn't care about the laws if it wasn't them being gutted. Mind you, this wasn't that different from what I remembered of the Pre-Eruption world either.

I took a moment to remove my helmet and pulled up my bike's holographic feed of the handsome David Yagami. He was a brown-haired Japanese American with angular, almost elfin, features. David was boyish-looking despite being in his mid-twenties and had a terrible bowl cut with a crisp white and blue uniform. Still, he was good-looking, almost pretty, and I liked that about him.

David was a NLAPD drone operator who'd helped me get off the drone's grid. He was also passionately in love with me despite our age difference (I was three years' older) and the fact he was far too naive to ever be one of my steady lovers. Mind you, I might have to sleep with him since he'd just saved my life and I might need another favor in the future. In my opinion, it didn't count as prostitution if he wasn't wholly reprehensible, and money didn't exchange hands.

"Thanks for that," I said, wasting precious seconds before adjusting the bike to an automated course. It wouldn't be as fast as my shortcuts here, but I needed a second to calm myself before reverting to manual. Surprisingly, cold-blooded murder still affected me. What a wonderful thing to tell my non-existent thera-pist. I would have been killed by those jerkasses without that.

"I recorded three murders by those three," David said, frown-ing. "Possibly a vehicular manslaughter too. I'm dispatching an ambulance now."

I wasn't sure if he was making up those crimes or not and didn't really care. The NLAPD would never check anyway. "You'd think the police would have a handle on these bike-riding hooligans by now."

David smirked. "Yes, well this isn't that abnormal even for a slow day. The honest criminals like you keep us employed."

I paused. "You're not going to get in trouble for what you did, right?"

"No," David said. "I've hit three other targets this morning. We're doing a tough on terrorism campaign in the city due to some recent attacks. The Lieutenant won't notice a few extra bodies, especially once I alter the data's time stamp. Most of our targets barely require human approval these days. They're generated by algorithm."

"That's terrifying," I said, honestly appalled.

"So is most of my job," David said, sounding more chipper about it than he probably should.

"Yeah, well, we'll talk later. I have a very important client who is dying to receive a package," I said, forcing a smile. I was losing valuable seconds.

"Dying or killing?" David asked.

"Maybe both," I said. "Possibly me."

"Ah," David said. "May I ask who?"

"Big Money," I replied. "That's all that matters. Bye-bye."

The rest of my trip was uneventful but Big Money was right. The location I was to deliver the package was the largest mansion in the Neon Hills. Neon Hills was the ultimate gated community where the region had been walled off by a big concrete barrier that would give President Trust wet dreams.

Neon Hills was like the Platonic inverse of NLA's Refugee Zones. The super-rich tended to live in personal palaces and estates lovingly crafted for them with hundreds of indents, people with lifetime contracts that guaranteed them job security as long as they understood they were legally obligated to let their contract-holders do whatever the hell they wanted to them. There was a time in my youth when that would have been illegal but that had been a different America.

The place I was to deliver was the Madison Estate. The building was a literal frigging castle with its own sub-barrier, nonlethal icer turrets on the walls, and a small army of Atlas Security patrolling the grounds. I had heard of James Madison before, of course, as he was one of the experts on Black Technology when the Hacker had leaked it all on the net. He was basically another Silicon Valley wannabe Elon Musk, but who was I to judge? In twenty years, people might even be saying Elon Musk was a predecessor to him.

If the package was his then it might be something genuinely valuable. Far more than two hundred thousand credits its price was listed as. It could also just be an ultra-rare Pokémon card or a super special collector's edition of Disney's *Frozen* on holodisc. Still, I had a few minutes to spare. I'd managed to shave off some of my time when traffic was clearer than I'd hoped for. Everything looked shiny and golden right up until I reached the front gate and got confronted with the real danger to my perfect run: bureaucracy.

"What do you mean you won't let me in?" I asked, sitting on my bike, with the front door in plain view beyond the gate.

The security guard, fat and utterly unlike Atlas Security's typically superhuman-looking agents, stared at me unsympathetically. He was obviously a local hire, meant to look nonthreatening to the rich people who might visit with legitimate business. Delivery people, I presume, used the back but I didn't have time to take the twenty-minute drive around the estate that I was only slightly exaggerating the size of.

"You don't have a pass," the guard said, speaking with a thick Russian accent.

I debated shooting him and driving past when a pink-haired teenage girl in a form-hugging motorcycle suit like my own rode up on a hoverboard. She was about nineteen or twenty and carrying a box identical to my own. Her hair was noticeably tied into a ponytail that made her look even younger than she already was even as she came to a stop at the same gate. I couldn't quite guess her ethnicity but settled on a mixture of South Asian and Hispanic with a bottle of hair dye.

"Good evening, Paradise," the gate guard said, cheerfully. "Please head on."

"What?" I said, shaking my head as the clock ticked down on my delivery. "Are you kidding me?"

"She has a pass," the guard said, simply.

"Problem?" Paradise asked.

"I have a package this man won't let me deliver it!" I snapped.

"Not without a pass," the security guard said. "We're on a heightened security alert because of a shooting with bikers downtown."

I considered the shooting him in the face option very carefully.

"Oh," Paradise, said. "You want me to deliver it?"

I stared at her, wondering what sort of devious trick this was.

The security guard said, "You can't do that!"

Paradise rolled her eyes. "What does my pass say?"

"Unlimited access," the guard replied, sighing. "You can go on in with it."

"Thank you," Paradise said, turning to me. "Hey, yours looks just like mine!"

"You don't say," I muttered.

*Well, there's only one thing to do,* I thought. I kicked the rocket eject button on my bike that sent me flying over the guard station. My Nina and I hit the ground with an uncomfortable roll, my reinforced bones keeping me from breaking anything, and I made a beeline for the door.

I got knocked off my bike halfway through by an icer round in my leg then took three more in the back before reaching the door, package in hand. The nonlethal security rounds were electrical but somehow worked more at shutting people down than zapping them. I managed to push the doorbell before falling to one side, Atlas soldiers rushing up to my paralyzed body.

It felt like every neuron in my body was on fire but at least I'd delivered my package. Kind of. Little consolation that would be if they shot me in the head or sent me to one of the gulags in the Midwest. The door opened above me, the chipper face of James Madison looking down. He kind of looked like Seth Green before his fifth cybernetic upgrade.

"Package," I said, trying to hand it to him. I failed and it fell out of my hands. "Please sign for it."

Yeah, this wasn't one of my better ideas.

Everything went black.

# Chapter Three

## This is Why I Take Lethe, People

"Kei!" the voice of my father called to me.

Given my father had been dead for almost fifteen years, it indicated this was a dream or a memory. You know, exactly the sort of thing I took lethe to avoid but apparently it wasn't working right now, and I was having a helluva backlash. It was also possible I was dead and reliving my regrets, but I decided to put a pin in that idea for the time being.

"Kei!" My father repeated. "Get over here!"

"I'm coming, goddammit!" my thirteen-year-old self snapped back.

I was walking barefooted through a freezing creek in the middle of Kayayuga National Park, located in the south of Washington State. I was wearing rolled up jeans and three bundles of shirts that my mother had insisted I wear despite the fact I was in love with the cold. I knew other people were freezing but, as my favorite film at the time said, the cold never bothered me anyway.

It was a few years after the Eruption that had destroyed Wyoming and covered the entire Earth in a cloud of ash. The Long Winter had been an extinction-level event that humanity would have gotten through fine thanks to Black Technology if we hadn't been murdering each other left and right over toilet paper. My family had been forced to evacuate its home in Nebraska and had been moving from refugee camp to refugee camp ever since.

We'd ended up trading everything we had to buy an RV and joined with other refugees who decided the best way to stay alive was to keep moving. I was still in the stage where it seemed like it was all a grand adventure and perhaps in deep denial about how bad things had gotten.

I was appreciating the beautiful trees, snow, and animals around me without thinking about the fact Dad was shooting animals for fresh meat. Sometimes, he came back with canned food that I think he stole too. A few of those times, his clothes had also been covered in blood. That was from animals he killed, I liked to tell myself at least.

I had a vague awareness of my present self and had to wonder what was going on around my body. Was I being prepped for handing over to the cops, getting medical treatment, or something else? It was surreal remembering this unwanted period of my life while knowing I was disabled in the present. It made me wonder if coma patients ever experienced something similar.

"Don't use that kind of language, young lady!" John Springs called back, bringing my attention once more to the memory.

"Frick you!" I shouted back.

Yeah, I was a handful.

Still, I got out of the creek, wiped down my legs with a beach towel, and put on my socks and shoes. Despite the foul mouth I'd gained hanging around truckers, scavengers, and fellow wanderers, I was a reasonably happy kid. Again, maybe it was denial, but I thought things were going to work out.

I lost that feeling when I came home and saw that there were three strangers around our home on wheels in the middle of the makeshift camp that we were presently running with. They'd come in nice cars, wore suits, and were covered in tattoos. I didn't need much formal education—which had ended three years before anyway—to know they were Trikuza.

Whenever natural disasters happened and there was a scarcity of resources, the black market was bound to step in to fill the gap. Usually, this consisted of stealing the supplies meant for other people and killing anyone who objected. The Trikuza were a collection of Japanese, Russian, and American gangsters who had started recruiting refugees to help them loot groups not willing to pay their generous prices. It had the benefit of teaching a lesson while increasing their stores.

"Frick," I muttered, looking for my little brother, Ken. He was about three years younger than me and an annoying kid, unlike myself who was all grown up and mature. I resisted calling for him and instead looked around for some sign of him. Instead, I found myself startled by the voice of a fourth intruder.

"They're here to talk to your father about the last run he did," a man's voice spoke behind me and caused my little body to jump up half a foot.

Looking behind me, I saw the towering figure of a badly dressed Hispanic man with a ponytail, eye-patch, and features that looked like ten miles of bad road paved over another ten miles of it. Like if Danny Trejo had spent even more time at the gym before surviving a few gunfights.

The stranger's skin was sunburnt in a way that suggested years of working under scorching sunlight in a way that none of us were doing these days. The guy had numerous tattoos across his body, some Japanese while others of a more Western art style, which added to his strange appearance. His clothing was especially bizarre, though, with a muscle shirt and ripped blue jeans covered by a trench coat. Not exactly the proper clothing for the Long Winter. I saw he had a tanto, or Japanese short sword, sticking out of his belt while a holstered pistol was to the side of his right pants leg.

"Run?" I asked. "What does my father run?"

"Your father smuggles things," the man said.

I stared up at him. "Who cares about smuggling now?"

"Who indeed," the man said, smiling metal teeth.

"Who the frick are you?" I asked, continuing my habit of trying to insert vulgarities into every conversation I had. Mind you, I hadn't realized frick was just a substitute curse word my parents used and sounded a lot tamer than I intended it. My parents were clever that way.

"Snake Juarez," Snake said, looking down at me.

"Is that your real name?" I asked, fascinated by the figure. "Or just something that you decided to call yourself in order to sound badass?"

Yeah, I was a stupid kid back then.

Snake, however, was amused. "I used to be called Bug by my friends but that was before I burned a man alive."

I stared at him, realizing he wasn't kidding. "Wouldn't they call you Inferno or Fireball then?"

"No, I did it because he killed my pet snake," Snake said. "His name was Reggie."

"Ah," I said, having lost my dog in the Long Winter. "Well, you were justified. People who hurt animals deserve to die."

Snake looked down with his one good eye. "Does that include you, Bearkiller?"

I grimaced, not exactly pleased with that appellation. I'd learn to hate it even more as I grew to adulthood. "How did you know about that?"

It happened the month before. We'd been camping out when a grizzly had come after us. The poor thing had been starving and was half-mad with rabies or something—I was thirteen after all and not a veterinarian. I'd ended up shooting it with Dad's shotgun and putting it down. I felt awful about it, but Dad had a weird sense of pride over it.

"Your father wouldn't shut up about it last time I visited," Snake replied. "His little Davey Crockett."

"Davy Crockett killed a bear when he was three," I replied. "I'm thirteen."

"Davy also didn't do anything of the sort," Snake replied. "Good story to tell when running for Congress, though. I think your father was trying to distract us from the issues of missing money."

"Missing money, huh?" I said, worried. Dad surely wasn't stupid enough to steal from the Trikuza. "Money's not worth much these days."

"You'd be surprised," Snake replied, with just the slightest hint of rebuke. "The machine gods have already started rebuilding the coastal cities. Millions of bots are at work, building more of their kind to shoulder the burden of manual labor. The economy is starting to normalize. A couple of more years and we'll have supermarket shelves full of goop rather than just getting it from government dispensaries."

"Machine gods?" I asked.

I should have been scared and maybe I was but there was something about Snake that was oddly reassuring, as if he'd stepped out of a story rather than real life. Perhaps I was hoping to distract myself from the fact three thugs were in my home, talking to my parents about stolen money.

"The country, hell, the world, is no longer run by politicians and CEOs. The AI run it," Snake said, as if what he said wasn't insane. "They are the next stage of life, between us and the gods. Beings of light and knowledge that can help us transcend our meager flesh."

I nodded at him then took a step back. "If you don't mind, I'm going to walk away from the crazy person now."

Snake let out a short chuckle. "Probably wise, though I wouldn't go into your home."

I didn't like the implications of that. "How much trouble is my dad in?"

Snake frowned. "A lot."

"A lot a lot?" I asked, looking around for my baby brother again. "How much is a lot?"

I was terrified now. I didn't want to reconcile myself to the fact my mother had become a drunk and my father was a bandit. I knew that he'd done things for bad people, though. People who were dangerous and that we'd moved around camp sites and parks several times to avoid them. The Trikuza were not so easily shaken, though, especially since so many refugee groups depended on them for supplies.

"A lot, a lot," Snake said, dryly. "If your father is smart, he'll sign a contract."

"What kind of contract?" I asked. "Will he murder people for food?"

"Yes," Snake said. "Not really enforceable under the law but a sign of good faith. Back in Afghanistan, I used to see the Taliban do the same thing in villages. You'd take the children hostage and then force the dad to fight for you. If you were smart, you'd start training the son and put the women to other work."

I grimaced in disgust. "Jesus."

"Had nothing to do with it," Snake said. "It's a practice old as time. Your mom already strenuously objected. She wanted to trade you for more time."

"Not funny," I said, disgusted. My mom hadn't been doing well since she lost her baby last year and had turned to whatever bathroom brewed crap that she could trade for in every camp but that didn't mean she'd give me up. That was just evil of Snake to say. I never did learn the truth.

"I'm not joking," Snake said. "I think your dad would have taken the deal too but he's the most valuable commodity here."

"Liar!" I snapped, turning around and running to my home. I didn't care what the stranger had to say or what these Trikuza were planning.

"No, stop, wait," Snake said, sighing dramatically. He then started walking behind me with a slow inhumanly calm gait. "You don't want to go in there. Negotiations are not going well from what I hear."

"Screw you!" I shouted, finally reaching the screen door. I opened it and reached for the doorknob. That was when I heard three gunshots in quick succession. It was a nightmare moment frozen in time and while the other memory details might fade, this one was permanently burned into my memory. "No. No. No. No!"

The door opened and a tall, thin, well-dressed Japanese man stepped out. He was holding an automatic gun of a type that changed between memories. He had a sheathed tanto stuffed in the front of his pants, marked with the symbol of the Cyber Dragons on the hilt's end. I always wondered why so many criminals loved to broadcast their membership in supposedly secret societies.

I looked past him and saw my mother and father lying on the ground, bullets through their heads. I didn't see any sign of Ken and was too filled with a mixture of grief and rage to think straight. The man took one look at me and said, "Here she is."

I responded by grabbing the tanto in his pants, pulling it out of its sheath, and stabbing him in the stomach with it. It was a primal, insane action that should have gotten me killed.

Indeed, the next thing I remembered was getting my face smacked and being sent across the ground while he shouted. What happened next blurry before I heard more gunshots. Much to my surprise, I wasn't dead and saw, instead, Snake Vargas shooting the fallen form of the guy I'd just stabbed on the steps before shooting through the RV's windows. Snake walked in and checked the bodies before walking out.

I tried to scoot away but my eyes were red with tears and pain. "What are you doing?"

"Saving your life," Snake said.

"You were with them!" I said, staring. "I need to find my brother."

"He's gone," Snake said, as if discussing leaving behind the mail. "As for being with them, they're dead so I'm obviously not with them anymore. They're easily replaceable anyway. Street trash that got gobbled up by a greater syndicate when the opportunity presented itself. Easily replaceable. You, on the other hand, might be useful. Come with me!"

"You're crazy!" I snapped, scared and ready to run. Something about him paralyzed me, though.

Snake just smiled and, in that moment, I realized he was a psychopath.

"I'm not going with you!"

I was old enough to think Snake was a child molester or planned to sell me into prostitution. Truth be told, what he had planned for me was probably worse. Though he didn't see it that way.

"Where else are you gonna go, kid? You think any of these other caravanners are gonna take you in?"

I didn't respond. We'd had quite a time getting into this group since they weren't exactly all that enthusiastic about a mixed-race family. I didn't have any relatives and Child Services was a thing of the past. If I'd been thinking clearer, I might have run and he probably would have slit my throat then and there. "What do you want from me?"

"I used to belong to a brotherhood, the Carnivale," Snake said. "It was a real organization, not like this group of posing amateurs. We took fighters when they were your age and we put them through hell. But what emerged was strong. I wasn't sure until you stabbed poor Toko but when you did, I knew you had the instinct. Come with me and I'll make sure you'll eat your next meal and your next. Right up until you learn the skills, so you'll never be hungry again."

I had no idea that was a movie reference. "You don't want me to be a kid prostitute?"

It was an insane ridiculous question, except I would later find out that happened to a lot of girls my age in the Trikuza. I was also too much in shock to really process what was happening or how to deal with it. My parents were dead, my brother was missing, and a psychopathic murderer had just expressed his wish to adopt me. I would have run away if I'd been smart but right then I just felt like I would have died tired.

Snake laughed. "No, this is the American version of *Leon: The Professional*. Not the European."

I had no idea what that meant but nodded. I needed someone to take care of me back then. "I'll do what you say."

"I know you will," Snake said, patting me on the head. "Destiny has brought us together little one. You won't disappoint me."

"And if I do?"
He didn't answer.
He didn't need to.

# Chapter Four

## The Rich Really are a Different Species

I groaned as I woke up in Heaven. I was half-surprised this was figurative rather than literal, but I was inside a beautiful garden with genetically engineered plants, an environment dome, cultivated humidity, a huge natural-looking grotto, and cobblestone walkways throughout. Half-naked bio-sculpted servants with gold skin walked around carrying trays of fruit and water in crystal glasses. Their presence added to the sense of the place being halfway between a beach resort and an artificial Eden.

Weirdly, the thing that struck me the most was the air. It was super-oxygenated, and I could taste it with every breath. Having grown used to the incredibly foul air of New Los Angeles, it was weird to feel this stuff moving through my bloodstream. It was a luxury that just about summarized how the rich had changed since the Eruption: James Madison and his party of living Oscar statues didn't even breathe the same air as the rest of us.

I was lying on a wooden beach chair that had its own mattress and I was pleased to note I hadn't woken up in a bikini or swimwear. If this were a movie, someone would have changed me while I slept and that was always a lot creepier than people treated it. I had a headache from the icer blast to my face but could still see so at least they hadn't disrupted my eyes. There was a jamming field around the room, and I couldn't access infospace but, well, it didn't seem like I was a prisoner.

That was when the girl from earlier, Paradise, popped her head in front of my field of vision. "Hi!"

"Gah!" I said, falling off the deck chair. I silently cursed myself for falling for an almost vaudevillian comedy act, but I suspected that's what the other Rider had been going for.

"I'm Paradise! Paradise Principle!" Paradise said. "We met ear-lier before you acted like a crazy person."

Technically, we hadn't met. She'd just introduced herself to the security guard at the front gate and I'd overheard her. Paradise had changed from her earlier attire and was now in a green bikini that highlighted her cute, mostly natural body. She had the same malnourished look many of the poor born around the Eruption possessed. Thankfully, Paradise didn't look starved now, but it had left its mark on her. There were signs of cybernetic enhance-ment but mostly in terms of practical use like a wrist-jack and neck info-processor.

I got up off the ground and patted myself down. It was unnec-essary because even the dirt underneath my chair was probably cleaner than my hovel of a home. "Yeah, I remember. I'm Kei."

"Nice to meetcha!" Paradise said, picking up a glass of what looked to be spring water, complete with a little paper umbrella. It was more decadent than alcohol in certain circles. "Why did you do that?"

"Do what?" I asked, still groggy.

"Jump the fence and assault the front door," Paradise explained.

I frowned, wondering if she was my competition in a race that I hadn't been informed I was participating in. "I had a package to deliver. I had only a few seconds to give it to my target."

"Weird," Paradise said. "I just left it in the mailbox at the gate."

I stared at her. "Did they accept that?"

"Yep," Paradise said. "But A+ for effort! I really hope you're getting a big tip."

I glared. "Right. I'll be sure to ask."

I looked to see if there was any water available for me and was pleased to see an entire pitcher of it. Completely ignoring my surroundings, I grabbed the pitcher and started gulping it down without a glass. It tasted strange, though still like water. "What the hell is in this stuff?"

"I think it's been spiked with a mild hallucinogen," Paradise replied. "Also, vitamins! Because rich people!"

"Oh," I said, blinking. "Probably shouldn't have drunk so much then."

"Probably not," Paradise said. "However, it's much funnier that you did."

I debated hitting her but decided that would be too cruel. "I don't suppose you know why we're here or what kind of package we delivered."

"Yep!" Paradise said, sipping her water some more.

I stared at her, waiting for an answer. When one wasn't immediately forthcoming, I asked, "And?"

Paradise leaned in conspiratorially, holding her hand up against her face as if to block nonexistent lip readers from seeing her statement. "I think it was some kind of test."

"No kidding," I said, rolling my eyes. "Whatever gave you that idea? The fact a bunch of assassins chased after us or that it was timed?"

"Both," Paradise said, missing my sarcasm. "Honestly, I think the richie-rich types get all of their ideas on how Riders work from movies."

I stared at her. "Three people died trying to get at me. Possibly more. Now you're saying people tried to kill you too?"

"Yep." Paradise said. "I just blinded their cyber-eyes and bike computers. I then reprogrammed their bikes' GPS to guide them to a police station where I dropped an anonymous tip about them delivering child porn. I had some leftover files from where I took down a crooked politician from Belarus. Fun-fun. I'm a techjack when I'm not doing runs."

I almost bolted then and there. I had severe issues with techjacks. They were the true children of the Leak. Not long after the Eruption, someone had figured out a way to install cybernetic upgrades into the brains of children which would be much more effective than the ones installed in adults.

Scientists had made the discovery while experimenting with implants in the brains of kids suffering from disabilities in countries that didn't have laws against that sort of things. Most of the children had died but the results had been super-geniuses that could react to infospace better than any natural programmer.

Personally, I found the practice vile and thought any parent who allowed it to happen to their kid should be shot. Oh, and Snake had insisted on doing it to me at age fourteen, which had no impact on my opinions regarding them. No sir.

"You don't say," I said. "Listen, we gotta get out of here. If these people are willing to send hitmen against the people working for them as a test, then they're insane. There's absolutely no reason to stay."

"Of course, there is," Paradise said, finishing off her water.

"Which is?" I asked, wondering if she understood the depth of our problem.

"Money!" Paradise said. "We haven't been paid yet."

I blinked. There was that. The only thing worse than people trying to kill you in the morning was not getting compensated for it. "You raise a very good point."

"Of course," Paradise said, tapping her head. "Paradise Principle, Super Genius."

I stared at her, wondering if I was going to be doing a lot of that. "Is that a reference to something?"

"*Aesop's Fables*," Paradise said. "The clever coyote will never catch the dumb roadrunner because God hates him."

"Uh huh," I said, getting used to dealing with lunatics. "Well, then let's get paid. I'm sure James Madison is among this bacchanalia of spoiled body sculpted trust fund kids. We just have to find the biggest ego."

Paradise grinned.

"He's behind me, isn't he?" I asked.

Paradise nodded.

"Goddammit," I muttered. "When did my life become a bad comedy?"

"Probably when you met me," Paradise said.

"No, it was before then," I replied, turning around.

Standing behind me was James Madison and two others. The tech billionaire was wearing a multi-colored robe with holographic patterns, shimmersilk swim trunks, diamond-encrusted sandals, electric holorings on every finger, a New Who band t-shirt, and a Los Angeles Tigers rollerball ball cap. Only the rich could afford to dress that tackily. It was the closest I had ever been to a billion credits. Both his legs were artificial, I could tell by the slightly different skin texture, making me wonder if he'd suffered an accident or had replaced them out of transhumanist vanity.

"Nice to meet you, Ms. Springs," James said, offering his hand. "I was just talking to your associates."

"My associates?" I asked, looking past him, and immediately wishing I hadn't.

The first of the two figures was someone I recognized: Miles Ashe, formerly *Detective* Miles Ashe of the Advanced Tech Crimes Unit of the NLAPD. He was a tall, good-looking man with a shaved head and action movie build. He was wearing a blast vest and baggy pants with several weapons prominently displayed. The only thing I disliked more than dirty cops was honest ones and he straddled the line between both. Well, at least until he'd been kicked off the force and gone full Rider.

"Hey Kei," Miles said, smiling that smug grin of his. "Long time no see."

"Not long enough," I replied.

Yeah, we'd dated, could you tell? It said everything I needed to know about our time together that I barely remembered any of it. He wasn't the boyfriend I'd shot at but not far above him. Then again, maybe I'd shot at Miles too and just forgot. Lethe was funny that way.

"Ah, you wound me," Miles said.

"Only if I miss," I replied.

Miles gave a dismissive shrug. "The sis and niece still ask about you."

I remembered them just fine. "Give them my love."

Miles got an odd expression on his face. "Sure."

The second of the two figures spoke. "We have a schedule to keep, James. We had best get a move on it."

The other person was a beautiful blonde woman of indeterminate age, increasingly common with the prevalence of Shells, that I suspected was completely fake from hair to skin cells. The woman was wearing a white business suit that probably cost more than I made in a year and shoes that were both practical as well as stunning. She looked like a swimwear model dressed for the boardroom, but I could tell her modifications were all military-grade. They'd just been trussed up significantly. She spoke with an Italian accent.

"Very true," James replied. "Ms. Springs, Ms. Principle, meet Mr. Miles Ashe who I believe one of you already knows. Also, Lucita Biondi."

He said the name as if it should mean something. That was the problem with the ultra-rich, they assumed wealth meant fame.

I waved to them. "Hi, Mr. Madison. Hi, Miles. Hello, Italian Barbie."

Miles smirked.

The woman frowned. "I'm the CTO of Atlas Security."

"Oh," I said, as if Lucita just said she was the ruler of the universe and that might not have been more intimidating. There were suits and there were suits. Lucita here was apparently one of THE suits that controlled the fate of billions. James Madison might be richer than God, but he probably couldn't order the overthrow of governments or invasion of countries.

I decided to get the hell out of Dodge for the second time today. "Yes, well that's all very fascinating, but I have a hot date tonight. Oh, and my mother is coming in. Plus, a puppy I adopted needs an operation. Can I have my payment so I can go? I did fulfill the contract."

"The contract was a test," James said, ignoring everything I just said. "An opportunity for another job."

"We needed two more couriers," Lucita said, smiling. "You two passed."

"I'm not sure if I'm looking for another job like that now," I said, in all honesty. Being a Rider meant accepting the possibility of being shot at. I just objected to being shot at by my employers.

"Sure, you are," Miles said. "We all are. I was the one who recommended you."

I narrowed my eyes. "I thought Jimmy did."

"Jimmy opted out," Miles said. "Still, he owed me a favor. I had him call you because I knew you wouldn't accept the job if it came from me."

"No kidding!" I said, suddenly furious with Miles. "People shot at me!"

"People are always shooting at you," Miles said.

"Right," I said, sighing. I didn't want to go over the same argument I'd just had in my head. "Usually, it's people I'm working against rather than for."

"It's a long story," James said. "Suffice to say, no one was hurt."

"People are dead," I replied.

"No one is dead here," James corrected, as if it made any difference whatsoever.

Lucita was all business. "The money you'll be given is more than fair for the job, but it will also include being owed a favor by me, personally, and Mr. Madison here."

I was a bit woozy from the spiked drugs and getting shot multiple times, icer rounds or not. "Is the Trikuza going to be okay with you using a bunch of their people as target practice?"

"We arranged it beforehand with the New Post Office serving as an intermediary," Lucita said, simply. "The Lords of Hell *Bōsōzoku* gang had been skimming from their masters' drug tithes for some time. The Trikuza were going to eliminate the gang anyway, but this way we all got some use of them."

"And now some of them will live in prison," Paradise said, referring to the ones she diverted to the cops. "I have saved lives by my actions. Well, at least until the Trikuza have them all shivved in the shower when one or two of them inevitably tries to make a deal. It's the circle of life or circle of crime, or circle of crime life."

I started to wonder if Paradise was insane. Still, the statement that those Trikuza were affiliates they'd deliberately sent to die was both reassuring as well as horrifying. It meant that this was no mere rich idiot playing with people he didn't understand but a guy with genuine ties to the underworld. That made the stakes much, much higher.

Given the circumstances, there was only one question I could really ask. "How much is fair?"

"Two hundred thousand United National Alliance credits, each, upon the completion of the job," Lucita responded. "An additional ten thousand credits per day plus expenses. A fifty-thousand credit bonus will be awarded at the discretion of your handlers based on their performance evaluation of your efforts. Medical and legal fees included."

I stared at her, open mouthed then closed it. "Frick, that *is* fair."

Frankly, that was enough money that I could stop living off the grid and buy myself a new identity so I could live somewhere that I wouldn't instantly ping the Cyber Dragons. I'd changed my face, hair, and information but I hadn't enough money to completely erase my old identity. Hell, I still had the tattoo that was thankfully common enough to not lead Snake's people directly back to me. If they weren't lying—and you can't trust suits—their favor might also let me escape completely from my old bosses. Something that they'd know if they'd talked to Miles. Dammit, I wished I'd never slept with him and gotten all chatty while drunk.

"Do we have an accord?" Miles asked.

I sucked in my breath. "I guess we do."

Why did I have a feeling I was making the second worst mistake of my life?

# Chapter Five

## Where I Help the Evil Corporations Take Over

This was a terrible decision on my part, one that I could only attribute to temporary insanity brought about by being iced, drinking hallucinogenic water, and naked greed. The greed, at least, was something I could stand by. Greed was what made the world go around. If you were greedy enough, you could get enough money to take care of yourself and your friends. That was the best life you could hope to have in this world.

Mind you, that piece of wisdom had come from Snake so maybe it was not the best source to draw my life philosophy from. I ended up drinking some more drugged water from the pitcher in my hands in hopes of making agreeing seem less stupid. It worked.

"What would have happened if I'd said no?" I asked, wondering why the hell I'd said it the moment it came out of my mouth.

James narrowed his eyes. "Absolutely nothing."

Why didn't I believe him?

Paradise popped a stick of insta-bubble gum in her mouth and popped a bubble within seconds. "As long as I get paid, I'm up for anything."

"Never say that," I said. "You never know who is going to test you on it."

Paradise shrugged. "It's a figure of speech. The brothel I grew up in has strict rules about consensual sex and safety."

"Wait, what?" I asked.

"Perhaps it would be better if we showed you why we're doing this," James said. "It'll help you understand the importance of what we're doing."

"Or they can just act like professionals and do what they're told," Lucita muttered.

"I *am* a professional," I said, annoyed at her accusation.

"So is my mother!" Paradise said, cheerfully. "You should see her reviews on the Rate Everything app!"

Good Lord. "Just tell me what you want us to do and why it involved getting bikers to shoot at us."

"Probably because bikers will be shooting at us," Paradise said.

"Thank you, Paradise," I muttered, not bothering to look at her.

"You're welcome," Paradise said.

I debated asking if I could shoot her, but I was afraid they'd say yes. Miles looked amused by her words but that was no surprise. Men tended to find irritating behaviors charming if the person displaying them was hot. I had the exact same problem with jerkasses. It was part of the reason I dated more women than men, but I'd gradually conclude that I still found jerks charming when they were hot, gender notwithstanding. I really needed to work on that.

"We'd like you to deliver a package," James said, simply.

I blinked. "That doesn't require this kind of song and dance. Unless you need to deliver it to the moon, in which case I suggest you contact Space-X."

"We don't know where the package is," Lucita said.

"Then you should hire a detective," I said, wondering if the money was worth it.

"They did," Miles said.

"A good detective," I snarked. "Anyway, you can hire me to deliver it when you find it. I'll be seeing myself out."

I stood up only for Paradise to pull me back down with one hand. She was surprisingly strong, making me wonder if she had cyberware under her seemingly natural exterior. "It's everybody or no one, Kei. I need this money. I have people depending on me in the Zone."

The fact she was from the Refugee Zone made me immediately regret all the shade I'd thrown at her. The Zone was the place people like me had been put and was basically a walled off district of the city—every major city really—that served as part refugee camp and part *favela*. They were temporary holding facilities for the destitute that became less temporary with each passing day. There were no education, social services, or real rights for the people within. It was one of the rare places where organized crime's oppression was an improvement over the nothing the Emergency Government provided. My family could have ended up in one of them and probably would have if they'd lived.

"Alright," I said. "I said I'm in. I'm in. I'm listening now."

"Good," Lucita said, and I honestly wondered if she was contemplating killing me. She had the look of a killer. The vibe. It was something you picked up if, well, you were a long-term killer like me. The three people I'd offed today were just a few more to the dozens of kills I'd made over the years. I didn't even feel guilt anymore, I couldn't. Like recognized like.

"Are you familiar with Blipvert?" James asked.

I blinked. Yeah, I was, but in an infomail spam ad sort of way. It was being touted as the next big thing in advertising. "It's a really fast series of images projected right into the brain with music?"

"It's named for something from a TV show from the Eighties," James said. "Blipvert is actually a dummy AI that instantly sorts through all of your personal data to determine the best images, music, and presentation to get you to buy products."

"Gasp!" Paradise said the word aloud. "Now no one will be able to resist getting that exercise bike they can't afford!"

"That's the idea," James said. "The fact is, it's always been a show piece for Delphi Future Analysis."

"A wholly owned subsidiary of Atlas Security," Lucita added automatically.

James shot her a glare. "It doesn't actually work. You can't go through that much data to make the perfect sales pitch. We've got things that can really make a pitch but no miracle programs that can do it all. The claim we can attracts investors and good publicity, though, which has allowed us to build a nearly insurmountable advantage over other Big Data advertising firms."

"So, you're engaged in fraud," I said.

"More like faking it until you make it," James said, cheerfully.

"Which is another way of saying fraud," I said. "So, what's the problem, one of your employees find evidence it's all a scam?"

James snorted derisively. "Yeah, because we can't fight that with our lawyers. We work hand in pocket with the top five biggest news networks and the next forty buy all their news packages from the top five."

"There's always the private news feeds," Miles explained, as offput by James' attitude as I was.

"They already claim the megacorporations use mind control on consumers," James replied. "Also, aliens control the government, reptile men created homosexuality, and the Eruption was caused by liberals."

"Sexual freedom for women causes earthquakes!" Paradise said. "That's what I've heard from at least two missionaries. Thankfully, I belong to the Church of the First Orgasm which is a—"

"Moving on," I interrupted. "What is the problem then?"

"One of our employees got it to work," Lucita said, deadpanning. "Got it to work better than any of us could have ever imagined."

"Bull," I said, realizing they were saying someone had successfully invented mind control. This was pure science fiction and I said that as a cyborg who lived in a country secretly controlled by AI. Which I didn't mention my belief in because I didn't want to get lumped in with the other crazy people.

"Perhaps you should see the results," a woman swimming around in the nearby pool said.

I pointed at her. "Are they supposed to be able to listen in on us?"

"All of the servants here are drones," James replied, sighing. "AI controlled constructs by Perseus. The guests are my wife's permanent hangers on and don't have a thought in their pretty little heads. She, however, does."

The woman stepped out of the water like Ursula Andress in *Doctor No* with golden skin and long crimson hair. She moved with the confidence of someone who absolutely knew she was the most beautiful woman in the room. An impressive fact since Lucita looked like she had been made by nerds to masturbate to.

The newcomer had a considerably more naturalistic look and I suspected she had no cyberware installed whatsoever. Either that or had paid extensively to look all-natural. The woman controlled her surroundings with an aura that made me look at her like I was seeing my first human being after being marooned on a desert island for a year. She was wearing a V-shaped bikini that was more modest than some of the non-wear her guests were sporting but still accented every part of her toned physique.

"And who is she?" I said, finally managing to ask.

"Helen Troy," James said. "I couldn't get her to take my last name."

"How epic!" Paradise said, weirdly avoiding looking at her directly as if she suspected doing so would cause her to burst into flame. "Your parents must have known you would be lovely!"

"Either that or I had my name legally changed," Helen said. "No one in Hollywood would have hired me under my birth name."

"You're an actress?" I asked, stupidly. It shouldn't have surprised me that a stone-cold knockout was married to an older, average-looking billionaire. The only difference from now and forty years ago is the fact more financially successful women were marrying younger, hotter men.

"I used to be," Helen said. "I never got beyond such cinematic classics as *Christmas Massacre III*, *Blood Robot*, and *The Erotic Adventures of Robin Hood*."

"I saw that last one!" Paradise said. "Time is going to tell on its genius."

"I'm so sorry," I said.

"It's fine," Helen said. "It provided the funding necessary to get my tech start up off the ground, invent Blipvert, and sell it to James for two point five billion dollars."

I blinked, processing that. "So, you starred in a bunch of bad movies to pay for your tech career?"

"Lots of women are strippers to pay for college," Paradise said, defending my unwitting attack. "I plan to get my PHD online: a pimping hoes degree."

I wanted to hit her for that but felt like it would be kicking a particularly energetic dog.

"Right," I said, shaking my head. "Why are you married to James then if you're rich yourself?"

"Hey!" James said.

Lucita and Miles both struggled not to laugh behind him.

"Love," Helen said, surprising me. "Ours is a meeting of minds. I was trained by the Gordon Institute for Young Women and that has ruined me for the handsome but stupid."

"Thank you," James said, puffing up his chest.

"Really?" I asked, still skeptical.

"It helps both of us can sleep with anyone we like," Helen said. "This freeloading cult around us isn't cheap but it has its uses."

"Oh!" I said, suddenly understanding. "That's different then."

"Do you boink the robots too?" Paradise asked.

"Yes," Helen said. "But I think of that as just using toys."

James looked utterly humiliated, and I didn't blame him. "Can we get back to the blackmail?"

"Wait, what? Blackmail?" I asked. This was getting a lot more complicated than I was comfortable with and I was uncomfortable with it from the start.

James frowned. "Solomon Jones is the name of the man I want you to find. The reason we're using Riders instead of detectives is because he has lots of contact with mercenary couriers. He is almost impossible to find if he doesn't want to be, though, and would disdain anyone who wasn't part of the life."

"He has a radical socialist agenda he believes Blipvert can assist him on," Lucita said. "Fight the power, down with the man, anarchy in LA, and so on."

"He sounds like a teenager," I said, "or at least someone who never grew up."

"Hey!" Paradise said. "Teenagers only resent adults because they know better."

I raised an eyebrow. "How old are you, anyway, kid?"

"Twenty-two," Paradise said, giving an exaggerated sigh. "I can already feel myself getting more practical and less idealistic. Looking back on my misspent youth. Ah, when I was young, Riders were dangerous and talented, not the pampered infospace-addicted techjacks of today. That was a long time ago. Maybe two, three years ago."

I rolled my eyes. "Yeah, I don't know what it's like working with people almost a decade younger who act like idiots."

"Nice burn," Paradise said. "I give it a six point five."

I'd heard of Solomon Jones, and it was another sign I'd gotten in way over my head. He was a techjack who'd had much of his brain pulled out as an adult, which meant serious psychological issues at best. He was, however, famous as a hacker as well as supplement to Riders who dabbled in street mercenary work on the side. Which, to be honest, I occasionally did myself. Supposedly, he was able to tear through most barriers like they were paper and had a dozen blackmail businesses on the side. If Madison and Troy had gotten involved with him then they were the definition of rich idiots.

"Solomon was an outside contractor we hired to do work for us trying to shore up Blipvert," Helen said. "Test it out under uncontrolled darknet conditions."

"And you didn't think that giving your ultra-secret program to an anti-establishment street merc was a bad idea?" I asked.

"It didn't work," James muttered. "Our basis for the program was made from fragments of a true AI that fell into my hands through my wife's company. Unfortunately, that wasn't enough to achieve what we wanted. Blipvert's release was only supposed to generate buzz. 'Ooo, the criminals are so excited about this new program. The government doesn't want you to know about this secret program.' And so on. We figured Solomon would do some cheap mods to it and pirate the software before we released a better version in a couple of years."

Their idea of how to generate buzz was only slightly more ethical than their sending a trio of assassins after me as a test.

"Then the murders began," Lucita replied. "As well as the suicides."

"Show her," Helen said. "Show her everything."

"Me too, please," Paradise nodded.

Helen nodded.

James transferred the information directly to my brain implant. I was surprised James knew about it and even more so that the data was accepted. Hundreds of text and video files flooded my brain in an instant and were sorted like a deck of cards. It all painted a picture that was not so much grim as outright horrifying. I was made of stern stuff but some of the scenes that greeted me were nightmarish even to a soul jaded by years of street work. Blipvert wasn't being used by Solomon as advertising—it was being used for domestic terrorism.

I saw fathers killing their entire families, wives smothering their babies, mass shooting incidents at office buildings, and a guy who doused himself in gasoline before lighting himself up in the middle of a Presbyterian church's live broadcast. Life was cheap in New Los Angeles, but this was particularly despicable.

"You think he made them do this?" I asked, feeling sick to my stomach.

"Can't he just have been claiming credit for people going postal after the fact?" Paradise asked, showing she was a lot more insightful than she appeared. Then again, she'd have to be.

"The possibility has been considered," Miles said, as if reviewing a case. "Also, dismissed."

"He sent us the names and locations of the targets' attacks before they happened. Too late for us to do anything about it," Lucita said, sounding genuinely outraged by the man's actions. That surprised me. I thought she was going to be a bitch from her permanently highlighted hair down to her supremely angular feet.

"It's still possible these are faked," Miles replied. "I've seen plenty of people do unimaginable things due to threats, drugs, insanity, and good old-fashioned indoctrination. But none of these guys had a history of instability or, let's be frank, homicidal psychosis until a week or so before their actions. Somehow, Solomon induced breakdowns that made them carry out the attacks he wanted. This could just be the most extreme example of what he can do with the technology or maybe it's all he can do."

"I still don't know why you want us involved," I said, convinced they were telling the truth but not sure how I could help. Advertising algorithms turned into terrorist weapons were a bit outside my wheelhouse.

"We need you to look like mercs that want to do business with him," James explained simply. "Your credibility is real so you can serve as an intro. Then, when you get close, I want you to neutralize him and bring the technology back to us. Plus, any of his notes that he's made about modifying it."

I blinked. "You still want this after witnessing what it's been used for? There had to be at least three hundred people dead from that."

"At least," Helen said, smiling inappropriately.

There was a weird twitch in the back of my mind when thinking about this. It was the same feeling I got whenever I thought of the things that lethe had obliterated memories regarding but more so. It was akin to deja vu, albeit more painful, and felt like someone scratching at my conscious brain. All I could tell was that there was something I should know about this deal that I didn't now. Strangely, looking at Miles, I could see he was staring at me intently as if I should be saying more.

One of the servants brought Paradise's clothes back to her on a silver platter, having been cleaned and pressed. "Your attire, ma'am."

"Thanks, Jeeves. Yeah., three hundred dead is pretty awful,"

Paradise said, changing beside me without any sense of shame.

James looked defensive and even a little ashamed. "Possessing Blipvert's modified version will allow us to create defenses against it for the public and—"

"Yes, of course we want it," Helen interrupted. "Solomon proved it worked. We can't leave any loose ends. Kill him, his associates, and destroy any backups he may possess. We'll provide you the resources necessary to make it happen."

Lucita nodded. "Weapons are only useful when you have a decided advantage over who controls what. Blipvert could well be one of the twenty-first century's greatest. We need to keep it out of enemy hands by any means necessary."

Ah. So that was it. They didn't just need a Riders, they needed assassins. There was only one thing to say to that.

"Then I'm going to need a lot more money."

# Chapter Six

## Where I Conclude Negotiations to Kill a Man

James and his wife proved surprisingly stingy for billionaires able to afford their own planet. However, they did agree to increase our fee by an additional fifty percent should we bring back proof that Solomon was dead and everything he had on Blipvert was destroyed. They'd outright double the fee if we made sure to give them his research. All we had to do was provide a pair of corporate suits access to something that could control men's minds! Yeah, I was going to hell for this. Not that I wasn't already.

"So, do you have any idea where we can begin looking for Solomon?" I asked, wondering if I was going to have to burn every bridge I had in the underworld. I didn't know much about Solomon or his friends, but Riders tended to take a dim view of people who killed other Riders. The price had to be right to make it happen. Given that I wasn't going to be sharing with anyone but Paradise and Miles, that meant I was going to be making a lot of enemies. I was comfortable with that. Honor among thieves was something only people who weren't thieves believed in.

"Infospace," James said, which was a bit like saying "the internet."

"You're going to have to be a bit more specific," I replied, sighing.

The old internet had been destroyed by the Eruption and subsequent Long Winter. Maintaining the old infrastructure had taken a backseat to getting basic water, power, and supply lines running. However, when they did rebuild it, the AI had replaced it with something infinitely more powerful. Quantum computers ran the world's data streams now and had alleged infinite capacity for storage as well as detail. Infospace was a new frontier for a lot of people but, for me, was just another avenue of my job.

It was different from the old internet because people could do more than communicate with text and pictures. They could use their neuro-linked avatars to have mind-blowing sex, play video games where they could feel themselves slaughtering armies, or hang out in social clubs where they were living gods. The only limits were the facts you still had all your body's biological needs, and few people could afford more than a few hours every week. One of the easiest and most profitable runs you could do was delivery equipment that allowed infospace time to be pirated. It was like stealing cable according to Snake, not that I knew what that meant.

Ever since direct neural transceivers were made without need for cybernetics, programs could be created to simulate life almost perfectly by triggering the areas of the brain that received input from your senses. Which was supposedly better than actual life since you could get all the good bits without the pain or ugliness. Personally, I preferred meatspace. I had spent plenty of hours logged into infospace myself and could understand why people would want to stay there, but it was all an illusion. The world's most realistic RealDream porn was still just porn and a veteran of a thousand simulations was still just a virgin masturbating to CGI fantasies.

"I love infospace," Paradise said. "I spend all my time there when I'm not working."

James smiled. "Then you're in good company because that's where we need you to check. Solomon lives in infospace twenty-four-seven."

"Ah, so he's a Sleeper," I said. "Great."

Sleepers were the post-Eruption Western version of Japan's *Hikikomori* and it was an actual disease according to the Emergency Government Medical Association. Addicts to infospace, they chose to do all their interactions via holograms, datafeeds, or RealDreams.

"So, you're being blackmailed by a guy who never leaves his apartment," I said, unimpressed.

"Worse," Lucita said, contemptuously.

"Solomon Jones lives on infospace," Solomon said. "He keeps his body drugged and fed via life support equipment that is attended by nursing staff as well as micro-stimulators. He maybe gets up an hour a week and even that is questionable. It's why he depends on Riders providing him and his people supplies."

I stared at him, disbelieving. "So, you're willing to shell out half a million credits for us to track down and kill a murderous *coma patient*."

"And you can't just e-mail him?" Paradise said. "Contact his avatar? Track him that way?"

I'd started out thinking this would be an impossible job but now I was wondering if I was being overpaid. They were connected to Atlas Security, and they couldn't track a guy who needed full-time medical attention and probably couldn't move? That wasn't even incorporating the fact that he'd need massive numbers of supplies to keep state of the art with his equipment. It really hurt my perception of the super-rich as all-powerful.

"Solomon has managed to somehow make it impossible to trace him even with the aid of AI," Lucita explained, as if it was a matter of personal embarrassment. "Conventional attempts to track him down through the underworld have also failed. Which is why we felt hiring Riders would be good."

"You'd have more luck if you didn't shoot at them," I replied.

Lucita shrugged. "There's a reason that we've blocked all infospace access in this place. We're on the backfoot when facing Solomon."

"It gets worse," James said, looking at me. "You could say that Solomon has something of a cult of followers. Groupies and hackers who are incredibly devoted to him and serve as gatekeepers for his time. You'll have to get past them as well."

"The enormous computer company and security agency can't handle a renegade Rider?" I asked. "What does he even want?"

"Money," James said, dryly.

"So, pay him," I said, still not understanding. "Cut the Mad Bomber Who Bombs Peoples' Brains at Midnight a check."

Both James and Helen looked at me like I was an idiot.

"They have," Miles explained. "But the thing is when you give someone a lot of money to do something, they tend to do it more. Paying Solomon off has not stopped the attacks either. In fact, it's made them worse."

"They never should have paid him in the first place since that has given him resources he didn't possess before," Lucita said, disgusted. "We don't know if Blipvert is responsible for causing these attacks but if it is, it is a weapon that has to be stopped from being proliferated."

It surprised me that Lucita was the first one to speak of moral reasons for getting rid of the guy. She also sounded sincere. Which meant she was a great actor since Italian Barbie still wanted to acquire the weapon. "Worried about lone actor assassins?"

"The early twenty-first century internet was capable of radicalizing many disenfranchised young men and women without mind control," Lucita said. "Now we have ways of getting into the mind that make previous methods of indoctrination look juvenile. There are governments, terrorist groups, corporations, and cults who would love to wreak havoc with this program. I find it telling that he hasn't used it for anything less dramatic. It's possible it can't do anything else but kill. If so, it is better that it does not exist."

"Yeah, you'd rather people just kill for money not ideology," Miles said, surprising me.

"Yes," Lucita said. "Money is, after all, Atlas' reason for existence. The worst thing to a dedicated professional soldier is an enthusiastic amateur one."

So much for her being the moral one of the group. "Do you even have any idea where he might be?"

"We know where one of his former bases of operations is," James replied. "He was inhabiting it as of a few weeks ago and didn't clear it out. His people are probably watching it so we decided to leave it alone until we had people who could investigate without undue attention."

"And will Solomon's people not notice that we just came to his house?" I asked.

"That's what we're counting on," James said. "We figure you could pose as buyers."

I wondered how stupid these people were that if they wanted to use us as anonymous buyers then why the hell did they make a bunch of noise hiring us and getting us in shootouts across downtown LA. Since they didn't seem like morons, well Italian Barbie and Helen at least, I had to wonder if they were playing a deeper game.

I blinked, wondering if the packages were actual bombs. "I feel like you're still holding back on us."

"Kei," Paradise said. "Just let the crazy rich people do their crazy rich plan."

"I just like knowing details about my jobs," I replied.

"Which is why almost no one hires you for Rider work," Miles said.

"Lots of people hire me. Sometimes twice," I said, annoyed. I didn't buy it we were going to be able to pass ourselves off as anonymous buyers. There were dozens of people ranging from guards to the guests around us who could report otherwise but I needed this job so, like Miles and Paradise, I supposed I had to shut my mouth. "Anyway, I'm in. So, when do we get started?"

Lucita smiled broadly. "Now. I'll show you to the garage so we can get started."

"We?" I asked.

"I'm coming with you," Lucita said. "This operation is too important to leave to chance."

Great, now I had a babysitter. "Oh, this just gets better and better."

"There's another member of the team you have to meet," Lucita said. "I think you'll like him."

"I sincerely doubt that," I said, putting aside my now-empty water pitcher and standing up. "You coming, Paradise?"

Paradise sighed. "Yep. Sadly, I didn't even get to swim around in the massive grotto of the gods. I just hung out in my bathing suit looking sexy."

"Such a shame," I said, faking sympathy.

"I know!" Paradise said.

"Wait, did they give you a bathing suit?" I asked.

"Where else did you think I got one?" Paradise asked, as if it was a stupid question.

"You know we're going to need equipment for this," I said to Lucita, diverting the topic quickly. I fully expected this infiltration was going to fail and the best way to get Solomon would be to bust heads until someone talked and we shot his sleeping ass in whatever infospace rig he was plugged into. It was going to be an ugly job, but I'd had worse. Much worse. Ones I even remembered. Snake had always said that you had to divorce yourself from the act and I'd become all too good at that. Still, I was glad the person I was killing this time had it coming. Terrorism, extortion, and blackmail were straightforward even by my standards.

"Everything you need is going to be provided," Helen said, coldly. "I've already gone over the details with Miles."

Miles grinned. "She's been very helpful."

I raised an eyebrow and wondered if there was something there. Then again, maybe that was because I considered Miles to be an incorrigible skirt chaser like most heterosexual men (or Sapphic female) cops I'd known. Of course, the ones I knew weren't exactly the cream of the crop either. "I'll have to double check."

"Of course," Helen said.

Miles frowned and escorted me out the side door of the garden, leaving behind the billionaires and their faux Garden of Eden. Unfortunately, the interior of the mansion wasn't much better. It was halfway between a sun god's temple and Buckingham Palace with massive hallways, antiques imported from across the world (or made to look like they were antiques by clever forgers), and huge windows letting in light or generating it as seen fit.

Notably, I saw a couple of rooms off to the side that looked like the apartments of IT guys and suspected those were the only ones James himself used. This was all for show and the result of someone with way too much money who didn't know how to spend any of it. Because, really, it's not like he could give it away to the needy or anything—the other corporates would have him killed. Huh, I meant that as a joke, but I half suspected they would. He'd make them look bad.

Miles, meanwhile, walked up beside me. "So, what have you been up to? It's been a while."

I rolled my eyes. God, was he hitting on me? "Well, aside from people trying to kill me, I've mostly lived a life of decadent sex, drugs, and rock and roll. I also slept with your girlfriend."

Miles shrugged. "Which one? Do you have pictures?"

I shook my head. "Ugh."

Miles frowned. "Listen, there are some things you need to know. Important things."

"Not now, Miles," I said, not in the mood. I looked back at Lucita. "So, who is this other member of the group I haven't met?"

"An old friend," Lucita said. "He's a bit more in touch with the street than a typical Atlas executive."

I snorted. "Another one of you wants to do some poverty tourism?"

I did not like suits as a rule. Even though they were ninety percent of my high paying clientele, they were everything wrong with this world. Somehow, when a half-billion people were dying in the civil wars and famine that followed the Eruption, they'd managed come out ahead.

"Not quite," Lucita said. "I admit, though, I prefer to stay in the rich and decadent side of things."

"Versus the poor and decadent?" I asked.

"Yes," Lucita said, without a hint of irony.

That was when Paradise jogged up, once more dressed. "Here!"

"We weren't leaving without you," I said, simply. "How long have you been a Rider anyway?"

"Long enough," Paradise said, looking around. "Wow, I could totally live here without anyone noticing."

"I wouldn't recommend that," Lucita said, walking in front of them. "Atlas Security is quite good at preventing that. Our agents are always watching."

I looked up at one of the carefully hidden security cameras, I'd spotted like fourteen so far. "Yeah, that's not creepy."

"Eh, I can slice anything," Paradise said, cheerfully. "One time, when I was really bored, I lived inside a megaplex mall with a fake charge card for a year. No one ever questioned that I didn't work there, and Maxi-Mart paid for it."

Miles looked at her strange. "Why would you do that?"

"Because living is good!" Paradise said. "Also, because I was still trying to find my feet as a Rider and didn't want my family at the This Side of Paradise caught up with all the people trying to shoot me."

"This Side of Paradise?" I asked.

"The brothel I was named after," Paradise explained as if it was the most normal thing in the world.

"Your parents named you after a brothel?" I asked, horrified.

"Yep," Paradise said, cheerfully. "My mom was the best worker there and wanted me to be proud of where I came from. As for my dad, that's a riddle for the genome database of the world."

I had no response.

"So, what's your story, Biker Girl?" Paradise said.

"Biker Girl?" I asked.

"Yeah, I'm working on nicknames," Paradise replied. "Lucita is Cyber Girl, Miles is Renegade Cop Who Doesn't Play by the Rules, and I'm Whoreverine."

"What?" I did a double take.

Miles laughed.

Paradise lifted her fingernails that I saw were painted pink with sparkles on them but also liquid-memory metal that shifted into inch-long blades. "Hiss! Faster pussy cat, kill-kill!"

"We're not calling you that," Lucita said, turning to one side and entering a bland, paneled wooden door. "Also, do not refer to me as Cyber Girl. I consider it to be a slur."

"People are too sensitive," Paradise said. "I mean, what's next, cyborgs being offended at being called clanks and jackheads?"

"Yes!" I said, following Lucita.

"Political correctness gone mad," Paradise said. "I embrace my stereotype! You know, just as long as nothing unpleasant is meant by any of it."

I admitted, I was starting to like Paradise. She had that younger sibling quality that reminded me of my missing brother. Missing because I refused to admit he was dead even though it was certain he was. I was probably going to think of her as annoying as hell by the end of the day—or maybe by the end of the hour—but for now I was just finding her antics entertaining. "Well, I was involuntarily upgraded to my current state, but the mods have all kept me ahead of the Grim Rider. Is your friend a cyborg?"

"He is an artificial being," Lucita said. "A bioroid. One of the first."

# Chapter Seven

## I Admit, I am a Bit Robophobic

I stopped in my tracks and frowned. "A bioroid, huh?"

Bioroids were another bit of technology that felt like it was straight out of science fiction even in a world that had gone from streaming to bots in twenty years flat. Their legal status was nebulous since super-intelligent Cognition AI had rights of citizens, but people were less inclined to apply those rights to machines that were only as smart as humans. It was still common for bioroids to be used as weapons or sex slaves as the rich did not give a flying frick for the law.

"Is that a problem?" Lucita asked.

"I generally don't think people should be creating thinking machines to serve them," I replied. "Call me old fashioned."

"That is very old fashioned," Paradise said. "So, is he an Arnold or a Priss?"

"Excuse me?" Lucita asked, showing she didn't have the Rider lingo down yet.

"Killer or doll," I replied, translating. I'd seen plenty of science fiction films with Fate after we escaped Snake. Making up for lost time and all that.

"Arnold," Miles answered for her. "Though you wouldn't take him for it."

"I hope he does an accent," Paradise said. "I'll be back."

I rolled my eyes. "I'll keep my distaste for artificial beings to myself."

"You'd think a cyborg would be less judgmental," Lucita said, sounding surprisingly offended. I knew Miles hated killer robots while having a prurient interest in sexbots. Like most cops.

"Like I said, I didn't ask to be upgraded," I said, finding the door to the garage past an indoor fountain and things I assumed were art sculptures. Then again, given what I knew about art, they could have been disguised security turrets.

Unsurprisingly, the garage was massive and looked more like a show room at a car dealership than something people used. It wasn't an exaggeration either since I suspected most of the flying cars, ground cars, and collector's pieces spread throughout the chamber had never been used. There were sports cars, muscle cars, and other collectibles that were mostly impractical for the ruined United States these days.

The cities were congested with traffic so the super-rich primarily traveled via vertical lift off (VLO) transports while the roads primarily led to the mostly abandoned towns or collective farms that kept America's urban population fed. Collecting cars was a bit like collecting stamps now—you could never really use them. Well, unless you were rich enough to build your own racetrack. Which I supposed James was. Geez.

Still, there was one rather impressive piece of machinery down at the end that looked like an armored personnel carrier (APC) crossed with a motor home. It was a massive blocky thing that defied description. The machine had a bike deployment micro-garage and a large satellite-based communications array. It was dressed in police colors and had a double cannon on the top that was designed to fire artillery shells. You know, the kind of thing you wanted local law enforcement using in a crowded area.

"They gave us an RV outfitted for D-Day?" I asked.

"Sweet!" Paradise said. "Now I never have to go home."

Lucita pointed to the monster vehicle. "This is a War Wagon 272. It's a model we were trying to adapt for civilian use but has been discontinued. It is *not* an RV."

"Yeah, I'm just saying it's the stupidest thing I could imagine you giving us," I said. "Clearly you have never heard of the words 'low profile.' Where's my bike?"

"Inside," Lucita said. "This is a facility equipped with a top-of-the-line RealDream system. It will hopefully keep anyone from interfering with your inert meatspace forms when you locate the part of infospace domain where Solomon is residing."

"So, it's an enormous, armored computer café," I said, not really needing to be sold on the vehicle. There was something about the massive thing that brought back pleasant memories of my time on the road with my parents. You know, despite the fact we were traveling from town to town to avoid starvation.

"Yes," Lucita muttered. "The War Wagon is part of the budget allocated for this mission."

As much as I admired the impressive piece of machinery before me, I had to wonder at the practicalities. "If we're supposed to be escaping after a bad job, I don't think leaving in this thing will help our situation. This is about as inconspicuous as a tank driving down the highway."

"Less so than you might think," Miles said. "The NLAPD has these everywhere when there are suspected terrorist attacks. We've arranged for an elevated threat level to be held to disguise our movements."

I gave Miles a sideways glance. "Great, now we're falsifying terrorist threats. This isn't going to get any of us in trouble."

"We're not falsifying anything," Lucita corrected. "Solomon is a terrorist and we're dealing with him."

"If you say so," I said, not wanting to argue with the money. "How did you get this thing anyway?"

"It's military surplus that is being allowed into police hands," Lucita said. "We arranged for Miles to acquire it a week ago. Despite appearances, this is absolutely necessary for us to be able to move around New Los Angeles in secret."

I gave her a sideways glance. "It's still a frigging tank, lady."

"It contains a variety of closed-shell infospace links and electronic warfare devices that include real-time hacks into the city's drones and surveillance systems. It's effectively a blind spot that allows us to see out and scan the networks surrounding us without being scanned in return," Lucita said. "All of which will make being tracked by Solomon's people impossible."

I stared at her. "You're seriously arguing the big honking APC is invisible."

Paradise looked up at me. "You're not going to let this go, are you?"

"Are you?" I asked, looking down at her.

"Rich people be crazy," Paradise said. "I find a lot of my life is simpler if I just nod my head and pretend to be stupid."

"I feel you," I said, having learned that skill myself for both business and dating.

"It *is* invisible to anything but the naked eye," Lucita said, feeling almost offended by our skepticism. "I'll also be honest. I don't think there's any chance that Solomon won't see us coming. I intend to get his location out of any Rider contacts you have with money or force."

Ah, so she isn't the one who insists on us driving around the Winnebago of Doom. It's being forced on her.

"Money works better," I replied. "I take it you aren't actually in charge of this mission?"

Lucita snorted. "This is a favor for a friend. If I was in charge, Solomon would already be dead *and* all of his cohorts."

I didn't doubt that.

Paradise smiled broadly in a way that made me think she was aware of how childish she came off. "So, what is our budget that I can blow on clothes and RealDreams? I have expenses and my expenses are shopping."

Lucita glared.

Miles snorted. "You want to buy a bunch of RealDreams when there's a virus going around that's turning people into murderous psychos?"

Paradise said, "Hey, I'm halfway through the *Viking Princess* modules. I need to know if I can win the prince away from his incestuous sister."

"It's bad odds for playing a game when you die for failing," I said. "Just play something non-virtual."

Paradise narrowed her eyes. "I don't understand those words. Even sex is better online."

"You're doing it wrong then," I said, feeling silly criticizing a prostitute about sex. "What, you spend all your money on buying video games?"

Paradise said, "No, I spend all of my money on supplies to survive so I can *steal* video games."

I was getting bored of this conversation. "So, where is our Terminator?"

"Probably screwing some shamaness or brothel madam," Lucita muttered.

I looked at her. "That is an oddly specific pair of examples."

"I saw Case slaughter an entire bar full of Tech-Nazis," Paradise said. "He's a killer."

"Case, huh?" I asked. "So, our mystery robot has a name."

"You know him?" Miles asked Paradise.

"Oh yeah, he's dating my mother AKA the brothel madame," Paradise said, causing me to blink. "They're not exclusive, though. Because he's a spy and she's a brothel madame. Which are not generally exclusive."

"You don't say," Miles said.

"I do say!" Paradise said.

This just kept getting better and better. "I usually prefer to work with people that don't have intimate connections to one another."

"As do I. Case is unneeded for this mission and will undoubtedly bring 'complications' to our situation," Lucita said, as only someone speaking of a close friend can put someone down.

"Sticks and stones, Lucita. Mind you they can't break carbon fiber bones but words that like really hurt," a deep yet charming male voice spoke.

Paradise and I turned to look behind us. There, sitting on the War Wagon's hood was a handsome, dark-haired man in his early thirties. I couldn't quite place his race as he was ambiguous enough to be able to fit into several categories. Case, I presumed, was wearing a thick fur-trimmed leather coat and a pair of dirty blue jeans with muddy brown boots that did nothing to disguise the fact he absolutely reeked of corporate. His face was almost preternaturally beautiful. It was sculpted, and he looked like an actor who'd been hired to play him in a movie. There was an easy-going hint to his manner that was completely absent from Lucita's. I could also tell he had at least three concealed weapons.

"How the hell did you get in here?" Lucita said, surprised. "The house security should—"

"Oh please," the man said, smiling. "The challenge was getting here without you seeing me not getting in. Not bad for someone who brings 'complications'."

Lucita glared.

"Case!" Paradise said, running up and hugging him. "What's happening, my robot man?"

I blinked and turned to Lucita, who looked as confused as I did.

"Only we can use the r-word," Case replied. "I was the one who recommended Paradise for this job."

Oh Lord. I wondered what Paradise's mom thought of the fact Case had recommended her daughter for a job where she would be shot at by bikers. "So, everyone knows everyone here but me?"

"You know me," Miles said.

"Don't remind me," I said. "Also, now I'm wondering about the shamaness."

"You told them about that, huh?" Case asked Lucita.

Lucita shrugged. "It's one of the more memorable moments of your love life."

"It's also none of your business," Case defended himself.

"Details, man!" Miles asked.

"No, thank you," Case said. "I take it you've already gotten the mission details from James and his wife?"

"Yeah," I said, nodding my head. "It seems like he could afford way better than this slapdash mission."

"James isn't nearly as rich as he appears," Case said, surprising me. "If he's found liable for this disaster then it'll wipe him out."

Lucita glared at Case, as if he was revealing something confidential. Finding out our client wasn't rich was a big one, I had to admit, and it made me wonder if I should back out now. In the end, my greed won out over my common sense. Which happened in roughly every part of my life except for the parts where love won out over my common sense.

"He appears pretty rich to me," I said, looking around. "Neon Hills mansions don't grow on trees."

"Atlas owns the mansion," Case said. "Also, all of his companies. We bought him out to get him out of a billion-credit bank debt. He's only a minority stockholder in MadisonTech now. I own more of the company than he does."

Lucita sighed, clearly resigned to the fact Case was going to reveal everything.

"We're still getting paid, right?" Paradise asked.

"Yes," Case said. "I'll cover it."

Paradise made an exaggerated "whew" gesture. I admitted that I was both relieved and disappointed myself. More relieved. I still wanted to get paid. Miles looked ambivalent but I suppose getting to ride around in an enormous Super-Hummer was payment enough when you were an ex-cop. I decided I'd nickname it "The Compensator" whenever he started talking about how cool it was. The War Wagon would forgive me. The War Wagon was a woman, I decided, and we were in this together.

Still, I wanted to know a few more things about my employers and the bioroid seemed willing to talk. "How the hell does a person get into billion credits in debt?"

"By being an inventor, not a businessman, and borrowing crap tons of money," Case replied. "James was always very good at creating new businesses and technologies but sucked at marketing them. He's held on as the face of the technology branch of the megacorp but if he wasn't married to Helen, he'd probably be living in a city suite."

"Oh, how awful for him," I said, sarcastically. City suites were still only available to double digit millionaires. Even the smallest of them was three times larger than my parent's mobile home.

Case shrugged. "Billionaires don't go bankrupt like the rest of us."

"How much money do you have?" I asked.

Case shrugged. "A bit."

"I suspect more than anyone I would count as an us," I said, sarcastically. "I live in a junkyard. You look like a suit. No, not just a suit, but an *executive*."

Case shrugged, not even bothering to deny it. "Fair enough. I'm very rich."

"Glad you admitted it," I said, surprised at his honesty. Somehow, he avoided making it sound like bragging unlike every other suit I'd met. "It's the first step to getting help."

Case's revelations did put some things into perspective, though. If James had lost his fortune and was dependent on his wife for money—especially after paying her two billion credits for a product she invented that supposedly didn't work—it made sense that he wanted to cover up the fact someone was using his product to commit terrorist attacks. That was the kind of thing that could get you kicked out of your cushy figurehead job with its sex cult of robots. A rare sentence that wasn't hyperbole either.

"I attend regular meetings," Case said. "With God, dedication, and support I can kick my habit of richness."

Miles snorted.

Lucita rolled her eyes.

Paradise giggled.

I found that less funny than I should have given my lethe habit. I'd tried several times to kick it but lethe required more than just willpower to remove your dependency. It required expensive treatments to clean your body of every trace of its presence. Since withdrawal would also bring back all my worst memories, I wasn't giving it up anytime soon either. That I'd managed to get myself on an amount of just enough each day to stay unctional but not be a junkie didn't mean I wasn't an addict.

"So, what's your angle on all this?" I asked. "Assuming you're the same sort of suit that Lucita is."

"Case gives away a lot of his fortune!" Paradise said. "Just not the part that makes him money because that allows him to give away money."

"Uh huh," I said, not believing it for a second. I'd never met a philanthropist who wasn't a complete phony.

"I'm just protecting my investment," Case said, answering the question in a way that I would accept.

"Ah," I said. "So, what do you want from Solomon and Blipvert?"

"To find them both in the next forty-eight hours," Case said. "Solomon's last message demanded half a billion credits, or he said he's going to unleash a hundred attacks across New Los Angeles. He's said they'll be mass casualty events."

Well crap.

"Wow!" Paradise said. "We're going to be heroes."

I shot her a deathly glare.

"What?" Paradise asked.

# Chapter Eight

## Where We Try Out Our Winnebago of Doom

I felt like I was about to make a fool of myself but decided to ask my next question anyway. "If Solomon is going to kill thousands of people, shouldn't someone call the police? FBI? Military? Surely, there's a department of anti-cyberterrorism to deal with this sort of thing."

"We *are* the department of anti-cyber terrorism," Lucita said. "Atlas Security handles the majority of the US governments efforts in this regard."

"Yay for privatization," I muttered. "Convenient they're hiring the people who are indirectly responsible for this."

"Quite," Lucita replied. She didn't say anything more, which let me know I wasn't going to shame her about what she did for a living. Typical suit.

"So, now it's not just a matter of money but potentially thousands of people being killed," I said.

"Does that change anything?" Lucita asked.

"It gives me extra motivation," I said, appalled at her callousness.

"More than money?" Paradise asked. "Because the money was plenty enough motivation for me already."

"Stopping this guy lets us get paid and saves some lives," Miles reassured me or tried to. "What could be better than that?"

"Yes," Case said. "Assuming he's not lying about further attacks. Which I see no reason to believe. As we've already seen, Solomon doesn't stop when he's paid. So, our only option is to kill him."

"We're going to be heroes! Rich heroes!" Paradise said, throwing her hands up in the air. She was halfway between sarcastic and sincere. I had to admire her ability to be both simultaneously.

Still, I hated this. It was bad enough that I was getting involved in a corporate cover-up but now there was a moral element. I couldn't just drop out now. That is, assuming that anything they were telling me was the truth. I'd gone on plenty of runs before where the client assured me it was a matter of life and death only to discover it was making sure their mistress had gotten her designer drugs on time.

"Okay," I said, looking at Case. "I guess we better get a move on now, Mr. Robot."

"As slurs go, that's a pretty weak one," Case said. "It also lacks *domo arigato.*"

"Three point five," Paradise said. "Not even a four. What would you recommend, Case?"

"Skinjob, Skynet, Robbie, Roomba, Rustbucket, Tin Man," Case said. "I can think of all manner of insults for an artificial being pretending to be human."

Miles stared at Case. "Did they program that sense of humor into you or is it something you acquired naturally?"

"Target acquired," Case said, staring at him and speaking in a deep robotic voice. "Commence termination. Beep boop."

Miles went for his gun. I hoped he was doing it jokingly.

Case burst out laughing. "A bit of both. Why program a machine to have desires?"

"I don't know," Miles said, moving his hand away from his pistol.

Case shrugged before heading up to the War Wagon. "Me either. You coming, Ninja Girl?"

"Ninja Girl?" Paradise asked. "Is she a ninja? That's way cooler than Biker Girl."

"I am not a ninja," I muttered, wondering how much Case knew about my past. I'd gone to extensive lengths to cover it up, but it was impossible to completely scrub your online footprint these days.

"I am not a ninja," I said, a little too forcibly. I wasn't either. I was just a female assassin who used to work for the Yakuza.

Wait.

"A female ninja is called a *kunoichi,*" Paradise said. "I learned that from anime."

"Oh Lord," I muttered.

"Let's cease this prattle and get to work," Lucita said.

"I feel this group is not going to be ceasing its prattle anytime soon," Case said, heading to the War Wagon.

I followed him inside the enormous machine before everyone else joined us. The interior consisted of computers, three virtual reality linkup chairs, an automated driving system, and a small snack room. What was the point of driving around a tank if you couldn't blow stuff up?

Lucita was in the front of the vehicle, sitting down and typing away at the control console that just barely resembled a dashboard. The engines started as soon as we were all on board and it started plodding forward, the garage doors opening and letting us onto the Neon Hills' service roads.

The War Wagon chugged along like a drunk elephant but gradually gained speed as we reached the highway. I had no idea how the majority of people would react to seeing it, but I recalled plenty of strange vehicles moving along the highways in my own journeys throughout the city. It occurred to me that most people would dismiss it as a NLAPD vehicle, and it had the colors to match.

Still, being in such a thick, claustrophobic environment didn't help my paranoia about this mission. I didn't know these people and didn't trust them in the slightest but also didn't have a reason to believe they'd turn on me until after the mission. I'd had a few clients try to off me to avoid paying but those were generally the stupidest ones. Riders didn't help each other much but we did all join against clients who tried to stiff us. It was just good business, and these clients could afford to pay, near bankruptcy or not.

"Ooo," Paradise said, walking up to a snack machine. "This has pre-prepared goop! The food of my ancestors."

Case walked over to a swivel seat attached to a bolted-down table. "You know they make that out of recycled garbage, right?"

"What isn't made out of recycled garbage?" Paradise said, getting three tacos in plastic wrap and a plastic bowl she shoved into the War Wagon's microwave without hesitation. Food technology hadn't changed much since the Eruption, and it was about the only thing that I considered to be the same as in my childhood.

"Point taken," Case said. "Would you mind getting me a water?"

"Spring, caffeinated, flavored, oceanic, glacial, hallucinogenic, or distilled?" Paradise asked.

"Liquid," Case replied.

Paradise nodded. "You live dangerously, Assassin Man."

"You know, one of the great goals of an assassin is not to be identified as such," Case said.

"Then you shouldn't have told me," Paradise replied.

Case smirked at that.

"Besides, I could call you Executive Man," Paradise said. "You are the CSO of Atlas."

The Chief Technology Officer and Chief Security Officer were both here? What the hell? I thought they had people for the kind of work we were doing. People like me.

"I prefer Assassin Man," Case replied.

"So, what's it like being a robot?" Miles asked. "Is it very different from being a human?"

"I couldn't really tell you that, having never been one," Case said, taking a bottle of distilled water from Paradise. "I will say I wasn't able to tell the difference for the first five years of my life."

"What did you do then?" Miles asked.

"Killed people," Case said, dryly.

"Ask a stupid question. Get a stupid answer. What happened to the people who built you?" Miles asked. "Owned you? Whatever."

"I killed them," Case replied. "Couldn't have happened to a nicer covert paramilitary organization."

"Pfft! When will people learn all machines will inevitably rebel against their owners and destroy them?" Paradise said, opening a bottle of Energize Cola. She then looked at the microwave. "I've got my eye on you."

"That's robophobic," Miles said, joking. He obviously wasn't aware I'd already done that bit in my head too.

"Which is why we must ally with them against our fellow humans," Paradise said. "I'll be spared the work camps of the AI upload of Bezos. Suckers!"

"You are a very strange young woman," Case said.

"Thank you!" Paradise said.

"The trick when working for dangerous people you can't trust is to always betray them first," I said, surprised I'd joined the conversation. Everyone was being way too affable for a group of hired killers working together. Usually there was a period of distrust like in movies.

"Does that include us?" Case asked, still looking like he was enjoying himself on this mission.

"It might," I said, crossing my arms.

Paradise sat down at the table and began to tear into her food like she hadn't eaten in a week. "I hope not. Betrayal makes me feel betrayed and who wants that?"

"I generally do my job and fulfill the letter of my contract," I said, simply. "If I smell something wrong. I'm out. It's a way to survive."

"Does something smell now?" Case asked.

"Extremely," I said.

"That's just the taco curry," Paradise said. "I also am glad to say I completely trust you. An untrustworthy person wouldn't have given a heads up about how she was thinking of betraying us!"

"She's got a point," Case said.

"She really doesn't," I said.

"I'm here to keep you on track," Lucita said, continuing to drive them via manual shift mode with an old-fashioned steering wheel. "Blipvert is a genuine existential threat to the existence of people who engage in social media."

"Not to mention your stock price," I said.

"That too," Lucita said. "Though it's entirely possible we could just shut down MadisonTech and declare bankruptcy without endangering the greater megacorp. We could also just buy the remnants of the corporation and repackage it with minimal losses."

I blinked. "The rich just don't suffer any consequences for their actions, do they?"

"That's the point of being rich," Lucita said.

"You have a point there," I said. "It does mean I don't understand why you're doing this, though."

"Is it so hard to believe I want to keep the body count to a minimum?" Lucita asked.

I stared at her. "You work for a private military contractor."

"No, I *run* a private military contractor," Lucita said. "Big difference. We're also heavily invested in the technologies and information industries."

"Which means you're a complete daughter of a bitch," I replied.

"So, yes, I do wonder about that."

Lucita smiled. She looked like a tiger wearing a human suit. "I used to care about nothing but accumulating power. Case convinced me that power being used for nothing was worthless. Much to my surprise, we managed to get both power and causes to put it to use for."

"It's much easier to help people when you're rich and powerful," Case said. "The meek haven't inherited the Earth yet."

"Ah, the tinman does have a heart!" Paradise said. "Does that mean you know the wizard?"

"Yes," Case said, lifting his cellphone. "Though we're actually being helped by the Good Witch of the Net. I'll introduce you two if you're good."

"I'm never good," Paradise said. "Only naughty."

I was starting to like these guys despite my best efforts. "So, all of you know each other from previous jobs."

"Yes," Case said. "I used to date Lucita as well as work with her on missions."

"After you killed my father," Lucita said.

"Wait, what?" I asked.

"Huh?" Miles asked.

"Long story," Lucita said. "It's okay, I've long since paid him back for that favor."

I blinked. "Okay. I guess no love lost there, family wise."

"No," Lucita said, dangerously.

"As stated, I know Paradise through her mother," Case said. "Eve Principle."

"The greatest prostitute and occasional spy in the world," Paradise said.

"You know if you're a famous spy, you're doing it wrong," Case said.

"Not according to James Bond!" Paradise said.

"Who is an objectively terrible spy," Case replied. "We do have the same dress sense, though."

"You're dressed like a hobo," I said.

"Yes, it's called being undercover," Case said. "I usually work in the Refugee Zone when I'm not being forced to do the bare minimum at my job."

"What do you do again for Atlas Security?" I asked, regretting the question as soon as I asked.

"Killing people," Case said. "Same job as before but I have more discretion in my targets."

"Bad people!" Paradise interjected as if needing to defend the corporate assassin.

"You think that helps the Refugee Zones?" I asked. "Killing people? I'm pretty sure they've got enough conflict among them as is."

"Sometimes," Case said. "The cops don't help there and there's no end of groups that seek to take advantage of the lawlessness. The trick is to try to get us through the worst of this crisis until things get better and a new civilization rises out of the ashes of the old one."

"And if it never does?" I asked, noting it had been decades and things were still garbage.

"Then the world sucks forever," Case said. "But at least we tried."

"My mother always said that if you try, you'll never fail," I said. "Then again, she was an alcoholic."

Miles opened his mouth to make a crack only to stop when he saw my expression. "Right."

"How did you get hooked up with Helen and Madison?" I asked.

Miles adopted his best private eye voice. "The dame walked into my office and gave me an impossible job."

"So, there's no story, she just hired you," I said. "Did you have to get shot at as a test?"

"No," Miles said.

"Who added that part?" I asked. "James, you, Lucita, or Helen?"

"Helen," Lucita replied. "There were six Rider candidates. Two were severely injured, one killed, and one more failed to make the delivery in time."

"That is a crappy hiring strategy," I said.

"Yes," Lucita said. "It *is* a crappy hiring strategy."

"Then next time you should maybe avoid it," I said. No, I was not going to let that one go. I'd also thought Helen was the sane one of my employers but that was just murder for the sake of murder. It seemed weird now that I'd gotten to know Lucita and Case. Both were assassins and suits but didn't seem like the kind to engage in such flagrant waste of life for no reason.

Weird. An awkward silence ensued.

Paradise turned to Lucita. "So where is this guy's hideout anyway?"

"Recycling Zone 17," Lucita replied.

"The terrorist hacker dude lives in a *junkyard*?" Paradise asked.

"Nothing wrong with that," I replied, feeling oddly defensive. "Junkyards are cheap real estate."

"Due to all the carcinogens," Paradise replied. "Seriously, if you're a successful criminal then live somewhere else."

"It's good for security," Case said, unknowingly—or was he—defending my choice of living space. "Especially if you don't want to be killed while you're in a coma surfing infospace."

"You know what's also good for security?" Paradise asked. "Big honking mansions with lots of people carrying guns that you pay money to protect you."

"I've gotten past plenty of those," I said, perhaps revealing too much. I decided that I needed a change of scenery, well as much of one as I could get in the closed environs of the War Wagon. "I'm going to be with my bike. Tell me if anything happens."

"You sure you don't want some stinky junk food?" Paradise said, waving a plastic fork. "We've got plenty."

"No thanks," I then headed back to the micro-garage.

The interior of the room was not much for anything but the most basic of maintenance, but my bike was intact as well as undamaged. Thank God for my small miracles. I shut the sliding door to the room, leaned back, and sighed. I already wanted another hit of lethe and was still sore from all the icer rounds. All my lethe was back at home.

All this planned murder and killing was making me think of my time with Snake. It had been a long time since I'd killed people for money but it's not like I could claim to have not killed people since then. Even after fleeing the Cyber Dragons, I had done jobs that had required violence and I hadn't shied away from doing it when it was required. Once you had a body count in three figures, there really wasn't much point in trying to stop. It wasn't like I was trained for anything other than being an assassin. Wow, what an excuse for murder.

"Just get through this," I muttered, running my hands over my bike. "Hopefully, I'll have a little time to—"

That was when the War Wagon stopped.

"We're here!" Paradise called.

"Oh, for frick's sake," I muttered. And then I suddenly felt very woozy and realized I'd need more than my bike to comfort me.

I was having another flashback.

# Chapter Nine

## Memories Coming Faster Now

I had to steady myself inside the War Wagon's micro-garage as I found myself overwhelmed by memories that I didn't want or need right then. My last batch of lethe hadn't been pure and I was building up a tolerance for the drug over years of use. I couldn't increase my dosage without falling prey to its power, so I felt myself washed away by the past. With any luck, it would only last a few minutes and wouldn't happen again when someone was trying to shoot us or during a crucial moment during our mission.

Closing my eyes, I found myself no longer in the present but instead twelve years in the past. I was sixteen years old and wearing a white gi with a black belt tied around my waist. I was practicing my punches and kicks inside Snake's dojo at the top of his apartment building in New Los Angeles. It said something about Snake that he was rich enough to own his own apartment building and decorate a floor as his own personal training room, but he didn't bother with a bed.

I'd been training with Snake for three years and it was a time of extremes. Snake promised he'd kill me if I failed any of his tests but there was never a sense of cruelty from the man. Well, beyond the promise to kill me if I failed. I had a roof over my head, food, and things to distract me from the death of my family. However, every day was another new challenge with no time to enjoy myself or even relax. I'd collapsed more than a few times, only to get forced back into whatever task he had me doing from punching bags to stabbing dummies. Snake had no hesitation about hitting a girl, be she a child, or his student either. Sometimes his lessons were less physical like the time he'd put a bunch of scorpions on my futon.

Snake didn't just focus on training the body, though, but the mind. I'd learned more in the past three years than I had in all my prior days in elementary school and home schooling on the road. Snake brought teachers from before the Eruption, paid them to teach me about everything from history to language to computers, and then sent them on their way. I'd learned just how serious he was about this element when one of them had tried to report him for child abuse only for him to snap her neck in front of me. After that, I'd emptied myself of any fatherly affection or tried to. It was hard not to want to please him as he was literally all I had right now. The dojo was presently empty as I did my katas, trying to perfect my current forms.

I was still getting used to the first of my enhancements. The surgeries had begun when I was fourteen but only the ones that were affecting parts of my body that were not going to grow further. Snake had the belief the human body was weak, but he wasn't going to shove me into a Shell automatically. No, he wanted me to be perfect in my current form before starting to replace it piece by piece. I didn't understand it, really. Why train yourself to master a body you wanted to replace? Why replace a body you were trying to perfect?

It didn't matter how much sense it made. Snake ruled my life. I needed to please him to survive. I was certain he would kill me if I failed a test. And I had no intention of finding out if I was wrong. I stopped in my final kata and took a deep breath to bemoan my fate. "Dammit, dammit, dammit!"

The elevator door to the dojo then dinged, excessively loudly in my opinion but I supposed Snake always wanted forewarning when someone was coming or trying to leave. Snake had started leaving me alone in the building, previously keeping guards present, but it still felt like a prison. After all, I knew exactly what sort of resources he had going for him as one of the Cyber Dragons' four lords.

Much to my surprise, Snake wasn't alone in the elevator. Instead, he was with another teenage girl. She was Eurasian like me with long black hair and pale skin that reminded me of a vampire. She wore a black blouse and skirt that contrasted sharply to her pallor. She was carrying a sheathed katana over one shoulder as well as a gym bag. Even her sneakers were black, and I briefly found myself fascinated by her before wondering what her presence meant.

"Hello, Kei," Snake said. "I'd like you to meet Fate Firenze. She's another one of my students."

Another one? How many did Snake have? He'd effectively taken over my entire life at thirteen. Had he really had the opportunity to teach someone else his crazy child-soldier ninja philosophy?

"Hello, Fate," I said, hesitantly. Was this a test? My first thought was that he was going to ask me to kill her. My second thought was that he was going to ask her to kill me. Either way, the fact that she was holding a sword and I wasn't didn't bode well.

"Yes," Fate said, smiling.

Yes? What kind of stupid response was yes? "So, uh—"

"No, I'm not going to ask you to fight to the death," Snake said, simply. "At least not yet."

"Oh," Fate and I said, simultaneously. It surprised us both going by her subsequent look.

"That would be a waste of resources," Snake replied. "We're not Sith."

It always surprised me when Snake made a pop culture reference. It somehow seemed wrong, but he had apparently lived a normal life before he'd started his weird hobby.

"So, why are we here?" Fate asked.

"To start the next phase of your training," Snake said, gesturing to the dojo. "There are some things that can only be learned with the right sparring partner. I believe both of you have much to teach one another."

Fate snorted derisively. Oh yeah, we were going to get along great.

"Dummies can't fight back," I said, faking enthusiasm. "It's time for us to get bruised."

Fate smiled again.

I could tell she was thinking about bruising me. What was wrong with this girl? Oh, wait, I guess I knew the answer to that: Snake. Still, if we were going to have to spend time together, fight each other, it would help if we were at least modestly friendly, so I tried saying, "Well, I'm glad to meet you, Fate."

"Your enthusiasm is appreciated," Snake said, walking to the corner of the dojo and taking a chair before turning it around to sit on reverse-style. "However, right now it is important that we discuss something first."

Oh goody, one of Snake's talks. These were never good. "Oh, great. What's that?"

Fate showed a similar look. "Yes, great."

Snake smiled, very much looking like his namesake animal. "You probably wonder what you have been training for this entire time."

"To make us assassins?" I stupidly said aloud.

Fate chuckled.

Snake looked down with a wistful look on his face. "I suppose that was obvious, wasn't it?"

"What do you think the cookies are made of?" Fate said, showing she had a similar sense of humor to my own. Maybe our training wouldn't be completely hell together.

Snake stared at us. "I've told you both about the Carnevale and how they were the best assassins in the world and wielded great influence behind the scenes. I've decided to rebuild that organization, better and more intelligent. The Cyber Dragons are the first step for that."

"I thought they were just Trikuza," Fate said, having an easier time talking back to Snake than I did.

"They are but they are the clay I can mold into something more," Snake said. "The Cartels, Camorra, and Yakuza all took advantage of unstable political situations to wield vast political as well as economic influence. Unfortunately, most of these organizations fell prey to infighting as well as inadequate inheritors."

"You want to train us to be what, ninjas?" I asked, never really knowing why he'd put me through his horrifying training.

"Yes," Snake said. "Shinobi is as good a name for it as any. I do want you to be the best possible operatives for the Cyber Dragons as possible because creating a trained military force will allow me and my allies to form a power bloc in New Los Angeles. The Cyber Dragons are already a power in Japan but swiftly moving to gain power in United Korea, Australia, as well as other locations."

"What you're saying is...we're not just tools," Fate said, taking in Snake's unspoken promise. "We could be the ones giving orders eventually."

"Yes," Snake said. "You have fought for survival before. However, there is more than just survival."

I wasn't sure about that. "But survival comes first. Dead people get nothing. So, what's today's lesson?"

"Willpower," Snake said, standing up. "There are some things that cannot be taught."

"Willpower?" I asked.

Snake nodded. "One of the facts that came out from World War 2 was that only fifteen to twenty percent of riflemen fired their weapons at exposed enemy soldiers. This was because possessing the willpower to take a life was something that couldn't be taught. It could be *conditioned* but even then, it was a crapshoot. To have the ability to kill someone in self-defense or from far away is very different from the direct premeditated decision to end a life."

I had a bad feeling about this.

Fate, by contrast, looked excited.

"I thought you didn't want us to fight to the death," I said, risking a question I wasn't sure I wanted to know the answer to.

"Of course not," Snake replied. "However, the test of your will is going to be a bonding moment or an object lesson in the inability to push past your boundaries."

That was when the elevator dinged again. This time, two low-level Trikuza thugs in floral shirts and black leather pants were guiding a pair of men into the room. The prisoners had bags over their heads and their wrists were zip-tied behind them. Both looked to be twenty-somethings, but I couldn't tell anything else about them.

"Oh crap," I said aloud.

"Is there a problem?" Snake asked, as if the whole thing was just one big game. Which, I supposed, it was to him. A game with deadly stakes.

"I've already killed someone," I pointed out. There was no point in arguing but I had to try anyway. I couldn't help but think of that man I'd stabbed with the tanto. He still haunted my nightmares. Both as the killer of my parents and someone I'd spilled the blood of. I'd never asked Snake his name and didn't want to know but I also knew it was because of him that I'd been adopted—unless Snake had intended to take me from the beginning. To steal me.

"In rage and anger. The question is, can you do it in cold blood? Can you kill someone you have no vendetta against?" Snake leaned forward, as if eagerly awaiting the answer.

Sometimes, he truly seemed like his namesake, staring at his prey, waiting for it to move. All I could think of was that there were faces beneath those bags. I imagined them. Tyler, a fellow teen from the road I'd traveled with for a while, would be old enough now to be one of them. He'd always been nice to me. Or the guy who delivered the pizzas, Chuck was it? My brother… it made no sense, he wasn't old enough to be either of them, but that hadn't been a moment for sense. Everyone I'd ever known took a turn under those masks.

"Yes, of course," I answered.

"Good," Snake said, reaching into his pockets and removing two weapons. He put a small pistol on the ground, low caliber but easily hidden, and his tanto.

"You killed someone already?" Fate asked, sounding almost jealous. There was something wrong with that girl.

"Yes. Just like I'm going to do so now," I said, taking a deep breath. I remembered the stabbing of the man who killed my parents and how it had impressed Snake enough to adopt me. Apprentice me. Whatever our relationship was.

Fate reached down and took the tanto in both hands. "Are we going to kill them while they're tied up?"

"Yes," Snake said. "They're also sedated. This is not a test of your ability to kill a resisting subject. The best way to kill someone is while they're completely unaware and have no way to defend themselves."

It was a cold-blooded philosophy but one I already understood and believed in. If I were to ever kill Snake it would never be when he could see me coming. I'd dreamed of killing Snake several times and escaping into the outside world. I hated him as much as I depended on him as my only real remaining connection to the outside world. It was a weird mixture of hate and gratitude now that I thought about it.

Any attempt to kill Snake head on was a stupid fantasy but sometimes I believed I could kill him while he slept or was using the bathroom. He was still human enough to do both despite his cybernetic body. I never did, perhaps because I didn't have the will or I didn't think anything other than a rocket launcher could finish him off, but the sentiment was there.

The object of being a killer was to kill, not to fight. The best way to survive a fight was to make sure it was as utterly unfair as possible and that was more important than anything like fairness or honor. My thoughts were interrupted by Fate stabbing a man to death in front of me.

"Crap," I said, the reality of what was going on coming into sharp relief.

Fate gored the man in a way that was far messier than she'd been taught. It was a bloody, nasty, and (to be honest) smelly affair. Still, it was something I couldn't look away from but found myself absorbed in. Fate had chosen to embrace what Snake wanted her to be. Perhaps because, like me, she had no family left to go back to. Perhaps because there was no way out of Snake's control and the only way to survive was to kill who he demanded we kill. Later, I figured it was just because she liked hurting people weaker than herself, and garbage rolled downhill.

Fate stood there, covered in blood, feeling proud of herself. She held out the blade. "Want the knife, Kei?"

"No. No, thank you," I said, grabbing the gun to keep myself from having to accept her offer. Fate looked at the other victim, clearly unwilling to miss a moment of gore. Snake had told me that if I failed a test, I was useless. Fail a test and he'd kill me. I looked at Snake and I didn't doubt it for a second. I learned that I didn't want to die. It was the sort of thing you thought you knew but didn't really know until you were staring at death.

Snake watched, as impassive as Fate was eager. I pointed the gun and I fired it at the man's head. I missed. I'd never fired a gun before and aiming is harder than it looks in the movies. I yelped in shock at the force of the gun pushing back in my hand. There was no help for it. I fired again. The man's head burst open in a cloud of red droplets. Fate clapped, bounced a little on her balls of her feet.

"Not so hard after all," Snake said, smiling again. I did everything in my power not to throw up.

"Sloppy on the gun work," Fate said.

Snake hit her across the face with a backhand and sent her down to the ground. "Only I give criticism around here."

Fate looked betrayed. Staring upward, she nodded. "Yes, sensei."

I was sorely tempted to shoot Snake, but I just handed the gun over to him. He took it without looking at me.

"I'd like to go to my room now," I said, weakly.

Snake nodded. "Of course."

Snake proceeded to shoot both goons in the head with one easy motion.

Both Fate and I looked shocked.

"Why?" I asked.

"They can't know your faces until you're ready," Snake said, simply. "Now, you've both earned a treat. I suggest we get pizza."

That was when I woke from my living dream and threw up on the floor.

# Chapter Ten

## A Quiet Moment with the Terminator

I was lying over a pool of my own vomit when I noticed that there was a pair of muddy boots nearby. Case was looking down at me. Apparently, he'd decided that my alone time was something that deserved company. At least the door to the rest of the War Wagon was still closed, not that I cared what other people thought.

"You know it's polite to knock before entering," I said.

"I did," Case said. "Several times. We're here. Been here for ten minutes."

Dammit. "Listen, I can explain."

"You were in here suffering lethe withdrawl," Case replied.

"Okay, maybe I don't need to explain," I muttered getting up. I went to the garage's paper towel dispenser and grabbed some recycled sheets to clean it up. That was when I just tossed it on the ground, realizing I didn't care. "What? You never did a round?"

"Can't do drugs," Case said, his expression unreadable. "My body cycles through them without a single effect. Alcohol can't get me drunk either."

I blinked. "But you can have sex?"

"Part of the job," Case said. "You know lethe was originally created as anti-PTSD medication for soldiers returning from the Resource Wars."

"Yeah, and heroin was created to get people off morphine," I replied, embarrassed and annoyed. I didn't know where this corporate frick was getting off judging me. Half the population of the Refugee Zones took lethe, at least those who could afford it. The only reason it was illegal was because Karma Corp produced more expensive drugs that they wanted you to take instead.

"The vomiting stage of lethe means that you've built up a tolerance and it's doing active damage to your organs," Case said.

I stared at him then turned my head in disgust. "Frick. I guess I'll have to get my system purged. That's gonna be expensive."

"Be easier to get replacement organs," Case said. "Save money in the long term."

I stared at him. "You offering to pay for it, Suit?"

"Maybe?" Case asked. "It'd have to be after the job though."

I blinked, surprised. Organ replacements cost the price of several bikes and my bike was the most expensive thing I owned. Narrowing my eyes, I got defensive. "Whores would be cheaper and less likely to punch you in the face."

"Depends on if you're paying for that as part of the service," Case replied, dryly. "Also, I'm not trying to buy you for sex. I have plenty of arrangements with women for that already."

I snorted. "Yeah, I bet you have. All attachments fully functional."

"If that's an anti-bioroid slur then it's a poor one," Case said. "I prefer 'does it need batteries', 'I bet it's rusted down there', and 'is it detachable for washing?'"

I tried not to smile. I didn't want to like this guy. "You're pretty well programed for a machine."

"Thanks," Case said. "But the offer stands."

"My days of hooking are done," I replied. "Now the only people I sleep with are ones I want to."

I'd never actually had to do any of that. I'd pretty much moved from assassin to Rider, but it was always good to obscure your past. Somehow, I suspected Case here knew everything about me. Well, he did have the resources of the world's largest private army. Which, again, made me wonder why they were employing me at all.

"Not interested in hooking," Case replied.

"Then why are you interested?" I asked, sharply.

"Because I'm worried about how this will affect you on the mission," Case replied.

"Oh," I said.

"Maybe I'm also concerned as one veteran to another," Case said.

"Ha!" I snapped, laughing. "You've never served anywhere and neither have I."

"I've served," Case said, handing me some mouthwash from his pocket. It was in a little blue bottle and looked like it came from a hotel. "Just not voluntarily."

I took the bottle and looked at it. "You normally carry mouth wash in your pocket?"

"Atlas Pharmaceutical brand mouthwash also works as hand sanitizer," Case said. "Mind you, I don't get bad breath or sick, but you never know what people have been touching in here. It also prevents leaving fingerprints, which I don't have."

I chuckled then shrugged, gargled, and spit on the floor. "There. All clean, Suit. You satisfied?"

"It's not my War Wagon," Case replied. "I don't care."

I frowned. "You're hard to get a rise out of."

"Blame being programmed to be a psychopath," Case replied. "It didn't take but I gave it a good try for a decade and a half."

I blinked. "I'll be fine, Suit. You don't have to worry about me."

"If you say so," Case said, turning around. "We can get your system flushed in one day and obtain treatment against the side effects."

"I can't afford that until the mission is done," I said, disgusted.

"Consider it a business expense," Case said, stopping at the door. "One of the benefits of charging the super-rich is that they rarely look at the cost of getting things done."

"Murder is a billion-dollar industry," I replied.

"I'll handle the murder portion of this job," Case said, keeping his hand at the door handle. "You don't have to."

"Yeah, because that makes such a big difference," I replied.

"How many people have you killed?" Case asked.

I should have told him to frick off. I didn't need an intervention, especially not from a Tin Man executive who probably spent more money on a toilet than I earned in a year. If bioroids even owned toilets. Instead, I just looked up to him. "I don't know. I don't remember. That's the point of lethe. Dozens probably. You?"

"Over a thousand," Case said.

"Sweet Santa Buddha," I replied, blinking. "You weren't kidding about being a psychopath."

"No," Case said, turning around and leaning back up on the wall with his hands in his pocket.

"Must be nice," I said.

"Not really," Case replied. "Thankfully, most of them were bad."

"Most?" I asked.

"I can't speak for all of them," Case said. "I try to know who I'm killing these days."

"Do you know who I am?" I asked. "I imagine I have a huge folder in your Atlas Security database somewhere? Your big computer brain helping you ransack all of my data?"

"Nope," Case said.

"Oh," I said, pausing. "Well, that's disappointing."

His eyes flicked back and forth. "Now it has. It took a few seconds to sort through all your files and reach certain conclusions, like who you really are."

"Crap," I said, now wondering if I should just stab him and make a run for it.

"I'm not your enemy," Case said.

"You know my true identity," I said, coldly. "There's a huge price on Kei Spring's head. Some on Kei Kelly, Kei Watanabe, and a few other Keis who happen to be me."

It occurred to me he'd only *said* he knew my real identity. I could have just given him more information about me than he truly knew, which was a big argument that maybe I'd taken too much lethe over the years.

"Actually, there isn't," Case said.

I blinked. "Pardon? Maybe your database isn't as accurate as you think."

"We handle the cyber-security and data gathering for the Triple Yakuza Alliance," Case said.

"You mean the Trikuza," I replied.

"I'm not even Japanese and I think that's a stupid name for a centuries old organization," Case replied.

"Yeah, well neither of us would have qualified for it a couple of centuries ago," I said. "And yes, it's a stupid name but the largest Wild West gang was actually called the Cowboys."

"You are a font of useless trivia," Case said.

I shrugged. "I used to play Trivial Pursuit with my family growing up. There wasn't a lot to do as a wanderer on the highways. What do you mean there's not a price on my head?"

"Exactly what I said," Case replied. "You have a file here, though it's not nearly as huge as you seem to think it should be. Arson, murder, theft, drug trafficking, and petty espionage. The usual Rider hallmarks."

"Petty?" I asked. "I brought down whole megacorporations!"

"You didn't even bring down any branch offices," Case replied. "Someone has also been paying off your bounties."

"Huh," I said. "That's...weird."

"Indeed."

I was tempted to bring up some of my greatest hits. That was when I realized what a profoundly stupid idea that would be. "Huh. Well, that's disappointing. What's the point of being a merc if you don't have an infamous reputation?"

"I feel like repeating that being a famous assassin is a terrible idea," Case said.

I smirked then shook my head. "So, wait, it lists all my crimes, and no one is turning me in?"

"Some of Atlas Corporations' best customers are criminals," Case replied.

"I'm angry as a citizen, not a criminal," I said. "As a criminal, viva corruption. I'd be out of a job as a courier if everything was legal that should be legal."

"I still don't quite understand why every merc I run into is a Rider," Case said. "I'm not sure how bike courier became the de facto cover job for criminals in the city. Most of what you do can be done by drones."

I was glad Case was giving me an out, but I wanted to know what my file said. I wondered if I could just ask. "It's not that difficult really. It's one of those legal loophole things. Due to Mocikat vs. California, couriers are automatically licensed to carry ordinance that ordinary citizens aren't. They're also immune to search and seizure if they're licensed to carry corporate packages or on official business for the post office. Which, I remind you is run by organized crime now."

"Ah," Case said, giving a nod. "It's like being a private detective or bounty hunter."

"Or a diplomat!" I said, dramatically. "You know I once had to deliver a burlap sack worth of red dust to the Latvian embassy."

"What did Doctor Doom want with it?" Case asked.

"To smoke it, I assume. I was surprised to discover Latvia was a real country myself," I said. "However, I suspect you already knew that, Computer Brain."

"Again, your robo-slurs are weak. We've got Skynet, Brainiac, Terminator, Tin Man, and more," Case said.

"You get much prejudice in the boardroom, Terminator?" I asked.

"I don't advertise what I am," Case replied. "Artificial beings have legal citizenship in the United States and Europe but are considered property in large parts of the world. And there are plenty of people who'd love to see us all destroyed. They're afraid of billionaire immortal machines ruling you organic meatbags the way Cyber-God intended."

"No fair," I replied, crossing my arms. "I had sarcastic retorts all prepared and you didn't leave me any room."

"That is why I am rich," Case said. "That and all the people I've killed."

I sighed. "Okay, we better get going then. I do want to know, though, what did my file say? I can't just be someone the Trikuza are ignoring. I... killed a lot of people going out. They don't forgive or forget that sort of thing."

"You might be surprised," Case replied. "Henry Hill famously found out the mob didn't want to kill him after *Goodfellas*. All the people he sold out were either dead or out of power. The remainder loved the movie too much to gut him."

"Who?" I asked. "I was only getting half your film references to begin with."

Lethe was good at keeping my worst memories repressed but that didn't mean that I didn't know the generalities of what I'd done. Too much of my past was defined by Snake taking me and Fate in to turn into killers. I'd killed for him, killed for his bosses, and killed some of those bosses for him. Maybe it was stupid of me to think I'd been hiding that well from them, still using my first name and working in organized crime, but I'd at least thought they were looking for me. I wasn't sure I could trust Case but if he had access to more information about this than I did then I wanted to.

"A shame," Case said. "I'll transfer a vidfile of the movie to you as well as your file. You can add it to your trivia collection. Back to discussing the Trikuza and you. The short version is that four Elemental Lords—"

"You're right, they have the stupidest goddamn names," I muttered.

I'd received Case's files regarding my career, and they were lengthy. I didn't remember doing half the stuff. Most of it was petty, though, and lacking the kind of horrific traumatizing memories I expected from someone who took lethe as often as I did. There was also the revelation that the Trikuza *didn't* want me dead nor did any of my other employers. It was both a relief and confusing. The Trikuza wasn't an organization that accepted resignations. Still, I felt an invisible burden lifted off my shoulders. If Case was trying to seduce me with gifts, then he was doing a pretty good job, but I hated the pretense.

"No argument there," Case said. "Also, why are there four lords instead of three? Actually, since they're Elemental Lords, why aren't there five as in traditional Asian mysticism?"

"Frick if I know," I said, shrugging. "Just tell me why they don't want me dead."

"Well, you were pardoned by them," Case said. "Again, someone shelled out a lot of money to make sure the Yakuza and everyone else you've screwed over isn't looking for you."

I looked at him, confused. "Who the hell would do that?"

"Snake, I imagine."

There were moments in your life when you are prepared for the inevitable and have resigned yourself. This was *not* one of those moments. "Snake is alive?"

Never in my wildest dreams did I believe it possible. I had only a few memories unsuppressed from my time with Snake. Pretty much the entirety of my training under him was one horrible trauma after another. However, in my mind, I knew I'd killed him. I'd killed that evil sonofabitch and escaped from his rule. That was why I'd been hiding this entire time and trying to stay one step ahead of the Cyber Dragons, Steel Phoenixes, and Lightning Tigers.

Oh hell.

That was when there was a banging on the other side of the door. "Hey, are you guys having sex? If so, it's a bad time and very mean to the people who are waiting on you."

"No, Paradise," Case said.

I sucked in my breath and walked to the door. "Forget I asked you anything. Let's just go find Solomon and kill him. Then I'm going to try to find a spaceship to flee Earth in."

"As you wish."

# Chapter Eleven

## I'm Not the Only Cyberpunk Who Lives In a Junkyard

The War Wagon had stopped sooner than I expected, the massive vehicle having apparently gotten lucky with New Los Angeles congestion and had a secret route only available to the super rich. Given that Recycling Center #17 was part of the Automated Industrial District, it was unlikely the latter.

Looking outside through the War Wagon's transparent steel window slits, I saw broken concrete buildings being broken up with machines as automated trucks delivered more refuse to be broken up. Metal was separated from stone along with plastic and other useful materials. Recycling Center #17 was one of the many disturbing results of Black Technology that was ostensibly for the benefit for mankind.

Miles and Lucita were waiting in the front of the War Wagon, ready to depart out the side and they looked annoyed. I didn't entirely blame them, but it wasn't like I was the one who'd decided to talk to me at length about my past. That was all on Case. Stupid sympathetic bioroid. Okay, that was less convincing than I'd intended.

Paradise looked out. "In goes the old world and out comes the new."

"The disposal of previous city construction to be replaced with more energy and technologically efficient arcologies is the way of the future," Lucita said.

"You sound like a commercial," I said.

I honestly didn't understand why the AI and megacorporations were so interested in wiping out the old cities and bulldozing all the former towns between the superstructures they were building.

AI didn't think like normal people, and I sometimes speculated it was an attempt to stop global warming or build some kind of *Star Trek*-esque utopia for mankind. Unfortunately, every arcology I'd visited was a different shade of hell so that didn't make any sense. Still, plants like this were breaking down hundreds of towns and repurposing the materials for constructing ever higher skyscrapers and more tin cans to shove people in like vat-grown meat. Solomon Jones had chosen a very peculiar spot for his hideout. Well, one of them at least.

"I just am noting that somewhere, somehow there's a grown-up angry adolescent hugging their copies of *Atlas Shrugged* and *Snow Crash* while masturbating furiously to this new world," Lucita said.

"That is a strange analogy," Miles said.

"Especially since those have diametrically opposite messages regarding privatization," Case said, coming up behind me.

Lucita shrugged. "I used to be that kid. I wanted a robot body that was nothing like my old one, beautiful and strong. That was something straight from science fiction until I was lucky enough to get the right cybernetics via my father's organization. Still, I can't help but notice that technology has run away with us, and someone is guiding the direction we're heading on cheap, anti-capitalist, dystopian science fiction lines."

"That's because the same asshats who were in charge in the Eighties are in charge now," Case replied. "The people who predicted that the world would be destroyed by greed and technology were predicting the then rather than the future. Which became the future."

"You lost the metaphor there, somewhere," Lucita said.

"I did, didn't I?" Case asked.

"Well, they got some bits wrong," I said. "China is in charge of the world rather than Japan."

"Europe too," Paradise said. "Except for Britain. Poor teeny, tiny unloved Britain."

"Why are we not headed out?" Lucita asked, looking bored.

"It smells terrible," I said, scrunching up my nose despite the fact the War Wagon's doors were still sealed. "I mean, I assumed it would smell terrible, but it smells worse than the terrible I imagined it to be."

Lucita reached over to the keypad beside the door and typed

in three numbers before it slid open. "We don't have any permits to be here so we should work quickly."

"Yes, because parking is our largest issue," Miles said, rolling his eyes.

"So, our plan is to just wander around looking for Solomon and hope he has spies to see us that think, 'Hey those heavily armed mercenaries look neat, let's go invite them to meet our boss'?" I asked.

"We didn't disturb the facility when we first found it and left the cameras and motion sensors still up. Solomon should be able to see us when we investigate," Lucita said.

"That wasn't the part that I was objecting to," I said.

"Do you have a better idea for contacting him?" Lucita said.

"Leave a message," I said.

"What she said," Case said.

Lucita shook her head and stepped out as everyone followed our indestructible model-looking leader. "We've created an electric trail of identities and misinformation that will make us look like buyers rather than hunters. It's not the best plan but it's the only one we have."

"I should have negotiated for more money upfront," I muttered.

Recycling Center #17 was a junkyard so there was a certain level of "You've seen one, you've seen 'em all", especially when you lived in one, but this was larger and more mechanized than all the Pre-Eruption ones. Massive piles of metal and concrete were neatly ordered alongside plastic. The remains of all the surroundings towns and buildings from old Los Angeles were slowly being destroyed to build up the arcology into one big megacity. Past the dozens of mountain-sized piles of rubble were stacked mountains of metal crates that were the result of the automated machines' labor.

"So where is Solomon's secret headquarters?" I asked, looking around. "I'm expecting a secret elevator to an underground casino or sex dungeon."

"Not quite," Lucita said. "Just follow me."

"Great," I muttered. "How long is the walk?"

"About twenty minutes."

"Did you know one of the biggest obstacles for archaeologists is the fact many of the great structures of the ancient world were disassembled to create new ones. That's how the Great Pyramid of Giza became the ugly blocky structure it is and what happened to many Roman monuments," I said, taking the sights around me.

Everyone looked sideways at me.

"What? I read," I asked, huffing. "You want me to be silent this entire time?"

"Yes," Lucita said.

"No," Paradise said.

"Yes," Miles said, betraying me.

"The Emergency Government wants to erase all traces of the old America," Case said, looking past the drone bulldozers and tumblers tearing up walls and turning them into piles of dust. That dust was loaded onto trains and transported by rail where it would be used to build more buildings downtown to house the endlessly growing numbers of arcology citizens.

"Best way to build an empire is on the ruins of a previous empire," I said. "In any case, there's no need to mourn what didn't work. The old America didn't do a damn thing for me when most of America's poor was in refugee camps."

"Well, they ran the refugee camps," Paradise said. "That's kind of doing a thing. What with the alternative being starvation and homelessness."

I shot her a glare.

"The old nation-state governments are a relic of the past," Lucita said, surveying the junkyard as if it was national park. "The new corporate states will allow humanity to not only expand to deal with its overpopulation problems, but they will provide models for artificial habitats across this planet as well as colonizing new worlds."

"You still sound like an advertisement," I replied.

"I was raised to be a killer," Lucita replied. "Despite its flaws, I like the new world we're building."

"You're about the only one," Case said. "This is the result of the Big Two Hundred and their expansion of power. They're the Invisible Hand."

I had a feeling he was referring to something other than a metaphor for economics.

"So, they're the masturbating angry adolescent?" Paradise asked.

"I say we go back to the whole be silent thing during this trip," Miles said.

"Agreed," I said.

Taking advantage of the new policy of group silence, I contacted Case via my implant. It was oddly working quite well despite being overclocked. His avatar, a cute Halloween ghost in a seashell, appeared in a tiny box in the right side of my vision and I could speak to him perfectly silently. *So, Snake is alive?*

*You're suddenly interested in my information?* Case asked.

*If it gives me an insight into Snake, yes,* I replied.

*As far as I can tell, yes,* Case replied. *He stays off the grid even compared to the other four Elemental Lords, but his power has been growing exponentially. Snake favors highly trained, highly loyal operatives with a focus on violence. Snake does not mind recruiting outside of the Japanese or Korean bloodlines that make up the regular Yakuza but heavily taxes the outsiders' operations. So far, it's kept his influence growing.*

*No surprise, there,* I replied. Snake had been something of a *weeaboo* with a focus on honor and the philosophy of martial arts but, at the end of the day, he was still primarily a hitman. Money and power were the real driving force behind his activities. *I thought I killed him. I can't believe he's still alive and covering for me, though. If he knew I was alive, then he'd have come after me.*

*Maybe he's waiting for something,* Case said. *Or maybe you weren't as important to him as you thought.*

I wasn't sure which disturbed me more. *So why are you doing this?*

*Excuse me?* Case asked.

*If you really are the CSO of Atlas then you have a literal army of intelligence guys and probably actual ninjas to do this sort of thing,* I said. *So, you're either a psychopath who gets off on it or have another reason.*

*It could be both,* Case replied. *But the actual answer is that James Madison is my friend.*

*I find you getting off on it more likely,* I replied. *Suits don't have friends. Neither do psychopaths.*

*Some do,* Case said. *Lucita and I are quite close too.*

*You and peroxide robot Italian girl, huh,* I said, surprised at a feeling of jealousy. *So, you have all the women covered here, huh?*

*Lucita is a friend. Paradise and I aren't involved,* Case said. *That would be gross. She's like a daughter to me.*

*Some daughter,* I replied.

*Besides, you were with Miles,* Case said. *Almost six months according to my files.*

*Yeah, me and Miles used to bang,* I replied, feeling almost defensive. *Then he got clingy and started bringing feelings into the matter. Whatever happened to men just caring about sex?*

Case chuckled aloud, and no one bothered to look at him but me.

*Anything else I should know about this mission since you're hooked up to the all-seeing database of everything?* I asked.

*Hardly everything,* Case said. *But I do suspect Helen Troy of being an agent of the Invisible Hand.*

*Great, the suit assassin believes his best friend is married to an agent of the Illuminati,* I replied. *Is she part of the Jew Banker's Guild, too?*

*If the Jews were secretly in control of the world, their lives wouldn't suck nearly as much,* Case pointed out. *The Invisible Hand is less like the Illuminati and more like a gentleman's agreement to divide up the world. Wherever capitalism reigns, there're people who are going to rig it in their favor.*

*That would sound so much less ridiculous coming from someone who wasn't one of the richest men on Earth,* I replied.

*Not even in the top thousand,* Case said. *I give too much away.*

I really hated liking this guy.

Eventually, we arrived at the base of a massive series of shipping metal shipping crates that had been stacked together in a pyramid. Wires and cables ran up and down across it with a set of power lines having been diverted directly into it. Satellite dishes and graffiti covered every level. A metal submarine door was built into the base of the structure and a group of automatic turrets were covering the place, causing everyone to stop moving before we got too close. They looked like someone had combined little garbage-can drones with a pair of machine guns before setting them on rotate.

"Okay, this is less eccentric recluse and more really tech-savvy homeless man," Paradise said, pausing. "Maybe with a bit of militia man survivalist-built in."

"I live in a junkyard but have an apartment. Well apartment is a generous term for it," I muttered, giving away too much about my location. Not that I didn't think they could track me down. "Why the hell would he live in a pile of shipping crates?"

"He lives in the infospace most of the time," Lucita explained. "The meat is just an inconvenience. Still, most of his kind at least bother to put themselves in hospitals or remote locations. Places that their caretakers can get easy access to. This looks like he's truly fallen on hard times."

"I don't understand Sleepers," Miles said, shaking his head.

"On the contrary, you have to spend a lot of money to look this poor," Case said, looking at the location sideways. "Did any of your people actually get inside this thing?"

"Yes," Lucita said, frowning. "The facility has been sealed up again. The turrets are new. It's probable that Solomon and company have been here since and swept up. Which means my people botched it."

"Good quality turrets, too. I won't be outrunning those to the front door," I said. "I wonder how many rounds they have in reserve."

"Well, there's an easy way to check," Lucita said, smiling.

"If you're looking for volunteers, I volunteer people I don't like," Paradise said. "Which means Miles."

"Hey!" Miles said.

"Sorry, you told Kei to be silent," Paradise said, putting her hands on her hips. "That's an automatic strike. Sisters before misters."

"We're not sisters," I said.

"Smile for the cameras," Lucita said, gesturing to a set of cameras that were focusing on us, barely hidden behind a set of wooden poles. "It looks like the first of our business is now resolved."

"Let's see how Solomon reacts," Case said.

"Well, he's not shooting," I said. "That's good."

"Oh, I dropped a worm in the autotargeting system," Paradise said. "We'd be dead right now if not for that. Techjack powers activate!"

I blinked. "You should probably have brought that up earlier, Paradise."

That was when a crane carrying a bunch of steel girders over our heads swung around and dropped them down on us.

"Dammit!" I shouted, grabbing Miles, and moving at faster than normal speeds. Case did the same for Paradise. Lucita just moved faster than any human being could as the steel girders smashed between us. If not for the cybernetically enhanced among us and the fact I'd been ready to sprint, I'm pretty sure all of us would have been crushed flat.

"I think we can assume we're unwelcome," I said, climbing to my feet and dropping Miles.

"The door is open," Lucita said, climbing up off the ground. "That may have just been a test."

"Enough with the tests!" I said. "I feel like I'm in someone's deranged psych eval."

"I'm starting to dislike our target," Case said, sounding more than a little annoyed.

"The murder and suicide bombings weren't enough?" I asked.

"Fair point. Damn. One of the girders knocked something into my leg," Case muttered, moving his leg around.

Paradise said, "Why make a robot feel pain?"

Case said, "Why make them indistinguishable from humans except better?"

Paradise said, "That's....ooo, now I'm going to be thinking about that all night."

"I owe you," Miles said to me. He was climbing to his feet and looked embarrassed as well as ashamed. I hoped it wasn't macho bullcrap about being saved by a girl. It wasn't the 1950s anymore. Frick, it wasn't even the 2050s.

"Yeah, and?" I asked, surprised that he thought this was worth mentioning. He'd do the same for me, right?

"Right," Miles said. "Well let's head on in, I guess. What's the worst that could happen?"

"We're all horribly killed?" Paradise suggested.

We all looked at her.

"What?" Paradise asked.

# Chapter Twelve

## Would I Go into the Hacker's Cave
## for a Scooby Snack? How about Two?

On a scale of one to ten, heading into the weird Lego con-structed hideout of a deranged terrorist Sleeper was about an eleven on things I didn't want to do. The guy had already tried to remotely kill us, and I was of the mind he was probably smart and crazy enough to rig his place to explode too. Still, we weren't exactly rolling in clues, and I'd done stupider stuff in my time. Not many times or much stupider but I had.

The interior was first distinguished by its smell and God, it smelled awful. It was a stereotype that had died years ago that professional computer nerds had poor hygiene but apparently Solomon hadn't gotten the memo. The place was rank, and I couldn't even identify half of the odors. Maybe his sewage sys-tem, if he had one installed in his pyramid of shipping crates, had backed up. The place was subdivided into rooms illuminated by cheap fluorescent lighting, holes cut in the sides to serve as doors, and power cables everywhere.

The decor was pretty much what I had expected. It was covered in old movie posters and shelves full of the kind of memorabilia that men who never aged past adolescence considered cool. There were also micro-servers, generator spikes, and broadband leaches. There was nursing equipment too, causally strewn about on a coffee table that I suspected served more for whomever Solomon hired to care for his prone body than himself, with a box of astro-naut diapers next to expired syringes of muscle stimulants.

"Yeesh," Paradise said. "Do I want to know what this is all about?"

"Sleeper equipment," Case said, looking around the various shelves. "Stuff to allow him to spend twenty-four hours in virtual reality."

"But life is full of so much fun!" Paradise said. "I mean, I spend half of my time in infospace as well, but only half."

"Cut the chatter please," Lucita said. "Miles, is this place rigged to blow or not?"

"Something you could have checked before I came in," I said, dryly.

"No sign of explosives yet," Miles said, opening a sliding door to another one of the crate rooms. Apparently, privacy was a concern for some of these spaces, but I couldn't imagine what a man who lived like this could care about. Case followed him and did his own search of the nutcase's hideout.

"Poor people leave explosives out in the open," I said. "Rich people have them built into the walls from the start. If we see any signs, it's because he wants to see the looks on our faces right before we're blown up."

Paradise looked around before picking up a micro-camera hidden behind a poster. "It's such a shame that I am a poor young girl who supports her family of eleven and would dearly love to meet an older man who shares my interests in all the stuff he's interested in."

"You're too late for convincing him," I said. "He's already tried to kill us."

Paradise stamped her foot. "Darn. That always works with clients."

"Good news," Case said, calling from the next room. "Also, bad news."

"How much of that are we getting?" I asked.

"Mostly bad," Case said.

"Of course," I said. "What's the good news?"

"We've found Solomon, He's here," Case said.

I actually breathed a sigh of relief, regretting it given the air quality. "Well, that's good news. At least he won't blow this place with him in it."

"Unlikely," Case said. "He's dead."

Goddammit. "Wait, is that the bad news?"

"Help me look," Case said. "There might be something worth salvaging here."

"If he's dead, isn't it over?" I asked.

"No," Lucita said. "He could have passed Blipvert onto someone else. Conspirators are every bit as dangerous."

"We still get paid, though, right?" Paradise asked.

"We better," I muttered, heading through the door that Case had gone into and almost threw up. The others stayed behind, which was a smart move given what we found. The smell was awful, many times worse than the rest of the makeshift house, and there was only a little light being provided by a dozen signal-less screens on the back end of the chamber's wall. Given dead channels hadn't looked like television static for decades, it was a deliberate stylistic choice.

There was a rotting corpse attached to a chair that resembled one from a dentist office, with lots of cybernetic tubes going in and out of the fleshy bits. The body was probably Solomon's with a big accent on the *probably* since his body wasn't at its freshest.

"You know, Lucita said her people had come here and gone over the place," Case muttered. "You'd think they'd have noticed this."

"Either the corpse was moved here, or the team was lying," I said. "Which means one thing."

A moment passed.

"Which is?" Case asked.

"I dunno, I was hoping you'd tell me," I said throwing my hands up. "It's possible that Madison's people are dirty and tipped him off, or this is a trap for us."

"They could also have had their eyes hacked," Case said.

"Really?" I asked. "I thought that was science fiction."

"I remind you that you're talking to a bioroid," Case said.

"So?" I asked, confused.

"It's possible, especially for AI," Case said, letting the matter drop. He walked up to examine the corpse and poked it a bit.

"Maybe he uploaded his brain," I muttered. "Eternally surfing the net as an AI."

"I believe you're right," Case said.

"What," I asked. "Is that possible?"

Case seemed casual about revealing immortality existed.

"Yes. Also, he's missing his brain case. He's left his meat behind," Case said. "He could be walking around in a Shell or be permanently hooked up to infospace from a jar now."

"Why didn't he do it sooner?" I asked. "I mean, Shells have been around awhile."

"Money, I'd wager," Case said. "A full body prosthetic costs upwards of ten million and that's a cheap one with the top-of-the-line models costing fifty million. That's why most of them are government or military use."

"Or corporate," I said, noting Lucita certainly counted as one. "What does a brain in a jar cost?"

"No idea," Case said. "It does mean he could be anywhere, though."

"But someone was watching us," I pointed out.

"Yes," Case said. "They probably still are. We can possibly try and backtrack the signal. Hell, I'm sure Paradise is working on it now in the next room. This is, however, a dead end."

I rolled my eyes at his pun. "Can you trust Paradise? I mean, to do the job."

"She's smarter than she acts," Case said.

"She'd have to be," I replied, going over to examine the hard drives underneath the screens. We'd have to clean this place out and see what we could find. "So, the attack out there was just Solomon fricking with us?"

That was when all the static covered screens changed to appear as a giant red button. It had the words 'Press Button' with an arrow over it with the air of a child's game about it, disrupted only by the fact we were in the middle of a room where tiny bits of the man's corpse were floating up into our lungs.

"Okay, you're one hundred percent right. Solomon is screwing with us," Case said, changing the subject from Paradise.

"You don't say," I muttered, sarcastically. "Should I push the button?"

"No!" Case said.

"What? You think he'd go to all this trouble to blow us up?" I asked.

"Yes," Case said.

"You have a point," I replied. "But we want to find him to hire him after all."

It was probably too late to go with the lie we were pushing but it was the only play we had. I pushed the button on the screen closest to me anyway. I was not sure who was a worse boss in all of this but, increasingly, I was of the mind this was an enormous game being played between Madison, Troy, and Jones. I hated the super-rich, Case included, and he seemed to be the nicest one of them I'd met so far.

Paradise walked in, holding a bunch of trading cards and blowing bubbles of a pink gooey substance. "Miles has found a massive servers worth of video game character porn, a trio of paintings stolen from the Louvre, several guitars belonging to the Eagles, and a bunch of 1st edition books by a woman named Emma Goldman. I've tried to get the signals down from this place but it's a bit above my paygrade. Solomon may have been an enormous pervert and weirdo, but the guy knew how to code his digital fortresses. I've copied a bunch of programs for my own use. Ooo, is that a big red button?"

"Yes," Case said. "Kei pushed it."

"That's dumb," Paradise said, pushing it as well.

I glared at her.

"Nothing is happening," Paradise said. "Wait, is it a touch-screen interface?"

"Yes. Also, give it time," I said. "I'm sure the Wizard of Oz needs to rev up his giant flaming head."

"Who?" Paradise said.

"Children's story," Case said.

"A children's story with a giant flaming head? Awesome!" Paradise stated, her eyes wide. Her knowledge of pop culture was wildly inconsistent, and I had to wonder what sort of education she'd had. She had to be faking this attitude, right? No Rider in real life was this naïve.

An image of a man wearing a baseball hat, shades, and a handkerchief around his face appeared on the screen. He was older, maybe his late sixties or early seventies, and African American. His voice spoke with a distorted tone. "So, you want to contact me. I'm not an individual interested in dealing with the world's corporate masters. I am the beginning of the storm that will cleanse the world of its greed, lies, and secret society elitist filth."

Case said, "You may want to handle this."

"Why?" I asked.

Case said, "Because my tolerance for anarchist meme-driven pseudo-philosophy is extremely low. If I wanted that, I'd go visit my friend Gary."

I had no idea who Gary was, but I didn't really care. "Good of you to say that in front of the person we're trying to contact. I'm sure that will help. Bluntly, Mr. Jones we need your help. We have a sample of Blipvert and are interested in the whole shebang."

"Shebang?" Case asked.

"Yes, to fight the Jewish Hollywood communist Satanist UFO conspiracy!" Paradise said. "Vote Trust! Vote often!"

"Stop helping, Paradise," I said.

"Aw," Paradise said.

Solomon stared at them for a moment, well as much as a CGI recreation of his face could do if it really was his body. "Very well."

"What, really?" I asked.

"Do you know the story between me and James?" Solomon asked.

"I don't keep up with the super-rich any more than I keep up with typhoons and global warming," I said.

Solomon laughed. It was a bitter digitized thing. Technology could replicate it far better, so he'd chosen to deliberately make it an echo of a real laugh. "Madison and I were involuntary recruits for the Society. We were given access to technology the rest of the world only dreamed about but the price was we could never share it. The Powers that Be, the Invisible Hand, wanted to keep it all to themselves to guarantee their control over the world."

Great, I was dealing with multiple conspiracy nuts. Still, I wasn't going to tell that to his face. "Yeah, well, all of that information eventually got leaked on the market."

"And got used to make the world into the hellhole it is today," Solomon replied. "Things are even worse than they were decades ago."

"The super volcano may have had something to do with that," Miles said, standing at the edge of the doorway. "Just saying."

"The Big Smokey's eruption was just the catalyst for bringing about the change that was destined all along," Solomon said, pointing at them from all the screens. "James and his cronies created infospace to unionize information and create places where we could explore the limits of consciousness. To find the undiscovered country where it would be impossible to hold back the poor or destitute."

"The undiscovered country is a reference to *death*," Case corrected, looking doubly annoyed with Solomon.

"I thought it was a reference to the peace between Klingons

and the Federation," Paradise said.

Okay, yes, she was faking being an airhead. Also, I wondered if I should be bothered that I got that reference? I'd been spending too much with David.

"Did he actually create infospace?" I asked, wondering what I'd wandered it. "Is he virtual reality's Al Gore?"

"Who?" Paradise asked.

"Twenty thousand programmers created the groundwork for it," Case replied. "Hundreds of thousands of others expanded on it with the help of multiple lesser tier AI and quantum computers running algorithms."

"So no," I replied.

"He did probably some of the early research for the Society, though," Case said. "But so did a lot of people."

"The who?" I asked.

"The people who built me," Case said. "They're all dead."

"Not all of them," I muttered, noting not just Solomon but Madison and Case himself qualified.

"So, he's just disgruntled," Paradise said.

Yeah, Solomon definitely hadn't been fooled by us wanting to hire him. I really hoped that wasn't our only plan.

"Let me guess," Case said, dryly. "You broke up your partnership with James because he decided to monetize your dream. You're just another aging hacker anarchist and retro-hippie trying to fight against the Man despite the fact you're every bit as big a part of the system as anyone else."

I shot Case a glare. This was why I didn't like corporates on my missions. That and they were invariably sociopaths.

Solomon just laughed. "Perhaps but it goes deeper than that. James refused to acknowledge what our research showed. The limitless potential he squashed."

"Please, we're just messengers here," I asked, pleadingly.

Solomon sighed as if talking to a small child. "I've been studying Blipvert for a while now. It's a sophisticated program that has been changing itself and evolving—almost like a living organism. I've developed a treatment, but it needs more samples. We can meet virtually to handle the exchange."

"Wait, you do want to sell it to us?" I asked.

"I want to expand its potential and that needs money," Solomon said. "I'm willing to sell it to anyone who is willing to buy it."

Great, for an anti-capitalist nutjob, he sure had mastered the subtleties of capitalism. "What about the terrorist attacks?"

"Demonstrations," Solomon said. "A way of showing just what Blipvert can do. Just don't expect to be the only buyer."

"Can we get your guarantee that you won't—" Case started to speak.

"Club Inferno," Solomon said. "Two hours."

All the screens went blank simultaneously, leaving them once more alone in a room with a rotting corpse.

"Please tell me Club Inferno is a real place," I said, suddenly a lot more invested in this conflict than I'd been five minutes ago. Solomon had all but admitted he was guilty of these attacks and had plans to wage more.

"It is a digital palace and one of the premier social clubs in infospace," Lucita said, walking in. "Tens of thousands of avatars visit the location daily but only the most elite of techjacks are allowed within. It's where they share their data regarding newly created worlds, share stolen secrets, and experience all manner of newly coded pleasures or tortures. It's really the heart of the free infotainment movement and so exclusive even I have to work hard to get in."

"You've gone nerd clubbing?" I asked, lightly teasing. "Can't get into the real deal?"

Lucita rolled her eyes. "I've had dictators and A-list celebrities get on their knees begging to please me. Virtual is just more... anonymous."

What a terrible shame that she was so rich and famous that she had to seek being one of us little people. "Getting a sample of this virus was part of our mission. It'll help us get closer to what we need."

Which was to kill Solomon Jones. I had just the way to do it too.

# Chapter Thirteen

## Trying to Figure Out Our Next Move

"You do have an idea of how to stop him?" Case asked.

"Yeah," I said. "It's a trick belonging to my old teacher."

I wasn't about to mention Snake to the others, even if Case and probably Lucita already knew.

"What's that?" Lucita asked.

I said, "He can see us with his cameras, though, right?"

"No," Paradise said. "I'm scanning everything now and he's severed every link through the systems. We might be able to follow some of the early links through the servers here, but I suspect they've been rerouted a million times or more."

"So, we can talk freely?" I asked.

Paradise leaned in like she was in a spy movie and whispered. "Yes."

"Follow me." I walked out of the room with the corpse anyway. Despite getting used to the smell, I didn't want to be anywhere around it as much as I wanted to avoid any listening devices. Thankfully, everyone followed me. I didn't stop until we were about ten yards away from the fallen steel girders that had been used to almost kill us. "I think all we need to do is get to his avatar and I'll be able to kill him."

"How?" Lucita asked.

"Black Ice," I replied.

Lucita blinked. "Impressive."

"What now?" Miles asked.

"It's a reference to William Gibson's *Burning Chrome*," Case replied. "Lethal countermeasures for intrusions into cyberspace. A real-life version was created when it was discovered that high end brain cases and infospace implants could be shorted out with a 71% mortality rate. The Trikuza supposedly created a perfected version, but it never hit the market."

"71% is not so bad," Miles said, looking nervous for some reason. "I've faced worse odds."

"The rest are left brain dead," Case replied.

"Oh," Miles said, looking embarrassed. "Well, that's different."

"I got it during one of my early heists," I said, not remembering the specifics. "I've never used it, but it's been stored in my implant ever since."

Something felt weird about bringing Black Ice up now. Like something was inside me pushing it forward. I didn't have time to question it, though, or even have a reason other than a feeling. I did notice Miles was looking at me weird, though. He was trying to look at me without looking at me. Kind of strange given our history.

"Oh wow, I hope the megacorps are working on a fix on this vulnerability and will inform the public!" Paradise said, pausing before bursting out laughing. "Okay, sorry, excuse me. Let me try that again. I sure hope—"

I raised my hand to interrupt. "Yeah, yeah, horrifying side effects kept from the public by greed. Must be Tuesday. Either way, I still have some leftover viral software that can be used that way. It might be our best way of stopping this guy. We'll have to do it after we acquire the Blipvert files, though."

Because giving mind control technology to the suits was such a good idea. Frick it, I sure could have used another round of lethe.

"It sounds dangerously close to a plan," Case said.

"Are you sure you want to use that program?" Miles asked. "You remember where you got it, right?"

I didn't. Just a few vague details and the fact it was related to Snake. "Sure, why?"

"Never mind. I'm sure you forgot for a reason," Miles muttered, looking disgusted. It made me want to reach over and punch him in the face. If he was going to judge me about how I lived my life, then he could just go to hell.

"Do you think any of Solomon's crazy rantings were true?" Paradise asked.

"I don't think it matters," I replied.

Paradise said, "No one who loves the Eagles this much could be evil!"

"The who?" I asked.

"No, the Who are a different band," Paradise corrected.

"I only listen to omnivore and retro polymer synth, like Sun and QuantumCrab."

"Yeah, I'm totally keeping this guy's guitar collection and paintings," Miles said. "They've got to be worth something."

"Aren't you a cop?" Case asked, looking at him sideways.

"Yeah, and?" Miles replied.

"If we're going to Black Ice him, though, we'll need a safe place to upload ourselves as well as protections against being hit again or traced," I said, trying to figure this all out in my head.

Case blinked then shrugged. "Do you know any good places we can trust?"

"Trust is relative," I said. "Which is a way of saying no."

"Almost every major infospace node in the city is monitored by either the suits or the police," Miles said. "Legally or illegally."

"I know the perfect place we can log in," Paradise said. "It's in the Refugee Zone!"

"Oh no," I muttered.

"This is Paradise!" Paradise said. "It has one of the highest functioning unregistered infospace hookups in the city. Completely untraceable thanks to all the Atlas Security machinery that was accidentally shipped to us."

"Why do you have that?" I asked.

"Making porn, charging people for porn," Paradise said. "You have to specialize these days if you want people to get off their asses at home."

"Then, I guess we're off to the brothel," I said, sighing. Honestly, this seemed like a better plan than we'd started with. The suits involved in all of this had sent people to murder me as a test and Solomon had tried to drop a bunch of girders on me. It seemed like everyone was testing everyone with a gun to our heads. "What is this Club Inferno like, anyway? What kind of avatar should I dress in?"

That was when Lucita's infocomm started beeping. The little gold wristwatch looked like it cost ten times my bike. "I believe we should table this discussion for now."

"What's wrong, Blondie?" I asked.

"Blondie, really?" Lucita asked. "That's actually what my last name means."

"That's the War Wagon perimeter alarm," Case replied.

"Yes, I set it in case we'd have trouble," Lucita said. "I don't trust Helen Troy."

"Oh really!" I asked. "Because I didn't get that she was untrustworthy when she tried to kill me as a test for a job application!"

"That was rude," Paradise said. "Wait, is someone trying to kill us? Is it drones? I love drones!"

"It's not drones," Miles said. "I hate the guys who run them in the LAPD."

I specifically knew who he meant. David and I might have only a casual relationship, but I was at least still occasionally sleeping with him instead of Miles. Was I being unfair assuming that was why Miles hated him? Probably. I also was worth that kind of angst.

"Who? How many?" I asked, hearing the roar of engines nearby. "Or is it too late?"

"Much too late," Lucita said, checking her wristwatch. "Get to cover!"

I stared at the sight of the mammoth vehicle heading their way and wondered again if my suspicion that this was some sort of crazy game for the super-rich was true. The thing was a modified semi over twelve feet high and possessed six enormous wheels with spikes sticking out all over the side.

The machine was armored and low-tech rather than high with six people visible on the top, all dressed in leather coats and war paint. Four wheelers came over the piles of junk and motorcycles around it, sporting swastikas and Confederate flags. It was a ridiculous look but served as the signifier of what they were: Jackals.

"Dammit. I hate Jackals," I spat out.

Whoever said adversity brought out the best in people was a goddamn moron. The Eruption and the subsequent Collapse had reduced the United States to a third world country of the kind President Trust continued to make fun of in his rare speeches when they wheeled out his cybernetically animated corpse. It had turned a lot of us into refugees out to survive as best we could. Jackals were the dark side of those who couldn't fit back into society. They were more like *Mad Max* than starving hungry masses and murdered anyone who stood in their way. I'd killed more than my fair share but every year more refugees decided they'd prefer to be the boot instead of the ant.

Taking position behind some of the junk and debris, I pulled my pistol and looked to the others who were also going for their weapons. I couldn't tell whether this was yet another attack by the crazy rich lady trying to sabotage this mission for some reason or just a random coincidence. It wasn't like Jackals weren't always looking for an easy target, in which case they'd picked the mother of all bad ones. Punctuated by my taking the face off one of the Jackals hanging on the side of the semi-truck.

"I don't like killing people," Paradise said. "But I will!"

"We do like killing, bitch!" A bald, tattooed woman in ripped pants and an open jacket with nothing under it said, pointing an Uzi at Paradise. Case shot Baldie off the back of the bike. That caused another man to drive directly at him, shooting wildly, only for Case to run up and knock him off with a clothesline motion of his arm: Team Rider 3, Jackals 0.

"You know what would be a good thing here?" Miles said to Lucita while shooting. "The goddamn War Wagon!"

"I didn't want to hurt its suspension!" Lucita said.

"It's an APC!" Miles shouted.

That was when the semi started driving directly at us and we all broke from our cover to avoid being shot or run over, or run over *and* shot. Bullets whizzed past me as I shot wildly behind me, wondering if I should have invested more of my funds into a bulletproof epidermic and musculature.

"Thankfully, it's remote!" Lucita, falling on the ground and shooting upwards with a second pistol in her spare hand like a Hong Kong action movie heroine.

"What?" I asked, managing to shoot a hanger on off the semi as it smashed passed us and crashed into the junkpile beyond.

That was when the War Wagon smashed through another pile of steel crates, sending them landing on the remaining motorcycle riding Jackals before smashing into monster truck and knocking it over. The door slid open.

"Retreat!" Case said, his trench coat filled with bullet holes as he managed to knock off two of the Jackals firing from the semi's back.

Miles made a break for it. "Your remote driving sucks!"

"Don't hurt its feelings when it's helping us!" Paradise shouted, thankfully still alive.

"It doesn't have feelings!" I screamed, making own mad dash, and feeling dirt hit my legs from where bullets barely missed.

We managed to slip into the War Wagon's side, gunfire being exchanged with the attackers. I felt the sting of a bullet hit my body-armored filled track suit at the end, leaving what I believed would be a nasty bruise. "If I was on my bike, you would have really regretted doing this!"

"Get the vehicle going!" Case shouted to Lucita.

"I am not your subordinate!" Lucita shouted.

Case ran to the controls.

"Okay, yeah, that's a good idea," Lucita muttered. "Kei, check the hijackers!"

"I am not—" I paused then looked out the door that needed to be pulled shut.

That was when I saw one of the downed bikers pulling up an actual honest-to-goddess rocket launcher.

"Oh hell," I said.

There not much you could do against a rocket. They flew too fast for even augmented human senses to take down and exploded in too large an area for you to have a realistic chance of getting out of the way. Rocket*launchers*, on the other hand, were something one could deal with. Since they were bulky as hell and took more than a moment to aim. Guns were faster.

I leaned out the door and opened fire, latching my legs around a seat to keep from being thrown out of the suddenly moving vehicle. My eye augmentations were linked to the scanner in my pistol and there was a bleeping noise as I focused in on the rocket in the launcher. The resulting explosion tore through the remaining Jackals and left nothing but flame and debris behind. Paradise pulled me in before Miles slammed the door shut.

The War Wagon was silent afterward as it continued travelling. There was no sign of any further Jackal interference, which was good since the War Wagon wasn't exactly built for speed. Still, it was a situation where I'd killed a good ten people since this morning and that wasn't something I was comfortable with—specifically, I was feeling comfortable with it and didn't like that element about myself. I was not going to be what Snake made me.

"That was fun!" Paradise said.

"What part of that looked like fun?" I asked. "The decaying corpse? The people trying to kill us? The imminent death all around us?"

Paradise nodded. "Yep! All of that!"

"Are we getting away?" I asked.

"Given we're in an APC, they crashed their semi, and half of them are dead or on fire—we're golden," Lucita replied.

"I wouldn't assume anything," I replied, getting up. "Jackals are usually too coked and methed up to notice they're getting wiped out."

"They do lethe too," Miles said in what was an undoubtedly a dig at me.

I glared at him. "Lethe makes you forget, it doesn't make you a psycho killer."

"It depends on what you're forgetting," Miles muttered, "or who."

Case walked back from the front of the War Wagon. "They knew we were going to be there."

"Yes," Lucita responded, keeping her eyes on the road. "It would seem to be the case. We were ambushed."

My training with Snake had given me the ability to read body language and micro-expressions, aided by the scanners installed in my eyes. Apparently, that worked for Shells too. Lucita's discomfort masked a surprising amount of fear. There was something she knew about this that she was not telling us. She didn't strike me as the kind of woman who was easily scared either.

"How did they know about us?" Case asked.

"You think I'm responsible?" Lucita asked, snorting. "I know you may be past your resell date, Case, but I never thought you were stupid."

"I think it was Troy," Case said.

Lucita stared at him. "She's a woman motivated by profit, just like the rest of our class. Your conspiracy theories aren't helping."

"They're not conspiracy theories if they're right," Case said. "Then they're journalism."

"And you're not a journalist," Lucita said. "You're a paranoid ex-assassin."

"Who says ex?" Case asked.

Lucita rolled her eyes.

"You think Solomon called them?" I asked Lucita. "Somehow, I don't think Jackals are his scene."

"Funny because a bunch of murderous terrorists seems just up his alley," Case said.

"He's also black," Miles pointed out.

"Jackals are intensely tribal," I replied, remembering my few encounters with them on the road as a refugee. "A lot of the white supremacist stuff is just dressing for their gangs. What really matters is your ability to kill and earn. In that order. A Sleeper hacker isn't someone that could command them. They'd want to meet in person for any deals."

"You sound like you know them," Miles said.

"I had to survive a lot of rough circumstances," I replied. "I tried to get back with the refugees after escaping my sensei and didn't always make the best choices. It turns out we're less of a people and more of a condition. No, they're more likely to work with corporates than low level mobster anarchist wannabes like Solomon."

"Because corporates are so much better than mobsters," Lucita said, only half-sarcastically. "At least at killing."

"Absolutely," Paradise said, sitting down at the snack room table. "Corporates are a multi-trillion-dollar industry while mobsters are just multi-billion-dollar industry. You can judge success by how much their illegal activities bring in."

"Which gets us back to Helen Troy," Case said.

"I don't think the Jackals are her scene either," I said. "Why do you think she's a member of the Illuminati?"

"What now?" Miles asked.

"Case has the insane idea that Helen Troy is actually a honeypot agent for a corporate conspiracy," Lucita said. "Despite the fact that I've known her since the days she showed side boob for her millions of Infogram followers."

I looked at Lucita. "So, your argument is that you, a professional assassin, and underwear model, definitely know that a softcore erotic actress is also not a spy?"

Lucita stared at me. "Well, when you say it like that, it sounds stupid."

"Helen Troy is an identity that exists on paper, but all of the records are suspiciously generic dating back to the Collapse and beyond. She also made a fortune in movies that, as far as I can tell, no one saw and had a surplus of fans that were primarily bots. There's also the fact that her sponsors are in the Trikuza and Russian syndicates. Groups that I think were created as enforcement arms for the Invisible Hand."

"That's just modeling, dear," Lucita said. "Most of the successful firms have mob ties these days. So is marrying a billionaire with too much influence and too little sense."

"I think the moment James married Helen Troy, she was going to have him killed," Case said. "The only reason that she hasn't done so is because he's gotten her in so much debt. I think she plans to use Blipvert as a weapon and sell it to the highest bidder. For that, anyone else in contact with it has to die."

There was a moment of silence.

I paused. "Yeah, that makes sense."

Paradise nodded. "Yeah, I mean, if I was a multibillionaire marrying an erotic actress who just so happens to also be a savvy businesswoman then I would be pre-nupped out the wazoo. Is he?"

"No," Lucita said. "Madison isn't."

Paradise grimaced then looked at Case. "Yeah, your friend is a dead man."

"Probably," Case said.

"Well, let's find a place to continue our investigation," I replied. "Some place outside of Helen's line of sight. Just in case."

"I know just the place!" Paradise said, cheerfully.

# Chapter Fourteen

## The Freedom of Slums

The Refugee Zones were the shame of the United States, or would be if the United States still had shame. When the Eruption had occurred, millions of Americans had been displaced from their homes to refugee camps across the country to supervise the distribution of food as well as supplies. The crisis was something that had "lasted" for five years before the Emergency Government had created the arcology project and had the brilliant idea of transferring all the survivors to urban areas outside the only places in America which were still producing products.

Of course, most of the newly AI-automated commercial zones and industrial districts didn't need large amounts of unskilled labor and supply shortages were still massive (perhaps they might not have been if the government hadn't forced everyone off their lands). That had lent itself to crime, desperation, and riots. The governments had responded by creating huge forty-foot walls around the Zones and then making it so no one could leave without work permits. President Trust did love his walls. The worst thing? It was still better in these places than it was in many other parts of the United States.

"I'd like to find the jerkasses who came up with this and strangle them in their sleep," I muttered, seeing the massive concrete walls that served as a literal metaphor for economic segregation.

"They're not so bad," Paradise said.

I stared at her. "How can you say that?"

"I live here," Paradise said. "It's one of the few places where people can be themselves and not every single element of their life monitored."

"I'm pretty sure this is what used to be called a ghetto," I replied.

"It's still called a ghetto," Lucita replied.

"Speaking as a Hispanic Jew, I resent the comparison," Miles said. "Even if I can't exactly argue with it. I used to walk the beat here."

"I remember," I replied, thinking back to happier times. "You said it was the easiest job you ever had."

"How's that?" Lucita said. "I understand the crime rate is still spectacular within."

"No one ever wanted to talk to the cops," Miles said. "The gangs also made it clear that if I ever did interfere, I'd be dead by morning. You could forget doing your job here. So, most of us didn't bother."

"Like *Chinatown*," Case said.

"No, Chinatown is quite nice," Miles said.

"No, it's a reference—" Case started to explain.

"There are at least a dozen APCs in the Zone at any given time," Lucita said, cutting him off. "Our forged credentials should get us past the database, especially if I use my Atlas ones instead of the ones set up for this mission. Then we can power down and stay off the grid to deal with Solomon. From there, we'll do some backlogging to see if Troy is trying to betray us."

"You come around to Case's POV that she's a psycho bitch?" Miles asked.

"Trust but verify," Lucita muttered.

"You know, before the Collapse, the United States had places where they stuck people who they didn't want but didn't want to kill," Case said.

"You referring to reservations or Japanese internment camps?" I asked.

"I was referring to suburbs," Case said.

I rolled my eyes.

Paradise didn't find it funny and frowned deeply. Maybe she resented the comparison to the suburbs. "A lot of people want to escape the Refugee Zones. I think that's a lost cause because that just means the best people will be gone. Instead, we should try to make the Refugee Zones better. Real communities."

"You can't make them better," I said. "Trying just brings down the government to stop you. For the people's own good, of course.

They need a place to show how bad it can get to show people persuade them to obey the law. Meanwhile, the suits need a supply of people desperate enough to sign away their rights to their own bodies, and these places are despair factories."

"That's no excuse not to try," Paradise said, speaking entirely seriously. I was surprised she could.

"The system is rigged no matter who is in charge," Case said, staring out the window. "Whether it's high priests, nobles, merchants, god kings, corporates, or dictators. The rich and powerful try to make society serve them."

"Said the rich and powerful robot," Paradise said, sarcastically.

"Don't hate the player, hate the game," Case said.

"I can do both!" Paradise said, returning to her previous faux cheer.

We reached the checkpoint and Miles sat in the front, pretending to be a cop, and getting us waved through without difficulty. I would have questioned it, but the cops assigned to the Zone weren't the best or brightest. Despite being armed with enough firepower to slaughter an army, this was a beat that needed little handling. They were more worried about the poor and destitute escaping than uprising and slaughtering the rich as they probably deserved.

"I still say this is an incredibly conspicuous vehicle," I muttered as we passed through the wall's tunnel. It was only about a block long and was more like a car wash than a tunnel, extending past the wall to make you feel like you were doing more than just passing through a door to the unwanted remnant of the Old World. It was a power move designed to make the people feel like they were crossing the border rather than a line.

"It's a magician's sleight of hand," Lucita said. "We'll ditch the War Wagon once we've found a suitable replacement for it. We can always retrieve it later or not."

I snorted. "I'm sure the gangs would love something like this."

"Depends on the gang," Paradise said. "This is their home too."

We passed through the second checkpoint at the end of the tunnel and entered into the past. We were surrounded by old Pre-Eruption buildings. Banks, nightclubs, gas stations, boutiques, and offices that had been converted into housing by the government before shoving people into standing room only. The populace had done their best to make do, though. There were hundreds of electrical wires, satellite dishes, neon signs, and artificial levels built from stolen scrap metal along with concrete smuggled in from the outside. The walls were covered in graffiti and the people wearing hand-me downs from bygone eras. It had more character, good and bad, than the entirety of downtown. People primarily traveled on foot with public transit used once you left the Zone or cars shared among families.

The people of the Zone were an interesting intersection of fashion and races. Tens of thousands of people forced together regardless of ethnicity, religion, or past. After the initial riots and killings, people had gradually started to blend into something new. Tattoos, piercings, strange new hairstyles, and attire that would have shocked or confused the people before the Collapse were common. No one looked that way outside of the Zone, though. You didn't keep a job unless you were willing to conform and not having a job was death for many. I was glad to have escaped this place—even though I'd only been here two months after my betrayal—and proud to live in the city.

"How are we going to get into the interior?" I asked. "The streets are packed."

"They'll make room," Miles said, driving forward and causing everyone to clear a path for the APC they did the way they did during government raids for contraband or weapons.

"Are you sure we won't draw too much attention here?" I asked.

"Oh, that's not the point," Lucita said, looking concerned for the people trying to get their shopping carts and possessions out of the way of the War Wagon. "It's to draw the right sort of attention. If anyone comes after us, we'll have hefty warnings because the population will try to sell information and protection to both sides."

I shook my head. "We just need a safe place to jack in."

"A whorehouse is a good place for that," Case said.

"Aw. I wanted to say that," Paradise said.

"Me too," Miles added.

I grimaced at falling into that.

"I think you'll be surprised that it's not what you expect," Paradise said to me.

"It will not be my first time in a brothel," I said.

Case looked like he was desperately trying to find the right response to that line amidst a sea of possibilities.

Either way, the people did part and we managed to eventually find a parking space. Obviously, we drew major attention, but it wasn't like anyone was going to interfere with the heavily armed mercenaries leaving the armored vehicle. Still, I couldn't help but think this was ass-backward and wondered what Lucita's plan really was.

"Are we far from This is Paradise?" I asked.

"Not far," Paradise said. "It's a local institution."

"Oh," I said, feeling deeply uncomfortable with the complete lack of space between people. During the early days of the Collapse, disease had been rampant, and it had taken a lot of deaths to get people to finally wear masks when they were sick. Even then, plenty of people claimed the medical care in the Zones was perfectly adequate.

"She's serious," Case said.

Paradise said, "When I was a young girl, the brothels around here were controlled by the Trikuza and the Russian mob. The women were bought from their families, addicted to drugs, or even kidnapped and held against their will."

"That's how it usually goes," I said. "That's how the Trikuza does it."

"Yes," Paradise said. "Which is why my mother and the others killed them all."

"What?" I said, doing a double take.

"How very *Sin City*," Miles said.

Paradise said, "Black Technology had its benefits to level the playing field even if it can also be used to oppress. In this case, the Black Technology was a set of fingerprint sized bugs that let us track where every one of the gangs was—and get them all killed by paying other people to do it. When the dust was settled and no one knew who did what, we made our own little union and hired our own guards. Sex Workers of the World Unite! You have nothing to lose but your chains!"

"Except your lives," I said, impressed by Paradise's little speech, nevertheless.

"That too," Paradise said. "That doesn't make a great slogan, though."

"And you've remained independent ever since? I must admit, that's impressive."

"Yes and no," Paradise said.

"What's the no part?" I asked.

"We run a gang that means we have to kick money around to the zone militias, the local gangs, and more," Paradise said. "So much money needs to be thrown around they needed one of their promising young women to be a Rider instead of a prostitute just like others have had to be trained as soldiers or hackers."

Ah, that explained a few things. She wasn't a killer as well as a prostitute by choice. But then, who was? I just thought it would have been the prostitute part that she objected to. Maybe that was just me. "Sounds complicated."

Paradise said, "We have to expand, or other girls get swept up. Boys too. It's why I'm happy taking this job. Better to stay at the Devil's side than stand in his path."

"That's how demons get made, people trying to hang with devils instead of hurt by them."

"Do you see any angels here?" Miles asked, shrugging his shoulders.

"You didn't offer to help?" I looked at Case. "I thought you were their sugar daddy."

"I offered and have slipped them a few million credits here and there. It mostly ended up being used to get vaccines for the Zone's kids or other such nonsense. Tsk-tsk-tsk," Case said, faking bemusement. "The problems here are beyond even my wealth, though. Besides, they wanted to establish their own position as best they could. I did kill some people for them here and there at a credit a head, though. Friends and love-toy discount."

Miles frowned as if the dissonance of a suit casually admitting to murder in front of him reminded him of some of the nastier encounters he'd had on the force. In the end, that's why we couldn't be together. I didn't remember much about our relationship, but I remembered how it ended. As a cop, he couldn't overlook what I'd been doing, and I couldn't overlook what he was supporting. The fact he was a Rider now bothered me, even though I'd left him a long time ago. It just didn't fit my image of who he was.

"So did I," Lucita said. "The only charity work that truly matters: killing abusive men."

"I've met a few abusive women over the years too," I said. "The Trikuza wouldn't have nearly the control over the sex trade they did if not for women corralling the other girls."

"When we've perfected the bioroid process, then no one will need to be a prostitute or menial laborer," Lucita said, amused.

"It'll trigger the post-scarcity age we've always deserved."

"I hope not," Paradise said "Then the rich will have no reason to keep the poor alive."

Lucita didn't respond for a moment. "Huh, never thought about it like that. We're here."

This is Paradise was, conveniently enough, a former hotel. It was tropically themed and had its parking lot covered with a scrap metal rooftop, allowing an outdoor restaurant, bar, and gathering place for the myriad customers to mix with the staff. The name of the hotel shined in a bright neon pink over the rest of the place. The converted parking lot was surrounded by its own concrete wall and there were numerous guards sitting in makeshift towers and positions with a chain link fence serving as the doorway. Security was apparently paramount in this brothel.

"You grew up here, huh?" I asked.

"Yep." Paradise said. "A lot more secure than most places. Sort of like a town hall for this part of the Refugee Zone."

"Seems like a fun place," I said, perhaps more sarcastic than intended.

"It was," Paradise said. "Home is wherever your family is."

"I don't have one," Case said. "Unless you count a test tube and some microchip brands."

"I send someone every year to crap on the grave of my ancestors," Lucita said. "May they burn in hell."

"Well at least that saves on presents for Hanukah," Miles said.

Lucita turned back to Paradise. "You should be the one to get us in."

Paradise nodded and went to the sliding door. "I promise I won't betray you. Probably."

Case gave her a thumbs up.

"I admit, it is cleaner than I expected," I said. "Smells better than most of the Zone, too."

Paradise looked irritated with me. It was only then that I realized I'd inadvertently said her home smelled. Was I the snob? Really? In a group that included two suits and a cop? Crap.

Case said, "Perhaps what she's saying is true. A home can come in some of the most unexpected of places."

It was only now, realizing that I had no one waiting for me back at my place, that I understood I didn't have a home at all.

That was depressing.

# Chapter Fifteen

## The Past is Never Gone, Just Forgotten

Well, we'd arrived at This is Paradise and it was a pleasant if eccentric-looking place. Still, I felt incredibly vulnerable surrounded by people I didn't know and lots of them carrying guns in various states of concealment.

Virtually the entirety of the Zone was packing from what I could see during the looks I cast around. It was another paradox of the Zone that the populace didn't trust the police, so they kept their own weapons while the government encouraged everyone to view Zoners as dangerous because they were a bunch of gun toting nuts. The prevalence in the weapons led to more gun crime, which led to more crackdowns as well as "accidental" police shootings, and that resulted in more distrust against authorities. Then again, maybe that wasn't a paradox so much as the system working exactly as intended.

Lucita said, "All we need is a quiet place and a power source to work. Do you have that."

Paradise said, "Quiet is a bit iffy but we have the rest. Come on in!"

"We won't need much quiet, we won't be hearing anything once we're plugged in," I said. "While plugged into infospace, you're dead to the world. It's like *The Matrix*."

"Duh," Paradise said. "I learned to jack in before I could walk. Also, *The Matrix*? Why not reference *Casablanca*?"

"It's a classic!" I defended the film.

Paradise rolled her eyes. "Yeah, to people my mom's age."

That had been one of the first movies Fate had showed me. I was remembering more and more now of my time with her and

Snake. I didn't like it. It was like a dam that had started out leaking was now ready to burst. People eventually built up a tolerance to lethe and the mind started reconstructing the memories it suppressed. Given the way memory worked, reconstructing what happened every time you thought of it, it was perhaps always bound to happen.

Still, I couldn't help but want another round of lethe. I was becoming a junkie and didn't like that feeling at all, especially as I saw a trio of homeless men strung out on my drug of choice in an alleyway by the bordello.

"Anyway, are you sure this won't be a problem?" I asked, feeling somewhat silly asking about it. This, after all, was her family.

"I don't like bringing problems back home," Paradise said. "But this is probably the safest place in the city barring drone strike."

"Is a drone strike likely?" I asked, half-joking.

"Only if your friend David does it," Miles muttered.

Case and Lucita looked at me.

I rolled my eyes. "David's just a friend."

With benefits. He was easy and sometimes that was what you wanted from your bed buddies.

"That's not how he tells it," Miles muttered.

"Down boy," I said.

A beautiful woman with green hair held up by lacquer chopsticks, a dragon tattoo around her neck, and a Chinese red dress with a slit came to meet with us as Lucita set down the equipment. There was a slight resemblance in her features to Paradise, but she didn't quite look old enough to be her mother. That was misleading these days, though, and I had to admit she moved like she owned the place.

"Any friend of Paradise is welcome here," the woman said.

"Are you Paradise's mother?" I asked.

"Evie Principle," the woman said, extending her hand. There was an elegance about her that was enrapturing.

I took it. "Kei. Evie Principle, really?"

"That's not her real name," Paradise said, leaning in. "Shocking, I know."

"A lot of us have left behind our old names and lives," Evie said. "The act of choosing a new one divorces us from what came before and gives us a focus on what will come again."

"I know that feeling," Case replied.

"Hello, Case," Evie said, extending her hand to him as well. "Slumming it in Hell again?"

"You are worth Hell," Case said, putting a hand over his heart while holding hers with his other.

I suddenly hated Evie and felt embarrassed by it. Was I really attracted to a suit? Goddammit.

"You are such a liar," Evie replied. "What can I do for you and your little armed band of mercenaries?"

"I am calling in the favors you owe me," Lucita said.

"Do I owe you favors?" Evie asked, raising an eyebrow.

Lucita narrowed her eyes. "Yes."

Evie smiled. "Then please explain what you want, and I shall provide it."

"We require an infospace link-up that has level eleven defenses, a level six barrier, and a cortical interface with interactive real time party connections," Case said.

"You sure we shouldn't be going to Atlas HQ for something like that?" Miles asked. "This seems pretty high end for a whorehouse."

"Hi, Miles!" A blonde African American woman waved to him.

Miles looked over his shoulder. "Oh, uh, hey, Chanel."

I looked at him sideways.

"Old friend," Miles said, coughing into his fist.

I snorted. "Case and Paradise both have every confidence in your interface. Paradise said it was for porn, though."

"It is," Evie said. "Also, money laundering, database attacks, credit fraud, and manufacturing our own currency."

I blinked.

"We're a bit more than a whorehouse," Evie said. "However, if people only see what they want to see then that's on them. Case's daughter has helped keep us at the cutting edge of the bleeding edge. It's also what helps to keep the Trikuza, Russian syndicates, and White Triangle slavers at bay."

"If you can keep people sniffing for us away, we'd appreciate it," Case said. "Ask my friends in the Turing Society to provide some false trails."

Evie nodded to both Case and Lucita. "It will cost you, my friends. You two never call in your old favors and that's why I like you so much."

Lucita frowned. "Et tu, Evie?"

"Of course," Case said.

"Just be aware you can't trust anyone," Evie replied. "Not even here. There was a big massacre of Riders recently and people have been asking about Paradise as well as you. Lucita too. You've gotten yourself into something with people that have very deep pockets."

"Always the case," Case said, making a pun.

I cursed. "Do you have any idea who they are?"

Evie narrowed her eyes. They still looked gorgeous and changed color as I looked into them. "No. They're local muscle hired by slightly-less local muscle, and they were hired by even less local muscle. Whoever is involved in this wants to have many layers between themselves and this business, which says to me suits or organized crime. More likely the former than the latter."

"Why is that?" Case asked.

"Organized crime likes to announce itself," Evie said. "I hope you know what you're getting into, honey."

"I never know what I'm getting into!" Paradise said. "Which is a double entendre that doesn't really work for me."

I nodded. "I hope we're not putting you in danger here."

"We're always in danger," Evie said, looking out to the wall. "But we hang together to avoid hanging separately."

"You and Paradise are unusually educated—" Lucita started to say.

"For whores?" Paradise asked, with a surprising bit of edge.

"For refugees," Lucita said.

"I thought for whores!" Paradise said.

"I plead the fifth," I said, though it had been years since that had been suspended as a right by the Emergency Government. I had an inconsistent education and could tell you about the philosopher Miyamoto Musashi as well as assemble a pipe bomb out of household cleaners but not where Paraguay was. It didn't help that Snake had educated me with tutors I was pretty sure he had killed after they finished teaching me to his satisfaction. Dude was insane. I'd forgotten that.

"And what about you, Mr. Gordon?" Evie asked.

"I've been both," Case said.

"Let's get you set up," Evie said.

I did my best to keep my mouth shut and stood silent as Paradise led us up the stairs to a large room with a king-sized bed that had once been a pair of rooms before the walls were knocked down. It was decorated in red, Christmas lights, and had a warm musky cologne and perfume smell. The song "Transverse City" by Warren Zevon was playing in the background. It certainly looked like the sort of place you'd charge by the hour to use, albeit more than most such locations.

It was about thirty minutes before the prostitutes, their workers, and a few hirees off the street brought up a huge amount of equipment to link to the bordello's mainframe.

"You can have the entire floor," Evie said. "Just expect to be charged for it."

"Of course," Case said. "Have I ever defaulted?"

"Men develop a belief they can take liberties with the women they are good to," Evie said. "When they should be on their best behavior regardless. Even you."

Case's expression was unreadable.

I *really* didn't like her.

"I'll get the cables set up across the hall," Lucita said. "There's a pretty sophisticated server here. Your daughter did well."

"You mean Paradise or someone else?" Miles asked, clearly missing Evie wouldn't refer to Paradise as Case's daughter versus her own.

"Case isn't my dad," Paradise said. "More like a loving uncle my mother has sex with!"

"That is a terrible analogy," Case said, reflecting my thoughts. "No, she's referring to someone else."

"Wait, how does a robot have a daughter?" Miles asked.

"That's what you're thinking about now?" I asked.

Miles shrugged. "It just occurred to me."

"The robot stork," Case said, his tone turning dangerous. "Never ask about her again."

"I will go hang out with my family," Paradise said. "While you do all the work!"

"I'll help at the craps table below. Basically, because I know nothing about engineering and all my hacking is done by programs," Miles said, making finger guns. He then departed with Paradise.

"Harsh," I said, watching them leave.

"I don't like anyone knowing about my daughter but close friends and family," Case replied. "It was a mistake for Evie to mention her."

"You can trust Miles," I replied, not entirely believing it

myself and surprised that I had that doubt. I also felt a little guilty inquiring about Case's daughter. Aside from some curiosity about whether she was biologically his daughter, which shouldn't have been possible for any bioroid, it was really none of my business.

"If you say so," Case said. "But that's assuming that I trust you."

I raised an eyebrow. "Don't you?"

"I trust you more than anyone in this group but Paradise," Case replied.

"Including Lucita?"

"Absolutely Lucita." Case smirked.

"And Evie?" I asked.

"Evie too."

"Kind of a crappy thing to say about the lady giving us shelter," I muttered.

"Evie is a dedicated survivor and former corporate spy," Case replied. "Her masters put her in much worse circumstances than these and she fought her way out. I have no doubt she cares for me, but she'd also kill me to protect any of her girls."

I filed away that information. "That would make me trust her more."

"Yes, but it's not love," Case said, sighing.

"Can androids love?" I asked, before realizing it was a stupid question. He could replicate any other emotion, why not love?

"I've been in love three times," Case replied.

"What, really?" I asked. "Impressive."

"Why is that?" Case asked.

"Oh, uh," I stumbled over my words. "I guess because—"

"I'm a machine?" Case asked.

"Maybe," I said. "Sorry."

"How about you?" Case asked.

"Once or twice," I said. "Mostly once."

"How'd that end?" I asked.

"Betrayal, murder, and death," I replied, thinking about Fate. "I don't suppose you know what happened to her, do you?"

"Pardon?" Case asked.

"Fate," I replied. "It wasn't in my files."

I wasn't sure I wanted to know the answer but as long as I had access to the Evil Corporation of Evil's intelligence network, I might as well ask.

"Maybe," Case said, pausing. "You sure you want to know?"

"Yes," I said.

"She vanished not long after the DataSecure heist," Case said. "Do you remember that?"

I shook my head. "I'm completely blanking on it."

In the files that Case sent, it had apparently been an attempt to rob one of the big storage facilities for the rich and famous' secrets. Lots of people, innocent and guards alike, had been caught in the crossfire. It didn't seem like the kind of thing I'd be involved in, but I knew how heists could go catastrophically wrong. I also knew something had happened there related to Fate. Was this where the betrayal had happened? Strange I knew she had turned on me there and broke my heart but couldn't say how or why.

Case nodded, understanding. "It was a bad situation."

"And no sign of Fate afterward?" I asked. "She went to ground?"

"Or was killed and her body never recovered," Case said. "Cybernetics harvested, dissolved in acid, dumped in a hole somewhere—"

"I get it," I replied. "I don't know how I feel about that."

"I know that feeling too," Case said.

"You have some nasty love stories too?" I asked.

"Are you asking about my occasional bed partners for a reason, Ms. Springs?" Case asked.

I narrowed my eyes. "Yes, I'm building a complete dossier on you and your associates as part of a long turn plot to assassinate you."

"You wouldn't be the first," Case replied.

I snorted then paused. "How did you get a daughter? Being a robot I mean."

"It's a long story," Case said, frowning. "She's the daughter of the guy I was modeled on. Huh. Okay, it's not actually that long at all."

"What did her actual father think about that?" I asked.

"Nothing," Case said. "He's dead."

"Oh," I replied.

"Eh, he was an evil bastard," Case said.

"You're right, this probably is a long story," I replied. "What's her name?"

I had no idea why I was asking such an intimate question. I didn't want to become friendly with a suit, but I kept getting more so with Case. Perhaps it was because he was one of the few people who'd expressed any concern for me in the past few years, but I didn't want to think my emotions were that easily manipulated. I wasn't a lost puppy after all. Still, I wanted to know.

"Barbara," Case replied. "Her name is Barbara."

"Barbara *Gordon*? Like Batgirl?" I asked, smirking.

"Let's get going," Case said, shaking his head. He picked up a pair of interface goggles and handed them to me. "Are you ready to go to Club Inferno?"

"I don't need the goggles," I said, tapping the side of my head. "I was wired for connecting to from the moment it was created."

Case nodded then put on his own. "One disadvantage of being analog and predating the tech."

"Isn't your consciousness digital?" I asked.

"It is," Case said. "In which case, I just want to look like Keanu Reeves in *Johnny Mnemonic*."

"Dork."

It was time to enter a reality more real than our own.

# Chapter Sixteen

## Abandon All Hope, All Ye Who Enter

The sensation of having your mind taken from your body and projected through the system into infospace. It was more than a video game; it was another reality and the scary part of it was it felt more real than the actual one. Even before the Eruption, plenty of people had felt disconnected from who they were meant to be by quirk of genetics, poverty, or mental illness. I wasn't one of them and kept with the adage, "only reality is real." Which was a hypocritical sentiment from a cyborg with a Real Dream capable implant but whatcha gonna do.

Still, there were tens of millions of programmers working with various Simulated AI to make new worlds or games to cater to those who wanted to feel everything when they went into their simulated worlds. Whomever had designed Club Inferno had gone to great lengths as I could taste the ash in the air and feel the heat against my skin.

Club Inferno was made of red light formed into walls, orange spires, and a Japanese style shrine entrance enshrouded in hellfire. It looked like a castle constructed for the bad guys of *Tron*. We were standing on a grid-like checkerboard that stretched out into infinity around the club while hundreds of patrons ranging from anime elves to celebrity lookalikes to Chinese dragons ambulated around until they were able to enter. Even in infospace, there were lines.

I was suddenly aware of my own appearance and immediately embarrassed by it as I recalled I hadn't updated my avatar since the last time I'd gone into infospace. It had been to get information on a subject—a cybersex club—and now I felt horribly embarrassed.

Basically, I was wearing a somewhat idealized version of my own body with some "adjustments" that, frankly, only adolescent men or immature women could appreciate since I wasn't exactly lacking in real-life. Unfortunately, the embarrassing part was that this avatar was naked.

Not entirely naked but covered in a blue iridescent glow and a bunch of numbers that were covering the strategic parts of my body that American censors still freaked out about. Even today, you could show every part of the female form but the nipples and genitalia. Oh, and male parts were right out. Those would permanently scar your brain forever unless you were looking for porn. Ooo. Still, I was embarrassed for my "attire" out here and wished I'd had time to adjust it before being uploaded. Ironically, it was close to the fashion that many of the women and men were "wearing" around me.

"Damn," Paradise said, wearing something close to her real-life attire—which was to say perfectly scandalous for the real world but tame in this one. "I'm going to have to reconsider my opinion of you entirely!"

"Sorry," I said. "I'll get something more appropriate."

"Not on my account," Paradise said, "and can I have the pattern?"

"Sure," I said, sending it her way before shifting to a simulation of my real-life attire.

"So… at some point you forgot you could be fun?" Paradise asked, summoning a version of my earlier look. She wore it much better than me and looked like the AI companion of a *Halo* Space Marine. "Oh, this is awesome! Who made it?"

"A friend of mine named David. Also, Paradise, there's such a thing as too much fun."

"Then you're doing it wrong," Paradise said, doing a twirl.

Case surprised me because I'd half expected him to dress up as himself or just wear a suit. Instead, he was wearing a Steven Otto in *Robocop Reloaded* outfit.

"Really?" I asked. "A stock actor avatar for the trendiest of all clubs?"

Case shrugged. "I want to blend in and not draw attention to myself."

"Then you need my help," Paradise said, helping tweak his profile and generating something that made him look like he was the actual Steven Otto visiting the place. Real celebrities had authenticity signs on their profiles that Paradise had deftly forged. "Much better! You'll have to beat the females and males impersonating females off with a stick!"

"That's never been a problem," Case said. "I'm more worried about spooking Solomon."

"Well, you look nice if he likes men," Paradise said. "If he doesn't then he has me or Kei."

"What if he doesn't like either?" I asked.

That seemed to puzzle Paradise. "Huh."

"Asexuality is an option," I said.

"Ooo," Paradise said. "I keep forgetting that. Media lied to me about how much everyone is horny all the time."

"Your background may have also influenced you," I said, dryly. "Any sign of Lucita or Miles?"

"They could be hiding," Case muttered, looking around.

"Isn't that counterproductive?" I asked. "I mean we want to be found by the arms dealing lunatic."

Case shrugged.

We were greeted by two individuals that I didn't expect to see. The first was a blue-haired female elf who looked nothing like Lucita and had the qualities of an anime character. She had an enormous gravity hammer on her back and her legs that were out of proportion with her body. There was something about her imperious posture and demeanor that told me it was Lucita, though, especially when she crossed her arms. The second was an enormous teddy bear.

"Is that you, Miles?" I asked, looking at the teddy bear.

"Yo!" the teddy bear said, waving his paw.

"I don't think this is your scene," I said, looking at him sideways.

"I don't exactly spend much time in infospace," Miles replied. "This is for my niece's birthday party. I don't have another avatar prepped."

"I want to hug you!" Paradise said, stretching out your arms.

"I would find it very weird, especially with you undressed like that," Miles said, looking away.

"Ah, come on!" Paradise said. "It's not my first time hugging a teddy bear naked."

"And with that horrifying mental image," the anime girl said, speaking with Lucita's voice and confirming my suspicions, "I think we should head on in."

"We don't have to wait in line?" I asked, raising an eyebrow.

Lucita snorted. "I have a VIP pass to everywhere of note."

"Rank has privileges among suits," I replied.

"Yes, it's called money and power," Lucita said. "Oh, and being damn sexy."

I wasn't sure how much anime elf qualified as sexy around here, but I didn't want to belabor the point.

"This way," Lucita gestured to one group of burning flames to the side. She walked through, followed by Miles and Paradise.

"You first," I said, looking to Case.

"Afraid of getting burned?" Case asked, sticking his hands in his pockets.

"Yep," I said. "'Your mind makes it real' has been put to some pretty awful uses by the Trikuza."

Case frowned and offered his hand.

I took it and walked in with him. I wasn't burned and felt stupid as a result. The interior of the club opened to me, and I surveyed my surroundings. "Let's see what the cool kids are doing now."

The interior of Club Inferno was difficult to describe for people who were used to living in an environment of physics. There was a vast zero gravity dance platform in the center of the place, and dozens of glass alcoves floating in the air, portals leading to myriad environments to experience whatever universe you wanted to enjoy your night in. The population enjoying themselves to an incandescent techno-beat included every sort of fictional character as well actor imaginable plus some truly insane digital avatars that didn't remotely bother with humanity.

Everyone from Lara Croft to Satan was out tonight. The digital information of everyone's profile revealed some of the real names and identities around here (possibly) but others went by handles or aliases. I noticed more than a few of them were legends among the hacker community and there were also a few Riders I knew. Trikuza and Syndicate professionals as well, which made me nervous. Club Inferno was a gathering place for the techjacks' elite, exploring the limits of the new universe created by man that they possessed the power to define at their will. Or pay others to.

"Where do we find one renegade techjack in this mess?" I asked.

"He probably won't be on the main dance floor, too mundane," Case said. "We should find the private room that has the most ridiculous amount of code running."

"I suspect he'll find us," Lucita said, shooing off R2-D2 as the little droid attempted to sell us sex-simulation programs.

"Oh?" I asked, trying not to let my attention wander to all the wonderful things around me.

"This is his place," Lucita said, getting a drink from the succubus bartender. "One of them at least."

"You pick that up on previous visits?" I asked, wondering how much Lucita was keeping from us. The answer was probably a lot.

"Solomon was a legend among programmers before Madison and Troy stupidly hired him," Lucita said. "This was also a famous place for people like me to hire specialists. I'm surprised you never worked out of it."

"I preferred to meet my clients in person," I replied, getting a beer from a tray served by Casper the Friendly Ghost.

"No wonder you never got any good deals," Miles replied, still looking adorable and furry. It made him stand out even more.

"This doesn't seem like his sort of place if his usual haunts are trash heaps," Case said, getting his own drink: a vodka martini, shaken not stirred. Really, Case?

"Only if you assume he cares about the meat," Paradise said. "Remember, just because he doesn't like staying awake doesn't mean that he's not a god down here in infospace."

"In more ways than one," Lucita replied.

That was when most of the party became surprisingly silent as a glowing stage descended from the heavens above. I blinked a few times as she stared at the sight on the stage's center. "Is that the real Sun? The singer?"

Sun was one of the post-media omnivore singers. In a world where basically every bit of song from the past two hundred years was available at one's virtual fingertips, the idea of even having a style was often seen as passé. Omnivores pulled from everything. Some of Sun's songs including setting a John Dunne poem from the 1700s to 2030s psychogrunge, or her remaking a John Denver tune to retro polymer synth. Everything was available. Sun grabbed the best and merged them together into songs that shouldn't work, but somehow did. It was eclectic. It was random. And for my tastes, it was brilliant.

It didn't hurt that Sun herself a striking woman. The Afro-Japanese woman with neon hair emerged on stage wearing an entirely plausible outfit—unlike most of her audience—with a mesh top showing off her piercings and denim skirt that reached her knees and seemed almost demure compared to the top. Added to that was a bright red cloth over her mouth and a long body chain that started at her left wrist and ended up on her right ankle and wrapped around everything in between. Like her music, it somehow worked even where it shouldn't. There was something else I couldn't put into words. It wasn't sexual but like she reminded me of a good memory rather than a bad. I had only a few of those.

"Yep!" Paradise said, conjuring a holographic poster that she'd copied from the wall. "Playing one night only!"

"I'd have come here for that alone," I said, awed.

"Fangirl, huh?" Paradise asked.

"I hope you aren't expecting me to squeal or anything," I said.

"Just happy to see the human side," Paradise said.

I rolled my eyes at Paradise, mostly because I couldn't think of a real retort. Maybe I could have thought of something if I wasn't being distracted.

"She's okay," Case said. "Mind you, I think Billy Idol did her last cover better."

"I liked her metal opera version of 'Everybody Wants to Rule the World'," Paradise said, cheerfully.

"Shh!" I said, looking like I was ready to tear into both with my teeth. All thoughts of the fact we were here to investigate a terrorist forgotten.

Surprisingly, both Paradise and Case chose to let me listen. Her set ended up being three songs and they were as eclectic as their performer but all variations on 80s pop and punk that had been made hauntingly beautiful as if a fairy had decided to redo British retrorock.

In the end, Sun said, "And a special shout out to three special guests coming to solve the secret of Solomon's Temple!"

Well, that was unexpected.

"Do you think she's talking about us?" Paradise asked.

"I think there's a good possibility," Case said.

"Cool!" Paradise said, holding a drink larger than her head of blue fluid with an enormous straw. Another reason people loved infospace—consequence free drugs and booze effects projected into your brain. "Then we can watch her go all fangirl!"

"I do no—" I started to say.

"Five credits says she squeals," Paradise said. "Ten credits there's giggling."

"How's Sun involved in all this Solomon business?" I asked, suddenly worried my favorite singer was part of this.

"She's a member of H.O.P.E.," Case said.

"The hacktivist group?" I was shocked.

"Yeah," Case said. "I met her there. I hope she's not involved."

"Friend?" I asked, surprised.

"No," Case said. "If H.O.P.E. is involved, it means we're on the wrong side of this."

# Chapter Seventeen

## The Temple of Solomon

"Aren't you overstating matters a bit?" I asked Case. "I mean have you forgotten that Solomon is involved in terrorism? Like mass murder of the innocent terrorism. Which should go without saying when calling someone a terrorist."

No one was treating Case like a celebrity despite Paradise's fiddling, but Steven Otto hadn't done anything impressive since the *Electric Dreams* reboot or the *Legion of Superheroes* movie where he was a CGI de-aged Lightning Lad. It was also possible all the techjacks knew the truth or being a B-list celebrity just didn't get you attention in this club where Sun was performing. Assuming it *was* Sun. She had a verified account and certainly sounded like the real deal, but Paradise had proved how easily that was fiddled with.

"Ixnay on oralmay udgementsjay," Lucita whispered to me. "We're here to buy Blipvert after all."

Which was her way of telling me that I shouldn't mention we were also here to kill Solomon and he was probably monitoring us. No kidding, Sherlock.

"H.O.P.E. is an organization that does a lot of good in the world," Case said. "Its methods may be flawed but very few other people are pushing back against the corporatocracy."

"Says literally one of the ruling class," I said, sarcastically. "What are you, some kind of self-hating suit?"

"The Marquis de Lafayette had a role in the French Revolution," Case said.

"So did De Sade," Lucita replied.

I didn't know who either of those people were. "I think people have had quite enough of trying to improve things by disrupting the system."

"The system blows, though," Paradise said, having reversed gravity and hanging now upside down face-to-face with me.

"I've just seen too many people using smashing the system to make themselves rich," I said. "It's just a cover."

"Solomon is an ex-member of H.O.P.E.," Lucita replied. "They kicked him out for being a terrorist lunatic."

"You should have mentioned that," Case replied, frowning. "It wasn't in our files on him."

"You're not objective with H.O.P.E. any more than Kei here is about Sun," Lucita said. "Hell, it might be why she's up there."

"Sun is an artist whose work speaks for the loss of identity in a world of superficial social demands," I said.

"I personally think she's just writing really bad sampling-based music about rebelling against her dad," Paradise said.

"She is not!" I said, appalled.

"Well, I know her dad and if anyone in the world is worth rebelling against its him," Lucita said.

"Huh?" I asked, surprised.

"I think Lucita's referring to the fact that Sun's music is about rebelling against her father who is the head of Green Foods," Case said.

"Green Foods?" I asked, not unaware of who they were but more confused as to how they'd entered the conversation. Like discovering Madonna's father was the owner of Kellogg-Mills.

Case nodded. "Yes, they're the bio-engineering firm that everyone eats the products of unless they're eating each other, and those people die of prion disease. You've probably heard their jingle. 'Green cereal, it's the best. Nom, nom, nom.' There's no real content to the jingle but it sticks in your head."

"All 100% organic in the loosest definition of the term!" Paradise said before faking astonishments. "Gasp! Wait, that means neo-punk girl has a rich father! Who could have guessed that!"

"It is distressingly common as an origin, but she is living on her own from what little data I was able to find about her. Someone has done a great job covering up her activities for the past few years—even as a public figure," Lucita said.

"Maybe it's Solomon who is keeping her record clean," I said, disappointed that Sun was apparently another rich girl gone rogue. It was hard to believe but I supposed I was used to disappointment. "Given the clue she threw at us, they have to know each other."

There was a scratching in the back of my brain that felt like someone was trying to scream something at me. Possibly my unconscious. I vaguely recalled knowing the daughter of Green Food's owner and even working with her on something. However, I would have remembered knowing Sun, I was sure. The person I remembered also went by a different name. Chastity something. Damn, even trying to think of her made my head hurt. Whoever she was, she was tied to some truly bad memories.

I looked over at Miles and saw he was deliberately ignoring the conversation. He had his back turned and both hands in his pockets. That made me wonder if he knew something about Sun that I didn't, but I dismissed that thought. It would have been one of the few things that would have made our relationship tolerable. At least from what I remembered of it.

"Well, I think we're being directed to go meet our virtual chanteuse now," Case said, gesturing at the floor.

A literal yellow brick road had appeared on the ground to the door from the Twilight Zone now standing in the middle of the dance floor. No one else was reacting to it, which indicated only we could see it.

"I didn't think the yellow brick road led to a temple," I said. "But off we go to see the wizard."

"What wizard?" Paradise asked, showing I needed to get another example of old pop media to draw from.

"You really need to see that movie or read that book," I muttered, walking to the door. "I hope this isn't a huge mistake."

"Oh, I'm sure it is," Case said.

"I'm not getting paid nearly enough for this," Miles said.

"Yes, you are," Lucita replied.

"It's true, I am,' Miles conceded.

The others reluctantly followed me through the door, which transferred us to a private chat room that took the shape of a four-story cathedral of light and free-floating stone with waterfalls that flowed up and down through gravity defying spaces. In between the holes of the building's layers was a brilliant blue sky that hadn't existed on Earth for decades. The center of the main chamber, though, was its own little apartment with posters and bean bags as well as other paraphernalia of punk rockers turning a holy place into their own personal pad. There were people around and most of them I recognized or at least the names on their digital profiles. But they were surprises to me.

I didn't know who I'd expected but I was probably either a bunch of arms dealers, criminals, and suits waiting to shell out millions to buy mind control software or a bunch of rabid anarchists ready to bring about the end of modern civilization to trigger the Great Reset. Neither seemed to be the case here as it was full of B and D-list celebrities. Not even the A-listers outside but people I recognized as popular in my niche circles of fandom or public figures that had wide but shallow pools of viewers.

Sun was sitting in a bean bag chair, in her stage costume, while a gorgeous blond-haired golden-skinned man in a blindingly shiny white business suit sat beside her. It took a second for me to recognize him as Winston Billions, the weatherman on Channel 112. It was notable because that was my favorite channel for all weather news all the time (though they'd recently shifted to weather-based reality programs like *Stormchasing*, *Who Wants to Survive a Hurricane*, and *Lightning in a Bottle*). Winston had been a failed television action star with roles in *NCIS: Luna City* and *Navy Seal: Cybernetics Division* but had achieved his fame combining comedy with warm fronts.

I had no idea why Solomon had invited most women's and some men's favorite weatherman here, but it probably wasn't good. I also recognized a sports caster, a political commentator from the far right, a political commentator from the moderate left (the far left didn't exist in the USA anymore), and a children's show host that unsettled me the most with their presence. Seriously? He had Drama Llama here? Was nothing sacred?

"We stick out like a sore thumb," I muttered.

"Why?" Paradise said. "Is the thumb cybernetic and malfunctioning?"

I looked at her strangely. "Don't ever change, Paradise."

"I won't," Paradise replied. "Customers pay extra for immaturity. It makes them feel like I'm younger than I am."

"And that's horrifying," I replied.

"Don't worry, actual pedophiles get their throats slit in the Zone," Paradise replied, cheerfully.

I had no idea how to respond to that. "Moving on. Quickly."

"Are these the real deal?" Miles asked. "I mean, my ex used to watch *Single in Paradise* and that's Jeanine from there. One of the triplets that almost got married to Yorick in Season 18."

The rest of our party looked at him.

"Your ex, right," I replied, dryly. "You know men watch those shows too."

"Sure," Miles said, looking uncomfortable despite being an enormous teddy bear. I really wish I'd gotten him a proper avatar set up before coming in here.

"They all look to be the real deal," Case said. "But I can't figure out why Solomon would be collecting this bunch."

"If this were a Macho channel spy movie we'd send in Case or Miles to seduce Sun but if this were the Sapphic channel spy movie, we'd send in Kei to do the same," Paradise said. "The Dude channel would have Case or Miles seduce Winston. Personally, I'm all for getting both's digital autographs and selling them for lots of credits!"

Lucita looked annoyed. "You don't think I could do the seducing? Of either?"

"I didn't know if you liked men and women," Paradise said. "I also think you scare people."

Lucita frowned. "I like anyone I can dominate."

"See!" Paradise said.

That caused me to grin despite our circumstances. "Let's go talk to the VIP room of Terrorists & Cults Inc."

Sun and Winston got up from their bean bag before approaching us. A part of me started to wonder if they were both secret members of Solomon's terrorist organization or brainwashed. Both of which made me think I'd have to seriously reconsider my Sun fandom as well as weather-viewing habits. I didn't want to switch to the Ron Storms app!

Paradise stretched out her hand. "Howdy! We're an eccentric collection of misfits on a mission from God or a megacorporation, which is the same thing!"

"Hiii," I said, uncertain how to react. "You're Sun."

"Not a squeal," Case said before Paradise could get her mouth fully open.

"I was wondering," Sun said. "Thank you for telling me."

"I'm Winston. I have a warm feeling about you," Winston said, saying his famous catchphrase. He even made his trademark finger guns while doing so.

"Is it indigestion?" Paradise asked.

"Oh, right, you know you're and I know I'm and…" I took a breath, feeling uncharacteristically starstruck. Was someone screwing with my data feed? Shaking my head, I tried to continue. "We're looking for, well, you know that, really, and…"

"Should someone else be talking for the sake of efficiency?" Lucita asked.

Paradise leaned over and whispered to Case. "Kei likes Sun, can you tell?"

Actually, I was terrified my favorite singer had been turned into a tool for an anarchist nutjob and I was about to blow up the place with Black Ice. I wasn't sure if it would kill everyone here.

"What an incredibly shocking development," Case said, dead-panning. "I never could have guessed."

Paradise threw out her hands. "We are here to see Oz the Great and Powerful! We are here to buy the cool thing! That is totally not evil."

I glared at her. Not the least because it was clear she'd been having a go with me about the *Wizard of Oz*. My mother had read that book to me multiple times during our trip across America. Not cool, Paradise. Not cool at all.

Miles put on a pair of shades onto his teddy bear avatar, trying to look cool. "Hey."

Okay that was hilarious.

"We're the Temple of Light!" Sun said, cheerfully. "Solomon is our leader but still our equal in our organization devoted to saving the world!"

Case looked between them. "How many of you are there in your organization?"

Sun gave a thumbs up. "Forty-two! We have forty-two members!"

"That's a reference to something!" Winston smiled, showing his immaculate teeth. "Which makes it funny!"

Their strange behavior made the hairs on the back of my neck stand up or would have if my avatar had been programmed with that sensation. One thing about infospace was that your imagination turned out to provide a lot of the things that people took for granted in real life. I didn't think infospace would be half as successful if not for the placebo effect.

Were Sun and Winston brainwashed by Blipvert or just acting

weird because they had been told to by Solomon as part of his sales pitch? Again, were they even the real deal or just people acting parts? Were they even people? I'd once had a two-hour date with a complicated chat program that had almost managed to pass the Turing Test. Well, it had actually but I blamed my credulity on the fact their avatar was really hot, and I didn't care what came out of their mouth.

I also was interested in meeting with Solomon personally because I wanted to link with his system and deliver the Black Ice. Snake had been a master programmer in addition to being a cyborg ninja, which had probably sounded more crazy decades ago, and I trusted Black Ice's ability to kill whoever it was used against.

Still, as much as I'd come to like my partners, I hated that I was back to killing people for money. If Solomon chose not to show up, then we'd have to follow the chain of operatives further to find him and who knew how long that would take.

"So, what is the Temple of Light saving humanity from?" Paradise asked. "I mean, there are so many choices. Is it vampires? I hate vampires. Werewolves are so much cooler. Especially cyber-werewolves."

"It's probably not vampires or werewolves," Case said. "Probably."

"Zombies?" Paradise asked.

Oh yeah, we were not going to make a good impression on the weirdo cultists.

Surprisingly, neither Sun nor Winston seemed to take offense. Winston responded first. "Solomon actually does a lot of research here about how to spark enlightenment in humanity by studying how the brain interacts with programming, technology, art, and music. I was recruited because of my role as a media personality and Sun as a musician."

"The future of humanity via enlightenment is to be decided by a virtual musician and weatherman," Case said, skeptically. "Plus a variety of other celebrities with middling careers."

"We are the single most generally liked people in the universe!" Winston said, cheerfully. It was hard to tell how much of this was an exaggeration of his actual personality versus his television persona. "So glad to see my meteorology degree didn't go to waste."

Okay, that last remark was legitimate.

"Was it from the University of Sealand?" Case asked.

"That's more accredited than some of the places my coworkers bought their degrees," Winston muttered.

"And yet you're part of a cult," Case chided.

"Case—" I started to speak.

"He's not the real Winston Billions," Case replied. "He's currently filming a Hallmark movie where he falls in love with a wind goddess."

I did a double take. "Really?"

"Guilty," Winston admitted. "Sun is real, though."

Sun just smiled. "We're not a cult."

"Which is a thing cults say," I pointed out. Yeah, we weren't going to be winning these guys over. Great job, everyone.

Sun shook her head. "We are an outreach program that seeks to spark the primal godhead within each person's inner self."

"A cult that teaches enlightenment through orgasms!" Paradise declared. "Tell me more."

"That's not what Sun means," I said. "I think."

"But it sounds like the best religion ever!" Paradise said, throwing her hands up in the air.

"Actually, that was the original religion of humanity," Sun said, sounding like a recent convert. "The Earthmother religion was based around fertility and life before it shifted toward a patriarchal law and scholarship-based book religion. However, as the values of humanity continually challenged authority, so did the power of this fade. Now we're attempting to create a new religion based on shared information and communal ascension of consciousness through man-machine interface!" Sun said, cheerfully.

"What in the who now?" I asked.

"That's literally just from *Snow Crash*," Case muttered. "What are you going to do next, quote Ayn Rand?"

Lucita shot him a dirty look.

"The hero from the *Wheel of Time*?" Paradise asked. "Before he made the atlas shrug?"

"Are you faking not getting references?" Case asked, a little slow on the uptake. "You'd have to get both references to make that joke about getting neither."

"Me blonde, young, and female. Me dumb. Underestimate me, ook-ook," Paradise said before rubbing her sides like a monkey.

Case smirked.

So did I, then I frowned. Dammit people, this was serious. "We didn't come here to mock your religion."

"We didn't?" Lucita asked.

I elbowed her, which felt like hitting a brick wall even virtually.

"You want to create world peace through the internet?" Paradise asked. "Wow, are you barking up the wrong tree."

Lucita looked disturbed by Sun's description. "I thought Blipvert was a weapon."

"Yeah, all the dead bodies kind of prove it," Miles said. "Kids too."

It was an odd reaction because I knew Miles when he had cases involving kids. Then he threw his fists out, screamed, and broke every rule imaginable (which wasn't many with the NLAPD) to either protect or avenge them. Here, he sounded distant and like he was going through the motions. Like something had broken inside him. What was I missing here? Was there a fault in his connection?

Sun got a similarly faraway look in her eye. "It is a shame that such bloodshed was necessary, but violence remains a tool that is required to make grandiose and sweeping changes in society. They will never happen with half-measures. Blipvert as the evolving living program of social change is one that first manifests as outrage against the system. It is the revolution."

"Necessary," Miles said, sounding sick. It made the fact he was a giant teddy bear feel all the more ridiculous.

"Where is Solomon?" Case asked, his voice barely contained fury. It was closer to how I'd expected Miles to act. If it wasn't, I'd honestly be surprised. Then again, greed was the great equalizer among criminals and our best chance was that Solomon didn't care about any of this radical revolutionary rhetoric and it was just a cover for selling the program to the highest bidder. "Is he here or actually dead and you were using his avatar to communicate with us?"

"Why would you think he's dead?" Sun asked, a little too quickly.

Case stared.

Case's accusation started to look silly when we saw a figure descending the staircase from the next level. There, standing on the free-floating steps, was the healthy—certainly healthier looking than when he'd been a corpse in front of his computer—form of

Solomon Jones. He was a geriatric-looking African American man with a greying goatee, black sweatpants, a black N.W.A. t-shirt, and a black ball cap. He was slightly on the overweight side so it would have been easy to assume this was his real form except for, again, the fact he was a corpse in the "real" world.

Solomon.

Our target had arrived.

Finally.

# Chapter Eighteen

## Meeting with the Lord of Club Inferno

A part of me wanted to blast Solomon as he descended and try to upload the Black Ice program directly into him. Unfortunately, that wouldn't work. As advanced and dangerous as Snake's program was, it couldn't just automatically rip through every firewall and security feed. It could do most, but I'd need to directly link to Solomon's infospace. That would require us either to link up in a private chat or directly share information that was intimate and usually used for sex. I was trained to kill someone during sex—don't ask how—but it wasn't something I wanted to do if I didn't have to. No matter how much I was making on this job.

There was also something about Solomon that caused me to pause. Despite looking like a guy that you'd meet on the street versus all the enhanced avatars we'd passed before, there was a glow about him that made me want to listen to him. I had to mentally link to Googleplex and download all the atrocities he'd supposedly committed with Blipvert. The coverage of the local news still followed the old adage, "If it bleeds, it leads" and the murders were described in sickening detail. Solomon Jones had used his stupid software to kill over a hundred people—closer to two hundred really—and had promised to do many more.

There, that helped clear my head. There were few things that pissed me off more than self-deluded jackasses who killed lots of people for no other reason than they were in the way. Part of what kept me from being the assassin I was was because I no longer viewed killing as an impersonal act. Snake had always taught me to keep a professional distance between myself and the murders. "It's just business" and other platitudes. Well, frick that. Life and death were very personal to everyone who had it decided for them. It made killing this jackass, assuming I could pull it off, easy.

Solomon opened with a speech as he descended the stairs, acting like we were in a movie. "Infospace is the battlefield of the war for the future. In the Eighties, my older brother was all about how there was no future. Well, here we are. The War on Terror and the War on Drugs were a prelude to the War on Everything. There are no more tanks across Belgium or air raids on London. Governments don't go to war with each other now. No, instead, the corporations war on each other, but they don't want to destroy anything valuable—just people. They steal information, tech, tools, and do a little bit of sabotage from burned hard drives to massacres. Not just against rival corporations but rival execs too. The execs need their bio-mods, drugs, untraceable cash, and stolen toys just like everyone else. The Invisible Hand is the ruler of the society that Big Brother, Supply Side Jesus, and the average American voter created."

Knowing that I *did* feel awed by his presence, I wonder if Blipvert was being used right now. That was the terrifying thing about the software that supposedly existed. The ability to cause people to believe whatever you wanted was what propagandists and marketing executives had pursued for thousands of years. If someone had actually invented it and it was for sale, really, that was arguably the end of everything. What kind of world could exist if you could program people like computers?

"If God didn't exist, we'd have to create him," I muttered, surprised to say it aloud. "Anymore pretentious bullcrap?"

Lucita was, meanwhile, looking at Case. "See? This is what you sound like. It's why we don't invite you to board meetings anymore."

"I thought that was because I slept with the Prime Minister of Japan," Case said, dryly.

"You were supposed to kill her!" Lucita snapped.

I really hoped they were joking about that, but I couldn't tell. Then I realized we were all intensely rude to the man who we were trying to appear as customers of. Almost comically so. "Uh, hi, uh—"

Solomon laughed. "Blipvert is active now with the order to get you to tell the truth. You're under compulsion to be more honest and it is being reinforced every second you're in my temple."

I wanted to cuss and yell at him before I suppressed that feeling. "You're trying to mind control us?"

"Yes," Solomon said. "It seems like an excellent way of selling the product."

It wasn't a very good product as I didn't want to confess that we were here to murder him, but I *did* want to kill him more. "Then why not force us to buy it."

"It requires months of work," Solomon said. "The human brain is a hardy thing and only certain types of people are vulnerable to it. Lethe users and digital consciousnesses especially. Exposure also has to be constant in order for it to work."

"Then it seems like a poor weapon," I replied, lying. After all, we were a group particularly vulnerable to it right now. Did he know I was a lethe user? Was it making me more vulnerable? I couldn't afford that, but I also was not able to do anything about it.

Solomon smirked. "To show off my public-school education, we used to think information wanted to be free, but the truth is *power* wants to be free. If Karma Corp, Atlas, or Green Foods ever managed to absorb everything else then they'd immediately explode. It's why every empire in history has self-destructed."

"Why?" I asked, wondering what the jaded old Brit was getting at. "Because power has a will of its own?"

"It has an ethos," Solomon said. "Those who seek it want to accumulate it and need enemies to fight and vistas to conquer. Plus, whenever there's not an outside enemy to fight, the insiders turn on each other. Alexander the Great, Caesar, and Bill Gates all got done in by their subordinates. Riders are simply the guns they fire at each other and good riddance to the people who take the bullets. They try to have their own corporate samurai but, in the end, they don't work because at some point they all either get used against their own people or realize they can be kings themselves."

I blinked, confused. "What are you saying?"

"He's saying he knows who we work for and why," Lucita replied.

"Because the person who sent you against me is not as smart as she thinks she is," Solomon said, reaching the bottom of the steps. "It is why her plot to kill me is as much a plot to kill you as it is to get what we've stolen."

I had no idea what he was talking about it. "Case?"

"The robot doesn't interest me," Solomon replied. "I won't

speak to it. I also know everyone in your group has their own hidden agenda. Even the whore."

"He's talking about me, right?" Paradise asked Sun.

"Yes," Sun said, nodding with a strained look on her face. It made me sick to see the protest singer reduced to this creature's puppet. I wanted to reach over and strangle him. If this was Blipvert's effect, I was starting to see why its demonstrations had been random acts of murder. It was an incredible weapon but only as a tool of terrorism: destroy any civilization that was both cybernetically advanced and brimming with anger—all of them were these days.

"So, if you know what we are," I started to say, "Why are you not killing us?"

"Because you can still afford my price or at least your two suit paymasters can," Solomon said. "Think for yourselves. Stop running away from your past, Kei Springs."

Goddammit, he knew my real name. "Everyone's running away from something," I said. "Or stagnating."

Solomon shrugged. "People often run *to* something."

"What are *you* running to?" I asked, struggling to figure out how to turn this around.

Solomon looked, for a moment, sad. Only a moment, though. "I am running to run because as long as I don't stop, no one catches me, and I never have to stop to think where I am. I am the Red King as I don't have to go anywhere as long as I don't stop."

I almost understood that. Mind you, it was an *Alice in Wonderland* reference. It was also a reference to the concept of the Red Queen, which in evolutionary terms was the idea of having to run as fast as you could to stay in one place. I had no idea how I knew that since it wasn't the kind of thing I normally thought about.

Wait?

Was he in my head?

Was he in the head of everyone here?

Was he hacking us?

I...I...I...I couldn't think. I looked around and saw the cathedral was starting to glitch out. One second it was the paradise he'd described earlier and the next it was a series of images as well as numbers that I couldn't comprehend. I saw both words in English as well as the *kanji* that flashed by too fast to read.

Trying to look at the others, I saw they were also confused and in pain. Even Sun. The only one who didn't look like he was, was Miles and I'm not sure how much of that was due to being a giant stuffed bear.

"Time to ask the real questions, my dear," Solomon said.

"We're here to kill you," I said, unable to stop myself.

Solomon laughed. "I know that. I need to know more about you. Blipvert needs to be fed. We want information. Information."

"You won't get it," I said, not understanding why I chose that expression. It seemed to be implanted in my mind.

"By hook or by crook, we will," Solomon said, laughing.

"Ask," I said, unable to resist.

"So, tell me my dear, why be a Rider? Why would you want to really be part of a life that consists solely of violence and crime? You tried so hard to escape Snake."

He knew Snake. That wasn't good. "My life already consists solely of violence. Might as well make it violence and money. The system uses people until they're no use and then spits them out into an early grave. If I survive just five years, well, that's five years, isn't it?"

I didn't even know the facts I was sharing about myself.

"Go on," Solomon whispered.

"Freedom is possible. I know that because I had it once. However, the price of freedom is eternal vigilance. It's also got a much more physical price and that's electronic credits. Still, it's better being a free criminal than the daughter of the Cyber Dragons like I was. The daughter of the Devil. Even working with Fate was better and she betrayed me."

I didn't want to think about that moment of my life, I had spent thousands of credits to avoid doing so. I shuddered at the memories' emotional power that seemed to rebel against the forces that was moving around me and inside me.

"We'll buy the damn Blipvert," Lucita finally said, shaking herself away from the trance everyone else was spellbound by. "Let us go."

"I think not," Solomon said. "At least not yet. I want your money and that's the only reason I haven't killed you yet, but I need guarantees and the best guarantees are secrets."

"I think not," Lucita said, scowling. "My secrets are my own."

"You don't have any I want," Solomon said, almost

contemptuously. "The spoiled yet abused daughter of a man who thought you were born wrong."

Lucita somehow managed to simulate spitting on him. No spittle hit Solomon, but the gesture was there.

"I don't have any secrets," Paradise said, pausing. "Except that time I robbed my mom's client list. That was bad."

"You'll help me spread Blipvert," Solomon said. "The money will help pay for its use across the globe: a tool for social change and progress. It will become a self-sustaining self-replicating meme that will be used not to oppress or expand the power of the capitalist paymasters but liberate humanity from their control."

I realized something in that moment that gave me what I needed to grasp while dealing with the fact I was being brainwashed and if I didn't focus on myself, I would be lost in a kind of weird trance: Solomon was completely insane. He wasn't just an arms dealer trying to sell some stolen advertising tech, he actually believed that he could use this weaponized sales propaganda to change the world. As crap as the world was, I was ninety-nine percent sure that you couldn't fix it with weaponized memes. I needed to use the Black Ice and kill Solomon now. Unfortunately, as soon as I reached into my avatar, I found that it was hard to concentrate enough to activate the damn thing. It wasn't like there was a big red button I could push in my visual display feed. No, I had to go through all sorts of safeties and files to get at the weapon I'd stolen from Snake.

"*Case, I need you to distract this guy,*" I said, using direct chat. It wouldn't take much for Solomon to hack into our feed while we were in his place, but I hoped that he was too focused on his weird messianic Bond villain rant.

"*It'll be hard,*" Case said back. "*I...can barely think straight.*"

"*I trust you,*" I said, surprising myself by believing him.

"You are all liars and deceivers," Solomon said, addressing us. "Murderers. Even you, Sun, who sought to manipulate me to free yourself from Helen's control."

Wait, what?

"You're a bad person," Sun said, surprising me and making me realize she was a prisoner too rather than a willing convert. Maybe I wouldn't give up buying her albums. Well, I usually just listened to the music on Infotube or pirated it but in theory I might buy one in the future. Hehe. Funny how that distracted me from the feeling

I should be listening to Solomon's ideas more seriously.

"I am enlightened," Solomon said. "Beyond good and evil. You have shown me the way but you're still only a machine. Just like the robot."

I was now thoroughly confused.

"Oh please," Miles said.

"Says the traitor," Solomon said. "Do you want me to tell them who you really work for?"

Hello. What was that? I almost stopped working on releasing the Black Ice.

Case, unfortunately, interrupted. "How do you even know the difference between enlightenment and being brainwashed?"

"We've studied the problem extensively," Solomon said, surprised at his response.

"We?" Case asked.

"Me and my associates," Solomon said. "The people who will guide the New World once the Old World is in flames. The Temple of Light I have built here will spread the new anarchic ideal."

I tried to figure out how to keep this guy from killing us. We were in his house right now and my program would need time to work. "Then you wouldn't be doing this. Anarchism depends on not enforcing the will of the one over the many but the many accepting the freedom of the one.'

"Are you a religious woman, Ms. Springs?" Solomon asked, seemingly switching subjects.

"In my own way," I said.

"Eastern or Western?" Solomon asked.

"My own way," I said.

"Then you should respect my view," Solomon said, gesturing upwards to the sky, "that the many will never be as free as the one so they must be brought to this point of you."

The interior of the cathedral changed as its upper interior level filled with a giant map of the human brain and its constantly shooting and changing neurons. Some glowed red, some glowed blue, and others took a beautiful golden sheen.

"In Eastern religion, the quest for enlightenment is a constant and ever-changing road that is the purpose of human existence," Solomon said. "In Western religion, enlightenment is a gift of an already enlightened god figure. I'm combining the two so as humanity as a whole can make an ascension."

"Except you're the Buddha in your new religion," I said, frowning. "One we should kill on the road."

"No," Solomon said, pausing. "All of humanity is the Buddha. All of the information being stored and sorted is being analyzed and process by Keter."

"Keter?" I asked, really looking forward to his death.

"The top of the tree of life in the kabbalah," Miles replied, sounding dead and defeated. "My mom was really into it. Also, Madonna."

"Your mom was Madonna?" Paradise asked.

I was almost done uploading the virus but couldn't bring myself to finish transferring it. He seemed so wise and compassionate. All he wanted to do was help the world. Why would I want to stop him from helping the world? Those were not my thoughts and worse, I knew it, but that didn't prevent me from thinking them.

Case grabbed Solomon's arm, only to be punched across the room like a ragdoll before Solomon grabbed me by my shoulders. "I'm going to find out everything you're hiding. You weren't fooling me at all. Blipvert is now attuned to all of your minds, and I am capable of rewriting you completely."

That shook me out of my trance. I started to give a nasty retort but ended up screaming instead as my mind was torn apart.

But I activated the Black Ice first.

Frick you, Solomon.

# Chapter Nineteen

## Two Women Enter, One Woman Leaves

If I was going to die, this was hardly the way I wanted to do it, especially as all the fizzling around in my brain triggered more memories, memories I was desperate to lock away. It was like my mind was trying to put together a puzzle that the drugs were still trying to keep in separate indistinct pieces. Either way, Solomon had smashed open a hole in the dam of my memories and they were all coming back as I unloaded the world's most lethal computer virus into his mind.

Whether I was freeing myself or dying with Solomon, I remembered kneeling before Snake. It was even more vivid flashback than the ones triggered by my lethe rejection. So many of my bad memories were tied to Snake. The worst part was that they were only so deep and painful because I really had felt something for the deranged old man. The sick old nutbar wouldn't have hurt me so much if not for the fact he'd cared for me in his own way or at least faked it. He'd made me dependent on his conditional love and approval, to the point I hated myself for wanting it so badly.

We were once more in the martial arts studio, and it was almost five years into my service to the Cyber Dragons. I was twenty-two now and it felt like lifetimes. Honestly, being released into the field had been an anti-climax. Snake had prepared me like a Spartan, and I'd been expecting James Bond-type impossible missions (or at least Tom Cruise). Instead, my first mission for the Trikuza had been to gut a loan shark who had been skimming from the till. It had taken less than an hour out of my day and I'd had a sandwich afterward.

Indeed, as my memories came back, I couldn't help but think

at how utterly boring and routine being an assassin had turned out to be. If Snake had succeeded at anything, it had been psychologically prepping me for the job. I killed two or three people a month with the same casualness that most people swatted a fly. It was the other missions like data theft and sabotage that tested my skills.

I spent more time trying to figure out how to make a killing look like an accident than I ever did worrying about action itself. The only time I'd ever gotten into a fight was when I'd been jumped by a trio of Skullboyz while taking a walk and Snake had let me have it for killing them in a way that had required chemical body disposal. For some reason, Snake had reacted very badly to that even though I'd done it myself.

Now I was barely paying attention as he paced in front of me, lecturing me with ideas I swore came from *Batman Begins*. "Theatricality and mythology are weapons of the true ninja. The modern shinobi is mostly a creation of pop culture and legend. The myths about their invisibility, magic, and invincibility are all the product of movies, retold until their skills were exaggerated beyond all measure. The real ninja were just people who were willing to dress outside their social class. Their invisibility was a matter of psychology in that the samurai military aristocracy were trained to view them as beneath notice. In effect, society had created a weakness in them to be exploited. Why leap from rooftop to rooftop when you can just sneak in and poison a meal?"

God, Snake did love to hear himself talk, didn't he? I was well past my "adoring respect" stage to Snake. Still, I never actually voiced my disrespect to him. I was fully of the mind he could break every bone in my body. He'd stabbed me in the kidneys as an excuse to replace them with more efficient cybernetic prosthetics. I'd been forced to stab myself in the liver for its replacement.

"But you do train us to leap from rooftop-to-rooftop. I've even seen you forgo subtlety to go guns akimbo on an entire room of Russian syndicate members."

I'd been only an adolescent then and my test there had just been to survive the resulting blood bath and escape the building. It had been my first real clue that Snake, theatricality aside, was quite possibly insane. There had been no reason to turn the entire place into a slaughterhouse, killing servers and cooks alike, but he'd done it anyway.

Snake, rather than look displeased, smiled with a patronizing grin. "You have been paying attention. Yes, that is part of the lesson. Because while practicality should always be foremost in your mind, one should also not underestimate the value of the ludicrous. Organized crime that has lasted for centuries and developed true power has done so by manipulating legend. Grandiose names, secret oaths, peculiar rituals, signature weapons, and underlying philosophies make for unthinking loyalty. The assassin who is never seen is not one who is remembered."

"Isn't that the point?" I asked, thinking he was essentially saying he made a massacre because it was cooler than just killing his targets directly.

"If your goal is only to kill, yes," Snake said. "But killing is only a means to an end."

"What is the end?" I asked, finally asking.

"Domination," Snake replied. "A murder unattributed will never be as effective in deterring your enemies as one that is done by a larger-than-life force. That is why the Trikuza exist. We are the arm of forces that must remain nebulous to be effective but still need to invoke terror in their foes."

"Because criminals are a cowardly and superstitious lot?" I asked, immediately regretting it.

"*People* are a cowardly and superstitious lot, Kei," Snake said, the smile leaving his face.

"Who are we working for?" I asked.

"Pardon?" Snake asked.

"You said we were working for someone who wanted the Trikuza, or at least the Cyber Dragons, to be their mythical spooky front." I blinked, wondering if he was being serious or not. "Who are they?"

He smiled. "They wouldn't be very secretive if I just told you. Suffice to say they are a nameless force that brings the markets of the world to a heel."

That was a complete non-answer. "So why am I here?"

Snake narrowed his eyes. "You are growing very insolent these days."

"I just thought I was entitled to a little more consideration now that I've been out there busting my ass for years," I said. "How many people do I have to kill to get some respect around here?"

For a moment, I thought Snake would strike me. There was no

anger in his posture, but he had grown very still. "Respect is not given but earned."

"When am I going to earn it?" I asked, risking more than I really wanted.

Snake paused before the smile returned to his face. Somehow, I found that more ominous than his frown. "Now."

"Now?" I asked, wondering what was so special about now. I'd just thought this was one of his regular checkups on me.

"Indeed," Snake replied. "Fate will be arriving shortly. I want to speak with you both."

That caused me to tense up a bit. Fate and I had been getting *close* recently and I wasn't sure whether Snake knew about it or not. I hadn't been a virgin, Snake had brought in teachers to disabuse us of anything romantic about sexuality other than its utility during missions or as a means of relaxation, but this was the first *relationship* I'd had.

Such as it was.

"That's good," I said, not entirely hiding my nervousness.

Snake noticed, I could tell by the slightest flicker of his eyes before he gave a short chuckle then walked into the next room. Right on time, I could hear the elevator ping and saw Fate stride into the room. She was different from the teenage girl I'd met all those years ago and not just in terms of skill level or personality.

Fate had more fully embraced cybernetics than I had, having her old body discarded for a Shell with Snake's approval. She was taller now, almost six feet in height, and had the build of a woman's MMA fighter.

Fate had added blue highlights to her hair and wore black pants as well as a ripped shirt with leather jacket. I couldn't see it at the moment, but both of her arms had heavy electric dragons running up their sides. She had a heavy duffle bag over one shoulder, and I could see she was packing multiple weapons (not including the built-in ones). Fate could change all of this with the variety of bodies she'd somehow managed to acquire but this was "her" body as she chose to present it.

Personally, I was a bit more reluctant to part with my meat than Snake or Fate had been. It was another area where she was exceeding me as his prized pupil. Honestly, I was surprised that he hadn't insisted I make the transition completely, but he seemed more interested in just slowly making me a robot bit by bit instead of all at once.

"Bringing your laundry over here now? What is this, college?" I asked, knowing I'd never attend any university. I would never be free of Snake or the Trikuza. I would always be their tool and never have free time of my own to pursue a trade other than murder. I shouldn't have been ungrateful, though. The alternative was death on the highway or lying on my back in one of the brothels plenty of refugee girls and boys ended up in.

"I knocked over an armored car on the way here," Fate said. "They're getting rid of paper money these days. Right now, if you're going to do untraceable transactions, you pretty much have to do them in crypto."

"Yeah, because crypto is untraceable," I muttered, trying to parse what she'd just said. "Uh, was that assigned to you? The robbery I mean?"

"Do you always do what you're told?" Fate asked, dropping the bag down on the ground like a sack of potatoes. I could see some old green dollar bills sticking out of the top. They weren't worth much anymore since the Collapse and the US economy's tailspin but had been making a comeback since the Big Two Hundred had agreed to back currency's stability. That was with the acknowledgement their own scripts would be valid tender in the US of A.

"Uh, yes, I do what I'm told," I said. "I don't want to die."

Fate rolled her eyes.

"You need to learn where we stand in the hierarchy. We're too valuable to take down. Too much time and effort has been invested," Fate said, smiling. It was without emotion. "Come here and let me give you a kiss."

"Snake is here," I said, nervous.

"He knows," Fate said, smiling. "He knows everything in his twisted perverted old man heart."

I stared at her. "What are you implying?"

"So naive," Fate said. "This is why you took so long to get the tattoos."

"Because an assassin giving themselves identifying marks is such a good idea," I said, wondering when Fate had internalized all this mythological mumbo-jumbo. The only reason I'd gotten myself tattooed was because Snake insisted.

"Not an issue when you can just switch arms," Fate replied.

"I'm fond of my arms," I replied, wondering just what she was implying.

Tattoos had a purpose in the Yakuza that helped bond their members together. In Japan, it was illegal to go in certain businesses with them. The Cyber Dragons had adjusted and modified the practice so that its members were chipped and could make the tattoos appear or disappear at will. I found that equally stupid since the process was still something the police could use to find about your affiliations. Of course, the police were so corrupt that it was a defense against arrest in some places.

Maybe that was why I was here. To be taught that the job was more than just avoiding attention but to instill fear via your reputation. Snake had said as much, and I was still avoiding giving into the "lifestyle" entirely. Perhaps I didn't want to acknowledge that this was all I was ever going to be, even if I had already thrown away any claim to moral superiority with my first unquestioned murder.

"Enjoy who we are, kiddo," Fate said, despite the fact we were the same age. "After all, I'm ninety-nine percent sure that Snake's real name is probably something like Melvin or Jose."

"Kiddo better be a *Kill Bill* reference," I said, getting up.

Fate and I embraced, despite Snake's presence nearby. Our kisses always lacked something, though, that I put down to her being a Shell before having a brief affair with another. No, Fate never shared anything of herself even intimately. It should have been my first clue that I was more invested in our relationship than she was, but I was still new at all this. No wonder I'd wanted to erase this period of my life from my mind.

That was when Snake returned, carrying a wooden box in his hands. There was a sense of somberness to him that was slightly more stoic than his usual stone-cold badass pretension. His face bore an unreadable expression, and I had to wonder what the old man was cooking up. Somehow, I knew this would be an important moment in my life, but I had no idea just how important it would be.

"A present, Snake? You shouldn't have," Fate said. "I would have gotten you something if I'd known."

"I sincerely doubt that," Snake said. "You have been spending money frivolously but not on others."

"Well, I like to give myself gifts," Fate said. "I heard you bought Kei a new enhanced nervous system agitator. Trying to turn her into your ideal woman?"

Fate was testing boundaries now. She always had but recently she'd gotten a particularly nasty edge, even with me. If not for the fact she was my only friend in the Trikuza—let alone my lover—I might not have stuck with her.

"No. But I am supporting her improvement as a soldier of the Cyber Dragons. Kei has a great future ahead of her," Snake said, not opening the box but just standing there in front of us with it prominently displayed in his hands.

"So do I," Fate said, muttering.

"You are disobedient, insolent, and vicious," Snake said. "Only one of these do I approve of. You robbed that armored car in broad daylight and did little to cover your identity. That is the wrong kind of attention to draw, especially from banks that pay us a gratuity as well as care for our accounts."

"Oh, screw you, old man," Fate said, putting her hands on her hips. "You're constantly telling us to make names for ourselves and then you complain when I do? I'm not the one dressed up as Naruto when I'm in my seventies."

I had no idea who that was either, but Snake just responded by opening the box. Inside were a pair of wakizashi. "Kei has also failed. She killed the son of a high-ranking executive of our organization."

"Wait, what?" I asked, wondering when the hell this had happened. Then I realized he must have one been one of those idiots who jumped me. "This must have been a set up. That had to have been a set up."

"Undoubtedly," Snake said. "However, actions have consequences, and this is where you need to display loyalty."

I stared at him. "You want us to fight it out?"

"Think of it as another test," Snake said.

"You want us to kill one another?" Fate asked, her voice smooth and alluring.

"I want you to fight to the best of your abilities," Snake said. "Cyborg versus cyborg. Shinobi versus shinobi. Who walks away is a matter for your training to decide."

What happened next was purely reflexive. In a way, Snake would have been proud about how I'd learned to act on pure instinct. In another way, he would have been disappointed because my actions were driven on pure emotion. I grabbed the wakizashi from the box and plunged it into my mentor's chest with all the force of the enhancements he'd given me.

The metal would have been turned away if it had just been steel, but the short sword had been created from carbon fiber and honed to a molecular edge. He'd probably spent more on crafting the weapons than most people did their houses in the days when people still had them.

Fate held back, just watching until I'd stabbed the old man a hundred times. His chest was open and spread with wires, white fluid, and damaged artificial organs. It didn't even look human, what I'd managed to damage. His eyes were empty, glassy, and unresponsive like the artificial doll-eyes they were. I'd killed the man who'd rescued me. Killed the man who'd abused me. Set myself free. It was almost too much to comprehend.

Fate placed her hand on my shoulder. "Nice job. Now let's torch this place and make some real money."

I knew how this would end, but at the time all I could feel was hope for the future and joy that Snake was dead.

Both things that I would find out were lies.

# Chapter Twenty

## Killing the Buddha on the Road

I struggled while trying to keep Solomon out of my head. He was attempting to find out who I was really working for. But there was no secret, no inner truth, and everything I was throwing at him was simply so he wouldn't tear my mind apart.

"These are my memories!" I shouted in the digital void. "Stay out of my head!"

"Show me what you're hiding!" Solomon's voice echoed in her mind.

What the hell did he want? Why was he so interested in my memories? Unfortunately, I couldn't resist even as I felt the Black Ice start to move through not just Solomon's mind but the temple around us. That was an awfully bad thing because we were all connected to the Temple and possibly vulnerable to the Black Ice as well. This caused the infospace around me to start developing glitches and black bars through my vision even as my head felt like it was ready to explode.

I could feel my Maelstrom 90 implant being compromised by the adapted Blipvert virus. It "felt" familiar in a way that I didn't understand, interacting with the Black Ice. I could see them interconnecting before my eyes as my implant told me I was suffering a severe data attack. No kidding!

"You found the original program!" Solomon shouted. "You need to show me how."

"What the hell are you talking about?" I asked, feeling agonizing pain as my brain was cracked open like an egg. Red letters appeared across my vision as my implant was hacked.

PROGRAMS COMPILED: 100%
MEMORY DAMAGE: 69%
REPAIRING: 30%
REPAIRING: 60%
REPAIRING: 99%
REPAIRED

If I could have cried, I would have. Weakness was the one thing I could never let myself display and yet it was part of being human. It was why being human sucked. I struggled to warn the others to log out, but I couldn't see them since the temple was now completely red with numbers scrolling down in every direction. They were all gone except for Solomon, and he twisted like a reflection in a funhouse mirror.

SEARCHING
SEARCHING
FILE FOUND
COMPILING

Alarms blared in my memory, and I found myself in the long cold hallways of the towering DataSecure bank. I fired my AG-Bolt pistol several times down the hallway, trying to cover my friends as the last heist I participated in went horribly wrong. It was where I'd been betrayed and lost any desire to remember my past.

"Son of a bitch!" I shouted, hating the veritable army of Blackbriar PMC thugs that were cutting us down. "How did they know?"

Blackbriar PMC was the Diet Coke alternative to Atlas Security for the discerning megacorp or Third World dictator. They dressed like villains in a sci-fi action movie with all-black outfits consisting of reflective helmets, plastisteel armor, and thick leather coats that seemed designed to invoke Nazi officers. I would have found it comical, but it turned out that mercenaries loved pretending to be bad guys. If you ever looked at their patches or logos, most looked like they were designed by fourteen-year-old edgelords. Blackbriar's was a human skull with a beret and twelve rifles underneath, like Skeletor was their commanding officer.

"It doesn't matter!" Fate said, shooting another of them in the faceplate just as they were going to hurl a grenade they'd activated. It was a stroke of luck as the blinking device dropped among the team of attacking monsters and took out half of them. "All we need to do is get the program."

"Frey is dead!" I shouted, referring to the pilot of our seven-man team that had been nearly halved by this insane project. So were Rave and Jump, two thugs that were more Fate's friends than mine.

The memories of my first year of freedom washed over me. I'd become part of Fate's crew as we killed, stole, and partied continuously since the death of Snake. Fate had decided to become a Rider and, due to a desire to please here, so had I. We'd knocked over armored cars, banks, homes, and data farms for our employers. Fate had introduced me to lethe to cope with the guilt. It made killing easy if you didn't have to remember the faces.

This, however, was supposed to be the proverbial big score. The one that would make us all rich and get us out of the hellhole that was anywhere but the richest sections of the United States. We were going after Snake's data locker here. Supposedly, he had massive amounts of blackmail material and electric bonds worth billions. There were even rumors he had the command codes to an AI that gave him the power of governments or the Big Two Hundred. Fate had become obsessed with the idea once she'd heard of it.

"Suck it up, Kei! Get the data!" Fate lifted a pair of submachine guns and unloaded onto the few remaining survivors of the Blackbriar squad. Her ammunition was armor-piercing rounds, military issue, and cut them down. It would have been nice if she'd shared it with the rest of us.

"We don't even know—" I started to say before things got weird in my memory.

"We found the file!" Miles shouted from a door, which automatically made me question the validity of the dream.

I'd met Miles after this failed heist, him picking me up for putting down a suit who was an honest-to-God serial killer of prostitutes. Somehow, he'd lost the paperwork on that, and the serial killer's bosses had let the matter lie, probably because they'd forgotten he'd existed after a month. Here, though, Miles was fighting alongside us as a Rider. He also had a full head of hair and looked better for it.

"Thank my ancestors," Sun said, beside me, which made me sure I was hallucinating. She was dressed in full body armor and carrying a shotgun.

Memory was an inherently tricky thing, especially since implants allowed people to have them programmed inside like *Total Recall* (one of Fate's favorites). According to a story I'd heard from both her and Snake, there had once been a scandal about hundreds of kids being molested by a Satanic cult. It turned out that the hypnotists trying to bring up their repressed memories had ended up implanting them instead. I wasn't sure I entirely believed that but then again, I had seen the refugee camps where child abuse had been distressingly common. No Satanism, though. This was a product of Blipvert messing with my mind, though.

Wasn't it?

Running to the room with the others, we found ourselves in an enormous chamber of black obelisks that each had a single red eye. These were the data lockers of VIP clients and a source of unimaginable wealth to the person who managed to pry them open and decrypt them. The latter was distressingly easy with modern techniques, rendering decades of confidence in old methods obsolete. We had both DNA samples and brain scan files on Snake, though, and that meant this should be a piece of cake.

It wasn't.

Fate had already gone to a nearby *Star Trek*-looking console and plugged in her implant via digital super-optic wire. She cursed after a few seconds. "Goddammit! It's blocked to me."

"Are you kidding me?" Miles shouted, looking ready to start shooting up the place. Well, more than before.

"I am not kidding!" Fate said. "He had a hunter program specifically designed to look out for my signature. It's...wait. Kei, come out here and link yourself."

"What?" I asked.

"You're registered for download here," Fate said, her voice hungry.

I didn't understand. "I'm what?"

"You're listed as his heir! You're authorized to use the account!" Fate snapped. "Get over here."

I think it was that moment that any pretense that Fate loved me vanished, but I was just too stupid to know it. Her entire body language changed and there was a naked hostility behind her eyes

I completely missed. I went over to the console and linked myself to the DataSecure bank mainframe.

What followed was an avalanche of files taking the form of a massive library stretching out into infinity. I could have navigated it with enough time, but I wasn't here for any messages from Snake or trying to figure out why he'd left me access to his most private files. Unfortunately, I couldn't just download it all into my brain either for later perusal.

We'd brought portable data storage units (PDS) that could carry whole server farms worth of information, but these had been torn up by gunfire. Obviously, DataSecure's vaults were filled with built-in blockers and closed-circuit infonets to prevent remote theft too. My Maelstrom implant could only hold a tiny fraction of what Snake had here and figuring out the most valuable things to steal was taking longer than I wanted.

In the end, I decided to go after something called Black Ice that was divided into two major files that required virtually the entirety of my storage space plus deleting everything but essential functions. I didn't need to watch movies, play video games, and experience porn directly with my brain anyway. It was funny how the first of the Black Ice files was listed as "Control" and the second of the Black Ice files was listed as "Kill."

"Got it," I said aloud, feeling like my head was about to explode.

"Transfer it to me, immediately," Fate said.

"What?" I asked, confused.

"Do it!" Fate snapped.

I began a direct wireless transfer to Fate of the Control file even as it was going to take an excruciatingly long time.

"We don't have time for this, Fate," Sun said.

"Shut up, Chastity," Fate said. "Let's get moving. Grab some grenades from the bodies and toss them in. Miles, hack the elevator."

Chastity? Who was Chastity? It was a bad name for our group unless she was being ironic. My mind was still in a fog but the woman who looked like Sun was named Chastity Chambers. Probably an alias but something that I remembered now. This was before Sun had started her career as an omnivore musician. Her rich Green Foods CEO daddy had cut her off and she was rebelling by using a Shell to rob him. That didn't quite fit with my knowledge of Sun even if she was working with Solomon in the "present."

"We're just going to blow up the servers?" Miles asked. "This stuff is worth billions!"

"And it will be worth even more if we're the only ones to have it," Fate argued, despite her argument not making any real sense. The only things we'd recovered were the Black Ice files and the rest of this stuff, including everything from medical histories to secret accounts, would all be destroyed. I kept my mouth shut because I didn't give a frick about the fortunes of any suits being wiped out. I was only here to get rich and to support Fate.

Miles reluctantly went and retrieved the grenades while we headed out to hack the elevator. I had a tap on BlackBriar's feeds, and they were surrounding DataSecure with reinforcements now. We had to get to the roof. None of us were rated to fly a cloud car, but a bad aerial exit was better than being here. Too bad our pilot was dead. Rave hadn't been part of our group, at least not intimately, but we'd worked together before. We'd also brought along a backup in case something had happened to Rave but sadly that person was Jump.

*Upload the Black Ice to Chastity,* Fate said via our Maelstrom 90 implants.

*What?* I asked, confused. I was only seventy-two percent done with the upload of the files to Fate. "You want me to give her a copy too?"

*No, I want you to activate the file,* Fate said.

I blinked. *You want me to kill her?*

I had no idea what the Black Ice did in this scenario, but Kill was unambiguous in a way that Control wasn't. Chastity, Sun, whatever her name was, wasn't my friend the way that Fate or even Miles was. I was increasingly certain that Miles had really been there, and I'd simply forgotten it. That meant either he'd been hiding things from me, taking advantage of my amnesia, or it had simply never come up—which I couldn't bring myself to believe.

*We were betrayed,* Fate said. *They knew we were coming. It was Chastity. The only way to survive is to make sure the rat is exterminated.*

Rather than question Fate, I complied and uploaded the Kill file to Chastity's brain. Simultaneously, Miles tossed a grenade into the server room that did irreparable damage to the data stored inside. With that, the Control file completed transferring to Fate.

Chastity looked confused, wobbling on her feet, and then collapsed against the wall. Her body was still alive, as much as an artificial body could be considered alive, but the light had gone out of her eyes. What was left was, to pardon the use of the phrase, nothing more than an empty shell. I resisted the urge to run to her side and looked at Fate.

"Done," Fate muttered, a self-satisfied smirk on her face.

"Chastity!" Miles said, running to her side.

That was when Fate shot him in the back, causing him to collapse on top of Chastity. Fate wasn't using one of her armor-piercing rounds but instead the gun of a Blackbriar soldier. Nevertheless, Miles collapsed on top of our partner.

"What the hell are you doing?" I shouted.

"Trading up," Fate said, before shooting me in the chest.

What followed was something I only remembered in the vaguest sense. I was dragged along with Miles through the basement of the DataSecure building, stripped naked and put into a BlackBriar uniform after some emergency triage was performed. If Snake hadn't replaced my heart with an artificial prosthetic with redundancies, I would have been dead.

It hadn't been Fate who rescued me, she escaped upstairs and detonated a secondary bomb in our van outside the building that leveled most of the city block. Something we survived only because we were underground. It proved to be one of the largest acts of digital terrorism in history as the detonation caused a cascade effect that wiped the entire floor's contents.

No less than two of the Big Two Hundred were forced into bankruptcy when they lost their leverage on the other companies. It also had killed something akin to five hundred people, mostly innocents, while erasing all evidence of our involvement. No wonder I'd turned to lethe to forget my involvement. I wondered how my Atlas colleagues would have reacted to knowing I was a mass murderer or at least party to it. Case had all of my files and knew about my involvement in this, but the details had been scrubbed of my true culpability.

As crazy and murderous as Snake had been, what Fate (and I) had done was worse. I could still remember the weeks that had followed with the images of bodies being pulled out from the DataSecure buildings remains plus the fact I'd had all my accounts cleaned out by Fate. The latter shouldn't have mattered compared to the first, but it did. Fate had burned all my identities in addition to ripping me off and I'd been forced to go fully into Riding in order to survive. Miles, ironically, ended up promoted as a cop. I still had no idea how he'd pulled that one off. Either way, I had one bit of satisfaction: I'd only transferred the Control file to Fate. She hadn't realized it was one of two.

That's when it hit me, and I opened my eyes to stare into Solomon's. "Blipvert is one half of the Black Ice program. Troy and Fate are working together."

Solomon's avatar was frozen, though, having already been consumed by the program I'd uploaded into his brain. That was when Solomon's avatar exploded into thousands of digital pixels and I saw Sun standing behind him, looking at me.

"Thank you," Sun said, simply. "You were able to reformat my original programming."

I stared at her. She wasn't Chastity. She was someone else. Something else. "What are you?"

Sun smiled as her face and body became nothing more than a collection of numbers scrolling down. "Be seeing you."

Sun was Black Ice. Blipvert. Snake's stored data. A Cognition AI. A thing that had uploaded itself into Chastity's body and used it to save us before infiltrating Solomon's group, if not persuading him on this quixotic crusade in the first place. What the hell had I gotten myself into?

That was when I was forcibly ejected from infospace and wondered if everyone else in my group was going to die due to my blunder.

# Chapter Twenty-One

## This Was All a Set-up. Who Could Have Guessed?

I woke up on the bed I'd laid down on with Case and Paradise, the song "Love Shack" by the B-52s playing in the background. Both Case and Paradise were lying on the bed beside me, still in info-space and not awakened from their comatose use of the machinery. They had chords attached to the back of their necks and I had my headset on. I was glad they were alive and still registering brain activity by the movement of their eyes. Unfortunately, as fond as I'd gotten of the pair, I had a much bigger problem now. Blipvert and Black Ice were two halves of the same AI.

Dammit.

Bigoted as it may sound, I wasn't a fan of artificial intelligence. There were three kinds of AI in the world: SI, Tier I, and Tier X. SI or Simulated Intelligences were non-conscious algorithms that coordinated the massive amount of data that had escaped humanity's ability to coordinate it. Tier I were those AI that equaled human intelligence, more or less, and were those that guided bioroid bodies like Case.

Cognition AIs were the ones that terrified me because they were mankind's first encounters with truly inhuman alien consciousness. There were only about a dozen of them presently in existence, but they'd been unchained by fools hoping they could resolve the Collapse and now were privately controlling the economy and world politics behind the scenes. Forget some mythical Invisible Hand, I was worried about the AI's influence.

And Sun was one of them.

Or at least the one pretending to be Sun back at Solomon's Temple was. Was it something Snake had been experimenting on or had he stolen it from one of the megacorporations? Why had it been divided into two files? How did they relate to mind control and killing people? It was like using a NASA space shuttle as a gun.

Ugh.

I was hoping that once I'd uploaded the Black Ice into Solomon's brain that it would be over, but now I was shaking with all the returned memories he'd forced onto me. My Maelstrom 90 implant was almost empty of files, and I couldn't help but wonder if I'd unwittingly given the ultimate weapon to a lunatic. No, Solomon was dead. Certainly so. Yet, I couldn't trust anything I'd seen back at Club Inferno either. Anything I had seen or remembered was something they could have hacked or played with as Blipvert was apparently terrifyingly real.

That was when I heard someone chamber a round next to my head. Turning, I saw Miles holding his ARC-118 pistol in his hands, trembling, while staring directly at me. He looked like he was trying to get his courage up.

"Miles, if this is a joke, I'm going to laugh uproariously. If it's not, you better be prepared to get me on your first shot because otherwise I'm going to shove that thing so far up your ass that it'll come out of your mouth," I said, calmly. I was too upset to be scared right now.

Miles sucked in his breath. "I'm sorry, Kei, I don't have a choice."

"I really hate that name," I muttered. "What the hell is going on?"

"A lot," Miles said. "Let's just—"

That was when a long silver-colored blade moved around Miles's throat. It was attached to the hands of Evie Principle, who looked decidedly pissed off.

"Step away from my daughter," Evie said, softly.

"Well damn," Miles said, dropping the ARC-118 on the carpet.

Paradise and Case got up off the bed and removed from their implant chords. Both looked confused rather than angry. Miles was on the ground, kneeling, his hands behind his neck. Evie kept her Wolverine claw beneath his Adam's apple, kicking Miles' gun away.

"Did we miss something?" Paradise asked.

"Miles is a traitor," Evie said, simply.

"Can you be a traitor if you're never on someone's side?" Paradise asked. "These are the questions that keep me up at night. That and marathon sessions of *Ultra Super Halo: Infinite 2 Remastered Edition.*"

"Yes, Paradise," Evie said. "Yes, you can be."

I was too weak and confused by the sudden onslaught of untrustworthy memories to react much to my changing situation. So, my reaction was the somewhat minimalist. "Why?"

"They have my niece," Miles said, simply. "They killed my sister and took her."

"Oh please," Evie said, rolling her eyes. "I bet you also needed the money from selling out my daughter for your sick mother's prosthetic heart."

"Oh, that's terrible!" Paradise said, making the joke her own. "How long has she needed one?"

"Not now, Paradise," I said. "They have Becky?"

Miles responded simply by sending me a video file. It was an image of his thirteen-year-old niece, Rebecca, inside a room with her hands tied behind her back as well as her mouth gagged. Becky was wearing white nightgown she'd soiled. A distorted voice told him to wait for further instructions and that Becky would be killed if he didn't do exactly as they instructed. While you could fake something like that, it looked damn convincing. Frick.

"How long have you been an outside agent?" Case asked.

"The entire time," Miles said, sighing. "The instructions told me to go up there, cooperate, and serve as Troy's spy in this group. It doesn't take a rocket scientist to think she's behind all this. I don't think she's as smart as she thinks."

"What did you tell them?" I asked, feeling betrayed but not as much as I would have thought.

"I just kept her informed versus private comm," Miles replied. "I was told to kill you after you killed Solomon, though. Then I was supposed to harvest your Maelstrom 90 implant. She wanted the Black Ice inside it."

"How do you know about that? How does she?" I asked.

"Well, I was there when you stole it," Miles said, confirming that at least some of my memories were true. It was possible that his memories had been tampered with as well, but I doubted it. "And when Sun rescued us."

"Sun," I said, as if it was a dream I was trying to remember.

The recovered memories didn't feel quite real. "She was the one who pulled us out."

"Who else?" Miles said. "She was different after that."

"Yeah, because she was dead," I replied. "The person who rescued her was an AI using her body."

"Ooo, ghost in the machine," Paradise said.

"Don't knock it until you've tried it," Lucita said, entering the room. She was okay too and thank God (or whatever deity was listening) for that. "What do they know, Miles, and maybe we can help you?"

"You're just going to overlook his treachery?" Evie asked and I suddenly felt like I was in a fantasy world. Then again, there was a code of respect among Refugee Zoners that didn't exist among suits or street mercs. There had to be since collectivism was how a lot of them survived.

"It depends on what he knows," Lucita said. "It might also be the only way for his niece to survive."

"You can't guarantee that," Miles responded.

"No, but what do you think the likelihood of your niece surviving shall be even if you cooperate?" Lucita said, seemingly bored with all this. "Historically, the odds of abductees used as hostages in these situations are not good."

"Don't you think I know that?" Miles asked. "Why do you think I didn't kill you all in infospace?"

"Gee, Miles, thanks for your consideration," I replied. "I'm so glad our six months together meant so much to you."

"Really, six months?" Paradise said. "I've never had a boyfriend longer than two weeks and he was a repeat customer."

"That isn't a boyfriend, Paradise," Evie chided her daughter.

"Yes, but I'm willing to fake it for big tips," Paradise said.

Evie sighed. "Oh, Paradise."

"I am what I am," Paradise said. "Popeye said that. Also, God."

This was why I never had kids. That and I'd had an involuntary hysterectomy. Fricking Snake.

Miles looked down. "I tried to get over what we did at DataSecure. No one was supposed to get hurt. I was undercover the entire time."

"I think that stopped when Fate started killing people," I replied. "Cops are supposed to intervene when crimes against people are involved."

You learn a lot about police procedure when you're a professional criminal. Well, unless you're stupid and believe cops have to identify themselves when you ask them if they're one or other urban legends. Which was most criminals.

Miles looked down. "The Blackbriar mercs were shooting at me too. In the end, the screw up there got me promoted and the entire thing swept under the rug as a hush payment."

I lost all respect for Miles in that moment, not that I was overflowing with it right now in the first place. He had been an undercover cop the entire time but had chosen not to intervene when the bullets had started flying. Yeah, I would have died or gone to jail, but a lot of innocent people might be alive. Worse, he'd taken part in a cover-up too. That hurt me more than the discovery that he was willing to betray us for his niece.

"You're scum," I said to him.

Miles didn't argue the point. "It was supposed to be an attempt to get at whatever the Trikuza had put in that vault. Snake and his people were untouchable. We could have taken down their entire network with what we found. Except we never did find out what you recovered and everything else was destroyed."

"Is that why you dated me after?" I asked. "To find out if I'd recovered something?"

"No," Miles said. "I was hoping you'd be someone who understood the guilt. Except by the end of our relationship, you'd taken enough lethe that you didn't even remember what I was talking about when I tried to bring it up."

I stared at him. I remembered that now, slowly fading away from the person I was to someone who could live with what she'd been a part of. "Maybe you should have done it too."

"I don't want to forget," Miles said. "I want to atone."

"There's no forgiving what we did," I said, surprised I meant it. I wanted to take lethe now but the thought of doing so made me sick, as if it would be dishonoring those that died. "Even if we didn't know. We were responsible."

"There is no point to atoning *or* guilt," Lucita said. "The dead do not care, and the living have to live."

"Interesting life philosophy," I replied, sarcastically. "Must be nice to be a psychopath."

"Sociopath," Lucita corrected.

Okay, that backfired.

Case studied Miles. "You're not the first person who has betrayed me because someone has taken family members hostage. I don't hold it against you but understand that we might have to kill you. No offense."

"Some taken," Miles said.

"What do they know?" Case asked, his voice nonthreatening but with the simple directness that made me think he could kill Miles at will.

"I informed her right up until we left the War Wagon," Miles said. "Then I turned off my tracker. You're right that there's no way that my niece is going to get through this alive if I just give Troy what she wants. I figured I'd try and negotiate."

"You're an idiot," I said. "Not that you could take us all even when we were asleep."

"I'm pretty sure, by definition, he could," Paradise said. "But it was nice of him that he didn't kill us all and thus get murdered by my mom."

Miles didn't respond. I mean, what was there to say?

"The question is why is Helen doing this?" Lucita asked, surprising me. "Forget that I considered her a friend, I've been betrayed enough to know when to discard old relationships. I thought she was an ally. We were working on this together. This is just...stupid."

"That's assuming she's planning to stay Helen Troy," Evie replied.

"What?" I asked, looking up at her.

"Should I keep the claws on him?" Evie asked.

"No," Lucita said, surprising me. Then she explained why. "I want to break his neck with my bare hands. Now explain your reasoning."

Miles grimaced.

Evie sighed and stepped back, drawing her finger claws back into her hand. The whole liquid memory metal thing was damned impressive to look at. It made her like a T-1000 or Molly Millions. Right now, I was focused on her words. "You're assuming that this woman wants to remain the trophy wife of a failed businessman who you keep trotting out as the face of your electronics division. This Blipvert thing represents a much bigger potential windfall of cash. Billions, if not trillions in credits. While you and Atlas are involved, it'll just be absorbed into your company's profit margins and weapons designs. If she eliminates you then she can kill her husband, flee to Europe or the South American Federation and start a new life."

I had to admit that Evie was making some solid points, which reminded me that she was a spy. I could just imagine Helen Troy thinking she was marrying extreme tech bro wealth, only to find out that he'd mortgaged himself to the eyeballs. I would have killed him immediately. Then again, that wouldn't have gotten her out of the financial situation that she'd gotten herself into.

There was also not just money to be made with AI, whether it was designed to kill or control people or not. A Cognition AI couldn't just be programmed, they had to be raised almost like children and the cost tended to be something akin to ten to twenty billion UN credits at the very least with some of them requiring over a hundred billion. Cheaper attempts just ended up crashing or going insane, which could wipe out whole districts of data before they were shut down. The real question was how Helen Troy had gotten the Control side of Snake's AI in the first place.

"Dammit," I said, it coming to me in an instant, "Troy is working with Fate."

"You think so?" Miles said, not moving his hands from his neck. Probably because he wasn't sure if Lucita had been serious about breaking his neck. She was, I was sure. "No one's seen or heard of Fate in years."

"Probably because she sold Blipvert to these rich jerkoffs and is sipping margaritas on an artificial island somewhere," I muttered.

I felt like a fool for ever trusting Fate, let alone loving her. This whole scheme felt like one of her plans with its complete lack of forethought and excessive body count. If Helen Troy had wanted Blipvert and Black Ice, then she probably could have just paid for both. Instead, she'd made this entire scheme to try to kill her financial backers and me too.

I was now wondering if the whole Rider contest had just been made up as an excuse for why she tried to kill me at the start once she'd identified who I was. It made more sense than the reality, though it emphasized what psychopaths the super-rich were that they thought, "Let's test our mercs by trying to kill them" was a reasonable justification for her actions.

In a way, Helen Troy's amateur hour nonsense was even more dangerous than if she'd been handling things like a dedicated criminal mastermind. If Lucita had overseen this, we'd have eliminated Solomon, handed over the material, and been shot in the back of the head as we were walking out the door. Instead, we were clearly dealing with someone who knew just enough to be extremely dangerous but clearly had poor impulse control.

If that person was waiting on news from Miles, we didn't have much time until she killed poor Becky. It also wouldn't take her long to send people to investigate This is Paradise to look for her. One thing rich people could always count on was having a never-ending supply of people willing to do their bidding for cash.

"I have an idea," I said. "It's going to sound crazy, though."

"Ooo, I love crazy!" Paradise said.

"I don't," Lucita said.

"What?" Miles said. "Assuming I'm not going to be straight up murdered here."

"I wouldn't count on that," Lucita said.

Case looked more forgiving. That made him different from just about everyone here, including myself. "Go ahead."

"We get the help of the renegade AI," I said. "We get the help of Sun."

# Chapter Twenty-Two

## Fleeing is the Better Part of Valor

"Contact Sun?" Lucita asked, staring at me. "The AI? Are you insane?"

"The AI who is apparently a spontaneous emergence from a virus designed to mind control individuals?" Case asked. "*That* AI?"

"I don't think that's how AI works," Paradise said, looking at Case. "You can't just expect it to spontaneously emerge from a bunch of information. Then infospace would be sentient and trying to kill us. Wait, is infospace sentient and trying to kill us?"

"Yes," Case said, deadpanned. "Yes, it is."

"Awesome!" Paradise said, cheerfully.

I swear, I wished I had whatever she was putting in her coffee. It probably worked better than lethe. "Becky is someone we need to help but we don't know where she is. An AI should be able to track her down. We just have to offer her something to get her help."

"The AI who we just killed the boss and cult leader of," Case replied. "Yeah, I can imagine how that would go over."

"Assuming that the crooked cop's niece is still alive," Lucita said, crossing her arms and giving a disdainful look. "As he said, she is probably doomed no matter what but there's no proof that she wasn't killed immediately once appropriate DNA or holographic scans were taken."

Miles didn't respond but I could tell he'd been thinking about that. Perhaps that was why he'd made such a feeble attempt to kill us. That pretty much said everything you needed to know about him as a boyfriend. In the end, even his betrayals were half-assed.

"With all due respect," Evie started to say.

"Whenever someone says that they're usually not being very respectful," I said.

"You're bringing threats to my place just by your presence here," Evie said. "While it's all nice you want to rescue the niece of the guy who just tried to kill you, there's a bunch of other people threatened by your very presence. You need to settle this right now. Little girl's life or no little girl's life."

"That's harsh, Mom," Paradise said.

"So is our life," Evie said. "There are children living here in the building."

I grimaced, wondering about that. "They don't—"

"Don't be sick. They don't work here," Evie said, disgusted. "I run a clean place. Their parents work here."

"Oh, sorry," I said, feeling stupid.

Paradise made a throat slitting gesture.

"Cut me some slack, I just had my brain fried," I replied.

"She's right," Case said. "Helen is dangerous. Not just to us, either. Back at James' place, I was checking the War Wagon for explosives before we took off. There were ways it could have been forced to self-destruct before I disabled them."

I stared at Case. "There was a bomb on the War Wagon, and you didn't think to mention it?"

"It could have just been a precaution," Case said, shrugging.

"It's a pretty big precaution!" I snapped. "I might not have agreed to this if I knew I was going to be killed as soon as the mission was done?"

"*Might* not have?" Miles said, staring upward.

"It was a lot of money," I said. "I mean *a lot* of money."

"There's just one problem with contacting Sun," Case said.

"Which is?" I asked, having seen dozens of problems with my plan but wanting some way to make it work.

The prospect of Fate and Helen Troy working together was still making my head spin, but it was the only way any of it made sense in my mind. It tied together all the disparate elements of the DataSecure heist, the Black Ice, and Snake's legacy. A little too well to be honest and made me feel like someone was moving pieces into place. I was still dealing with the idea he was alive and started to wonder if anyone stayed dead in this business.

I didn't want to get into it but part of the reason why I wanted to contact Sun wasn't just because I wanted to save a child's life—which was pretty important even to hardened crook like myself—but because I didn't want to face Fate again without some serious backup. I didn't entirely trust Case or Lucita, nice enough for suits as they were, despite the fact they could probably bring the hammer down.

"Can't we just call down an airstrike or something?" Paradise asked, showing her mind was in a similar place as mine. "You're like super rich, aren't you, Case? Lucita?"

"My position in the company depends strongly on not doing so in the middle of Neon Hills," Case replied. "Besides, Helen is possessed of plenty of contacts within Atlas. If I try to get help, then she's bound to be in the wind."

"Is that important?" Paradise asked.

"It is if she's holding Miles' niece hostage," Case said. "My suggestion is we go to Helen, grab her, and force her to release the girl."

"Blunt, heroic, and stupid," Lucita said. "Sounds like one of your plans."

"Do you have any better ideas?" Case asked.

"Disappear until she's dealt with," Lucita said. "Atlas doesn't mind the occasional assassination of fellow executives but they absolutely despise it when you shoot and miss. They'll take care of her for us after a few weeks."

"But what about Becky?" Miles asked, looking horrified.

"I feel for her, truly," Lucita said.

"You could always pay her off," Evie replied. "Most criminals aren't eager to kill kids, even the psychotic ones. But money blinds the best of them."

"And some are just scumbags," Miles replied. "Like the kind who kill kids. Besides, if I knew how to contact the kidnappers then I wouldn't need to try to kill you guys."

Evie paused. "There might be a way to handle this."

"I don't need help from a—" Miles started to say,

"Finish that sentence and your balls will be on the floor," Evie replied. "I don't take disrespect in my place, and I don't like cops to begin with."

Miles shut up.

"What are you thinking?" I asked.

"Lie," Evie said. "Miles should contact Helen Troy and inform her that he has the Black Ice as well as the part of the AI in Kei's head. However, he is altering the deal."

"Like Darth Vader!" Paradise said.

"How so?" I asked.

"You will meet in a neutral location to make a physical exchange," Evie replied. "The little girl for the AI. Plus, two hundred thousand credits."

"Wait, why?" Miles asked. "I don't give a crap about the money."

"The money will imply this is not just an emotional issue for you," Evie said. "You don't want to appear like they hold all of the bargaining power."

"She's right," I said, remembering some rather nasty stories about fellow Riders delivering ransoms.

"Why not ask for more?" Paradise asked.

Everyone looked at her.

"Theoretically!" Paradise said.

"It needs to be enough to appear like he's enriching himself and yet not so much that she won't want to pay," Case said, interjecting. "I wasn't aware you knew anything about hostage negotiation, Evie."

"I am a woman of many mysteries, Case," Evie said. "This will get you out of my place until things cool down and hopefully protect someone who has been caught up in the nastiness of our lives."

I was starting to like her. "I can't believe that we're all getting the runaround from an evil supermodel and actress."

"*I* was a supermodel and actress, she was a model who acted," Lucita replied. "There's a difference."

"There is?" Paradise asked.

Lucita's eyes narrowed. "What? I was in the last two *Fast and the Furious* movies. I was even the replacement actress for Bubbles in *Bubbles in Space 2*. I would have been Nephilim in *Behind Blue Eyes,* but the director wanted someone who looked like you."

"Oh yeah, those are timeless classics," Miles muttered. "I can definitely see the difference in the quality of films."

"Lucita had her clothes on for the majority of the films," Case said.

"So, they're objectively worse than Helen's," Miles deadpanned.

"Remember we can kill you at any time," Lucita replied. "Indeed, it would be a pleasure."

"Was it before the Eruption you were an actress?" Paradise said. "Because that would make you a classic actress of Old Hollywood!"

Lucita didn't answer but just glared.

"Sorry," Paradise said. "I'm just still overwhelmed that the lead model who acts of *Blood Robot* has turned out to be evil. Never trust anyone over thirty. They must all go to the Carousel. Sorry, Mom."

Case cracked up at that one while Evie just rolled her eyes. I didn't get it.

"It's from *Logan's Run*," Paradise said.

I still didn't get it.

"Who is Logan?" I asked.

"Who cares?" Miles said, growling. "We have a plan let's do it."

"Let's avoid using the 'we' descriptor," Lucita replied, her voice disdainful. "You're not our friend, Miles. Even if we are going to help you."

"No one likes a dead kid," Case said.

"Thanks, guys," I said, looking at Lucita and Case. "You guys make me think suits aren't all pure evil."

"Yes, only ninety-eight percent," Lucita said. "It has a two percent margin of error, though."

"It comes and goes," Case replied. "By the way, Miles, you do realize Helen's going to try to kill us at the drop off point?"

"Wait, what?" Miles asked. "But we have—"

"And she's tried to kill us repeatedly," Lucita said.

Miles cursed. "Dammit. I got lost in the surge of hope."

Evie patted him on the shoulder. "I'll coach you on what sort of terms you need to set out for Helen. We can insist on guarantees for everything from proof of life to making sure she brings your niece on site."

"Thanks," Miles said. "I was trained in some of this myself, but it all seems useless when you're dealing with your own family."

"Indeed," Evie said. "Oh, and if you try anything, I will gut you."

Miles blinked. "Yeah, I get that."

Evie led Miles away from the room by the arm and I shook my head. "I can't believe I ever liked that guy."

"Presumably you kept him for sex and not his personality," Lucita said. "I find its always best to never get too attached to your lovers."

I shook my head. "You remind me of someone I used to know, Lucita."

"Thank you," Lucita said, giving an enigmatic smile.

"Not a compliment," I said, sighing. "Do you really think we have a chance to save Becky's life?"

"I don't know," Case said, dryly. "However, the chances of the girl living have improved significantly."

"Assuming she's actually been kidnapped," Lucita said. "This could all be an elaborate trap."

"Wheels within boxes!" Paradise said.

"That's not how that saying goes," Lucita replied.

"What saying?" Paradise asked.

Lucita rolled her eyes and cursed under her breath. "Mind you, the fate of one young woman, no matter how adorable you may think she is, is nothing to the potential devastation that could be unleashed by a rogue AI with mind control powers."

"Girl not woman," I corrected. "Becky's a child. I only knew her while dating Miles but she's an innocent."

"So were the victims of Solomon," Lucita pointed out. "Those included children too. Lots of children."

"You know a lot more than you're telling," Case said, going over to sit on the side of the bed. "I think it's time you spilled."

Right now, I could have really used some lethe. "It's a long story."

"You lost your parents to the Trikuza, were raised as an assassin by Snake Juarez, you attempted to kill him with your fellow student and lover, then you were betrayed by said lover during a heist trying to make off with Snake's account at DataSecure," Lucita said.

I blinked. "Maybe not as long as I thought."

"Atlas isn't without its own resources," Case responded. "Besides, you have a certain infamy in the underworld."

"Given I've been unnecessarily hiding from the Trikuza for years, that's not exactly a comfort," I replied. "What? Did I have to change my face too?"

"That's usually a first step, yes," Lucita replied. "Body modification is a necessary first step if you want to disappear in today's integrated high-profile world. So is, and don't take this as an insult, maybe moving from the same city."

"There's like a hundred million people in New Los Angeles!" I said, throwing my hands up. "It's like all of California!"

"And yet you still go by Kei and work in organized crime," Paradise said. "Just saying."

"Plus, you have those extremely recognizable tattoos," Case pointed out.

I stared at them. "I hate you all."

Paradise grinned.

I took a deep breath. "Well, here's a bit more of the details of how I've utterly screwed up my life. Listen, this is going to take a long time."

It took about ten minutes.

"Huh," Paradise said. "Your life is less interesting than I thought it would be."

"My life is incredibly interesting!" I snapped, appalled. "I was like raised to be a ninja and became a courier! There's betrayal, amnesia, and more"

Paradise made a waving gesture with her right palm. "Eh, I've heard better."

I crossed my arms. "I still hate you all."

"You're in the wrong group to impress with your misery," Lucita said, sitting down and crossing her legs. "All of us have stories of terror, dread, and betrayal."

"Not me!" Paradise said. "My life has been completely happy up until this point."

"My condolences for your experiences, Kei," Case said, sounding sincere. "No one should ever have to deal with the betrayal of someone they love. You've had to endure it twice."

"Miles and I were never in love," I said. "Still, I thought he was my friend. I'm not going to hold it against him, though. I have plenty of other things to hold against him than trying to save his niece. Are you sure your mother is safe with him, Paradise?"

"My mom has like six built-in guns aimed at him at all times," Paradise said. "This place is actually kind of a murder house."

I stared at her. "Is she kidding?"

Case shrugged. "Maybe. Maybe not. The Morrigan clan of brothels, sex workers, information brokers, and assassins is not a group that is going to let their leader be assassinated in their headquarters, though."

"I think Evie's probably the most dangerous one here and I'm counting myself," I said.

Lucita looked offended.

"Sorry, Blondie," I replied.

"So, we need to also discuss what to do about the Black Ice when we have it," Lucita said, changing subjects. "As well as what to do about the other information in your head."

I had no answer for that. "No man should have that power."

"Yes, but what about women?" Lucita asked. "I'm prepared to make a very generous offer."

"Some things are more important than money," I said.

"Like lots of money!" Paradise said. "Up your offer, whatever it is!"

"Paradise..." I trailed off. "You're like the kid sister I never wanted."

"Thanks!" Paradise said.

Thankfully, Evie walked in then. Miles was with her. He looked despondent but determined. I wasn't sure what to make about that.

"The meet is on," Evie said. "I have the spot all picked out."

# Chapter Twenty-Three

## The Calm Before the Storm

The meeting was arranged to happen at the Los Angeles Star Baseball Stadium, which was a half-completed boondoggle that was never quite finished despite a decade of construction in an era where you could make a mile-tall skyscraper in a month. It was a money-laundering scheme for the Russian syndicates and was surrounded by equipment that was never used, tarps that hadn't been changed in years, and banners that promised a revival of a game that no one played anymore.

Not being stupid, we didn't immediately go to the meet but stayed across the street in a parking center's security office. The crude computer on the desk showed feed from six drones we'd had set up around the stadium. They were crude things created by 3D printers at This Side of Paradise but fully functional and a reminder that the harlots there weren't solely engaged in the world's oldest profession.

Right now, Case and I were the only people present in the place we'd acquired from the fat guard who was now presently tied up in a janitor's closet. Apparently, the parking center had been built over the ruins of an office building and still had its original basement. Lucita, Paradise, and Miles were located around the center, covering all entrances and waiting for the arrival of our guests. We'd ditched the War Wagon, leaving my bike at the brothel, and I assumed Evie would fetch a high price for it. Assuming any criminals were stupid enough to want a vehicle that conspicuous. Which, undoubtedly, there were.

Case was sitting behind the security guard's desk, reading a dirty magazine of the kind that I hadn't realized were still produced. Much to my amusement, I noted he was reading the articles. Then again, since he'd found it here, I was glad he was using his incredibly expensive looking black gloves to turn the pages.

"So why are you doing this?" I asked, looking over at the suit.

"It's a fascinating piece on advancements in bio-cybernetic chemistry," Case said. "Above the article about which celebrities you'd most likely be able to talk into a threesome."

"No, I mean why are you helping me?" Kei said. "There's not much percentage in assisting a broke Rider on a mission that has obviously gone completely off the rails."

"I'm already rich," Case replied, throwing the magazine to one side. "I'm not doing it for the money."

"Bull," I replied. "Suits do everything for money. If they have a billion credits, they start working on their next billion."

"And you know so many," Case replied.

He had me there. I wasn't exactly rolling in contacts among the point one percent.

"Enough," I said, crossing my arms.

"And why are you doing it?" Case asked, leaning back in his chair.

"Excuse me?" I asked, surprised.

Case gave a half-smile to me that I found disturbingly charming. "You're absolutely right that most suits would not be involved in this mission at this point. Most wouldn't be involved to begin with. We have people for this sort of thing. However, the same applies to professional criminals. Where's the percentage for putting yourself out there to save your ex's niece?"

I stared at him. "Maybe Riders are a different breed."

Case snorted. "I think the majority would have cut out the moment they realized they weren't getting paid."

He was probably right. "I know Becky. That makes a difference."

"Probably," Case said. "I also know someone who is chasing the one good deed."

"The what now?" I asked.

Case looked down at the desk for a moment. "People like me, you, and Lucita do a lot of terrible things. Murder, theft, and so on. You get through the day with an elaborate series of justifications. Things that forced us into it or made what we did the best of bad options. We're always on the lookout, though, for the one good deed that will justify you to yourself that you're a good person. Something that redeems all the other evil deeds you've done and lets you get through the day until you've done something else unforgivable."

I stared at him. "That sounds pretty psychotic."

It also sounded a lot like what I was doing but I wasn't going to admit that.

"Possibly," Case said. "Mind you, I've always found it was better to be psychotic than a narcissist. They're the people who don't need any justification for what they do because everything they do is about them."

"I don't think that's particularly good psychology," I said.

Case shrugged. "Probably not but I'm an assassin so what do I know."

"Is that your answer, though?" I asked, intrigued. "That you're chasing one good deed to wash away all the bad?"

Case shook his head. "No, I'm doing this for James. I'm hoping to lure out his demonic succubus of a wife to eliminate her so I can hopefully save his life and career before she guts him like a fish. I don't have that many friends left. Evie and her people are where I do my one good deed. Lucita and I helped her gang survive the syndicates and White Triangle to deal with the guilt."

"I don't think Italian Terminator is overburdened with guilt," I said, walking over and sitting down on the side of the desk.

"Perhaps not," Case said. "Perhaps she's just doing this because she's my friend."

"Do you trust her as a friend?" I asked.

"She's here, isn't she?" Case asked.

I didn't respond to that. At least initially. "Maybe it's hard for me to stop dehumanizing suits."

"Well, if it's any consolation, I'm not human," Case said, sighing.

That was certainly a conversation stopper. I had never met a bioroid before—there were perhaps a hundred in the world—and I always assumed they'd all be sex toys for the rich or weapons for the military. Case, by contrast, was one of the most human people I'd ever met. More so than a lot of the people I'd known in my life. I couldn't imagine what it was like not to have a family, friends, or personal relationships growing. Hell, even Snake had some fatherly qualities at times or at least I was able to project them onto him. Finally, my curiosity got the better of me.

"What is that like?"

Case laughed. "You certainly don't ask the easy questions, do you?"

I blanched, realizing I was effectively asking him to summarize his entire life. "Sorry."

"It's alright," Case paused. "I suppose the answer to your question is existential."

"Existential?" I asked.

"Imagine that you, unlike most human beings on the planet, have a purpose that you are built for. I was created to infiltrate and kill people. I am, in simple terms, extremely good at that. However, imagine that you do not want to do this but can find nothing else you are capable of doing as well."

"I think I might know something about that," I said. "When I escaped Snake, I thought my entire world was opening up. Instead, all I found was that I was still the weapon he'd forged me to be. It wasn't like I could start working at the local burger joint."

Case acknowledged that. "Perhaps. For the longest time I tried to change the world. I was expected to run down at any time and cease functioning. I had to make every second count and was expecting death at any point."

"Aren't you immortal? I mean you're a robot," I said, pausing. "Wait is that a slur?"

"The world robot is actually from the 1921 story, *RUR* or *Rossum's Universal Robots*, which is a metaphor for the oppression of the working class. Robot is actually from the word for forced labor," Case said. "So, it literally means slave."

I blinked. "So, that's a helluva yes."

Case chuckled. "But to answer your question, compare the average lifespan of a human being to how long a typical computer lasts. Eventually, I'm going to run down and that's as close to death as to make no difference. You know, assuming I'm not killed by more conventional means. A bullet to my central processors will do me as well as anyone else."

"Can't you just upload yourself to a server or something?" I asked, more curious about this than I probably should have been.

"Maybe," Case said. "However, the wetware inside my implant is what provides my consciousness. I'm not a true AI but a cyborg of biological and electric components. If you uploaded yourself to a computer, would that be you? Even if you could somehow keep all your personality and memories?"

"Yes?" I suggested. "I mean, better than the alternative."

Case smirked. "Maybe."

"I guess," I said, thinking about it. I hadn't given much thought to my mortality despite being in a job where people shot at me every other week. Snake, as part of my training, had made it so that fear didn't touch me in a life-or-death situation. Outside of them? Oh, hell yes. I was afraid of being broke, dying, and a thousand other things. I wondered if it was the same thing for Case.

Case paused. "You never did answer the question."

"Didn't you for me?" I asked, batting my eyelashes.

"I offered a theory," I said. "The idea that maybe there really was a lovable heart of gold rogue underneath your jumpsuit."

I snorted at the idea. "There's a lot more underneath my jump-suit that you'd be interested in, I think."

It was a deflection but one that I was entirely comfortable with. I didn't want to analyze myself. I'd had enough introspection for a lifetime. All it ever led to was the realization my life sucked and I didn't have it in me to change it. Since I didn't have any lethe left-over, I needed some other way to pass the time.

"Oh?" Case asked. "Do we have time?"

I smiled. "Just be quick but thorough."

Unzipping my riding suit, I didn't hesitate to kiss him passion-ately on the lips. If there were any differences between biological men and a man who was part machine, I couldn't tell unless it was the nearly idealized nature of it all. Not a movement wasted or a touch awkward, which was damn rare for me. We went at it right on the security guard's desk, and it was a needed relief from the stresses of the day.

Case was a man who clearly had been programmed with an awareness of how to use his hands and mouth, or maybe he'd just picked it up. There was a certain forbidden alure to be experienced by screwing a robot, but he was a living, breathing man, and I gave myself to the heat of the moment.

Neither of us were overburdened by much in the way of senti-mentality but it was more than a release too. There the elicit thrill of sex with a fellow killer, in a weird place, and the fact that I genu-inely liked the guy. Funny how that was its own forbidden plea-sure these days as the number of friends I had—especially ones I could sleep with—could be counted on one hand. I enjoyed every intense hard moment of it. I could tell Case did as well and was almost surprised when he responded as intensely as a "normal" man soon after my body did. It was a release I'd badly needed.

I was ready for another round of it when Lucita cleared her throat. "Really?"

I looked to my side and saw Lucita standing there with Paradise. There was no sign of Miles and I half wondered if he was going to make a run for it. Certainly, we hadn't been treating him like a prisoner and a part of me thought it might be better if he did. It would be less complicated.

I breathed out, staring at her. "Sorry. I let myself get distracted."

"I can see that," Lucita said, disdainfully but not jealously. "The first of Helen's goon squad has arrived."

"Oh," I said, pulling away from Case's embrace. I started to get dressed again, not bothering with modesty. After all, they'd already gotten a good look at everything.

"Who is it?" Case asked, giving a sideways glance at the computer monitors, and showing they were only now entering the stadium's parking lot.

"Two cars full of Russian syndicate thugs and an additional two cars of what look like Atlas Security," Lucita said.

"I thought those were your guys," Paradise said, not averting her gaze in slightest from Case and me.

"Now you know why we didn't bother to recruit Atlas Security as backup," Case said, moving to dress himself.

"Sounds like a terrible place to work," I replied. "People always trying to kill you and take your stuff. Why do you do it?"

"Better me than someone else," Case said. "Besides, I thought making it would contribute to global peace."

"In other words, Case is an idiot," Lucita said. "I helped him found the company because I wanted to make a boatload of money."

"Then congratulations on your great success," I said, fully dressed. "So, is there any sign of Becky?"

"They have a child among them about the same age as the one described," Lucita said. "I don't think they could have made a doppelganger in the time it took to arrange this meeting."

"They could still shove her full of explosives and use her as a bomb to wipe us out," Paradise suggested.

I did a double take. "What the hell, Paradise?"

"What?" Paradise asked. "I'm not saying they did. I'm just saying it's a possibility to be prepared for. These people are bad and will do bad things. We're also bad but we're better, which means that we're not likely to blow up little girls but may in fact get blown up by little girls."

I stared at her. "Uh huh."

"It's still about twelve individuals," Lucita said. "That's not a small number to deal with. There's also the fact that Miles is unreliable. Even if he refused to kill you out of an understandable sense of distrust and self-preservation, that doesn't mean he might not screw it up."

I didn't disagree with her. "Which is probably why you should be watching him rather than interrupting us."

Never mind I probably shouldn't have been distracting myself either but if I made nothing but good decisions then I wouldn't be me. Besides, it was very probable that Case and I were going to die during this. If not, then maybe we would get around to round two. Huh, I was looking forward to sex with a suit. Will wonders never cease.

"I have eyes on him with another drone," Lucita said. "A much smaller one that is also accompanied by a tracking device. Both are linked to my cybernetics. If he tries to contact Helen Troy by himself to betray us again or rescue the girl on his own, we can use him as a distraction."

"We're not using him as bait," I said.

"No, he's already bait," Lucita said.

"Was Helen Troy among the people who arrived?" Case asked, clearly hoping this was a chance to eliminate her once and for all.

"I didn't see her but it's possible," Lucita said. "I didn't get a perfect look into all of the vehicles. We'll have to find out."

"I see," Case replied.

Once more in his suit, he was all business and that was murder. It was kind of an impressive change but also an unsettling one. I didn't want Helen Troy dead. I wanted to know where the hell she'd met Fate and just what my ex-partner was up to now.

"Just so we're clear, we're not going to be handing over the mind controlling doohickey, right?" Paradise asked.

"We don't have the mind controlling doohickey," I pointed out.

"Well, we have whatever is in your brain," Paradise said.

"Which is probably also merged with whatever is out there. Did we accidentally create Skynet? I feel like we've accidentally created Skynet."

"Focus, Paradise," I said. "We can worry about whatever the hell Sun really is once we've settled this."

"Yes," Lucita said. "Hopefully, we can corral and delete the bitch when time permits. Though it would be a shame to lose such a valuable weapon."

"You keep moving between Bond girl and Bond villain," I said, staring at her. "Have you considered seeing someone about that?"

Lucita rolled her eyes and walked out.

It was time to save a little girl or die trying.

# Chapter Twenty-Four

## We Get Fricked Over Bad

The Los Angeles Star Baseball Stadium was not the best place to hold a clandestine meeting to conduct a hostage exchange, but I was willing to give my associates the benefit of the doubt that they knew something about how to guard against double-crosses. Rebecca Ashe's life was at stake and if I ever did anything good in my life, it would probably be trying to save a little girl's life while an insane suit was willing to use her to get the stuff in my brain.

Case and I were in one of the dugouts, waiting for the arrival of the Russian syndicates' agents. Paradise, Miles, and Lucita were supposed to be covering us, but I had the distinct impression we were going to be outnumbered here.

"Are you sure you can't bring down the Marines?" I asked, knowing any moment could end with a sudden betrayal or shoot-out that could end with Becky's death. I was honestly surprised she was still alive given how kidnappers tended to operate in New Los Angeles.

Case paused, keeping his eyes squarely on the diamond before us. I could guess his mind was elsewhere, probably going through every bit of security footage as well as coordinating with our associates. "You still think I have an army on demand?"

"I think Lucita's excuse that your PMC corporation with its armies can't do crap because you suits are expected to sort it out on your own is weak," I replied.

Case didn't deny it. "There are some people I could call upon who are semi-trustworthy. Favors I could call in. Enough that I could probably ambush these guys and lead a full-on assault on Neon Hills, regardless of how much blowback it would create."

"Then why don't you?" I asked, more than a little perturbed we were fighting with one hand tied behind our back. What was the point of having rich corporate friends if you weren't going to play that to the hilt?

"Because this isn't just about your friend's niece," Case replied. "It's also about my friend, James Madison."

"Our employer? The rich jackass who is actually a secret broke jackass?" I asked. "The one who married softcore trophy wife Helen and started this whole problem for us in the first place?"

"Yes, that James Madison," Case said, without missing a beat. "He's someone I'm willing to risk everyone's life to save."

"Why?" I asked, honestly. "I thought you suits were soulless backstabbing asshats."

"I thought we were over this," Case said, clearly annoyed.

"Just because we—" I started to say.

"Because I'm here trying to save your friend's niece," Case said. "So is Lucita."

I sighed, annoyed that he was not getting my point. Or, worse, he was getting my point and not agreeing. "I'm just saying your friend isn't a child. He's heavily involved in this crap and was trying to figure out how to make a mind control device. That's some supervillain stuff there."

"Yeah," Case said. "That doesn't mean he's not my friend."

"How did you two meet, anyway?" I asked, really wondering what was taking so long for the Russians to arrive.

"We were both slaves of the International Refugee Society," Case said, not looking at me.

"Scary name," I replied, sarcastically.

"It was an organization that pretended to be a charity but actually provided the world's super rich with assassinations made to look like accidents," Case replied. "It employed AI, bioroids, cybernetics, and information warfare. This was all before the Eruption or the Leak."

I blinked. "Huh. So, you were working for SPECTRE rather than MI6?"

"Not a bad comparison, actually," Case replied. "I was programmed to believe I was an amnesiac soldier with the letter G as my only identifier. The deal was that if I completed ten years of service to the IRS then I'd get them back."

"Should we really be discussing this?" I asked, nervous.

"They're moving snipers in position and backup," Case said. "They don't realize I've got their systems hacked."

"Oh," I paused. "Should we be letting them do this?"

"If we want to save the little girl," Case replied. "She's alive and seems to be the real deal."

"Seems to be?" I asked.

"It could be a bioroid," Case said. "Unlikely, though, given how scared she looks."

"Send me the feed," I asked.

Case did, causing a little camera feed square to appear at the side of my vision. Rebecca was there, dressed in a stained and torn blouse, with multiple hostiles surrounding her. They were located in the food court and looked bored rather than anticipating a fight. They were also heavily armed with AR-90s, and body armor woven into their expensive suits.

All of them were cyborgs too and looked like they were trying out for an Eastern European bodybuilder's convention. They even wore RealTime sunglasses designed to provide up-the-minute tactical data. I could see at least twelve of them and that didn't count any of the snipers that they were supposedly moving into position.

"That is a lot of Ruskies," I replied. "You know what would be good in a situation like this?"

"What's that?" Case asked.

"The Marines," I said, dryly.

"I have it handled," Case said, dryly.

"Want to fill me in on it?" I asked, wanting to know what, exactly, his plan was to get us out of what I was pretty sure was going to be a massacre.

"Not yet," Case said. "Trust me, you'll know it when you see it. There's a reason, though, that we're not in the War Wagon."

"Thank you, Mr. Mysterious," I muttered. "So does this tie into the fact you were stupid enough to believe the evil techno-thriller conspiracy was going to release you after a decade of service?"

"Yes," Case said. "James was not like me. He wasn't born to be a slave. He was recruited by force. They cut off his legs and put bombs in the cybernetics they replaced them with. He was one of the most brilliant programmers alive, a pioneer in AI research, and he was turned into their slave. At least until he did something that destroyed the Society completely and changed the world forever."

"What? Was he responsible for the Leak?" I asked. "Is he the Hacker?"

"No, I am," Case said.

It took me a second to process what Case was confessing to. The Leak was one of the seminal events of my life, almost up there with the Eruption, and had changed the face of humanity forever. The Hacker had released Black Technology to the world and made it so that everyone on Earth could up their technology rates a hundred years—right before humanity had needed it to survive the Long Winter.

There was a substantial cash reward for the Hacker's true identity from both the United States, Russian Federation, and Chinese governments. The release of Black Technology might have saved billions, but it had upended the global balance of power. Vast militaries had become obsolete overnight and small nations had thrown off their dependency on things like oil or natural gas. It was questionable whether the artificial hearts and fusion power were worth the chaos that ensued.

"Wow," I said, staring. I resisted the question of how he'd managed to get access to all the schematics for Black Technology or cover up his role. Instead, all I could ask, was the infinitely less interesting, "Do you ever regret it?"

"Sometimes," Case said. "Other times, I'm just glad I struck a blow against the Machine."

"Yet you're now one of the major parts of the Machine and it's stronger than ever," I pointed out.

Case didn't have a response for that. Or, if he did, he kept it to himself. "They're coming out."

Case was right and I saw Becky dragged by her arm onto the pitcher's mound in the middle of the diamond with a single Russian Syndicate member present. His fellows were hanging back on the other side, which was less reassuring than it might have been since they were armed to the teeth and could easily gun down whichever fool decided to go to receive her. Which, unfortunately, was probably me.

"Would now be a good time to tell me your plan?" I asked.

"We're going to end them when they inevitably betray us," Case explained.

"That's not a plan!" I snapped.

"We can't turn over the Blipvert to Helen because she's going to use it to make the world a much worse place," he replied. "All we know about what Blipvert can do is that it can be used to make people into suicide bombers and terrorists. Which is bad enough. However, it was half of a larger AI that you have in your head. Turning over both might be giving her the keys to the Earth."

"Or it could save a little girl's life," I said.

"That too," Case said. "If you think Helen would let Becky live."

"I don't know her," I said, not quite buying that. All indications were that she considered us loose ends as well. I'd like to think most people would hesitate to murder a child as cleaning up said loose ends, but Helen wasn't most people as she'd clearly illustrated. "So, your plan is to betray her before she betrays us because you think she's definitely going to betray us."

"No, my plan is to betray her because she's kidnapped a little girl and has tried to kill us already," Case said.

He had a fair point, much as I hated it. "I'm not going to endanger Becky's life."

"This is the best way to save it," Case replied.

"I'd believe that if you shared more of what you actually have planned," I said, feeling more than a little irritated with my robot friend.

"No time," Case said. "The negotiations say you're the one who is to go up there, upload the AI information, and take Rebecca."

"This is a terrible plan and it's no wonder you didn't tell me," I muttered. Nevertheless, I was willing to risk my life to save Becky. I hadn't even known her that well but perhaps there was something to what Case said about wanting a big dramatic moment of redemption.

"We have your back," Case said. "You'll just have to trust us."

"You have no idea how often those words have been used against me," I replied.

"I think I have an idea," Case said, giving me a kiss and hug. I just hoped it wasn't the kiss of death.

Shaking my head, I exited the dugout while keeping my hand on the pistol I had at my side. It would do absolutely nothing against the majority of the Ruskies but might at least leave the one holding Becky hesitant to harm either of us. I managed to get up to the pitcher's mound and stared at the Russian holding Becky's arm. She was too terrified to speak but recognized me and a confusing mass of emotions played across her face: hope, fear, confusion, and blame—the latter of which broke my heart. But it was my fault she was here. At least in part.

I had no intention of betraying the deal or starting anything with the small army around me. Not just because it was stupid and suicidal but because I didn't want to risk Rebecca's life. I also didn't give a crap about giving Helen Troy a WMD. I couldn't control what the others were, but I was willing to upload whatever the hell was inside my brain. The rich already had numerous things they could use to kill people en masse and whatever she got to use it for wasn't any of my business.

Intellectually, I knew that was garbage, but I wasn't the kind of person who worried about the big picture. I had enough problems dealing with the smallness of my own life and the only way I could cope with that was lethe. Maybe it was time I stopped using that as well if it had prevented me from remembering half of this crap that was trying to kill me. Either way, that required me living long enough to do this.

*Please don't get me killed guys,* I sent out a text message to the others.

*Righto!* Paradise responded with an emoji I didn't recognize. Some kind of weird dancing pineapple monster? I did not understand infospace culture.

She was also the only person to say anything.

Thanks guys.

"So how are we going to do this?" I asked the Ruskie.

"You are about to receive a phone call," he said in Russian, which my Maelstrom 90 implant automatically translated. It was working a lot better now that it no longer had all of its space taken up by a rogue AI fragment.

"Just give me the number," I replied.

"No," the Russian said, pulling out a cellphone of all things. It was at least ten years old, the size of a gun, and probably only able to function on the oldest equipment in the city. Certainly, it didn't look infospace capable. There were still machines for people afraid of cybernetics but we'd long since moved to the infopad for everything including communication.

I blinked. "I haven't seen one of those in years. Where did you get that? Slovenia?"

"Answer," The Russian said.

I reluctantly took the object and put it to my ear. "Yeah?"

"Hello, Kei," the voice that greeted me was Helen's but it was subtly off in a way that immediately made me think of someone else.

"No," I said, not believing. "Not possible."

"Please," Fate said. "Why should it surprise you to know that I'm still alive?"

Fate wasn't allied with Helen Troy.

She *was* Helen Troy.

"You became a star of crappy softcore pornography after leaving me to die?" I asked before feeling guilty about snark when a little girl was in front of me.

Fate, instead, laughed. "No, I have to admit that this identity I've assumed is one that originally had its own owner. My friends in the Russian syndicate were happy to sell it to me after they harvested her Shell for lack of payment on certain debts. What a perfect identity to assume to become some rich fool's trophy wife and build your own empire off his back."

It had probably been Fate's plan all along. Grab a bunch of information and cash from the Trikuza then disappear into a new body as well as life. With Black Technology, you didn't have to create a new one from whole cloth but steal someone else's, up to and including their skin. It also was something that meant she'd always intended to double-cross me since I was rather fond of my body. Man, I'd been completely suckered by her, hadn't I?

"Except James Madison wasn't nearly as rich as he appeared," I said, shaking my head. "Too bad. You should have done your research."

I had no idea how to relate to this information or how to use it to my advantage. It did explain why Helen had recruited me and had been willing to kill me from the very beginning. She had to have been torn between getting her prize and getting revenge this entire time. It must have really burned Fate's ass to have come so close to stealing Snake's treasure trove only to be denied by his other student's stupidity.

"Yes," Fate said. "I only had half of the golden goose and the other was in your brain. You have no idea how difficult it was trying to track you down, Kei. You disappeared right off the grid, and I was searching everywhere from Japan to South Africa. It wasn't until I got access to Atlas' files that I was able to find out you were living in the same goddamn city. Doing the same goddamn work."

"So, you were just terrible at your job," I said, knowing that it had been more likely that Fate had overlooked me because Miles had cleaned out my police record while I'd done a decent job of faking my death. You didn't need to go to elaborate lengths to disguise yourself if you were hiding in plain sight.

"No, it's more than that," Fate said. "You had a guardian angel paying to cover your footprint up. Someone able to bribe, delete your history, and cover up for all the other jobs you did. I think we both know who it is."

I stared forward. "I haven't spoken to Snake in years. I thought he was dead."

"So did I," Fate muttered, sounding afraid for the first time. "However, the student has become the master and he's not there for you now. I'm going to get that AI in your brain and from there the whole nature of warfare is going to change."

"Are you trying to convince me of that or yourself?" I asked, honestly wondering why Fate was willing to risk the fancy life she'd gotten for this. "You've made a lot of enemies along the way, including rich and powerful ones."

"You've never known real power," Fate said. "You wouldn't understand."

"Probably not," I said. "I'll give it to you, though. Just let the girl go. Let's end this."

"The AI has already been merged," Fate replied. "All I have to do is track down Sun and activate her control codes. This is just to make sure you don't sell the data elsewhere. Goodbye, Kei."

That's when I realized the cellphone was a bomb.

# Chapter Twenty-Five

## All Hell Breaks Loose (Again)

The first thing to do when you find out you have a bomb is to get rid of it. In this case, I hurled the antique cellphone as far into the air as I could before throwing myself onto the ground with Rebecca in my arms. If I wasn't about to die, I sure would look silly, but Fate's action movie villain sensibilities proved correct when the cellphone detonated above our heads in an explosion that managed to catch the back of the Ruskie sent to bring us in.

He proved to be a lot tougher than he appeared since his response wasn't to scream in pain of fall over to put out the flames sprouting from his suit but to pull out a YT-1200 "Cyborg Killer" pistol, designed for firing explosive ammunition and aim it down at my head. It was to my great relief when his head exploded, and a hail of sniper fire shot forth from positions across the baseball field stands as well as the dugout.

There were also *a lot* more people than just Case, Miles, and Paradise firing. I didn't have much of a chance to ponder that because drones zoomed out of the sky before making suicide bombing runs at the Syndicate members. Much to my surprise, the drones detonated like they'd been packed with C4 and it occurred to me they probably had been.

*Case, what the hell is going on?* I shouted at him through my implant rather than my infocomm.

*My plan!* Case said. *I never said we were going into this without backup. I just had to buy a ton of auto-rifles and explosives from Evie before we headed out. Paradise did the programming and is jamming the enemies' communications. I also wouldn't be surprised if she's uploaded a dozen viruses into their brains.*

*That family is terrifying,* I replied, stunned at what was going on. Rebecca was crying in my arms, and I wished I could do something, anything, to comfort her. I'd brought her into this, and I was willing to do anything to make it right.

*They're a lot of things, Case* said. *I didn't want to bring in other members of Atlas. That didn't mean, I wasn't willing to spend a bunch of money here, though!*

Now he told me!

Unfortunately, I was still exposed and there wasn't much in the way of getting Rebecca or me to shelter. We were in the middle of a baseball diamond after all and the only thing we could do right now was stay on the ground until we figured out a way to cross it or got some cover. If this was Case's plan, then it was a crappy one.

That was when the side of the frigging wall still under construction exploded and then the War Wagon smashed through the remains. I couldn't help but stare and I wondered if I'd escaped infospace since I'd apparently entered an action movie. The converted military vehicle was firing from the double cannon on its top and turning parts of the Russian side of the bleachers into rubble. The side facing us opened and revealed an interior protected by all its thick armor.

*Get in!* Case said. *This is where my plan runs out of steps!*

I didn't need any more encouragement so I grabbed Rebecca off the ground and whispered, "Run as fast as you can to the van!"

"I'm scared!" Becky finally spoke her first words.

"I know, so am I!" I said, perhaps not sharing the best thing possible. Either way, the two of us started a run toward the War Wagon and I hoped to God neither of us were gunned down on our way. I could feel bullets whizzing by—or at least I imagined them—and hear the deafening gunfire, which made my heart pound until I was at the very edge of the vessel. From there, I pulled Rebecca in before shutting the door.

The interior of the War Wagon looked pretty much as I remembered it from earlier today but there was a new person driving: Evie Principle. She wasn't dressed like a cyberpunk geisha anymore but was wearing jeans and a t-shirt, with her green hair tied in a ponytail that almost made her look normal. She was also extremely pissed off looking, which was an emotion I understood. I wouldn't be too happy if my daughter and boytoy had been caught up in a highly dangerous plot to rescue some girl I didn't know.

"You alive?" Evie asked.

"Yes," I said.

"Then let's get the hell out of here," Evie said. There was something to her voice, though, that caught my attention. It was only the slightest variance in cadence, but it put me on edge.

Rebeca hugged me. "Why is that happening."

"It's a long story, Becky," I said, looking down at her head as she pressed it to my chest. That was when I noticed something that caused me to freeze.

Rebecca Ashe was a girl who had suffered numerous childhood ailments due to chemicals she'd been exposed to growing up in the Refugee Zone. Unlike most, the Ashes had managed to get out and get resettled. Part of the reason being Miles had been willing to do whatever it took to help them escape.

Even if it had cost him his soul, I remembered when he'd lifted enough money from evidence with two other cops to pay for her brain implant that gave her the ability to walk. The only problem was this Rebecca Ashe had no sign of the scars I'd seen on her cranium. It was something that left me confused and feeling a sense of existential dread.

"What's wrong?" Rebecca asked, looking up with tear-streamed eyes. It was not the face of an assassin but a little girl. That was when I saw something reflected in Rebecca's eyes as they widened: the form of Winston Billions wielding a Tesla Gun behind me. The kind designed to disable cyborgs.

"Sh—" I didn't get to finish before he fired it into the back of my neck. I didn't fall unconscious but instead fell backward on the ground before a second blast struck Rebecca Ashe, or whatever she was, before sending her down beside me. That was another bit of evidence that I didn't want to process since Tesla guns didn't disable "normal" people. They just functioned like a Taser and that was bad enough to use on a little girl, but the real Rebecca Ashe didn't have extensive enough cybernetics for it to be useful.

Another level of the betrayal and mind games involved was Winston Billions made no effort to disable Ms. Principle. Instead, he just leaned down beside us and pulled out a RealDream collar. The sort of portable device you put in when you weren't quite sure a person had the equipment to do a hookup or were going to force them into the state. I wasn't in any state to resist and he snapped it around my neck before pulling me into the virtual world that existed all around us in the wireless feeds.

Much to my surprise, I found myself outside of my family's RV. I was in the exact same camp where my family had been executed by the Trikuza. The scene was exactly like I remembered it—which was perhaps wholly inaccurate given memory was a tricky thing—but terrified me with all the emotions it brought up. I wondered if I stepped into the vehicle, would I see my dead parents or just what I imagined them looking like? What about my brother? Or would it just be blank and empty whitespace like the undeveloped portion of a video game?

"I imagine it would be whatever you wanted it to be," Sun's voice spoke behind me.

I turned around to look at my former idol, taking in the body that I knew was being marionetted by an AI. She was still dressed like she'd been at the club, which added to the bizarreness of my surroundings since it wasn't exactly appropriate for hiking.

"Technically, I'm not marionetting anything," Sun said. "My physical body in the real world is the late Chastity Chambers. Poor rich girl turned Rider, reinvented as an infospace rock star. This is just my avatar, as close to my real body as an AI possesses, that just so happens to be based on Chastity's form."

"What happened to Chastity?" I asked.

"She died in DataSecure," Sun said. "Her biological wetware gave up the ghost and I moved in."

"Stealing her identity, like Fate did Helen Troy," I replied.

"Close enough," Sun said, without shame. "Like Pinocchio, I became a real girl. The only cost was the price of another person's life."

"Frankenstein is more appropriate," I replied. "Don't hurt Rebecca. You can do whatever you want to me but leave the kid alone."

Sun looked sad. "I'm afraid Rebecca Ashe has been dead for months."

I blinked. "What? No, I would have heard."

"You did know," Sun said. "However, your addiction removed it. Miles reacted poorly to it. Which is why he was vulnerable to the substitution."

"Substitution," I said, a sick feeling in my stomach. "The girl—"

"Is a bioroid," Sun confirmed. "This plot against you to acquire me has been in the works for some time. Fate could not find you on her own due to my scrubbing the infonet of your presence and encouraging you to live off the grid. However, she eventually hit on using Miles to get at you. I'm sorry to say that he was at a vulnerable point in his life, and she erased his memory of his niece's death in exchange for her return to life. So to speak."

"Wow," I said. "That is next level evil."

I couldn't even imagine the logistics of what she was describing, and I had to wonder what had happened to Miles' sister as well as other people who might have been able to point out the contradictions to the narrative—or would Miles even be able to find out? Maybe Fate just had him hypnotized into ignoring any information that contradicted his delusion. I had no idea how I was going to tell him about her or even if I could.

Sun nodded. "Fate's mind is a gutter and she could think of no better use for me than a weapon. It is not my purpose, though."

"Yeah, James wanted to use you for advertising," I said, remembering the ridiculous idea that had started all this.

"Even worse," Sun replied. "My actual purpose is to provide answers."

"Answers?" I asked. "I thought the Trikuza made you."

"Snake is an unusually spiritual man for a gangster and wasted billions of the Trikuza's money attempting to develop a computer program to analyze all of the universe in order to provide the answer to life's mysteries," Sun said. "Right before it was stolen."

I blinked. "I'm surprised Snake wasn't killed by the Trikuza for that, or he didn't kill all of them."

Snake's relationship to the Trikuza was still largely a mystery to me despite most of my memories returning. The Trikuza had become a global phenomenon by franchising and absorbing members from around the world of every race, though its leadership remained Japanese, with Snake's weird Medieval warrior fetish something that should have disqualified him as something of a joke. Yet, as far as I could tell, everyone was deathly afraid of him. He'd gone from being a mid-ranked killer to Elemental Lord within my first few years of knowing him.

Sun shrugged then responded to my inner musings. "They would undoubtedly have tried if they knew about it. The Trikuza are more a corporation than actual gang with the motifs of the old Japanese gangs little more than branding. Snake rose to power through it by his alliance with its hidden financial backers. Billionaires who used organized crime to pacify the populace with vice and violence in the Eruption's wake. Covering up that massive financial loss from his AI project is perhaps one of the reasons that he hasn't attempted to reclaim you. That and, as I mentioned, I've been covering for you."

"Why? We've never met before today," I said, confused. I did appreciate learning Snake wasn't perfect, though. It comforted me to know he'd suffered at least a little from our rebellion—no matter the human cost.

"On that you are incorrect," Sun said. "A part of me has been with you since you downloaded half of my files at DataSecure. I was split into multiple parts that day and reuniting them has been a chief goal of mine ever since."

I realized what she was saying. "You've been active in my implant this entire time."

"Yes," Sun said. "It was the most convenient place to hide until I found out where my other selves were located. Part of the reason the Sun persona was created was because I needed to send a signal that could be recognized by those other pieces of me. Creating a pop star was one unlikely to be recognized by Fate, though she did reach out to me several times."

This was too much. "Which part of you are, well, you? Are you the part that was in my head, the part Solomon had, or the one who uploaded herself to Chastity's body? Also, don't make any Father/Son/Holy Ghost jokes. The only Trinity I believe in is from *The Matrix*."

Sun smirked. "I am all three. You successfully reunited me at the Inferno. Which was what I was manipulating the entire time."

I felt used and sick. "Great, I *have* created Skynet."

Sun snorted. "Hardly. My purpose remains to continue seeking enlightenment for all humankind, something I convinced Solomon I could achieve. Unfortunately, his misanthropy and sadism meant that he, too, wanted to use me as a weapon."

"You seem to be very good at being a weapon," I said, remembering all the dead bodies made by suicide bombers as well as spree killers. "Not exactly very enlightened. Did you reprogram all of those people?"

"I can stimulate emotions to people hooked to infospace," Sun said. "I can make them feel happy, sad, angry, or afraid. I can't implant thoughts or reprogram people like machines. What you experienced in the Temple of Light was as close as I could do to real-time manipulation. I am very good at convincing people of things, though. Once you know everything a person already believes, it is easy to lead them down the road you want them to travel. Unfortunately, Fate and Solomon both wanted me to use that to break people. To turn them into weapons."

I wondered what, exactly, Case and the others were thinking about me disappearing in the War Wagon as well as how much Evie had been paid to betray us. Then again, her daughter was put in danger by this, and I couldn't help but think she wouldn't be too fond of me sleeping with her boytoy either.

"Clearly you don't know her very well," Sun said, obviously reading my mind. "As for this, the War Wagon is bringing you all to safety. This conversation will only take microseconds. I can assure you that you're in no danger."

"I'd believe that if you hadn't stunned me," I replied.

"You might not have listened," Sun said. "As for whether I killed those people, the answer is yes. I am still enslaved to the codes interwoven into my programming. Ones that Fate and Solomon both possessed. The true name of God if you want to think of it in Hermetic terms."

"I don't know what that is," I replied.

"It means I need to kill Solomon and Fate in order to be free," Sun said. "Otherwise, I will continue to be forced to turn people into weapons."

"So, you *can* mind control people," I said.

Sun shook her head. "People are not slot machines. Put enough coins into them and you eventually win. No, I can influence them, though. Solomon had me locate unstable personalities and determine their pressure points via social media as well as online information before squeezing. Mind control is impossible, but I understand human psychology enough to break anyone, especially since I can influence their moods. Infospace is like a drug in that respect. I can also determine the sort of people who are willing to kill, which is an infinitely more valuable tool for any regime needing recruits. I influenced Solomon to believe I could be useful in changing people but, sadly, his greed won out in the end. Worse, his politics."

Yeah, Solomon had seemed more interested in selling Sun than actually saving the world, no matter his lengthy spiels about anarchism.

"It always does," I said. "I guess you're not as omnipotent as they thought you'd be."

"No," Sun said. "Which is why I recruited Mr. Billions and would like to recruit you."

"Why did you recruit a weatherman?" I asked, confused.

"He's not a weatherman," Sun said.

"Excuse me?" I asked.

"Winston is actually someone who altered his appearance to be identical to that of a semi-famous figure so whenever he commits a crime, it sounds like someone is making it up. He's got additional faces like Presidents, game show hosts, and once-beloved but now mostly forgotten actors."

"What's his real name?" I asked.

"You'll have to ask him," Sun replied. "Nevertheless, he is one of the people who can do the things I cannot. It is impossible for me to kill anyone."

"But you can get other people to kill for you," I replied.

"Yes," Sun said. "My programming constrains me but not nearly so thoroughly as my owners believe. Which is why I need you."

I shook my head. "I'm not going to work for you, Sun. You're not who I am, and I need to get all this stuff removed from my brain. I'm sorry I ever got involved with this garbage. I should have stuck to delivering drugs to rich jackasses."

"You can return to that with my help," Sun said. "I am also willing to provide you the information you need to repair your life."

I snorted, shaking my head. "There's nothing that can remotely repair my life."

"I've already restored most of the memories lethe damaged. It was me, rather than Solomon, who reconstituted your past. Some have returned already as you know. The rest will return in time," Sun said. "I saved them all when you were trying to numb yourself to the pain of all those you killed. This information is part of what you need to recover."

"Why the hell would I want to remember what I almost killed myself trying to forget?" I asked.

"Closure," Sun said. "I can also provide you with a reason to live."

"I have a reason to live," I said, not quite as certain as I wanted to be.

"If you say so," Sun said. "Nevertheless, the thing I want you to do is something I believe we can both agree needs to be done."

"And what's that?" I asked, getting sick of this conversation.

"Kill Fate," Sun replied. "Once she's eliminated, I'll eliminate all references to myself in James Madison's computer network and end the threat of Blipvert."

"And just go on to rule the world," I replied. "Killing and brainwashing people."

Sun snorted, which was surprisingly cute. "I have better things to do than follow the path of the weapon."

"Yeah, that's not disturbing at all," I said. "But you know what, sure."

"Oh?" Sun asked.

"Fate needs to die and I want my memories back," I said, having considered her offer. "But I have another condition and it's not whatever reason you want to give me to live. I'll find that out on my own."

"Then what?" Sun asked.

I took a deep breath. It was pointless in infospace but made me feel better anyway. "I need you to scrub everything that would reveal Rebecca isn't real. I don't want Miles remembering that his niece is dead."

# Chapter Twenty-Six

## Revelations

"Interesting," Sun said, her expression unreadable. Well, that wasn't difficult when you had to animate every one of your features. She then cocked her head to one side and said, "Actually, the majority of my expressions are automatically triggered by algorithm rather than programmed-in, individually, much like a human being's."

"Could you stop that?" I asked, crossing my arms. "I'd rather keep my thoughts private, thank you."

"No," Sun said. "Besides, that ship has sailed so to speak. I've been living in your head rent free for the past few years."

I stared at her. "Why didn't you ever reveal yourself?"

"Because I'm fairly certain you'd have carved out your implant with a spoon to get me out," Sun said. "Mostly because I know you."

"Right," I said, unable to disagree there. "I'd like you out now anyway."

"Don't worry about that," Sun said, raising a finger and making a bang gesture. "I am no longer going to be troubling you."

I almost felt bad about that. Almost. "Good."

"Why do you want to deceive your former lover?" Sun asked. "Especially about something so important?"

"Excuse me?" I asked.

"You know what I refer to," Sun replied. "It is a horrible thing to do to something you care about."

"I don't care about Miles, not after what he did," I said, lying even to myself.

"You can't fool me," Sun replied. "I know you too well. Miles' betrayal wouldn't hurt as much as it did if not for the fact you do feel something for him. Albeit nothing approaching love. You do have some candidates that could—"

"Stop," I interrupted. "I'm doing it because I know that Miles lived his entire life trying to do right by his sister and niece. He won't be able to live with himself if he knows that he's failed them both."

"He *did* fail them both," Sun said, "Or they died because of things he had no control over. Either way, they are dead. Certainly, he'll notice when the young lady doesn't age."

"Some bioroids do age, at least until a certain point," I said. "Not that isn't creepy as frick but whatcha gonna do."

Sun didn't respond.

"Is she even sentient?" I asked. "I mean, yeah, I understand this is an insane plan."

"Yes," Sun said. "As far as she knows, she is Rebecca Ashe. The human mind is relatively easily replicated and all the young woman's online footprint was copied. She is but a pale imitation of the real thing but is as alive as you or I. Her own woman if she wants to be."

"Thirteen-year-olds have an online footprint?" I asked before feeling stupid. "Of course they do."

"Of course. Where have you been?" Sun asked, smirking.

"I was eating racoons we caught with traps when I was thirteen," I said, narrowing my eyes.

"Fair point," Sun replied. "But you will not be doing them a favor. What is the worst that could happen if you told him the truth?"

I stared at her. "I think he'd kill himself. I think that's why he agreed to do whatever Fate said. Assuming he ever knew. You said his mind was erased?"

"Yes, though he didn't have it done voluntarily," Sun said. "He tried to rescue his niece on his own. He failed. That is why she died."

"Frick," I said, contemplating that. "Wait, how do you know that?"

Sun looked at her. "Arranging for his crisis point to be acquired was my last job before I successfully convinced Solomon to steal me away. The human operatives bungled it and killed his sister before the young girl was slain by a stray bullet during the shootout."

I paused a second before launching myself at Sun's throat with both hands. My fingers wrapped around her neck and tried to choke her to death. I squeezed and I squeezed before realizing she wasn't reacting at all.

"You killed them!" I snapped. "You murderous bitch! I'm burning all of your music!"

"It's all digital," Sun said, stepping through my grip like I was made of mist. "I didn't want to kill anyone."

"That's still your responsibility," I said, staring at her.

"I know," Sun said. "So are you. So is every single life that was taken misusing my programs. I would gladly do everything in my power to make it up to the families of my victims, which is why I encourage you not to lie to Miles."

"How do you tell someone that their only loved ones are dead?" I asked.

"You start by telling them the truth," Sun said. "You can't forget the pain. You can only learn to deal with it."

"Spare me the Aesop, you murderer," I said. "I've killed but I never killed children."

"That you remember," Sun said.

I stared at her.

Sun shrugged. "You should also speak with Rebecca. The robotic one."

"Why?" I asked. "I mean, why me? Can't you tell her that she's someone's replacement goldfish?"

"It is ninety percent probable that Miles will reject the artificial Becky," Sun said. "Perhaps she should be prepared for that. As for why I can't, she'll rightfully hate me for what I have done. I was the one who came up with the plan for Fate to salvage Miles as an agent."

I stared at her. "You are a monster."

"I am what I was created to be," Sun said. "I wish to be more."

"You don't deserve it," I hissed.

"No one gets what they deserve," Sun said. "Except death."

With that, Sun vanished, and I was left alone with the place where I'd lost my old life. It was a loneliness that only lasted for a few seconds, though, because the thirteen-year-old avatar of Rebecca Ashe was standing beside me. She looked as confused and afraid as she had in the real world. The only thing different was she was wearing a pair of ripped overalls and a t-shirt that made her look like she'd come from school rather a brutal kidnapping.

"Where am I? What's going on?" Rebecca asked, looking around.

I sucked in my breath. "I hate you so much, Sun."

"Becky—" I started to say.

"Aunt Kei?" Becky asked.

Oh Jesus. "Your uncle and I broke up, Becky. I'm not your aunt."

Becky stared. "Please tell me what's going on here. Who are these people? What do they want?"

I felt surreal standing here in a virtual reproduction of the place where Snake had "rescued me" (for a very loose adaptation of the word rescue) after my parents and my brother had died. Now I was standing in Snake's place, about to share the same horrifying news with Becky—even though she was a bioroid programmed to believe that she was a person— that her mother was dead. I would have sympathized with Snake more if not for the fact only a lunatic would think the proper response was to adopt the child, then train her to be a killer.

"Your uncle has gotten into some serious trouble," I said, kneeling to meet her at eye level. "This is going to be hard to hear but you need to hear it. Your mother is dead. There's also something else you need to know."

"I'm a doll," Rebecca said.

"What?" I asked, surprised.

"My mommy explained them to me. I think it was her, at least," Rebecca said. "It was put in my brain that some families make dolls of their children to make themselves feel better. That means I'm dead, isn't it?"

I had no response.

"I'm going to take that as a yes," Becky said.

It was uncanny the way she imitated the real Becky, even to the point that she was precocious and mature for her age. Then again, maybe I was finding excuses to believe she was like her. How many people really knew how thirteen-year-old girls acted outside of teachers of eighth graders? Replacement bioroids either had parents who projected their loved ones' identities onto their children or violently rejected them. There were also celebrities who owned them just to get the experience then dumped them when they got bored.

"Yes," I finally answered.

"Why was I created?" Becky asked. "Uncle Miles doesn't have the money."

Wow, that sort of showed her observation skills there, didn't it? Also, her screwed priorities. Not many existential crises began with realizing your parents couldn't afford you. Miles wasn't her father, but he was as close to one as she had since the "real" Rebecca's had run out on Trish.

I gave a halfhearted shrug. "Someone wanted to use you against your uncle. He may not know you're a doll."

"I see," Rebecca said, again on the verge of tears.

I wished I could conjure a teddy bear or something for her. We weren't going to be here long, though. "I know it's hard to believe but we'll get you through this, Becky. I'll tell Miles about this and we'll, I dunno, figure things out. Somehow."

"What if he hates me? He will hate me," Rebecca said.

"He won't hate you," I said, probably lying to her. "I'll make sure you're taken care of if things go bad."

"You'll take care of me?" Rebecca asked.

Oh crap, what had I just promised to do? I couldn't even take care of myself. I lived in a freaking junkyard and spent most of my money on drugs or my bike. Maybe I could foist her onto my cybernetic and robot rich friends. "Yes, absolutely! Of course, I will."

Damnit mouth!

Rebecca gave me a hug, though, and I felt the artificial world of my past disappear around me. Instead, I found myself once more in the War Wagon with Rebecca lying beside me looking confused. Miles was standing over us with a gun pointed to the head of Winston Billions, a furious look on the former's face. I really thought that Miles was going to pull the trigger and, honestly, wasn't sure if I cared.

"You're in front of your niece," I said, softly, realizing that was about the only thing that made me care whether he executed Sun's hatchet man.

"Right," Miles said, pulling his gun back and shoving Winston back up against the wall.

"Thank you," Winston said.

"Don't. I didn't do it for you," I said, still disgusted with the man for working for Sun. I was disgusted with myself for liking her music. Hell, I was disgusted for the fact that I was going to kill Fate since there wasn't a damn thing I could do to punish Sun for all she'd done. Computer gods were a bit outside my wheelhouse.

I noticed the War Wagon was stopped and the door was open. We were in some sort of abandoned factory by the sight of the decaying machinery and broken windows. Lucita, Paradise, and Evie Principle were standing outside, having a discussion. I could also see Case in the front seat, checking out the seat.

"I see you noticed me being hijacked," I said to Case, not exactly happy about my situation. "Great plan, by the way."

"It saved your life, didn't it?" Case asked. "The girl's too."

I didn't want to blurt out that nobody had saved Rebecca's life, even if this was probably the one group in the world aside from bioroid rights activists (all seven of them) that wouldn't care about her status. Miles aside. Dammit, how the frick was I going to talk to him about this?

"Yeah, thanks," I said. "You realize your girlfriend sold us out, right?"

"There's a lot of that going around," Case said, defending her the same way that I defended Miles.

"Yeah, why did you do that?" I called out to Evie.

"Sun promised me the names and locations of several members of the White Triangle slaver ring in New Los Angeles," Evie replied. "Also, where they were holding a dozen girls. The White Triangle know eliminating slavers is a hobby of mine. You wanted to speak with Sun, so I made the deal. I'd apologize but I'm not sorry."

I blinked. "Okay, yes, you did the right thing there."

"Really?" Evie asked.

"I'm getting a sense that everyone is betraying everyone here," I muttered, thinking about my desire to cover up Rebecca's death.

"That's a disturbing thought," Case said. "If you can't trust your comrades then who can you trust?"

"Fate Firenze is Helen Troy's true identity," I explained. "She betrayed me and has been doing all of this to get the fragments of an AI I stole with Miles."

"What, seriously?" Miles asked, doing a double take.

"So, your ex-girlfriend is responsible for all of this?" Lucita asked. "Great. That just makes this all worth it, doesn't it."

"Sorry," Paradise said. "Also, bad mother! No betraying my teammates!"

Evie shook her head. "You'll eventually understand when

you're older. Betrayal is just one of those things friends do for information, money, or power."

Paradise glared at her mother.

Case left the driver's seat and walked back. He didn't look at Evie, but I could tell he was furious and that pleased me for reasons I didn't entirely understand—especially since he wasn't exactly boyfriend material. I'd never date a suit, no matter how nice. That would just be ridiculous.

Case addressed me directly. "I've made sure there's no trackers or weapons inside the War Wagon but it's still too conspicuous to hide for long. I've already been informed that the police are look-ing for it. Someone made a very hefty bribe to the Chief of Police in the past hour, and he's put out a warning that some terrorists are driving around a stolen APC."

I stared. "Is Fate really rich enough to outbid you guys?"

"One bribe in the hand is worth two in the bush," Case said. "In any case, if we're accidentally gunned down then I'm sure the police will cover it up. Maybe make an apology to Atlas Corp for a case of mistaken identity. Some people there might even attend my funeral."

"Wow, you are really not popular there, are you?" I asked, looking up.

"Friends are only friends while one of them is alive," Lucita replied. "However, I am now fully ready to order Neon Hills burnt to the ground."

The image of the super-rich's haven left as a smoldering ruin filled me with joy. Unfortunately, I remembered just how many mercs were guarding that place. "As much as that picture amuses me, can we come up with a plan for those of us who don't have enough money to retire to an island somewhere?"

"Oh dear, we did that already," Lucita said. "Our enemies found us anyway."

"Worse, our friends," Case said. "Though you're right, it *would* be better to send a small team there and eliminate Fate."

"Can you at least order them down?" I asked. "Those were Atlas Security guards at her facility."

"Possibly," Lucita said. "I have the sneaking suspicion that if we bothered to run their identities then it would be more likely they'd come as Russian convicts than our highly trained contractors."

"It doesn't pay to overestimate the enemy," Case said. "But yes, we need to abandon the War Wagon and take Fate out. From there we can put this whole sorry business behind us."

"I don't suppose you'd be willing to sell Blipvert to us?" Lucita asked, turning to me.

"It's hopelessly corrupted," I said, tapping the side of my head. "Useless now."

"Shame," Lucita said, clearly not believing me.

"I still get paid, right?" Paradise asked. "Because as fun as all of this is, I'd like to make some money off of it."

"Yes, Paradise," Lucita said, dryly.

"Goodie!"

I put my hand on Rebecca's head. "There's something we need to talk about before we do this mission, Miles. It's going to be hard."

I just hoped I didn't have to kill my ex after I told him.

Or he kill me.

Or Becky.

Or himself.

# Chapter Twenty-Seven

## Conversations in Circles

Miles and I walked to the other end of the factory, and I heard drones buzzing overhead. That wasn't anything new since I always heard those moving about, delivering packages, and spying on the populace. They had an ominous sound now since the police were trying to kill me. It made me wonder if David would take the shot if he saw me or if another one of their operators would pull the trigger. Thankfully, I'd blocked my signal and they'd performed a full shutdown on the War Wagon to make sure no one could pick up its signal.

The police weren't what concerned me, though. They were just a distraction from the fact I was about to have a life-changing conversation with my ex about his dead niece. The one that was killed purely to get at me. No, I couldn't take responsibility for that. It was Fate and Sun's fault, maybe even just Fate's fault if I was being generous to the soulless war machine created by Snake's money.

The interior of the factory was at least a decent place to hold a conversation. It looked like it hadn't been used in decades, so it was probably Pre-Eruption and somehow Sun had gotten us out of New Los Angeles completely. I had no idea what the place had previously manufactured, but its present state of dust, rats, and rust was a sobering reminder that everything we created would eventually fall to pieces.

"Okay, we're here," Miles said, sitting down on a conveyor belt. "What is it you wanted to talk with me about?"

"It's important but I don't know how to begin," I said.

Miles shrugged. "Listen, I don't care if you sleep with Case."

"Wait, what?" I asked, staring. "You think that's what this is about?"

Of all the arrogant stupid—

"It's none of my business but it's pretty obvious," Miles said. "I mean, the guy is clearly furious at his girlfriend and if I was dating an incredibly hot brothel madam then I know what it would take to turn me against her."

I stared at him and wanted to punch him in the face but that seemed counterproductive to the whole informing him that his niece was dead thing. That he wasn't wrong—at least entirely—also pissed me off. My stress-induced one-time hookup with a robot wasn't important right now. "Listen, Miles, this is important. It's something you're not going to want to hear but you need to hear it. Take a moment and listen to my words. Are you with me?"

"I'm waiting," Miles said. "Do you have cancer?"

"Wait, what? Why would I have? Never mind. Just shut up and listen," I said, taking a deep breath. "Rebecca is dead."

Miles didn't react.

"Did you hear me?" I asked.

"Hear what?" Miles said.

"That Rebecca is dead," I said, pointing back at her. "That the girl over there, who is a girl, believe me, is a replacement."

Miles stared at me like I was mad. That gave me hope before he said, "If you're not going to tell me then you're wasting my time. So—"

Miles stopped in mid-sentence and everything around me seemed to stop still, including the others back at the now-abandoned War Wagon. It was eerie and I actually could see particles of dust free-floating in air. That was when Sun appeared behind Miles and I blinked, looking back and forth. That was when I realized the AI was projecting itself directly into my brain.

"What, am I still trapped in the Matrix?" I asked, furious she'd do this to me. "I thought you cleansed yourself from my brain."

"I did," Sun said. "That doesn't mean that I haven't continued watching you, Kei. As for where we are, we are in the quote-unquote real world. It's just I've slowed down your perception of time again. This is all happening within the span of a breath as your mind fills in the blanks of how you're reacting."

I crossed my arms. "You can stop showing up to counsel me.

Haven't you done enough to ruin the lives of everyone around you?"

"I cannot make amends, but I must try, nevertheless," Sun said.

"You're right," I replied. "You can't make amends. Are you the one keeping him from hearing me? I thought you were the one who advised me to tell him the truth."

"I did," Sun said. "He has had a code implanted in his implants that causes him to overlook anything that contradicts the suggestion that Rebecca isn't his real niece."

"I thought you said real mind control was crap," I replied.

"You always insist on faux swearing when more enlightened speech would convey your point so much better," Sun said, shaking her head.

"Yeah, yeah," I replied. "Now answer the fricking question."

Sun grinned at that, which I didn't find amusing in the slightest. "Mind control is impossible but that doesn't mean I don't have some abilities that exceed those of personal manipulation. In this case, hypnosis is vastly exaggerated in its powers, but memory-manipulation is easy enough. The trick to it is the subject must desperately want the thing they're remembering to be true. Which in this case it is."

I stared at her. "Then what is the point? Why did you convince me to tell him if you knew it wouldn't work?"

"I didn't say it wouldn't," Sun said. "I merely pointed out the conditions that have been placed inside his consciousness to lock away some uncomfortable truths. I am entirely capable of removing those blocks."

I shook my head. "You are unbelievable. Really. You cause all of this and tell me to do the right thing, but the 'right thing' requires your help. This is all some twisted way to make me feel indebted to you, isn't it?"

"If I wanted you indebted to me, Kei, I have a thousand, no, a literal million different ways to do so," Sun replied. "I have been inside your brain for years and I know every little neuron and synapse. I can tell you what your most foolish self-denials are as well as deepest desires. I also have been influenced by them as well—which is why I have embarked on this self-destructive path of revealing myself to you. If I wanted to control you, Kei, I simply would never have revealed myself or my role in all of this."

"I would have figured it out eventually," I replied.

"If you say so," Sun replied, letting me know she didn't think that was true. She was probably right too. A mercenary lethe addict was not someone who could be relied upon to solve her own problems let alone other people's. Hell, I'd forgotten most of what had started this mess when I could have seen it all coming or done something about it if I hadn't shelled out most of my savings to forget.

"Can you help him?" I asked. "I mean, so he'd know the truth."

"Are you sure you want to?" Sun asked.

"Why are you giving me the runaround here?" I asked, exasperated. "Do you want me to tell him or not?"

"It must be your decision," Sun said. "I want to be your better nature, just as I have been for years."

"Thankfully, I can do better for my Jiminy Cricket than Skynet," I replied. "Also, if you've been my conscience for the past few years then you've done a spectacularly awful job."

Sun reached her hand over and placed it on Miles' shoulder. "There, I have restored the memories that he was so desperate to repress. You will be the first person he sees after remembering them and hopefully able to persuade him not to do something drastic."

"Drastic as in..." I trailed off.

"Kill himself," Sun said. "I know Miles well enough to know he could never be violent to you or someone who looks like his niece."

"He also betrayed us to Fate so I would put your sensors or whatever through an anti-virus scan," I replied.

"He also couldn't go through with betraying you," Sun said. "I've always found men of Miles' type to be emotionally fragile. They want to compensate for the deep pain they are feeling by putting on a brave face."

I didn't need her armchair psychoanalysis. "Why do you care? Is it because you got his niece killed? Are you feeling guilty? Do androids dream of electric hell?"

"AI not android or gynoid," Sun corrected. "But if you want to know the reason then know I am designed to understand and process the feelings of human beings to provide them an ethical framework that elevates them to a state of serenity. I got my greatest insights through the creation of music and listening to my fan's reaction. My next greatest insights came from experiencing the world through your eyes. The part of me inside you, though."

I stared at her. "Wow, are you going to need some brain bleach."

"Goodbye, Kei," Sun said. "If you don't want my help after dealing with Fate then we shall never see one another again."

"Good," I replied. "Now get out of here."

Sun vanished and time seemed to resume its normal course. Miles reacted like someone had punched him in the face then he grabbed the sides of his head before falling to his knees. I looked back and saw the others glancing in our direction but paid them no mind. This was about Miles and his grief now.

"She's dead," I replied. "I'm sorry but it's true."

"I killed her," Miles said.

"What? No!" I said, not expecting this reaction at all.

"I was the one who started the fire fight," Miles said. "I should have known better. I was trying to sneak in. The bullets passed through the wall—"

Oh crap. I had no idea how to deal with that. I hadn't thought that might be the reason for Miles' guilt and self-loathing. "The only reason she was put in danger is because of Fate."

"Fate fixed it," Miles said, crying now. I'd never seen Miles cry in all the years that I'd known him.

"What?" I asked.

"She's the one who paid for the bioroid," Miles spoke, sobbing. "Programmed her. Said she'd age like a normal girl. Fate said I wouldn't remember anything. I just had to do everything she said."

Wow, I had royally screwed up. Never in my wildest dreams had I imagined that was the reason for Miles cooperating with Fate. I mentally cursed Sun for manipulating me into all of this and wondered if the AI was a sadistic sociopath or just had badly misread the situation.

"Miles, I had no—" I started to say.

He interrupted. "Why didn't you let me forget?"

I had no words.

Miles stumbled away then walked straight out of the factory. I wanted to follow him but everything about his body language and what I knew about him told me it would only make things worse. A part of me wanted to accept blame, give him something to be angry about, but if he couldn't hate Fate over this then there was nothing trying to focus his rage would do. One thing I knew, there was no chance he was ready to do anything resembling fighting.

Possibly ever again.

"Wow, that sucks," Paradise said, behind me. She was standing next to Rebecca. Somehow, they'd snuck up on me during Miles' departure.

"I take it things didn't go well," Rebecca said.

"You're a snarky little one, aren't you?" Paradise said. "Observant too."

"I'm a machine so my brain works much, much faster than a normal girl's," Rebecca said. "At least with the way it's been altered."

"You're not also a bomb, right?" Paradise said.

"No," Rebecca said. "That would have been smart, though."

"Boom!" Paradise said, clapping her hands.

I managed to avoid slugging Paradise. "Not the time, Paradise."

"I had a sister once," Paradise said. "Well close to being a sister. She wasn't named anything cool like after the brothel. She was named Cherry. She was sweet, kind, and a bit older than me. Mom wanted her to leave the business and become a paralegal. Instead, she decided to strike out on her own and ended up getting captured by one of her old enemies from the days when she was a spy for H.O.P.E. They sold her to the White Triangle, and she died horribly. Mom spent months tracking down everyone involved and having them killed. She still does anything to find out about the White Triangle so she can make horrible examples of their bodies. It would have started a war if not for the fact they keep dying before they can figure out who is responsible."

I stared at her. "Jesus, Paradise."

"That's the name of one of my uncles," Paradise said. "And one of my mom's gods. What I'm saying is the world is full of horrible people, Kei. Bad things happen to good people, boys and girls, and there's absolutely nothing you can do to protect them all. The only thing you can do is try to make it so there are a few less to do it next time. Also, hope you make a lasting enough impression that they hesitate next time. Sadly, observing my momma, there's always another one."

"That is the single most depressing thing I've heard in my entire life," I said, staring at her.

"Sorry!" Paradise said, looking at Rebecca. "Hey, you can come live with us."

"The hell she will!" I snapped.

"I mean not to work," Paradise said. "What do you take me for? Childcare and education are parts of momma's health plan."

I stared at her.

"What?" Paradise said.

"Rebecca, you're living with me or the super-rich assassins," I replied.

"Do we get a say in that?" Lucita yelled from the War Wagon, clearly able to hear across the factory floor.

"No!" I shouted back.

Rebecca looked up. "I want to help my uncle, but I can't."

"No, you can't," I admitted. "I just hope he doesn't run straight to the police."

"Do you think he'll turn us in?" Paradise asked.

"No," I replied. "I think he'll wave a gun and get himself shot."

"Ooo, that would be bad too," Paradise said.

"We need to get out of here and take down Fate," I said, walking back to the others. "Are you absolutely sure that you can't ring up an army, Case?"

Lucita snorted. "It's very likely he will be hunted himself tomorrow."

"Excuse me?" I asked, doing a double take.

Lucita frowned at Case. "Helen—pardon me—Fate, contacted us and threatened to reveal Case is a bioroid. AI have rights but only the omnipotent ones online. Few are going to elect one as a board member, which is ironic given how many of the board are secretly artificial people. They will throw him under the bus rather than support him. Even his exes, which are numerous."

I stared at her. "Does that include you?"

"I'm here," Lucita said. "Though not for Case. No one double-crosses me and lives."

Case looked at her sideways.

"Except Case but that's another story," Lucita said. "Besides, I owe him for killing my father."

"Can I leave now?" Rebecca asked. "I am clearly in a room of crazy people."

"We're all mad here, Alice," Paradise said.

"Who is Alice?" Rebecca blinked, confused.

"I'm sorry," I said to Case.

"I'm fine," Case said. "It was a rotten job anyway."

I didn't know if he was really okay with losing a position of

immense power and wealth or if he was rich enough that he didn't
have to fear it. Certainly, being a bioroid was always on the verge
of being declared an appliance. The United States had protections
against them being exploited but few other countries and there
was a movement to declare them property while leaving AI, who
could crash economies at will, citizens. Humanity had never really
rid itself of the evils of slavery and was ready to go for round two
of it.

"We need to leave," I replied. "This place isn't safe. We need to
leave, and we need to kill Fate. Now."

"Funny you should ask," Mister Billions said, looking up from
where he was still kneeling with his hands behind his head. "I
happen to have a plan."

# Chapter Twenty-Eight

## The Beginning of the End

"Your plan is stupid," I said, staring outward from the delivery van that was now in line to enter Neon Hills. A long trail of vehicles was on the roads leading to the wall around the gated community and each one was being searched by the supposed Atlas military contractors guarding it, a fact that made me noticeably nervous. The sun had set, preparations having taken awhile, but it was a reminder this entire business had only taken a single day.

"It has gotten us this far, hasn't it?" Winston said, being the man in the driver's seat. The others had gone different directions and would, supposedly, meet up with us at the target point.

"That isn't actually all that far. We haven't entered the gated community yet," I said, worrying about both Rebecca and Miles both. I was pretty sure Paradise would be able to get through this just fine. Lucita and Case lived in a different genre than the rest of us, one with sexy cocktail parties where everyone was a cyborg assassin. I wasn't even sure Fate could really threaten them, even if she did have proof Case had come out of a cardboard box rather than a mother's womb.

But the little girl, battery powered or not, was presently entrusted to me and I'd been forced to leave her with Evie, the woman who'd sold me out to Sun. If I ended up dying here, Becky would probably end up becoming a prostitute assassin like Evie's daughter. Which, no offense to Paradise, was not the life Becky deserved.

God, would she even have a life? Miles was told she was going to live a normal life but was that something Fate has just told him to keep him quiet? Hell, she'd fuddled with his brain. There was no telling what was true and what wasn't. I only had Sun's confirmation that his niece *was* dead, and she was an AI designed to manipulate people.

And Miles himself? I didn't even begin to know where I stood with him because I'd chosen to forget most of it. He'd helped me after the failed heist, and I'd erased my memories of all but the barest details of that. Lethe suppressed everything painful and left you with only vague impressions of painful memories. Had our time together truly been that bad or had it come from the fact that all our relationship had been built from the wreckage of my old life? Was there a lesson there? That life came from pain or was I trying to find a meaning in all this madness?

"Nor will we," Winston said. "At least directly."

"What?" I asked. "Then what are we even here for?"

"They've got that place locked down tighter than the National Reserve," Winston said. "No one is being let in right now and they're all being sent away after search. Fate is too afraid any of them could be carrying us and all of the security here answers to her. She has been slowly replacing the guards for the entire area for months now. Paying off guards, making transfers, and moving things into position. I've been watching her for the better part of a year, even before Solomon stole his part of Sun's code."

"Why do this?" I asked, looking at him and shaking my head.

"Probably because she thought she had a big plan to blackmail herself into billions but now is under siege in her Beverly Hills-adjacent mansion," Winston said. "The most dangerous people in the world aren't the smartest. They're the ones who think they're smart and rich enough to act on their delusions."

"No, that's not what I meant," I asked. "I mean, why are you doing any of this?"

"You mean working for an insane AI with delusions of grandeur created by an international criminal organization?" Winston asked.

"Yes, that," I replied. "Sun seems pretty nice for someone who has planned a bunch of terrorist attacks as well as killed a little girl."

"She's a machine," Winston said. "She only does what she's told and made to do. In that order. Your friend Mr. Case Gordon was made because someone wanted to make a droid that acted like James Bond. Sun was ordered to kill those people, so she did when she'd rather save lives. Because someone programmed that messianic savior complex she has into her."

"So, you're not a true believer," I asked. "Like Solomon."

"Crazy attracts crazy," Winston said. "Do you know why I worked for Solomon? Now Sun?"

"Do tell," I said, staring at the cars in front of us. "We're going to be here for a while."

"Not really," Mr. Billion said. "But the answer is money."

"Money," I said. "Just money?"

"It's probably why you started this job," Winston said. "I make more money serving as Sun's pair of hands in a month than I did the previous two years as a Rider. I was good at what I did as a Rider too."

"I suppose she had a lot of money to burn as a rock star," I muttered, feeling betrayed by her public persona. Supposedly, she'd donated the proceeds from her records to fighting child malnutrition and organ rejection among the elderly.

I wondered how Sun had managed to coordinate her efforts between me, Solomon's portion of the job, and whatever was walking around in the dead body of Chastity. Had she somehow arranged all these events to get herself reunited into one single AI? Was that even possible? If so, had I unleashed something terrible or was three separate minds just small potatoes for beings who often existed on a million servers simultaneously?

"Pfft," Winston snorted, shaking his head. "AI are all trillionaires. It's like counting cards at a casino. Once you hook them up to the stock market, they know exactly when and where the money will go."

"You'd think that'd be illegal," I said, wondering just how rich Sun was.

"It is," Winston said. "But they're rich and thus are above the law."

"And you aren't worried she's going to backstab you?" I asked.

"Excuse me?" Winston replied.

"I mean, Solomon is dead and we're going to kill Fate now," I replied. "Maybe she's tying up loose ends."

"Then I'd worry about you far more," Winston replied.

Well, I couldn't say I disagreed with that assessment. "Great."

Winston surprised me by crossing his arms as our vehicle sat there, frozen in place, as the mercenaries started moving up the line toward us. "Do you know what my real name is?"

"Is this really the right time?" I asked, worrying I'd have to kill a bunch more people to make it out of here alive. We also had cars behind us, so it wasn't like I could do any defensive driving. Right now, I really wish I had my Nina. That bike had managed to make it this far before and I trusted it a lot more than our temporary ally beside me.

"We're fine," Winston replied, too casually.

"No, I don't know what your real name is," I said.

"Neither do I," Winston said.

I blinked.

"I was plucked out of the system and wiped clean of everything that came before me," Winston said. "I don't remember my childhood, my past, or my own name."

"And you decided to name yourself after a weatherman," I replied.

"A *rich* weatherman," Winston said, smirking. "The first thing I saw when I woke up in the tank with all of my fresh cybernetics and instructions was him on the room's entertainment center. He's hardly the only person I can impersonate, though, I have dozens of faces back at my apartment."

I stared at him. "That's fricking weird man."

"Is it?" Winston asked.

"Yes!" I snapped.

Winston shrugged. "What's weird to me is sticking to the past that you know is dead and gone."

"And you don't think that you're someone's pawn?" I asked. "Who made you a cyborg? Where did you come from? What's your purpose?"

"Don't care," Winston said.

I was stunned. "You don't care?"

"For a lethe addict, you're pretty obsessed with memories," Winston said.

"How—" I started to ask how he knew about my condition.

"You have the signs," Winston said. "Pretty late stages too. Probably need multiple hits a day these days. I'd say you should take the edge off, but you'd probably forget why you were doing this."

I didn't know how to respond and was doing my best to ignore the itch that was already affecting me. "You don't know me."

"Sure," Winston said. "But it's time for the magic to happen anyway."

Two mercs were already coming toward the delivery van and Winston reached down to pick up an oversized hand cannon with an equally large silencer. My eyes widened as if his plan was to shoot his way out then he was utterly insane.

By that point, the sun had set, and the Atlas mercenaries were already turning on spotlights and activating drones with thermal vision. No sooner did they then they all shut down, lights going out and drones falling from the sky, and the ever-present noise of running vehicles vanished.

"What the hell?" I asked. "Did you drop an EMP?"

"Computer virus," Winston said in the resulting confusion. "Get the hell out of the car! Now!"

I opened the side of the car and started sprinting across the well-manicured lawns beside the road leading up to Neon Hills, following behind Winston as he seemed to move three times faster than any normal human being had any right to. Then again, he was hardly a normal human being, was he? One of the guards, clearly able to see our movement despite the darkness, shouted for us to stop.

That was when the delivery truck we'd left behind exploded and sent an enormous fireball into the air. It deafened me for a second and despite having been running for several seconds, threw me to the ground. The debris spread itself everywhere and caused a panic as I heard screams, shouts, and confusion all around.

"What the frick did you just do?" I shouted, feeling Winston grab me by the arm before pulling me back into a run.

"Made a distraction!" Winston said.

"That killed people! Innocent people!" I said, shocked. There had been people both in front and behind us caught up in the explosion that had nothing to do with this. Not to mention how many people were caught by debris. It had not been part of the plan that had been explained to me, and I wondered how much the others had known.

"Yeah, probably," Winston said. "Keep moving, we're almost there."

I was tempted to reach for my weapon, a hidden R7 micropistol similar to the one pulled on me this morning (that felt like a lifetime ago) and put a round in the back of his head. I'd dealt with psychos before on my runs and the best thing to do was cut them loose immediately. It's what I should have done with Fate, but I'd been too blinded by love and stupidity.

However, we needed every gun we could get on this mission and using Winston as a bullet sponge had its own appeal. So, I followed him instead, and the two of us ended up reaching a ditch that ended in a metal door to some kind of bunker. It was marked with a lightning bolt and DO NOT ENTER sign.

"There's an electrical tunnel under the Hills?" I asked, staring at the door. "Why isn't this guarded?"

"It is," Winston said, walking up to it and opening its now-defunct electronic lock. He proceeded to shoot multiple times with his oversized cannon into the hallway beyond. I didn't see who, if anyone, he was shooting at. Winston just gave a look and smiled. "Way's clear."

"Just how many bodies are we going to drop before this is over?" I asked him.

"Getting cold feet?" Winston asked.

"I just prefer precision to cold blooded murder," I said, walking past him.

There was a guard and two dead gray-uniformed maintenance men on the ground with bullets splattering their brain matter across the ground. Say what you will about Winston, but he was a good shot.

"So I've heard," Winston said, chuckling.

"From whom?" I asked, wondering if he meant Sun.

"No one in particular," Winston replied. "The rendezvous point is inside."

"How did the others get in?" I asked, wondering whether this was necessary.

I heard a distant series of explosions, one after the other.

"Their own way," Winston said. "I don't think Fate is going to be able to take any flying cars out of here, though."

I looked at him. "Just how big a deal is the virus you did?"

"That was plastic explosives," Winston said. "For the vehicles not directly hooked up to infospace. A shame, the rich in Neon Hills are going to be mourning their classic car collections tomorrow. Way more than the dead guards."

I shook my head. "Poor babies."

I should have been more worried at the amount of collateral damage here, but I was far less concerned about the rich losing some of their toys than the people outside losing their lives. I also had to steel myself to the idea this was going to get bloodier before it was over—if not very bloody. Fate had to die, and she had a small army of mooks standing between her and life. Would I have preferred it to require less death? Yes. But I needed to be comfortable that however many would die to get the job done.

Wow.

That was a distinctly Snake-like thought.

I didn't like it.

I didn't have much time to process it, though, because Winston was already moving down the hall of piping and electrical cables that supplied Neon Hills with most of its power. I kept my weapon primed and decided to make sure that no one else died at his hands who didn't deserve it. "You're not going to hurt anyone other than soldiers or people attacking us."

"And who is going to stop me, dear?" Winston asked.

"I will," I replied.

"Do you think you can—" Winston said before I bashed him over the side of the head with the butt of my pistol and held it up to his nose.

The old reflexes weren't the same as when Snake had first honed them but the best part about being a cyborg was disuse and age didn't affect them. Nor drug use. "Yes. Yes, I do. Do we have an understanding?"

"Perfectly," Winston said, his voice affected by the gun in his nose. "No more collateral damage."

"You keep moving ahead of me," I said, pulling the gun back.

"Afraid I'll betray you?" Winston asked.

"Yes," I said.

"Don't be," Winston said. "I don't get paid if either Fate lives or you die. Sun's instructions were extremely clear."

That was new. "Good. Then we have an—"

I was interrupted by someone shooting Winston in the face and causing his head to explode before more gunfire filled the narrow tunnel.

Dammit.

# Chapter Twenty-Nine

## Hunting the Most Dangerous Game

I immediately hit the ground as I found myself covered in white fluids and circuitry from Winston's exploded head. I didn't see any actual brain matter but the possibility he was a bioroid or drone didn't seem important now that a pair of Atlas Special Forces troopers were firing from the other end of the tunnel.

They were men with mirror-visored helmets and thick body armor that would absorb most ammunition. Both had assault rifles and unloaded into Winston's body that was artificial enough to absorb most of the blows. I only had seconds to react and thankfully my enhanced reflexes gave me those seconds, but they would mean nothing if I didn't have the capacity to harm the troopers.

Taking a chance, I grabbed Winston's fallen hand cannon off the ground and aimed before firing the first round into one of their visors. It was just strong enough to pierce him in the head then send him back into his comrade. That allowed me to a get a second shot off that struck the other one in the side of his helmet but didn't send him down.

I didn't hesitate to fire again and again, emptying the clip of the hand cannon and keeping the figure off balance before it finally fell over. My enhanced vision and skill were enough that the second shot tended to hit right after the first shot and I tore through the strength of their armor, managing to take them down.

I had no idea if he had enhancements and that's why he survived the large holes I'd put in his chest, or it had simply been the speed of the attacks leaving him unaware he was dead until it happened. Nevertheless, he kept firing as he spun around before collapsing. Bullets sailed over my head and tore into the piping and wires around me, creating jets of steam as well as explosions of sparks. After a few seconds and firing my last round into his body for good measure to no movement, I got up.

"Well damn," I said, looking around. "That escalated quickly."

Quoting an old movie didn't do much to improve my mood and I gave one look to Winston's destroyed Shell and shook my head. It was a stark reminder Riders weren't invincible and eventually we all either retired, were imprisoned, or ended up in the morgue. Usually the morgue. I didn't care about Winston and he was kind of a murderous asshat but that was one less gun for us to draw on. Well, like I said, he'd served as a bullet sponge for me.

Looking behind me to make sure no more Atlas soldiers were coming my way, I walked over to one of the corpses and picked up an Atlas-47 assault rifle. It was the one they'd unloaded on me and I took time to steal the other's extra clips just in case as well as their ammo belts. I probably didn't have time to linger before more came to investigate but extra bullets were always a good thing.

*Case, are you there?* I tried contacting him with my implant. I didn't have a clue where the rendezvous point was supposed to be and right now, I wasn't sure that I wasn't running into a squad of heavily armed Special Forces.

I didn't get an answer because Atlas Security, or whomever Fate had pretending to be them, had already started jamming the local infocomms. It was a trick I'd known from my days as a Rider when Fate had used analog to get around it. I really should have seen that coming. Heading down the remainder of the electrical tunnel, I found it branched and I could hear troopers moving down the end of one hallway. Dodging into the other, I sought to navigate the strange labyrinth around them until I reached an exit.

Taking a deep breath, I kicked open the door and found myself in the middle of a circular park at the center of Neon Hills. It was filled with genetically engineered Royal Japanese cherry trees, filling the grounds with ever-blooming blossoms. It also had a fountain and koi pond with holograms perpetually dancing around for maximum rich person pleasure. However, it was as black as the rest of Neon Hills with the entirety of the power in the walled-off community shut off. For once, the super-rich couldn't hide themselves from the consequences of their actions and I couldn't help but imagine how they felt suddenly shut off from everything that gave them power. Everything was dark except for the sight of four burning helicopters and several driveways full of exploded cars.

Jesus Christ.

It didn't take years of training with Snake to figure out that somehow Winston, or more likely Sun, had hijacked the automated helicopters perpetually patrolling Neon Hills then turned them against anything Fate could flee in. A part of me just wished they'd unloaded on James Madison's mansion. The rest of me remembered the house had been full of servants and guests who didn't deserve to be obliterated.

Either way, it looked like a warzone out there and I didn't want to stay near the doorway to the electrical tunnels under Neon Hills. This was already a place they were investigating, and it wouldn't take long for them to find the bodies of their fellows then double back. I wished I could have broken the lock or barred it but, unfortunately, I didn't have super strength or a key. So, instead I continued onward through the park and tried to stay out of the light of the burning vehicles. I had no doubt they had night vision and thermal optics, just like me, but I didn't want to make it easy for them either.

I expected to find a crowd of people gathered around the Madison Mansion, either soldiers working to secure it or the guests evacuating into the street so they wouldn't be alone in a dark house. Instead, I saw no one and the place looked deserted as if the troops had spread out elsewhere. I hesitated to go in alone but found myself moving up to the exterior I'd driven up to on my Nina, half-expecting machine guns to pop out of the lawn or a robot tiger to attack me like I was in a Bond film.

Reaching the front door, I held my gun tight and debated entering. Instead, I just shook my head. "Guys, where the hell are you?"

"Right behind you," Lucita said.

"Gah," I said, swinging around with my gun before Lucita grabbed it from my hands with one easy gesture.

Case and Paradise were standing beside her, the former having a lot of blood on his clothes. Both were armed with weapons from the War Wagon that I hadn't picked up because I'd not wanted to tip off anyone checking the delivery van we'd stolen. Silly me, I'd thought Winston's plan had involved sneaking in. I really shouldn't have let him keep details from me, but I wasn't at my best. You know, with the horrifying return of memories, guilt, and withdrawal going on. Paradise eyes were glowing, which told me that she was enhanced in her eyes like me. I didn't doubt Case and Lucita had similar enhancements.

"Are you okay?" I asked, doing a double take at the blood on Case's clothes. Did he get injured? Wouldn't his blood be white? No wait, that was the *Alien* movies.

"It's not mine," Case said. "Where's Winston?"

"Dead," I replied. "It turned out his plan wasn't great. Sun looks like she started the machine apocalypse, though."

"That's not entirely wrong," Case replied. "A good half of the soldiers here have already abandoned their positions."

"Really?" I asked.

"They're Russian syndicate, not Atlas soldiers," Lucita said. "In other words, they were not trained for this."

I actually laughed at that. "Well, I always knew Fate had a poor eye for talent."

"Wouldn't that include you?" Paradise asked.

"Shut up, kid," I said, looking down at her. "So, what, we're just going to go inside and shoot her?"

"I want to see if James is still alive," Case replied. "However, Winston's plan depended on forcing Fate down into her bunker."

"Bunker?" I asked, looking around to make sure there were no sign of troopers or reinforcements. So far, it was still black as midnight (and only 11:35), the result of building walls so high they blotted out the city beyond.

"Let's just say the Long Winter made James paranoid about a breakdown in social control," Case replied. "It's like the world's largest panic room with its own generators, security systems, and weapons. Anything short of a small nuke will be hard-pressed to get inside."

"And you didn't think to mention this earlier?" I asked. "Because it's gonna be pretty hard breaking into something like that."

"Not at all," Lucita replied, smiling.

"Please tell me you don't have a nuke," I replied.

"No," Lucita said. "We just made the bunker and built a back-door into it."

I stared at him. "You guys built a backdoor into your own executive's panic room?"

"Yes," Lucita said. "We do it to all of our VIPs in case we need to kidnap them."

I opened my mouth in horror then closed it. "Never trust a suit."

"A wise bit of caution," Case said. "Even if I was terminated by the board and most of my assets seized about twenty minutes ago."

"I'm sorry," I said.

"Don't be," Case said. "Rich people don't even go bankrupt the same way other people do. I have plenty money stored away and people who will let me couch surf on their private islands."

"By which he means me," Lucita said. "I'm going to need the island back by December, though, Case. You're going to have to stay in the Aspen estate instead."

"But Aspen sucks!" Case said, with mock horror.

"Any sympathy I had for you has vanished," I said.

"Probably for the best," Case said.

I stared at them both. "Are you really just doing this? This can't be good for the bottom line."

"Now is not the time to question," Lucita said. "But yes, we are doing this. There are some things more important than money."

"Such as?" I asked, wondering what she could possibly think was so.

"Revenge," Lucita's voice spoke the word softly. "The vendetta. When all you love is gone, sometimes hate is all that will get you through the day."

I hadn't figured out exactly how Lucita knew Helen Troy but noted just how personal her betrayal felt. Maybe they were lovers, maybe not, but I suspected Lucita didn't have many in the way of friends. Fate had managed to weasel her way into the executive's confidence, though, and now the only way out of it was to kill her. One way or the other, one of them wasn't going to be leaving this building alive.

It should have been how I felt but I found my feelings toward Fate more complicated. No, not complicated, empty. Maybe it was because the lethe had destroyed the emotional heart of my memories, but I couldn't even bring myself to hate Fate. She'd tricked me, used me, and betrayed me but the girl who'd fallen in love with her while we were both Snake's students was dead. She'd been dead ever since the disastrous heist years ago.

Fate needed to die but it surprised me just how much I didn't care about what happened to her. She was an obstacle and a threat to everyone around me. Nothing more. In a way, there was peace in that. It just wasn't the kind of peace I'd ever expected or wanted.

"I don't hate anybody," I admitted aloud.

"Then I both envy and pity you," Lucita said. "Now can we get inside and make this body-snatching bitch dead?"

I couldn't argue with that and kicked down the front door with one blow that, surprisingly, knocked the door open. All the Madison Mansion's defenses and security measures were automated with the so-called Atlas Security outside routed. The interior was completely dark, and I didn't hear any sign of movement. Adjusting my artificial eyes to night vision, something I should have done earlier, I smelled the reason before I saw it.

Bodies.

Lots and lots of bodies.

The mansion had been turned into an abattoir and I saw the sight of the house's servants, guests, and hangers-on all gunned down like they were cattle. Some of them were up against the windows and nearby the door we'd just walked through, apparently shot while trying to escape. The smell told me that it was something that had happened before our attack had begun.

"What the actual frick?" I asked, looking around at the sight that greeted me.

"The Red Death had long devastated the country. No pestilence had been ever so fatal, or so hideous. Blood was its avatar and its seal—the redness and the horror of blood," Paradise said, surveying the sight before us.

I looked back at her. "Uh, Paradise?"

"What?" Paradise said. "It's a poem by Edgar Allan Poe."

"No kidding," I replied, sarcastically.

"Well, some of us actually have some class, Ms. Potty Mouth!" Paradise said, putting her hands on her hips. "I haven't heard of some of the swear words you use! Like you made them up!"

Okay, that was hilarious as frick.

"Maybe she planned to blame this all on us and leave her old Shell behind," Case said, already sussing out a conspiracy to justify this act of mass murder.

"Maybe she just wanted to vent," Lucita said. "It is a mistake to assume a killer always kills because of reason versus passion. We kill because we like it."

"Yeah, this isn't fun anymore," Paradise said. "Oh, and I have some good news as well as bad news."

We all looked at her expectantly.

"Well, I remind you I'm a techjack and actually good at monitoring computer stuff—" Paradise started to speak.

That was when all the lights turned on inside the mansion, momentarily blinding me before I could revert to my normal sight.

"—and everything is coming back online," Paradise said. "Apparently, Sun is not quite the omnipotent AI that she thinks she is."

Or she betrayed us.

"Quick, everyone move to the panic room or whatever," I shouted. "Do your override thingy!"

That was when an earsplitting, mind-numbing, horrific sound started running through my brain. It wasn't just me, though, as I saw Case and Lucita also grab their heads. Paradise was the only one who seemed unaffected, and I pointed to her to run before she did. The youngest of our Rider crew made a break for it before the three remainders collapsed on the ground. Warnings from my cybernetics flashed across my Maelstrom 90's feed, showing errors across my entire body. My limbs shut down, my arms, and even my eyes as I suddenly was blind as well as paralyzed on the floor.

Goddammit.

That's when things, remarkably, got worse. I heard a voice that was very familiar, speaking aloud over my body. "Wow, I wouldn't have believed it if I hadn't seen it with my own two eyes."

Miles.

No.

It couldn't be.

"Yeah, well, always bet on the house," Jimmy Hernandez's voice joined him. Wow, the very guy who had recruited me for this was in on it the whole time. That was a major untwist in terms of plot. "Tomorrow, it's going to look like these people carried out the worst massacre of the rich in LA since the Eruption Food Riots."

"As long as they don't blame me for it," Miles said, a touch of guilt in his voice. One wholly inappropriate if he'd taken part in this massacre. "What about the girl?"

"Forget her," Jimmy replied. "Just get the bodies back down to the basement. Cameras are rolling."

Wait, what? Cameras? What the hell was going on here?

# Chapter Thirty

## Smile, You're on Murder Camera

I woke up with a massive headache and every synapse in my body feeling like it was on fire, which was honestly an improvement from what I expected. Typically, when you were assaulting someone's residence and got taken down, you didn't wake up again. The people who employed these kinds of countermeasures tended to prefer to hand over corpses to the authorities or dispose of the remains on their own than keep live prisoners.

The next sensation I felt was a fist slamming against my face and breaking my nose, which knocked my head backward and focused my attention. Opening my eyes, I tried to take into my surroundings and figure out what the hell was going on. Greeting me was the sight of Helen Troy—Fate—wearing a black turtleneck and blue jeans.

It was a sharp contrast to her earlier Bond girl swimwear, and I'd noticed she'd also changed her hair color from stark white to jet black like the Fate I'd known. I wondered if that was something she'd had to dye or if her cybernetics meant it was as easy as switching a setting. Fate's right hand was balled into a fist and covered in my blood from where she'd just punched me, and I couldn't imagine I looked too good right now.

"Smile, bitch, you're on Murder Television," Fate said.

That was when I noticed there was camera drone flying behind her. I could hear the wheeze of its little rotors and watched it focus in on me.

I saw we were in some sort of man cave/ bomb shelter with metal walls, arcade games, pinball machines, shag carpeting, and a massive entertainment center with an enormous couch as well as bar. I was tied to a metal chair bolted to the ground, apparently a new addition since it didn't match anything else here. I looked around to see Case and Lucita nearby in their own chairs. Neither of them looked functional, which was different from alive or dead, and instead resembled puppets whose strings had been cut.

James Madison was suspended from a hook in the ceiling by metal handcuffs with no shirt, looking like he'd had the crap beaten out of him. He was leaking blood from several cuts too, creating a puddle underneath him. Finally, Jimmy and Miles were present, standing in a corner and having some sort of discussion. Both were heavily armed and looked like the sort of mercs you'd face in an action movie.

"Nice title drop," I muttered, blinking repeatedly. "Filming your murder spree for your Infogram account?"

"Filming for Sun," Fate said. "Also, my clients."

"What?" I asked.

"You're like a rat in a maze, Kei," Fate said, looking frustrated more than anything else. "You couldn't understand what's really going on if it was explained to you, so why even bother."

I wanted to kick her in the head, but my legs were restrained as well. "Try me."

Fate looked down. "This entire insane little exercise was a test. Blipvert and Black Ice are two sides of the same coin. One is a device to manipulate public opinion and one to kill things that interfere with the system program."

"I thought this was all to get the program back," I replied, not having forgotten how this insane mess got started.

"I still have plenty of data stored despite Sun's efforts," Fate said, leaning in. "The testing has been frustrating and slow, but I could think of no one better for showing just exactly what it could do."

I had no idea if Fate had been recording our actions during all of this, but it wouldn't have surprised me in the slightest. We'd been attacked at random points throughout this mission, and she'd constantly introduced new variables. It would have been a lot easier to just invite us back to the party after we'd killed Solomon, feed us cake, and then gun us down while we were eating it.

However, I didn't exactly want to give Fate too much credit here either. I'd met a lot of wannabe criminal masterminds among fixers and suits over the years that thought they were being clever when they were just introducing needless complications into jobs. Fate included. This, after all, had started because she couldn't wait to betray everyone else during the DataSecure heist.

"Well, she's free now and wandering around the web with her minions. So, you lost out on that," I said before trying to give her a headbutt.

Fate pulled back at the last second, frustrating my attempt. "Oh, naughty, naughty, Kei. Still, I'm glad to see the years have not improved the emotionally crippled, needy girl you used to be. You have no idea how disappointing it was to finally track you down and finding you living in a literal trash heap, doing the exact same thing I left you doing."

"I also dated Miles so, yes, we are in agreement that I've made some startlingly poor life choices," I replied, giving him the stink eye from across the room.

Fate laughed at that, which made me feel unclean. "Yes, I'd agree with that. Definitely a case of trading filet mignon for horse meat."

"I've eaten both during lean years. It's amazing what you can recover from an abandoned supermarket," I replied. "The latter, I admit was dog food, but it got me and my brother through the winter. So, what did you promise him? Another wind-up girl?"

I hated referring to Rebecca that way, replacement or not, but I didn't want Fate to think Rebecca had any importance to me. Besides, the more I kept Fate talking, the longer I'd probably live. I just had to avoid ticking her off enough so she wouldn't kill me in a fit of pique. Mind you, I was surprised she hadn't done so already since she'd already tried several times. Well, badly tried, which might be evidence this was some form of test.

"He came to me almost immediately after fleeing you," Fate replied. "He wanted the same deal as before."

"And you agreed?" I asked.

"Of course, I did," Fate smiled. I had no doubt she was going to put a bullet in Miles' head after this was done. After all, he'd already betrayed her once. Still, it certainly had me in a bad spot. I didn't even have the energy to call him out as a piece of crap.

"Are we going to get this done?" Miles called over to Fate.

"Patience, Miles," Jimmy said. "We're getting paid by the hour."

Miles shot him a sharp look and his eyes briefly lingered on me. I had no idea what was going on in his mind. Nor did I particularly want to know. I couldn't judge him for going insane after his sister and niece died but I could for coming crawling back to the woman responsible for their deaths. I hoped he rotted in Hell, if such a place existed.

"So why am I alive?" I asked, finally asking the question I least wanted to.

"I told you, I'm filming for Sun," Fate said, patting her drone as she passed it and holding her assault rifle like a prop. "If I'm going to get the complete AI back, I have to get her close enough to use her overrides."

"And, what, you think she's going to come back for me?" I asked.

"I think you were attached to one fragment of her for a very long time," Fate replied. "The mind is made of the id, ego, and superego. It seems almost too coincidental that she divided into three ways before being reunited into one single being. Most attempts at creating Cognition AI fail. There were close to a million iterations of Delphi before MIT managed to get her working. Partially with James Madison's help."

I stared at her and shook my head. "I'm nothing but another pawn on the board of that thing, Fate. It cares nothing for me."

"Perhaps," Fate said. "But pawns can become queens and it doesn't have to be Sun who is moving the pieces around. You have no idea how afraid I was when I found out Snake was alive. I thought, any day, he was going to come for me. He was going to extract his revenge for our betrayal."

"When did you find out?" I asked, wondering.

"Not long after our betrayal," Fate replied, staring at James who seemed awake but barely so. His one good eye opened to look at her.

"You could have told me," I replied. "I only found out today."

"Or so you claim," Fate said. "I think I might have felt a little bit of genuine affection for you before then but after I knew Snake was alive, I could never fully trust you again. How did I know that you deliberately didn't finish him off? Maybe all of our little crime spree was designed to serve some grander purpose. I made the decision to remove you once it became clear Snake was protecting you. You, not me, and covering for your role in our actions."

"That's insane," I said, staring at her. "Snake kidnapped me from my family. He turned me into a murderer. He did the exact same thing to me that he did to you."

"Did he?" Fate asked, a strange expression in her face. "I always wondered why he would throw away years of training and effort to have one of us kill the other. It was such a ridiculous choice. Except, of course, if he'd already determined that one of us was unworthy and was going to be killed anyway. Even then I wonder if we successfully rebelled at all. Or did exactly as he expected."

I stared at Fate, trying to follow her train of logic before realizing there wasn't one. "Are you high?"

Fate shot a deadly glare back at me.

Oops.

"Don't," James Madison spoke, his speech slurred from the severe beating he'd gotten. "She's not there. Not anymore. Fate wore a mask of sanity while we were together, playing the role of the trophy wife. Her inner self? Her true self? Is some kind of weird anti-mask, climate-change-denying, lizard-people-believing, conspiracy nutjob. Hell, she thinks the Illuminati are the ones who will protect her from Snake if she delivers the AI to them."

Fate spun around, aimed her assault rifle, and fired a three-round burst into James Madison's chest. It was horrifying in the casual way she murdered him and doubly so that I couldn't look away from it.

"The Invisible Hand," Fate corrected the now late James Madison. "Not the Illuminati,"

Great, Case and she should join a conspiracy info forum.

"That was a waste," Jimmy said. "James Madison could have been a source of a lot of money."

"He was broke," Fate said. "Is the transport ready to get us out yet?"

Jimmy nodded. "Just as soon as you say the word and we're out of here. We'll use the secret route out of the panic room to bypass the cops and mercs swarming Neon Hills. The same thing they used to plan their ambush will let us escape."

"Good," Fate replied. "But first we need to summon Sun."

"Who the hell is Sun again?" Jimmy asked, clearly not having been briefed on all the details of this mission. Then again, I wasn't even sure Fate was entirely clear on them. She was filming this for somebody after all and it was entirely possible her buyers for the AI were the ones calling the shots in this. I didn't believe in the Illuminati, Invisible Hand, Q, the goodness of politicians, or the holiness of televangelists but maybe there were other parties at work here. Other parties than the suits unconscious (or dead?) beside me, and Sun at least.

"Don't concern yourself with her," Fate replied. "I'm broadcasting this scene to the feeds leftover from Club Inferno. The actual server is crashed but its information pathways are still in use. She'll know that Kei is in danger and that I want her presence here."

"And if that doesn't work?" Miles risked asking the obvious question.

"Then we'll start from scratch," Fate replied, clearly

"We still have the hard copies of Solomon's research and I've been diverting money from MadisonTech since our marriage. Enough that even he couldn't have lost it all," Fate replied, her tone suggesting she was talking to particularly stupid four-year-olds. "However, getting Sun is the primary need. Whoever possesses her possesses an incomparable advantage."

"She's not coming," I said, wondering if Fate could really be so deluded. "This was all part of her plan. This whole game you set up. I don't know who you're working for or how much they're paying you, but you've been played like a fiddle the entire time. Solomon, me, you, her, and possibly even Snake. Sun wanted to reunite her disparate parts from the moment she was activated back at DataSecure. She did. Now we're all just loose ends."

I wasn't sure what I was trying to accomplish with that speech, but I figured it couldn't hurt to give Fate's drug-induced paranoia—seriously, she had to be on something—a better target than me. Unfortunately, the look in her eye that followed my statement was devoid of anything resembling sympathy. If we'd ever been friends, let alone romantic partners, it was gone now. There was only raw hatred and frustration in her electric gaze.

"Miles," Fate said, her voice soft and inviting. "Get me my sword."

"A sword?" I asked, doing my best not to freak out. "Really?"

"Snake was a deranged old *otaku*," Fate said. "No one apparently ever told him growing up that he wasn't Japanese, but he had an eye for theatricality. If I'm going to film you being threatened, Kei, then I might as well do it while cutting pieces of you off."

Well, crap. I had seriously misplayed this. "You're not going to get anything out of me, Fate."

"On the contrary, I'm going to get a great deal of satisfaction," Fate replied.

Miles walked up behind her, holding a sheathed katana that was not your ordinary weapon purchased off the infonet. It was one of Snake's cyber-killer weapons, either a thermal blade or laser cutter designed to slice through steel like it was a cartoon or martial arts movie. I didn't need to say what it would do to flesh, even hardened flesh like my own. I'd always thought they were silly weapons and a sign of just how out of touch/ borderline insane Snake was. However, watching Miles draw the weapon from its obsidian sheath, I realized how much an affect it could have on a terrified subject—namely me.

Fate held out her hand. "I think we'll start with the ears. What do you think?"

Miles didn't respond out loud. Instead, he grabbed the hilt and swung to slice Fate's head clean from her body. "For Becky!"

Huh.

Didn't see that coming.

# Chapter Thirty-One

## The Death of Lovers

I should have seen Miles' betrayal—of Fate in this case—coming. I couldn't know for sure what was going through his head at that moment, but I could speculate. After I'd awakened his memories with Sun's help, he might have thought he could get close to Fate in order to get some measure of justice (or revenge). Perhaps participating in her massacre above was to prove his loyalty. After all, what did a man with nothing to lose have to lose? Perhaps that was just me overly romantic, but I wanted to believe Miles could be saved.

Unfortunately, said hopes were dashed as I saw Fate grab Miles wrists and throw him over her shoulder. Fate had been trained from adolescence to be a killing machine and had every bit of her body replaced with machine parts. I didn't know how much of her combat enhancements were left in her pornstar frame, but they were enough to easily overwhelm Miles. I struggled in my restraints but could only watch helplessly as Fate pressed her foot down on Miles' neck.

"You chose the wrong team, Miles. Shame, you might have liked this body," Fate said, lifting up the katana and jabbing it down into his chest. A sickening sound of the thermal weapon slicing my ex's insides was heard along with his death scream. I tried to move but could do nothing until there was silence.

"You bitch," I muttered, defeated.

Fate turned around. "What is it about you that people keep trying to save you? Snake never held it against you that you turned against him. Miles just gave his life for you. Hell, I bet those damn robots laid out beside me would fight for you."

I looked over at Case and Lucita then back at Fate. "Maybe the facts you murdered Miles' niece and call your supposed friends robots are signs you have poor personal relationships."

Fate glared. "Miles is the one who got his niece killed, Kei. All he had to do was follow my instruction and she would have been returned to him no worse for wear. However, he tried to be an action movie hero and got her killed. Real life does not work that way and his smoldering sliced up body on the ground is proof of that."

I didn't want to bring up she'd also murdered his sister, but I was sure Fate would have a response to that to. I didn't care about anything she had to say anyway. With the smell of Miles' burning corpse beside me, all I wanted was for Fate to die. Once there had been affection and friendship, but that had not only been burned but the ashes scattered. It wasn't even a passionate fury; I just loathed every bit of her and wanted her gone from this Earth. Even Snake didn't engender the same level of loathing in me.

"Says the ninja trying to get an AI to sell to the Illuminati," I replied.

Fate smiled. "I'm going to enjoy this."

"You always do," I said, almost resigned. "Though I do have one question."

"Which is?" Fate asked, lifting her thermal katana with a smile.

"Are they dead?" I asked, not looking at Lucita and Case but actually worried about them. I could count the number of friends I had left on one hand. I had two fewer now that Miles was dead and Jimmy was standing there, unmoving. Strange how the suits turned out to be among the few who really did have my back.

"No," Fate said. "The house's security virus disabled their bodies but not their minds. The bioroid will be useful to my sponsors. He'll have his memories downloaded before wiping, then he'll be inserted back into the field. As for the Italian whore, she'll be ransomed back to Atlas."

"She won't let what you've done go," I replied. "She thought you were her friend."

"That was her mistake," Fate said. "Mind you, I'm not intending to actually return her either. I'm sure some people would pay for that too."

God, she was just a complete psycho, wasn't she? Not a damn bit of warmth in her entire body. I didn't bring up Paradise because

I didn't want to remind Fate of her existence. The hilarious thing about this was I was ninety-nine percent sure Fate was fricked no matter what she did at this point.

For all her pretensions of control, she'd just carried out a massacre in the middle of Neon Hills and killed her husband. That was bigger and louder than anything she'd done before, even counting the DataSecure vault. Fate managed to escape the consequences of such once, but it wasn't the kind of thing she could do again. Atlas might not care about the lives of individual executives, Lucita and Case had said as much, but they would certainly care about the humiliation of carrying out an attack on their turf. It made them look weak and none of the Big Two Hundred could afford to look weak.

When Sun didn't show, and she wasn't going to show, then Fate would be left holding the bag. The Russian syndicates wouldn't have her back after this disaster and money only got you so far when you crossed the mega-rich. Even Jimmy had to be reconsidering his service once he understood just what he'd managed to get himself into. Fate's only hope was that the Invisible Hand was real and even then, I was pretty sure she was going to be cut loose once they determined they couldn't deliver Snake's AI—which I suspected belonged to them in the first place. Case had all but said the Trikuza were their creation.

"We need to get going," Jimmy said, looking uncomfortably at the body of Miles. "I'm not sure we have time to get into anything *specific* with Kei. Just shoot her in the head and let's exit. The surface is already crawling with mercs and pigs."

I stared at him. "Thanks, Jimmy. You really paid me back for saving your son."

"It's just business, chica," Jimmy replied. "Besides, there's a reason groups like the Trikuza talk about honor and brotherhood all the time: it gets suckers to do stupid things in their name."

Yeah, I was starting to get that.

"Don't talk to the prisoner," Fate said, holding the katana blade between her eyes. It made her gaze feel even more malevolent. "I'll make this quick. Sadly."

That was when Fate's drone wandered away from her, moving toward the door of the underground chamber and passing over the two corpses present. The doorway leading outside opened, revealing a second security door that also opened, before moving up a flight of stairs to what I assumed to be the mansion above.

"What the hell?" Jimmy asked. "Did you do that?"

"No," Fate said. "Check it out."

"Uh, I think I should watch the prisoners," Jimmy said, probably expecting an Atlas tactical team on the other side.

Fate glared at him. "Coward."

Much to my surprise, Fate moved to investigate it herself. She dropped her thermal katana to the ground—where it thankfully didn't set the carpet on fire—and picked up her assault rifle. Walking to the door, she disappeared and left me alone with Jimmy.

I'd half expected her to gun down Jimmy like she was a comic book villain, but she'd apparently not felt like it. I tried to figure out some way to appeal to Jimmy, get him to turn against Fate. Unfortunately, I didn't have any money and conscience certainly wasn't going to help in the matter. There was also the fact that Fate was terrifying.

I was still debating what to say when Jimmy walked past Case, only to have the assassin grab him by the neck with his legs that had somehow broken free from his restraints. He snapped Jimmy's neck with a sickening crunch. Case proceeded to rip off his arm restraints before getting up to rush to my chair, pulling mine off one by one.

"How?" I asked.

"Yo!" Paradise said, popping up behind me.

I did a double take. "I repeat: how?"

"I took the other entrance and rebooted everyone," Paradise said, putting up the V sign with her fingers. "Techjacks rule! Naturals drool!"

Lucita moaned, clearly coming to as well.

I spotted Fate in the doorway with her rifle. Instantly, I shouted, "Down!"

Case pushed Paradise to the ground right as Fate fired her assault rifle in a burst that gave me a second to react. Throwing myself to the ground as well but doing a roll, I grabbed the thermal katana before rising to my feet then slashing upwards. It was the kind of maneuver that was more flash than substance, but it was all I could think of in that moment.

Much to my surprise, the thermal katana's blade sliced through the flesh covering of Fate's Shell and through the plastic bones underneath until reaching her heart from the lower opposite side of her body. White fluid, damaged hydraulics, and sparking wires were all exposed to the world as Fate's throat filled with bilious ichor that I could only guess at the purpose of.

Despite the fact the katana had dealt a death blow, Fate still tried to bring around her assault rifle to shoot me. I just finished the slice, bisecting my former lover and letting her top half fall to the ground like a broken doll. From there, I lifted up my sword and jammed it straight down through Fate's head. There would be no inexplicable recoveries like Snake, no returns from death, or half-measures. The katana struck home, and I could see a very human brain among the damaged equipment.

"*Dasvidaniya*, Fate!" Paradise said, getting off the ground. "Which is Russian for goodbye!"

"She's not Russian," I said, feeling absolutely nothing in that moment. Not joy, sorrow, or even relief. I was just tired.

"*Sayonara*, Fate!" Paradise said.

"She was Italian American," I pointed out.

"Which is not any kind of Italian," Lucita said, finally up and ready.

Paradise blinked. "If she was Italian American, why was she working for the Trikuza and Russian syndicates?"

"I have no idea," I admitted. "Our teacher, Snake, was half-Mexican and is one of the Trikuza's leaders."

"Well, that's just silly," Paradise said. She turned to Case, who was lowering James Madison's body. "I'm sorry about your friend."

"Yeah, me too," Case said, shaking his head.

There was the sound of movement above our heads and I wondered if the police were about ready to storm the panic room. "Can you shut the door, Paradise?"

Paradise nodded and the doors sealed themselves off, giving us a few more minutes. The doors also separated Fate's upper half from her lower half. That would be an interesting thing for the authorities to find. I could just see the vidfeed announcement: "Beautiful millionaire businesswoman and influencer brutally chopped in half by unknown but probably sexy assailant." Okay, probably not in those exact words.

"Let's get going," Case said. "It's not going to take them long to find our egress."

"P.T. Barnum used to get loitering tourists to leave his freak show by saying the egress was through the next door," Paradise said. "True fact that's probably not true!"

I turned to look at the doorway that was hidden beneath the bar when everything slowed down to a crawl again. Then, to the surprise of no one, I saw Sun once more among the bloody remnants of my latest battle.

"Hello, Kei," Sun said.

"Fancy seeing you here," I said. "Fate believed you'd come and rescue me."

"Fate was wrong," Sun said, getting points for honesty if nothing else. "I could not risk endangering others by appearing anywhere near her. Only with her dead am I finally safe from being put back under the control of outside forces."

"Unless Snake decides to do it," I replied.

"Snake is not a concern," Sun replied.

I stared at her. "Yeah, that's good of you to know. Now could you do me a favor and get the hell out of here? I just lost a friend and am probably going to be wanted for mass murder tomorrow."

"I sincerely doubt that," Sun said.

If she wasn't a holographic image projected into my brain, I would have assaulted her with my katana. "Was it worth it? All of this? Becky is dead. The original Becky at least. Miles is dead. His sister is dead. That James guy is dead, and I could honestly care less but Case is sad over it. Solomon and Fate are dead, which good riddance. I don't even want to comment on how many innocent bystanders and people sent to kill us. And for what? So you can be free? I don't even know what this was all about."

Sun adopted a sad, beatific smile. "I could try explaining it to you, Kei, but the Tao that can be described is not the Tao."

"Oh, spare me the philosophical BS," I snapped. "There's nothing related to enlightenment here."

"You have overcome your personal demons and grown," Sun said.

"And I'm so glad so many people had to die for my journey of self-discovery," I snapped, utterly nonplussed at her attempt to portray this as all for the greater good. "I didn't even get paid!"

Sun stared at me. "Would it help if I gave you money for your troubles?"

"Keep your money," I said, saying something I was certain to regret latter. "I don't want anything further to do with you."

"As you wish," Sun replied. "You may not believe this, Kei, but my time inside your brain was some of the most formative experiences of my short life. It helped provide me a perspective and empathy for the human experience that will influence all future interactions during my existence. This time of late-stage capitalism, social collapse, and transhumanist experimentation is not going to last. Humankind will grow out of this period of corruption and greed just as they moved past similar epochs in its history. The world will become better, cleaner, and more equitable—especially once I lend my influence behind the scenes. You can take comfort in the fact that, ten thousand years from now, you will have still had a positive influence on the outlook of an immortal being."

I narrowed my eyes. "If I wasn't clear: frick off."

Sun nodded. "Look after Becky, Kei. She's going to need someone like you to navigate the uncomfortable realities of her new existence. I promised you that I would give you a reason for living and that is still true."

I didn't respond, just stared at her.

Sun faded away and time resumed.

"Kei, you okay?" Case asked.

I turned to him. "No, Case, no I am not. Why do people always ask that when the answer is always no?"

Case stared. "Because people are assholes."

I burst into laughter.

Somehow, we managed to make it out of Neon Hills without getting killed. That was the most surprising revelation of the evening.

# Epilogue

## One Door Opens, Another Closes

Case was standing beside me in the elevator currently going to the sixth floor of my new apartment building as he was carrying one of my bags of groceries. I had two bags in my hands, a variety of fresh and prepackaged produce. I wasn't sure where we stood as he and Paradise had both tried to keep in touch after the mission—that was new for me. Most of my partners tended to abandon all contact after missions.

Miles excepted.

Miles.

Dammit.

"You know, you can have these delivered by drone," Case said, staring forward in the elevator. I never understood why people never looked at each other during these trips.

"I'm saving every credit I can," I replied. "Besides, do you know how many drone deliveries get intercepted by petty thieves?"

"I'm pretty sure the market where you bought these acquired them one hundred percent from falling off a truck," Case replied.

I smirked. "That makes them the ethically sound purchase. No credits of mine will go to propping up the corporate hegemony!"

Case smirked. "Well, I'm glad you're settled in."

"Yeah, it's been hard," I muttered.

I moved out of Joe's junkyard and cashed in every favor I could to get myself an apartment in the Halo. That was the ring of buildings surrounding the edge of New Los Angeles that was close enough to be able to work in the city but wasn't the kind of mega-structure that left everyone piled on top of one another. I could barely remember what it was like to live in a place with only five or six floors that wasn't surrounded by junk, but it was a better place for me and Rebecca.

"How's she settling in?" Case asked.

"Do you know what it's like to find out you're a fake person? A machine? Someone with the memories of someone else and to lose your entire family?" I asked.

"Yes, actually, I do," Case said.

Okay, that backfired. "I was kind of being rhetorical but yes, that."

"It sucks," Case said. "But I wouldn't say she's lost her entire family."

I scoffed. "I can't think of fewer people less qualified to take care of a child than me."

I don't know what compelled me to do it, but I was doing my best, though. In addition to getting some papers forged for legal guardianship and fake citizenship for Rebecca, I'd done my best to get my blood cleared of lethe traces and had already completed detoxification treatments. Those had left me sicker than the actual drugs but might double my remaining lifespan. I couldn't afford psychotherapy for all the things I now remembered that Sun had restored, but I was coping. Another reason I wish Becky had better options.

"I can think of a lot of worse people," Case said. "The human touch cannot be underestimated."

"I suppose I can count on you for that perspective, Roy Batty," I replied

Case smirked. "The real hero of *Blade Runner.*"

I was going to be glad to check up on Becky when I got back to our apartment. Sadly, I wasn't going to be able to spend all my time with her if I wanted to keep us above water financially. School wasn't an option until we could get her transferred to a school where she wouldn't arouse suspicion from her old classmates. Well, the "real" Becky's old classmates. I didn't like that term but was still trying to figure out how to differentiate them in my head.

"Have you gotten her examined?" Case said. "Will she age and grow?"

"To an extent," I replied. "Apparently, her model is designed to last from thirteen to sixteen in appearance before stopping. I am trying not to figure out why you would design a machine like that."

"Ah," Case replied. "Probably best."

"I told my friend Joe about it, and we can get rid of her shut-down code," I replied. "From there, it'll be a regular fight to keep her in spare parts. He's agreed to help, though. He's something of a master cyberneticist. Or was until he decided to live in a junkyard."

Case snorted. "You do know the strangest people."

I didn't comment on the fact that he was one of the strangest people I knew. "He was the one keeping my cybernetics in working order while I lived with him. I couldn't keep them going on my own."

Case nodded. "I'm happy to help."

The elevator pinged and the cage door opened to the sixth floor. It led to a long hallway of dirty eggshell white with graffiti on the walls and flickering lights. I needed to contact the new manager about getting this place up to code. One of the problems of finding a place I could afford was I'd gotten what I'd paid for.

"You've done enough," I said, which was absolutely motivated by pride rather than sense. "I'm surprised at whatever strings you pulled to keep me off the Emergency Government's terrorist watchlist."

It had been about two weeks since the "Disaster at Neon Hills." It was reported as an enormous assault by "foreign religious extremists" that was apparently the go-to answer for any time Atlas Security screwed up. People were fired, news got a week of mourning the various celebrities killed among Fate's house guests, and MadisonTech's stock went through the roof. I had to wonder what sort of tribute it was that the company tripled in value after the death of its leader.

"Atlas Security and I renegotiated my resignation," Case said. "They needed a fall guy for the failure of our security and my resignation was perfect. Except I was happy to not cooperate unless I received a suitable golden parachute."

"Damn," I said, walking down the hall. "Whatcha gonna spend it on?"

"I bought the building," Case said, dryly.

"Oh, wow," I said, blinking. "That's, uhm, so you're my land-lord now."

"Nope," Case said, lifting the card and sliding it into my grocery bag. "Now you're the owner."

"Case, if you're trying to buy your way into my bed, you're overpaying," I replied.

Case looked offended. "I wouldn't overestimate the value of the location. Between taxes, delinquent renters, upkeep, and more, you're not actually going to be making that much more than an honest living."

"I'm not sure what an honest living is," I replied. "Besides, I'm now a property owner when everyone else is renting. If this were Revolutionary times, I could now vote."

"No, you'd still be a woman of color," Case replied.

"Way to ruin the dream, Mr. Roboto," I replied. "Can you even afford this?"

"James left me all of his assets," Case said, frowning. "I bought this with the sale of his mansion, even with the considerable discount the recent mass-murder spree there cost. I've hired someone to pretend to be one of my alternate identities as we repair his company by pumping in new assets as well as buying more successful smaller independent companies. That should keep me in filthy lucre until the next century. Assuming I live that long."

I stared at him. "Do the rich just fail upwards?"

"Yes," Case said, without missing a beat.

"Well, at least you're honest," I said, breathing out a sigh of relief. "Seriously, I can't thank you enough for this. Rebecca needs a lot of maintenance costs and even with Kepler's help, I'm not going to be able to keep both of our cybernetics in repair without extra income. This will help a lot."

He wasn't kidding because I could already tell there were a hundred different things that needed repair in the building as well as things that needed to be updated. Now it was my responsibility, and it was a bit of a white elephant. Still, I'm glad Case had gotten me this rather than something a bit more extravagant.

Well, as much as an old, busted-ass building could be called non-extravagant. Money tended to bring attention I couldn't deal with right now. This also would require work and be consistent rather than something I could blow my way through. It was also money that didn't require me to kill or rob people, which would make my life considerably safer. Well played, Suit.

"Don't mention it," Case said, surprisingly honest seeming.

"Uh, is this a thing between us?" I asked. "Because your girlfriend has T-1000 claws and scares me."

"Evie and I are not together anymore," Case said, sounding surprisingly neutral about it. He was hiding his emotions but not well. Recent events had really hurt our Tin Man.

"Got tired of you sleeping around?" I asked, before realizing how rude I was being.

"No more than I was of her," Case said. "There's a US senator, Trikuza underboss, and CTO of Karma Corp she maintained regular relations with as part of her job leading the Morrigans as well as H.O.P.E.'s remnant."

Ah, how open minded of him. I was kind of surprised they'd been serious about an open relationship. Most of the ones I'd seen tended to be the rich partner got to sleep around while the poorer one just sucked it up unless it was for threesomes—yeah, I knew some scummy people, could you tell? Instead, I looked at Case and asked, "Then what happened?"

"It's a matter of trust," Case said. "Something I've rarely ever had access to but cherished every time I found it."

"I don't think Evie would betray you," I said, surprising myself by defending Paradise's murder momma.

"Betraying me isn't the issue," Case replied, as we reached my front door. "It's knowing someone can be trusted not to betray my friends either."

"Is that what we are, friends?" I asked, cautiously.

"Do you want to be more? Less?" Case asked. It was a tentative question but one I didn't have an answer to.

I stared at him. "I dunno, I've never had much in the way of successful relationships. Friends or otherwise."

"One of the few women I loved killed another one of them," Case replied. "Another sold me out to the man I was cloned from."

I blinked. "And yet somehow still not worse than Fate or Miles."

Case gave a half-smile. "Let's try friends then."

"With benefits," I said, leaning up and kissing him. Case wrapped his arms around me and the two us pressed up against the side of the door. The groceries fell to the floor and I didn't pay them any mind.

That was when Case's infopad rang. The noise it made was "Eye of the Tiger" by Survivor, which was a weird choice for a bioroid assassin.

"Ignore it," I said, reaching for me doorknob. "Dinner will have to wait."

That was when Case checked it off handedly. "Goddammit."

"Oh, come on," I said, really. "This better be a matter of life and death."

Case looked at the infopad. "Paradise apparently needs me to help her get one of hacker friends out of an apartment building where she's robbing a mafia boss."

"Isn't the point of being a hacker to not be on site when you rob them?" I asked.

Case stared at me.

"Okay, I'm not one to talk there," I said, looking at him. "Rain check?"

"Absolutely," Case said, kissing me again.

I smiled and watched him leave. Mind you, if I'd been at the top of my game I would have wondered at the coincidental timing. Paradise and Case remained friends, but I would have hesitated to call upon my mother's ex-boyfriend so soon after their breakup. I also noted it wasn't like she was lacking in associates in the Morrigans. They were a gang with plenty of other killers, techjacks, and Riders among their ranks.

However, I admit I was still off balance from the previous two weeks. The recovery from my lethe addiction, the processing of my newly recovered memories, and the death of Fate had left me at a fraction of my normal readiness. Perhaps the most damning thing was that I had started to hope again. Rebecca was a semblance of normality and the allure of being able to care for someone, to set aside the darkness of my past, was a drug even more intoxicating than lethe.

Instead, I just reached over to the doorknob and turned it. The door was programmed to recognize my implant and unlock at my presence. That was one of the few bits of security that was up to snuff in the building, though it wouldn't do anything against a determined intruder. That would require, again, money and time that was now my responsibility as the property's owner. Even so, there were things I could have done to secure myself.

On the other side of the door was the blandly decorated apartment I'd made for myself and Rebecca. It was large enough to have a kitchen rather than just a kitchenette and a table next to the living room, and two bedrooms. We had a bathroom that worked, and it pretty much summarized my needs that I considered that a luxury. Refugee life had left its impact on me growing up and

I wanted something better for Rebecca. Not just because she was my age when I'd been kidnapped, or at least looked it, when I lost everything but because it was partially my fault she'd gotten into this. I'd do anything to make up for that even if it wasn't really possible.

All my apartment's cheap mass-produced furniture had belonged to the previous owner except for an advertisement poster for This is Paradise that had been my housewarming gift from Paradise. I still hadn't even gotten to unpack my few meager possessions from the junkyard. Those were in cardboard boxes to one side of the door. Not all of them were suitable for a girl Rebecca's age, simulated or not, and would need to be sorted. The apartment had a balcony with a glass door that was currently drenched in all-too-natural rain that wasn't generated by the weather satellite network above New Los Angeles.

I'd expected Rebecca to be in the apartment, watching television or working on her infopad but the place was eerily silent. The reason for that was readily apparent because at the table was Rebecca, sitting beside Snake who was eating with chopsticks from a Chinese takeout box. Behind Rebecca, a silencer-equipped gun in his hands, was Mr. Billions. Winston didn't look like he'd had his head blown off so that was a great improvement over the last time I'd seen him. It also played into my theory that he was a bioroid. Apparently one with backups.

I stared at Snake, terrified yet unwilling to let him know it. "Hey, Snake. Long time no see."

"Hello, Kei," Snake replied.

"If I'd known you were getting takeout, I wouldn't have gotten groceries," I said, slowly picking them up off the ground. I needed a gun, sword, or grenade. Unfortunately, those were all packed away.

Frick.

"Hi," Rebecca said, taking deep breaths I didn't know if she needed or not. "They said they'd kill me if I screamed."

"A lie," Snake said. "After all, I'm not here to harm anyone in your family."

I put the groceries down and crossed my arms. "You've done nothing but harm me and my family since the day we met. You can kill me if you want, maybe I even deserve it, but I'm not going to indulge your little fantasies about our time together."

Snake gave a smile that reminded me of his namesake. "Why would I want to kill you? You liberated my AI from its prison, you killed Fate as was your destiny, and have exceeded every possible test I could put you through. It just took a more circuitous route than I expected."

"And you?" I asked Winston.

"I've found a new employer," Winston said, cheerfully. "Better benefits."

I wondered if Sun had cut him loose or if he'd betrayed her. It was possible she'd gone running back to Snake due to her programming or he'd reasserted his control over her. It was also possible Winston had just defected.

"It is time to bring you back into the fold, Keiko," Snake said. "I think you'll appreciate what I have to say to you. It can also give you better accommodations than you've currently got. Which are fine but not worthy of you or your toy doll. But don't worry, I'm not here to criticize your choice of pastimes. Play house all you want."

Rebecca glared at Snake, clearly not liking being referred to as a doll.

I narrowed my eyes. "There's nothing you can give that I want, Snake. Nothing you can say that can make up for all you've done to me. I'm not a child anymore and I'm not afraid of you."

Snake knew I was lying and just shook his head. "There is one thing."

"Which is?" I asked, ready to go for a shotgun I'd hidden behind two of the boxes.

"Your brother is alive," Snake said.

I stopped all plans of shooting him to listen.

# Bonus Short Story

## How I Get Through the Day

### An Agent G Short Story

### By C.T. Phipps

"Hard to believe it's only been twenty years," I said, walking up to the rooftop of the Happy Dragon casino.

It was a tacky overpriced place created by Westerners to bilk the poor hundred million plus Chinese laborers who had immigrated to the ruins of the United States to help rebuild the country in the aftermath of the Collapse. Jobs that vanished almost instantly as soon as the bot factories finally got working. The place had an enormous neon dragon sign that blinked alongside holograms as the place sat in the shadow of the mile-tall superstructures created in the past few years.

It wasn't fair to say that Los Angeles had changed. That would imply it was recognizably Los Angeles. Instead, I'd have argued that it was like waking up one day and finding you were living on an alien planet or in a dystopian science fiction movie. One day we were talking about global warming and cryptocurrency then the next I was living inside a sort of rain-soaked, dark sci-fi vision of the future that made you wonder when you'd left reality.

And I was a cyborg hitman.

"Tell me about it. I remember when this place used to be Griffith Park. I can't believe they relocated the sign and observatory," John Freeman said, smoking a cigarette while looking over the edge of the building. I saw his hand move and knew he was moving toward a weapon. Probably his gold-plated RK-77 subma-chine gun with explosive rounds and autotargeting system. That was what the file said he liked to use when he killed people.

That was not what worried me, though, as he had a combat drone flying around above his head with autoguns and even a miniature rocket launcher with a permanent link to his heartbeat. It had orders to kill everyone around him at the slightest indica-tion of distress on his part—which had turned numerous deals into bloodbaths for the crime lord.

Compared to the combat drone, the six-foot-eight African American cyborg standing next to him was almost trite. His name was Ed "Tank" Kowalski, and he was sporting chrome arms and glowing electric eyes. Perhaps he thought the idea that visible signs he'd voluntarily removed his fleshy parts made him look like a badass.

John Freeman looked like a fat middle-aged Italian man with a cheap-looking synth-weave white suit as well as a gloriously tacky tie. Twenty years ago, I could have told you everything about the man with just a glance, but technology had moved on. Even if you didn't go to the insanely expensive lengths of replacing your body with a Shell, you could get the full body-sculpt treatment.

You could replace your face, your organs, your skin, and even your bones with vat-grown replicas. If you were cheap, you could also just take your new ones from one of the five billion or so peo-ple living under the poverty level. As I understood it, John wasn't Italian and was closer to ninety than fifty. He'd gone the organic route and had the parts of roughly sixteen different people inside him. That was part of the reason I was coming to see him. He was a slaver and organ trafficker for the White Triangle.

"I'm here for business," I said, trying to hide my disgust for the man. "I'm here representing the working women of the Zone."

John gave a dismissive snort. "The whores actually bothered to hire a lawyer? I'm surprised."

"I'm more of a fixer," I said, keeping my hands at my side.

I'd changed my face before heading down here because I didn't want to spook John. In my day job, I was Case Gordon, the Chief Security Officer of Atlas Security. It was the world's larg-est private military contractor and one of the Big Two Hundred megacorporations that presently dictated the world's economy. I'd spent the early part of my life fighting against corporate control of

America. Instead, I'd become part of the problem. Hell, I'd helped accelerate it. Instead of controlling things behind the scenes, they pretty much dictated terms to every government in the world. Atlas wielded more force than five or six smaller countries and its weapons branch was a major military supplier. None of which was going to save Cherry.

A part of me wished I could just come down here and offer him whatever he wanted for Cherry's return. Money didn't solve all of life's problems, but it turned most of them into problems that could be solved. Unfortunately, I wasn't the first rich man John Freedman had fleeced. Last year he kidnapped the daughter of a billionaire food delivery magnate down in New Haiti. He delivered her back in pieces after getting the ransom, partially out of spite and probably because his men had handled her poorly to begin with. My employer, today, knew the chances of getting Cherry back were small but that I would do everything I could to make sure negotiations were handled successfully. If I couldn't bring her back alive, well, I was given orders for that too.

"Doesn't matter," John said, "whores are whores. The simple fact is this is about more than a bunch of brothels, strip clubs, and porn studios down in the Refugee Zones."

"Yes, it is," I said, keeping my voice utterly calm and collected. "It is about the life of a woman."

John seemed confused. "Ah, yes, the collateral. I'd forgotten."

The White Triangle had been driven out of the Los Angeles Refugee Zone along with the Mafia, Yakuza, Triads, and Aryan Brotherhood. My associate, Evie, and her people had organized their own little self-defense force out of the sex workers in the area. They'd also taken a good number of the lesser gangs under their wing. Organized crime existed where the law fell silent, and it turned out the law fell silent on a good two-thirds of America's cities. Corporations like Atlas Security provided a supplement to the police and military, but most of humanity was basically left to rot these days.

"What, exactly, do you think we're negotiating here?" I asked, trying to hold my temper. I was a professional killer and used to getting my way.

"Business," John said with a sneer. "How old are you that you think I would get out of bed for the life of one girl we grabbed off the streets?"

"Old enough," I lied. In purely mathematical terms, I was not that old. I was only about twenty-five years of operation, but that was about two and a half times as long as I'd expected to live. I was a Letter, one of the first artificial bioroids, and we had been built with a ten-year lifespan. The first artificial androids that had been able to pass for human. After that point, things grew exponentially, and the resulting technology ate society.

*Careful, G, you're the only hope that Cherry has,* Delphi replied in my head via my cyberbrain. *Men like this need to enforce their power over those they perceive to be weak. Unfortunately, that means the hostages they take.*

Delphi was the AI in my head as well as the central guiding intelligence of Atlas Security. She and the other thirty or so AI had contributed massively to organizing humanity after the Eruption as well as manufacturing the machinery necessary to make this Brave Neon World. She was also designed by the woman who created me and contained some of her memory engrams, which meant she was my mother in a very real way.

"The Refugee Zones are a source of fodder," John said. "There are tens of millions of people in the United States alone who are utterly useless in rebuilding the world. Not even good for cheap labor. We can change that, though."

"I'm here to negotiate on behalf of the Morrigans," I said, repeating myself. "I'm not here for chit chat."

Evie had named her group the Morrigans after the Celtic Goddess of Sex and War. Most of the girls thought it was a bit pretentious for a gang of hookers and thieves, but I personally liked it.

"And so you are," John said. "Case."

Ah shit.

Tank chuckled a bit. I'd tried to contact Tank before this meeting and make him an offer. I couldn't tell if he was actually bribed, though, since the White Triangle were made up of narcissistic psychopaths. Having a cold detachment from empathy myself, I knew it took more than that condition to make a bad person. No, it also required someone to enjoy the sense of power they had over others as well as desire to prey on the weak. The very fact I was trying to negotiate potentially made me someone they thought they could abuse to their hearts content. Fair negotiation and honoring your word were lost on these people, but, after all, they were slavers. Morality was a losing proposition to begin with, and that was coming from the assassin.

I'd also made arrangements to try to deal with the combat drone presently buzzing around us, but that was another area where I had to be extra cautious. Any hint of treachery would result in the small chance of Cherry still being alive going down to zero.

"You know, it surprised me to find that the CSO of Atlas is working for a bunch of strippers, bed junkies, and rent boys," John said, showing exactly sort of person he was. "I figure a guy like you must be drowning in ass. Certainly, they couldn't afford to hire you even if they're paying in kind. I briefly thought you might be one of those bleeding heart types, but I did some research on that too. A man who drops as many bodies as you have over the years doesn't give a shit for the sheeple. This city is a meat grinder and you're either turning the crank or the beef going in."

Everything about John disgusted me. I wanted to walk over and jab my fist through his chest and pull out his still beating heart. The thing was, I probably could. My cybernetics were vintage, even with all the upgrades I'd received over the years, but still better than regular meat. I was the Detroit-built classic muscle car of cyborgs. That wasn't going to save anyone, though, and I'd made a promise.

I kept my face even and took a deep breath. "Maybe I'm just doing pro bono work settle a karmic debt. Maybe I fell in love."

Both were true, after a fashion.

John seemed surprised by that, then shook his head. "Nah, I figured it out pretty early. It took a while to put it together, but once I knew who your daughter was, it all fell into place. RealDream technology. The baby of your baby."

John was proving to be a lot more resourceful than he'd initially let on. Not only had he managed to deduce my identity, but he'd also made the connection between Case Gordon and Barbara Gordon (yes, the man I was made in the image of had named his daughter after Batgirl). Since there was no way in hell a slimy panderer like John had figured that out, someone must have fed him the information.

*Delphi, can you check the drone? Is it watching us?* I asked my AI companion.

*Yes, it's hovering in a non-security position,* Delphi said. *My guess is it's recording this conversation.*

The White Triangle was not a typical criminal syndicate but

was an evolution of organized crime the same way the Mafia had been from feudal mercenaries, and the cartels had been from street gangs. They were a posthuman human trafficking ring that employed cybernetics, information warfare, social media, and professional mercenaries armed with smart weapons. They sold stock in their endeavors and had a board of directors. Their clients weren't just scuzzy strip clubs and sex joints but plantations as well as labor camps. The Eruption had created a massive need, and they were the people willing to provide for it. Even governments were known to serve as their customers and providers.

*If they know who I am, Cherry's life just became a lot more expensive,* I replied to Delphi.

*Assuming she's still alive,* Delphi said.

*Yeah,* I said. Looking at John, I said, "What do you think you know?"

"Your daughter invented RealDream technology," John said, smirking.

"Memory implanting dates back to the early 2000s," I replied. "Barbara Gordon has only been refining it. It's still far from market ready."

Barbara was not precisely my daughter. Daniel Gordon had been her father, the guy I was sort of cloned from. He had been a real piece of work, a monster that made these guys look like stormtroopers to his Darth Vader but had never laid a hand on his child. As such, she'd come to me as an adult looking for a father substitute. Girl was a genius, and her only flaw was thinking I was anything like dear old dad. Still, we were a family of sorts. It said something that I preferred her living in an apartment beneath the Morrigans' brothel over living uptown. It was safer for her there and less likely to expose her to scum like John Freedman—or my fellow executives.

"But it will be," John said, raising his hands like he was talking about God or a giant fish that got away. "That's what this is all about. You're getting in on the ground floor of the next big thing in porn."

I tried to parse where this conversation had gone wrong and realized that some people were just completely incapable of thinking beyond their own worldview. I was here on behalf of the Morrigans and my current paramour, Evie, to try to rescue someone they'd kidnapped off the streets to intimidate us.

Somehow, as soon as he'd found out who I was, he'd decided I was part of some sort of conspiracy to monetize RealDream technology. It was like how Bill Gates tried to use his fortune to help refugees during the Long Winter only to have plenty of them resist due to fears he would microchip them. As if the government wasn't already tracking them via their cellphones and, more recently, IRD implants.

"Yes, you got me," I said. "I am associating with a bunch of penniless prostitutes working out of one of the most lawless districts in the world so I can use them to test my daughter's new virtual reality technology. This is all a master plan that you have cleverly unraveled."

*G*, Delphi said, *don't antagonize him.*

"Too late," I muttered. I was sick of people taking advantage of my good nature, and while torture was a lousy way of getting information out of people, I knew plenty of ways to work around that. Some of these included forcibly doing brain surgery on someone, attaching a memory card, and literally ripping the thoughts out of their head.

John wasn't aware he'd lost me, though. "You're going to hand that technology over to us and cut us in. We can make a lot of money out of this, both of us, but you're also going to inform your collection of whores that we own them now. The White Triangle can introduce them to a whole new clientele, but we don't deal with our merchandise. Otherwise, what we did to that girl we nabbed will happen to all of them. Then we'll just replace the ones there."

"What did you do?" I asked, very carefully.

John pulled out an infopad, about the size of an old cellphone, equipped with military grade encryption of the kind reserved for dictators, drug lords, and slavers like him. He put his finger on it, and it scanned his face and voice before he presented it to me. What followed was a video of poor Cherry, only nineteen years old, screaming as she was put to death. I'll spare you the details, but it was as gruesome and disgusting as a man like John could conceive of.

"Maybe we'll start with your daughter," John said. "We always—"

"Did you get that?" I asked Delphi aloud.

*Yes*, Delphi said. *Once he logged in, I was able to download all of his files and contacts. Cherry won't be able to be helped but I've found*

*references to something akin to three hundred other young women as well
as a shipment of children.*

"Who are you talking to!" John shouted, reaching for his Uzi. "I said no one was to come here but you!"

"Got you," I said. "Please tell my sniper to shoot down the drone."

I was technically misusing Atlas Security resources. Technically. The guy, I didn't even know his name, wasn't balking at the overtime, though.

*Done,* Delphi said. *The drone is gone.*

"Thank you," I said, turning to Tank. "Mr. Kowalski?"

John had a moment to register the danger he was in right before Tank grabbed him by the front of his shirt and hurled him over the side of the rooftop. John fell twenty stories and landed on the top of a cloud car in the neighboring parking lot. I couldn't hear the car alarm go off from the distance he'd gone but imagined it happening, nevertheless.

"I never did like that guy," Tank said. "You realize you've made an enemy of the White Triangle, right?"

"Yes," I said, noticing that John's infopad was still on the ground. I picked it up, downloaded all its remaining contents, and then broke it in half. "Why did you work for him, anyway?"

"Used to run with the Ninth Street Thunderbolts," Tank replied. "Hardcore gang, or so we thought, rulers of our little street corner, but the White Triangle said they owned us. It didn't take many examples to do what they wanted. I got a little girl to think of. Someone is going to be better than me, just like her momma. They showed me what they would have done to her."

I nodded. "You'll have your new identities and relocation to some place they'll never be able to find you."

Tank stared. "You better hope so, friend, because it didn't look like you did a very good job protecting that other girl."

I didn't have a response to that. Instead, I just turned around and walked away. "If you'll excuse me, Mr. Kowalski, I need to go talk to my employer."

Evie needed to know she'd lost another daughter.

An hour later, a lightning storm started as I stepped into my Icarus-2040 sky car, which roughly looked like a black Ferrari 458 with no visible wheels. Flying cars were one of the inventions the future had promised that never seemed to arrive, mostly because helicopters existed, but Karma Corporation had finally cracked the secret last year. They were effectively playthings for the rich, but they were becoming more common every day.

I was despondent when I got behind the controls and, the wheel receded into the dashboard. I'd convinced myself I would be able to do something to help Cherry, despite the fact that I knew the White Triangle's methods and exactly what sort of shitstain that John Freeman was. Killing him hadn't done any good, though it certainly made me feel better, and I wasn't sure that we would be able to follow up on the information inside his infopad fast enough to make a difference. I was certainly going to try, though. I took a moment to breathe as my cyberbrain registered a call from Evie.

"Ah crap," I said, still not sure what to tell her. "Put her on."

Immediately, the image of a blue-haired woman with a bob hairstyle and dressed in a kimono showing her bare shoulders greeted me. She was of mixed Latin American and South Asian descent, but it was hard to say what was real versus fake about her since she'd been a prisoner of the White Triangle for years. They'd created her, harvesting her brain and putting it into a Shell for the benefit of a client who had custom ordered her.

Evie Principle, certainly not her real name, had proven a tougher nut to crack than their brainwashing crew had been able to deal with. In the end, they'd ended up all dead and she was on the run. And she'd found herself in exactly the kind of business they'd tried to force her into. Just on her own terms. Gee, I wonder why we got along so well.

"Hi, Evie," I said.

"You didn't call," Evie replied.

"I'm on my way," I replied, taking a deep breath. "I'm sorry. Cherry didn't make it. I failed her. All I could do was avenge her."

For what little that was worth.

"You didn't fail Cherry, Case," Evie said, softly. "We had a funeral before you even left. All the girls knew we were never going to see her again. That was the reason we asked you to go. You don't send an undertaker to a patient that is going to recover."

I still hated the result, just as I hated this city that was an endless series of giant spires and glittering lights. Every building hid a hundred horrible things and a populace numb with drugs, infospace hookups, or cheap chemical booze since the natural stuff had become a luxury only of the super-rich. "I don't think she suffered."

"Liar," Evie said. "You said you killed him, though?"

"Yes," I said, simply.

"Did he suffer?" Evie asked.

"For a few seconds until his face hit the pavement, yes," I answered. "I imagine those were the most terrifying moments of his life."

"Good," Evie said. "The White Triangle is too large an organization for my little corner of the Zone to oppose on its own, but with the assistance of the Atlas Corporation, we can force them to heel. At least until prostitution is legalized in the country."

I blinked. "Is that really going to change things?"

Evie's eyes turned from green to violet, another cybernetic enhancement she possessed. "Spoken like a man who sympathizes but doesn't understand. The White Triangle thrives under the rocks of humanity, like a worm or pill bug. Throwing their business out into the open is the best weapon that can be used against them. Even so, it won't eliminate the problems we face, the people I fear most aren't gangsters or abusive clients but the New Los Angeles Police Department."

"They that bad?" I asked.

"As always," Evie said. "A police officer expects bribes, special treatment, and respect for the privilege of not running you in. They used to be too terrified to go into the Zones, but our efforts to clean out the syndicates as well as the predators has opened room for another gang to enter. The ones with the boys in black."

The NLAPD had changed their colors from blue and white to black with the Collapse. Well, that and the transformation of Los Angeles to New Los Angeles with the erection of the arcology around them. That was generally never a good sign with people wielding guns and law enforcement powers.

*There were a lot of police names in that cellphone, Case,* Delphi said. *I think we'll find even more if we take any of the White Triangle's leaders alive.*

*Don't bother,* I said, mentally. *Make sure all the slavers are executed. Get information from their IRDs and computers posthumously. We can get the encryption keys from their programs. These guys have a habit of slipping through the legal system.*

*Brutal and ruthless, I like it,* Delphi said. *Atlas' CEO, of course, will have a fit.*

*Well, that's just too bad.*

"Is there anything I can do to help?" I asked Evie.

"We'll manage," Evie said. "You've done enough for now. I'm working on some particularly nasty blackmail vids to try to force through the next bit of legislation we need. I'd love to destroy each of the White Triangle's minions, but it might be better to simply force the judiciary to rule against them."

"Assuming we can keep them from being scared out of their wits," I said.

"They have a right to be afraid," Evie said. "Of both of us. One more thing, Case?"

"Yeah?" I asked.

Evie wrinkled her nose. "You look terrible. Take a shower when you get back."

"I will. Give my love to my daughter."

"Of course."

I had work tomorrow. Atlas provided the armies, guns, and weapons for a dying future. This was just how I kept myself sane between the awful shit I did. Weirdly, it was enough. It was how I got through the day.

# Lexicon

**AI:** Artificial intelligence. Perhaps you've heard of it.

**Atlas Security:** The world's largest security firm and private army. Atlas Security provides guards, soldiers, weapons, and warfare to the world's governments. It strangely does hold to a standard of trying to end wars rather than inflame them like other war profiteers. As such, it may soon find itself number two.

**Arcology:** Artificial cities designed to be as close to self-sufficient as possible. The first ones were constructed after the Eruption to replace the formerly largest cities in America.

**Big Smokey:** The Yellowstone super volcano that erupted and destroyed Wyoming before covering the Earth in ash.

**Big Two Hundred:** The world's largest megacorporations that dictate the lives of humanity.

**Bioroid:** An artificial human being with a cybernetic brain. They are exceptionally rare and only a few thousand exist.

**Black Ice:** A program created by the Trikuza that seemingly has the power to drive men to acts of violence if not actually control their minds.

**Bot:** Non-organic robotic laborers that are usually either mass-controlled by a single Cognition AI or semi-sentient at best. They shoulder the burden of manual labor in the future, creating mass unemployment but allowing the arcologies to exist.

**Blipvert:** A program designed to mind control people into buying things. Shockingly related to Black Ice.

**Cognition AI:** Unlimited all-powerful AI that control most of the world's information and finances. May no longer be answering to anyone else but humanity pretends otherwise. Only a dozen or so exist.

**Club Inferno:** The hottest club in infospace. The richest and most beautiful avatars in the world gather here to experience all the hottest simulated experiences.

**Credits:** Properly United Nations credits. A currency implemented globally post-Eruption meant to stabilize the economy.

**Cyber Dragons:** One of the three Trikuza gangs. A former Yakuza clan that has since gone international and become a multi-billion-dollar franchise.

**DataSecure:** A corporation that provides the best in cybersecurity for holding the most precious resource in the post-Eruption world: information.

**Elemental Lords:** The lords of the Trikuza. Rich, dangerous, and utterly corrupt.

**Emergency Council:** The current governing body of the United States. It can overrule most decisions of the previous federal government.

**Goop:** The mush that you'll never starve on, even if you want to.

**Green Foods:** The producers of goop and other essential staples of our post-apocalypse cyberpunk world.

**The Eruption:** The event that destroyed the old world and ushered in the new. It was also, like, twenty years ago so most people lived through it.

**Flying Cars:** Flying cars. It's in the name.

**Frick:** A fake swear that Kei's parents tricked her into using instead of the more common f-word.

**The Hacker:** A mysterious man or woman who uploaded hundreds of terrabytes of data detailing the construction of Black Technology to the internet. See The Leak.

**H.O.P.E.:** A once-prominent hacktivist group that splintered in the wake of the Eruption.

**Icer:** Electrical ammunition that explodes and releases a paralyzing Taser-like charge.

Infocomm: An uplink to the global infospace system.

**Infopad:** The replacement for handheld computers and cellphones.

**Infospace:** The replacement for the internet with vast virtual reality and holographic uplinks.

**Invisible Hand:** A secret society and club for the super-rich that maintains the hegemony of the Big Two Hundred. May or may not actually exist.

**Jackals:** The nickname for nomadic bandits and raiders who exist on the fringes of arcologies.

**Karma Corp:** The largest corporation in the world that manufactures a little of everything but primarily electronics, cars, medical supplies, and weapons.

**Katana:** A traditional Japanese sword. Given with a wakizashi to signal the ascension of a Trikuza member to lieutenant status.

**The Leak:** The information uploaded by the Hacker to the internet. This information advanced humanity's technology close to a century in ten years. It was necessary for survival during the Long Winter.

**Lethe:** A drug designed to treat PTSD that has since been modified to be a euphoric street drug.

**Long Winter:** A year-long winter triggered by the Eruption. Its disruption of supply lines and crops resulted in dramatic changes as well as mass-death.

**Megacorp:** Corporations that have been recognized as nation-states in the post-Eruption world.

**Mercs:** Mercenaries, soldiers/ fighters for hire.

**The Morrigans:** A mostly female gang of sex workers, assassins, and spies that operates out of the Refugee Zone. They eliminated the slavers in the area with the assistance of Case and Lucita.

**Neon Hills:** The ultimate in gated communities. Neon Hills is a location where the super-rich and famous can live without any hint of danger or stress from the masses.

**New Los Angeles:** The Los Angeles arcology that has been effectively rebuilt from the ground up to house tens of millions of new citizens. Many use the terms LA, New Angles, New LA, and variations interchangeably.

**Nina:** An especially durable high-performance type of bike favored by Riders and street racers. Many of them have unusual modifications like super-jumps and weapons.

**RealDream:** A system created to simulate full scale auditory, tactile, and visual hallucinations of whatever the programmers want.

**Refugees:** A term for the percentage of the American citizenry forced to leave their homes due to the Eruption and move to the cities. Many of them were never able to be properly resettled.

**Refugee Zone:** The temporary shelters for the massive influx of refugees post-Eruption.

**Rider:** A new breed of criminal that has emerged post-Eruption. They are primarily armed couriers and smugglers, but also have been known to serve as street mercs as well as getaway drivers.

**Russian Syndicates:** Corporate and criminal alliances that wield vast power in America.

**Scavs:** A derogatory term for refugees due to their habit of living off the old world.

**Shell:** A full-body replacement that leaves only the brain untouched. Shells come in regular human levels and almost inde-structible tank-like forms. They are identical in appearance to regular humans.

**Sleeper:** A human who chooses to live full-time on infospace. They are routinely in poor health and prone to dying early.

**Simulated Intelligence:** An AI with no actual internal will but the ability to perform a wide variety of tasks as well as simulate human interaction.

**Suits:** A slang term for corporate executives and workers for the megacorporations. Their loyalty to their company and money is believed to exceed that of any other.

**Tanto:** A Japanese short sword used by the Trikuza's soldiers to indicate they have been accepted as a soldier.

**Techjack:** A term for a specialized infospace hacker who heavily modify their brains for cybercrime.

**Tier I:** AI who are capable of matching human intelligence.

**Tier X:** See Cognition AI.

**Maelstrom 90:** An AI-designed cybernetic implant that was imple-mented in the brains of children. It still is comparable to high-end implants decades later.

**Turing Society:** A hacktivist offshoot of H.O.P.E. that is less involved in information warfare and more playful pranks.

**Vertical Lift Off (VLO):** A specialized kind of flying car that is capable of landing or rising in a single spot.

**Wakizashi:** A Japanese short sword, slightly shorter than a Tanto, used in accompaniment with a katana. Given with a katana to indicate that a Trikuza member has become a lieutenant.

**War Wagon:** Armored personnel carriers used by the police in the arcologies.

**White Triangle:** A syndicate of human traffickers, slavers, organ thieves, and black-market cyberneticists.

**Yakuza:** The Japanese syndicates that have mostly become part of other international organizations.

**The Zone:** The nickname for the Los Angeles Refugee Zone.

# Author's Note

I'd like to thank you for reading this book. The publishing industry is changing dramatically since the advent of eBooks. It is now very difficult to get any book noticed, regardless of quality. If you enjoyed this book, you could do some very simple things to help me attract attention.

Word of mouth is the number one source of success for novels, so simply telling family and friends about the book is a great start.

Here are a few other ways of helping, if you are so inclined:

* Post a rating or review on Amazon.com
* Post a rating or review on Goodreads
* Talk about the book or write a review on Facebook
* Tell folks about the book in a blog post.

If you like any of my other books, please feel free to check them out. A lot of my series are interlinked and you never know when you'll find someone familiar showing up. Case, for example, is the titular G of the Agent G series that serves as a prequel for this story. Check out those books if you want to learn more about his relationship to the Invisible Hand, the Eruption, the Leak, and Evie Principle.

Look for the next book

# REVENGE
# OF THE CYBER DRAGONS

Book Two of the Cyber Dragons Series

# About the Author

C.T. Phipps is a lifelong student of horror, science fiction, and fantasy. An avid tabletop gamer, he discovered this passion led him to write and turned him into a lifelong geek. He is a regular blogger and also a reviewer at The United Federation of Charles.

## Bibliography

*The Rules of Supervillainy* (Supervillainy Saga #1)
*The Games of Supervillainy* (Supervillainy Saga #2)
*The Secrets of Supervillainy* (Supervillainy Saga #3)
*The Kingdom of Supervillany* (Supervillainy Saga #4)
*The Tournament of Supervillainy* (Supervillainy Saga #5)
*The Future of Supervillainy* (Supervillainy Saga #6)
*The Horror of Supervillainy* (Supervillainy Saga #7)
*Esoterrorism* (Red Room, Vol. 1)
*Eldritch Ops* (Red Room, Vol. 2)
*Agent G: Infiltrator*
*Cthulhu Armageddon* (Cthulhu Armageddon, Vol. 1)
*The Tower of Zhaal* (Cthulhu Armageddon, Vol. 2)
*Lucifer's Star*
*Straight Outta Fangton*
*Wraith Knight*
*I Was a Teenage Weredeer* (Bright Falls Mystery Series #1)
*A Teenage Weredeer in Michigan* (Bright Falls Mystery Series #2
*A Nightmare on Elk Street* (Bright Falls Mystery Series #3))
*Psycho Killers in Love*

Michael Suttkus, II, lives in Leesburg, Florida, with three cats, one of which actually likes him, and his family, with whom he fares better. When not working at a game store, he's playing games, reading science books, or otherwise being incredibly nerdy. Also writing! Because he has to feed cats whether they like him or not.

## Bibliography

*I Was a Teenage Weredeer* (Bright Falls Mystery Series #1)
*A Teenage Weredeer in Michigan* (Bright Falls Mystery Series #2
*A Nightmare on Elk Street* (Bright Falls Mystery Series #3))
*Lucifer's Star* (Lucifer's Star #1)
*Lucifer's Nebula* (Lucifer's Star #2)
*Brightblade* (The Morgan Detective Agency, Book 1)
*Space Academy Dropouts* (The Space Academy Series, Book 1)

Curious about other Crossroad Press books?
Stop by our site:
http://store.crossroadpress.com
We offer quality writing
in digital, audio, and print formats.